CW01217649

Two Loves I have of Comfort and Despair ...
(Shakespeare, Sonnet CXLIV)

Part One: Autumn Term

O! therefore, love, be of thyself so wary
Shakespeare, Sonnet XXII

Chapter One

Every teenage girl, when she falls in love, thinks it will be forever. Megan was no exception. She and her friends in the sixth form had been a group who enjoyed socialising with each other: trips into Manchester, their nearest city, to check out the bargains at Afflecks Palace or sample the delights of Spud-U-Like; evenings in together, watching videos and eating crisps; and, in the summer months, hanging out by the reservoir, messing around in an old dinghy, or taking the bus to a not too distant park that offered putting and crazy golf. It was inevitable, then, that as the two years of their A level courses progressed, they would find companionship evolving into intimacy, friends becoming lovers.

Anita and Joe had been the first to succumb. Megan began noticing nuances in their interaction that hadn't been there before: flirty comments; a gaze held fractionally longer than with anyone else; Anita touching Joe's arm whenever she talked to him, as if staking her claim somehow.

It was no surprise then when she and Joe bashfully conceded that yes, they were 'going out', followed swiftly by Dave admitting that he 'liked' Megan and the two of them tentatively meeting each other without the rest of the group, for a date that began with a walk and ended with a clichéd kiss under a lamp post.

This was 1984 and AIDS and HIV were still relatively unknown, had not yet hit the headlines as they would a year later with the death of Rock Hudson and the sudden realisation that there was a new sexually transmitted disease to worry about. Nevertheless, sex wasn't on the agenda for Megan or Anita: the desire didn't enter their minds; and, although Joe and Dave sometimes dropped hints that they would like to take things further than the 'snogging' the girls enjoyed, they seemed prepared to wait – at least for the time being.

*

The summer holiday between Lower and Upper Sixth passed all too quickly. Anita and Joe had been a couple since April; Megan and Dave since June. They still met up as a foursome, sat together in the Sixth Form Common Room in their sprawling comprehensive school, but the dynamic had changed: instead of the girls spending more time with each other than with their respective partners, they had settled down into domesticity, choosing universities for their UCCA forms based on how far away they would be from the men in their lives, calculating the hours and minutes they would have to spend apart.

Despite taking the same A levels – French, German and English – Megan and Anita had chosen different paths. Megan wanted to take Combined Honours in English and French (literature had always been her passion) and was thinking of Birmingham, Sheffield and Keele – none of them too far away from Dave, who had been re-sitting Maths O level and wanted to go on to college for a City and Guilds qualification in Catering. Anita had her heart set on a double Languages degree: French and German at Bradford, Hull or Manchester. They had checked out polytechnics and colleges too, although their current grades seemed to suggest they would meet the requirements of two Bs and a C which they'd both been offered by their preferred universities.

"Where's Joe with the application process?" Megan asked her friend casually as they sat waiting one morning for their German teacher to arrive. She and Anita had both had interviews at their first choice universities and conditional offers of places; but Joe wanted to do Physics and she had a feeling that this course might demand higher grades at A level.

Anita shrugged. "He's still dithering over whether he wants to choose a university based in the course or how far away we'll be from each other." She sighed. "One of the reasons I chose Bradford was because I thought he wanted to go to Leeds – we could have seen each other easily then; but now he's talking about Imperial or UCL, and they're both in London. At least you know Dave's sticking around here if he's going to do his catering course at Rochdale College."

"It's still around two hours from Birmingham to Manchester by train though," Megan told her, "and that's without the journey from Manchester to Littleborough. You're talking two and a half hours at least."

"Maybe I shouldn't be planning my life around Joe anyway," Anita decided, pushing her hair out of her eyes. "I know everything's going well right now, but what if he falls for someone else at university? What if I do?"

Megan was silent. She wasn't looking forward to being parted from Dave in – how many months' time? This was February, so … She counted rapidly – in seven months; at the same time, she felt their relationship was sufficiently secure to withstand temptation. They'd talked about getting engaged towards the end of her First Year, when they would have been a couple for over two years. Dave wouldn't be contemplating marrying her unless he was really serious, would he?

"Do you think either of you is likely to fall for someone else?" she asked carefully.

Anita sighed again. "We get on really well and we're comfortable with each other. But that … *spark* … that we had at the beginning, when it was all new and exciting, well … it's just not there anymore. I still like kissing him, but it doesn't make me feel like I'm a firework display, the way it used to." She paused. "What about you and Dave? Are you still making him wait until after A levels?"

Megan flushed. She and Anita had both privately agreed that their A levels had to take precedence over anything else this year. That meant evenings were to be spent on homework and revision (thank goodness there was no coursework!) and not experimenting with sex. Since neither of them had been in a serious relationship before, this had been an easy decision to make. Chastity was straightforward if one had no concept of anything else.

Anita grinned. "I only asked! Do you think we're the only virgins left in the sixth form?" she mused next. "I know Katie's doing it; and some of the boys are awful: they go from one girl to the next, taking what they want and then dumping them. It wouldn't surprise me to find they've got some sort of contest going on to see who can sleep with the most."

Megan felt her eyes widen in shock. "But Joe and Dave aren't like that," she protested.

"No..." was Anita's measured response, "but they're both still human, Meggie. I wouldn't hang about for too long after A levels – you know, let Dave know what he'll be missing while you're away. That might help to keep him on the straight and narrow."

"Are you going to do that?" Megan asked her. "You know, *do it* before you go away to university?"

Anita nodded. "Even if it doesn't work out in the long run, I think I want my first time to be with Joe. We know each other far too well for anything to feel awkward."

Megan was silent, pondering what her friend had said. She thought she loved Dave, might possibly want to spend the rest of her life with him, yet something still held her back from making that final commitment. Was it fear of the unknown?

She resolved there and then that she would think about the issue again once exams were finally over in June.

*

Results Day. She had achieved an A and two Bs, easily matching and surpassing the offer she'd had from Birmingham. (She'd been awarded a B for General Studies too, but she was aware that a lot of universities didn't class it as a 'real' A level.) She was particularly pleased that her A was for English Literature, by far her favourite subject.

Anita, though, was not so fortunate, having only managed a D for German but Bs for English and French. What would happen to her friend now? Megan wondered.

Anita had already rung Bradford, who'd said that with those grades they could offer her French and Russian, but that French and German was out of the question.

There was, too, the whole issue of sex now that A levels were well and truly completed. Until now, she'd avoided Dave's gentle pressuring, removing his hands when they strayed further than her comfort zone, wriggling out from under him when his kisses became more insistent. They'd both taken on part time jobs to tide them over the summer – she waitressing in a local café; he stacking shelves at the nearby Tesco – and that had fortunately curtailed the hours they had together; but the warm August evenings inevitably led to them lying in a field, kissing, cuddling and – on Dave's part – groping. It wasn't that she was a prude, but the idea of taking things further when anyone could walk past and catch them at it wasn't the stuff her romantic dreams were made on.

"We could always go to your house, then, or mine," Dave suggested one evening as she pushed him away yet again.

She shook her head, aware that, location-wise, this field seemed the perfect setting: the sky was just beginning to take on a crepuscular tint; the hedge behind them was ablaze with yellow gorse, the grass scattered with wild flowers; yet it all seemed too open, too public.

"My mum wouldn't like it."

Dave was genuinely surprised. "We're teenagers. What does she think we're doing now?"

"Not a lot," Megan said honestly. Her mother belonged to the school of thought that reasoned sex only happened in a bed after 10pm at night – with both people suitably attired in nightclothes. She tried to explain. "It's not her fault. She's just part of a generation that didn't believe in sex before marriage."

"Your mum must have been part of the Swinging Sixties," Dave argued. "When was she born? 1944? Everyone was at it when she was our age!"

"Well, she definitely wasn't!" Megan snapped back. "I was a honeymoon baby, but I was a week early and she was mortified because she didn't want people thinking that she and my dad had done the deed before they got married."

It was true. To this day her mother hadn't forgiven her.

"Well, you're not your mum …"

He reached for her again but she turned away, adjusting her clothing, pulling her hair back into its customary ponytail. "No, Dave!" Her tone was sharper than she'd intended. "Not like this – not here."

"Where then?" He was beginning to sound sulky.

"Perhaps when I'm in Birmingham," she suggested tentatively.

"That's weeks away!" He was a petulant toddler, demanding sweets before his dinner.

"At least we'd have some privacy," she said softly.

He still looked moody, but there was nothing that would make her change her mind.

*

As it was, the next few weeks passed in a blur. The rest of August sped by, dragging September after it. It seemed like no time at all before Megan and Anita were enjoying their last 'girlie get-together' (Anita had eventually been accepted by Hull to do French and German; it seemed preferable to Bradford's option of French and Russian) before the final goodbyes with their respective boyfriends.

"What did you and Joe decide in the end then?" Megan was curious. She'd hardly seen Anita since Results Day, when the four of them had gone out as a group to celebrate (despite the D for German) but her friend seemed somewhat subdued.

"Oh, we've broken up," Anita said matter-of-factly. "Let's face it: it was never going to work with such a distance between us. It's better for us both this way."

She said it almost as if she believed it.

Megan was silent then, wondering if she and Dave would fare any better. Privately she was glad of all the hours she'd put in at the café: not only had her stint there swelled her bank balance – or, more accurately, given her something with which to start a bank account – but it had provided a welcome escape from Dave and his increasingly more persistent hands. She was dreading his visits to see her at the Hall of Residence in Birmingham, aware that she had finally run out of excuses not to sleep with him.

Why on earth was she so hung up about sex? she asked herself silently, miles away in thought so that Anita had to shake her arm to grab her attention.

"I'm sorry," she apologised. "I was just thinking about something."

"I was saying," Anita repeated patiently, "that you must be looking forward to going away and being out of your mum's radar." She grinned suddenly. "You and Dave will be at it like rabbits when he comes to visit you."

She stopped short, transfixed by Megan's horrified eyes.

"What's wrong?" Then, as comprehension dawned, "Don't tell me you still haven't …"

"We're the last two virgins in the sixth form, remember?"

Megan tried to make light of it, but Anita was shaking her head. "You're on your own there!" Laughing at Megan's dumbfounded expression, she continued, "I told you Joe and I had decided to have our first time together."

"But don't you feel terrible now you've split up?" Megan tried to imagine how she herself would feel if she'd been loved and left.

Anita was gazing at her pityingly. "We did it *after* we split up, not before. That way we knew it would be a one-off."

"I don't understand …"

"You really need to grow up, don't you?" Anita's tone wasn't unkind. "I know you're an incurable romantic, Megan: you probably don't want anything to happen with Dave unless it's in a four poster bed strewn with rose petals and you're in a long white nightie down to your ankles, but you can bet anything that's not what Dave's thinking. Why on earth have you kept putting it off?"

Megan was silent. How could she give an answer that she didn't know herself? But maybe Anita was right and she had to 'grow up' and see sex for what it was, not as part of some 'happy ever after' love story.

She would have to see what happened once she was in Birmingham.

Chapter Two

"This must be it, surely."

Megan's mother sounded fractious and Megan knew why: the journey to Birmingham had not been an easy one. The M6 had been almost at a standstill; Spaghetti Junction had been terrifying (and Megan wasn't even driving); and then they had taken not one but two wrong turns trying to navigate their way to Edgbaston from the City Centre.

Megan sighed. She loved her mum, but the two of them constantly drove each other up the wall. Megan resented being treated like a ten year old, despite being eighteen (nineteen in a few months' time) and now an undergraduate; whereas years of lone parenting, bringing up a daughter on her own after being unexpectedly left a widow when Megan was only a few months old, had embittered Mrs Jackson to the point where she had forgotten how to smile.

Still, they were here now: the blue signpost definitely read 'The Vale Halls of Residence' and Mum was swinging into the car park, narrowly missing mowing down a hitherto unseen student who just happened to have the misfortune to be in her way.

"Mum!" Megan shrieked.

Her mother tutted. "For goodness' sake, Meg! I've told you before that you shouldn't startle me like that when I'm driving."

As they pulled into a parking space, Megan examined the building before her. It was the first time she'd seen Ridge – or any of the Halls of Residence. Her interview some nine or ten months ago had been conducted on campus, in the Muirhead Tower, a tall building housing French on the third and fourth floors and German on the second.

Mum had driven her here for that too, circumnavigating the city centre by diverting them onto the M5 for a trip around the south side of Birmingham, coming off near the M42 and driving up through Kings Norton, Bournville and Selly Oak. It had fallen on Megan to map read, which she'd done rather successfully; so it was galling to think that this time she'd got it wrong and pulled them off the motorway slap bang into the middle of one of the UK's busiest junctions.

And at least this time she wouldn't lose the car! Her cheeks burned as she remembered the embarrassment from her initial visit. Mum had parked in the official university car park, right next to campus, but Megan had taken a wrong turn somehow after her (not very successful, she thought) interview and wandered round for over an hour trying to find both her bearings and her mother, the latter having opted to stay in the car and wait for her.

She looked at the building critically. Long and low, it was a modern red brick building studded with large windows that presumably demarcated bedrooms. Although not the prettiest of structures, nevertheless it wasn't aesthetically displeasing – until Megan noticed that one end seemed to be enjoined to a towering monstrosity next to it that was – she counted rapidly - fifteen, no! was it sixteen? floors high.

A pretty, curly headed girl in Andy Pandy striped dungarees was watching them with interest. As Megan unlocked the boot and gazed at her luggage, trying to decide what to unload first, the stranger approached. "Want a hand?"

Megan hesitated.

"My name's Ali," the girl continued by way of introduction. "I'm a Freshers Rep." Noting Megan's puzzled frown, she explained, "There's a group of us who're on duty, making sure that new people know where to go and what to do. Do you know what room you're in?"

Megan shook her head.

"There's a big photo board in Reception," Ali told her. "It's got all the room numbers on. A friend of mine's giving out the keys. I'll take you over."

Megan glanced uncertainly at her mother.

"Oh, go and make new friends." Mrs Jackson took on a martyred tone. "I'll just sit in the car until you're ready."

"Is she okay?" Ali asked Megan with a worried look.

"She likes suffering," Megan said primly. "And telling people about it."

She and Ali carefully lifted a large suitcase and a battered, old fashioned trunk out of the car – or at least tried to. Even working together, they couldn't shift the trunk.

"We'll have to get a couple of High over," Ali panted after subsequent efforts had failed equally. "How on earth did you lift in in there?"

"The next door neighbour helped," Megan explained. "He's a builder, with his own company. He got one of his boys to help him."

"Don't tell me they used a forklift truck!" Ali joked.

"Just muscle power," Megan laughed. Then, "*Who* did you say we should ask?"

Ali pointed to the tower next to them. "*That* is High Hall – and it's full of men, all seventeen floors of it!"

Seventeen floors? Megan felt ill. When the accommodation booklet had arrived through her letterbox along with the rest of the university bumf, she'd chosen Ridge because it was small (only 150 residents) and all-female. Now she was being told that she had - how many boys did seventeen floors contain? she wondered – lots of testosterone-charged young men practically on her doorstep. It wasn't fair!

Ali was misunderstanding Megan's consternation. "Don't worry," she said consolingly. "It might look like two buildings, but they're joined together. We share a big dining room on the ground floor: it's two separate rooms really but they always keep the dividing doors open; and a bar – well, a corridor with a bar in it – that connects both halls."

Megan could hardly believe her ears. Shared dining rooms. A bar corridor. (She had been too naïve to realise that most people's drinking habits would be different to her own, having assumed that there would be one student bar in the Guild on campus, not a bar for each Hall of Residence. Brought up by a teetotal mother, she had never tasted alcohol: she hadn't even been inside a pub, unless you counted the time she had been sent by her other friends to ask for glasses of water one hot August day on the way to the reservoir.) She might just have well have signed up for a Mixed Hall.

"Come on then!" Ali sounded impatient. "Let's see where you are."

She grabbed Megan's suitcase and half-dragged, half-carried it into the Reception area. A clever looking Chinese girl sat behind a large desk that held a cardboard box full of keys. Beside her, an outsize photo board displayed a hundred and fifty photographs of the Hall's residents, including, Megan noticed, one of herself bearing the caption 'Megan Jackson, English/French (1)'.

"That's me!" Ali pointed to the grinning photo whose inscription proclaimed her to be 'Alison Russell, Theology (2)'.

"Theology?" Megan's eyebrows shot up.

"I'm not training to be a vicar or anything," Ali laughed. "I was going to do History, only I didn't get the grades. But they offered me Theology instead, so I thought, Why not? Hey! Laurena!" She was accosting the Chinese girl. "Megan Jackson, new Fresher. The photo board says G30."

Megan looked again and noticed what she hadn't taken in before. Each girl's room number was printed next to her name.

Laurena pulled a face. "That's right at the end of the corridor," she commiserated. "It means you have to walk further to get to the dining room – or anywhere."

"Laurena likes her food!" Ali chuckled. "Even the stuff they serve here. A word of advice, though – sign up for the veggie option."

"But I'm not a vegetarian!" Megan protested.

"Nor am I," said Ali darkly, "but it's a lot safer than eating some of the dodgy looking meat they give you!"

"Perhaps I should take my key," Megan murmured politely, already feeling tired from all this enforced friendliness. "My mum's still waiting in the car," she added pointedly.

Ali's face clouded with guilt. "I am *so* sorry," she began. "I completely forgot ..."

But Megan had already taken hold of the key and was marching down the corridor in front of her, noting that it was lined on both sides with numbered doors, from G8 – "That's a double," Ali explained. "The one opposite's a double too - G36 – and the one opposite yours – G28." – down to her own tiny room at the end.

"The rest of the doors on that side are bathrooms and shower rooms," Ali continued, "and there's a little kitchen in the middle. It's not much: there's one tiny fridge which fills up really quickly, so you need to label all your stuff. There are some little cupboards too, but you'll need a padlock of your own. There are fourteen girls on your corridor but only twelve cupboards, so you need to get in quick."

Megan's mind whirled. It was too much to take in. And she hadn't even unlocked her door yet.

She didn't need to. Just as she was about to insert the key into the lock, the door opened and a tousle headed girl almost walked into her.

"Claire!" Ali greeted the newcomer as if she were a long-lost friend. (She probably was, Megan mused.) "What are you doing here?" she added, almost as an afterthought.

"Oh, I'm sorry! Is this your room?" The other girl's arms were full of jumpers. "This was my room last year," she explained. "I stored all my winter jumpers in the lockable part of the wardrobe, then lost the key so I couldn't take them home for the Easter holiday. They've been sitting there since last March!"

"Just as well you didn't need them in the meantime, then," Ali remarked chattily.

Megan felt like screaming. All she wanted was to go into *her* room, unpack *her* case, lie on *her* bed and try to acclimatise. This was well nigh impossible with so many people introducing themselves.

"Is Nick back yet?" was Ali's next question, directed again at Claire.

The girl nodded. "He's on car park duty in High. Just like I'm supposed to be in Ridge." She looked guilty.

"Pop over and ask him to lend us a hand," Ali wheedled. "Megan's trunk's going to need two men – it weighs a ton! Is Big Ron on duty too?" she continued. "We need all the muscle power we can get!"

It seemed only minutes until Megan was back in the car park, watching two strange men heft her ridiculously large and heavy trunk out of the boot of her mother's car as easily as if it had been filled with air.

"I'm sorry, Megan ..." Her mother's customary complaint filled the air. "I'm going to have to get out and visit the bathroom. I've been sitting in the car for over half an hour now and it isn't fair."

It was almost, Megan felt bitterly, as if she had forced her mother to sit there. Acting like a martyr was all well and good, but she objected to her mother then blaming her self-imposed suffering on her, Megan. People would think she was a terrible daughter.

Except no one did, of course. The two men who had been dispatched to come to her aid did what had been asked of them and swiftly disappeared, finally leaving Megan with the privacy she'd desired to start putting her room to rights – mother permitting.

Mrs Jackson surveyed the narrow room critically. "It's a bit poky," she remarked disparagingly.

Megan didn't care. It was *her* room and no one could take that sense of ownership from her.

"Do you want a cup of tea?" she offered, somewhat unwillingly.

Her mother sniffed. "I don't suppose you thought to bring a teapot, did you?"

"I can make it in a mug."

The look of horror on her mother's face silenced her.

"They might have had drinks on offer for parents who've driven a long way," she said petulantly, somehow making Megan feel that this absence of organised refreshments was also her fault. "I'll just have to wait until I get home."

She sighed, making sure that Megan appreciated her sacrifice.

"There might be a café somewhere," Megan said quickly.

Her mother shook her head. "I don't think so. It's never as nice as when you have one at home, and you can't guarantee the cups will have been washed properly. I'll wait."

And that was that.

Years later, Megan would realise that her mother enjoyed complaining to the extent that she had made it an art form: Mrs Jackson was never happier than the moments when she could find a cloud for every silver lining. At some point in the future Megan would learn to laugh at this attitude, playing 'Mother Bingo' by trying to anticipate how many times the woman would moan during a given time frame. But the potential irony eluded her at eighteen: her serious student self was sufficiently insecure to take her mother's comments and attitude to heart, so it was with a sense of relief (tinged with guilt) that Megan finally closed the door on her parent some five minutes later.

Now that she was finally alone, Megan stood and contemplated her room analytically. It wasn't the largest space she'd ever occupied: the width was only a few feet more than the narrow metal bed; but it was *hers*. She felt strangely excited to think that she could finally put her own stamp on something without her mother intervening and making Megan change everything.

She would start by dressing the bed with a brightly coloured throw and adding a couple of cushions to suggest that by day this was a sofa. Hurriedly she unlocked the ridiculously large trunk, rummaging around for the unwanted bedspreads she had brought from home. She threw a scarlet one over the tasteless brown and orange checked blanket that currently covered the bed. Although she had been hoping for a duvet, she knew that not everyone had succumbed to the lure of Scandinavian bedding.

Idly she pondered why it had taken so long for the British to warm to a custom the ancient Vikings had embraced centuries ago. The princess in Hans Christian Anderson's story had felt a pea through twenty duvets – was that why so many people in Britain today mistrusted them?

The next item of furniture to fall prey to her decorative touch was the wooden bookcase. She filled it rapidly with tattered yet cherished Penguin volumes, relics from her mother's Open University degree some years ago. 'Tess of the d'Urbervilles' and 'Jane Eyre' rubbed shoulders with 'What Maisie Knew' and a collection of short stories by Frank O'Connor. 'Middlemarch' and 'The Mill on the Floss' were flanked by 'Pride and Prejudice', 'Mansfield Park' and 'Persuasion' – each one an old friend, holding precious memories of her discovery of English Literature at the age of fifteen. She observed the empty shelves below the one she had just filled and shivered with the anticipation of the new books she would buy this term.

Delving into her trunk again, she unearthed the electric kettle her mother had bought her as a 'going away' present. This she placed on the corner of the large table that would serve as her desk, noting that there was a double plug socket conveniently nearby: room to plug in the kettle along with the reading lamp that had been thoughtfully provided. Her painted wooden mug tree (red, to match the coverlet) took pride of place on top of the bookcase with its six identical mugs: white with red spots. She didn't own a stereo, or even a small radio cassette player; but she had a Sony Walkman (bought with her mother's eighteenth birthday gift of fifty pounds) and she put this next to her bed, on the small set of drawers that resided there. She would use the drawers for her socks and underwear, she decided, and place larger items upon the shelves inside the wardrobe.

She was just getting into her stride, finding coat hangers for her meagre collection of blouses and dresses, when a tap at the door made her jump.

The knock sounded again. Somewhat unwillingly, Megan opened it. She wasn't really reclusive: she had just hoped to have some time to herself before being forced to meet the rest of her co-habitants.

A pretty dark haired girl in jeans and a striped rugby shirt stood there and behind her another girl whose short mousey hair and glasses lent her a serious air.

For a moment, all three regarded each other silently; then the dark girl spoke. "I'm Jen and this is Sally. We're your neighbours."

She gestured at the door opposite and Megan remembered: the double room. These two must be sharing.

"I'm Megan," she said hesitantly. "First Year English and French. What are you studying?"

Jen's face widened into a grin. "I'm English too. Sally's German."

Megan assumed the girl was referring to their courses and not their nationality.

"Did you get the letter about the Cheese and Wine get to know you session in the Arts Faculty?" Jen continued eagerly. "That's tomorrow at four o'clock. We can walk down together."

Megan felt vaguely alarmed. Cheese and wine? It all seemed very grown up. And what if one didn't drink? (She didn't.) Would she be given a glass of cheese instead? she wondered.

"Have you bought any of the set books yet?" Jen wanted to know next. Her gaze travelled over Megan's bookcase. "You like 'Tess' too. Did you do it for A level?"

"We did 'The Return of the Native'," Megan told her shyly, "but I read 'Tess' in the summer after I'd finished O levels, and I loved it."

"You've got 'The Go Between' too," Jen murmured, "and some Henry James – you *must* read 'The Wings of the Dove' if you haven't already; and who's this Frank O'Connor?"

"Irish short stories," Megan began, but Sally was already pulling a face.

"The two of you could stop being so cliquey for a moment ... There are some of us who didn't do English Lit A level, you know. How would you feel if I suddenly started spouting on about Goethe or Dürrenmatt?"

"You mean 'Urfaust' and 'Der Richter und sein Henker'?" Megan span round, her eyes shining. "I loved both of those when I did them for A level."

Jen groaned. "Thanks, Sally! I'm just as clueless about German Lit as you are with the English version!"

The corridor was beginning to fill properly now as more and more girls arrived, staggering under the weight of multiple bags and suitcases – although none of them, Megan noted, had brought anything quite as Gargantuan as her own monstrous trunk.

The sound of excited chattering was suddenly eclipsed by the peremptory tones of a small, round, red headed girl who seemed to have a whole retinue to carry her luggage whilst remaining empty handed herself.

"Be careful with that case, Cordelia!" she was saying bossily to a younger and blonder version of herself. "It took one ages to fold all one's clothes perfectly!"

Megan caught Jen's eye and smiled. What a dreadful girl! And how pretentious she sounded!

As if reading their minds, the newcomer turned to face the three friends. "One shouldn't have to make one's sisters act as porters!" she said indignantly yet with exquisite Received Pronunciation. Then, dropping her affectation slightly, "I thought the men from High were supposed to be turning out."

"You said that when we collected your stuff at the end of the summer term," Cordelia complained. "I wouldn't have come if I'd known I'd be pressganged into working as a removal man again!"

"How sharper than a serpent's tooth it is to have a thankless sister," muttered Jen to Megan, *sotto voce*.

Megan stifled another smile.

"Can we help?" Sally offered politely.

The redhead eyed her somewhat dubiously. "I don't suppose you have anything in the way of tea and biscuits?" Catching sight of Megan's kettle and mug tree through the open door, she continued, "*Someone* seems to have made herself at home very quickly."

Without waiting for an invitation, she sailed regally into the room and ensconced herself upon the scarlet bedecked bed. "I will, of course, issue an invitation to tea in my room once I've unpacked properly." She stared at the three girls expectantly.

"I was just going to put the kettle on," Megan heard herself saying. She looked imploringly at the other girls. Surely they wouldn't expect her to entertain this monster on her own?

"I've got some chocolate digestives," Jen offered, shooting Megan a sympathetic look. "I'll just go and get them," she added, disappearing so rapidly that Megan deliberated whether the mention of biscuits were merely a ploy to enable her friend to escape.

Silently Megan filled the kettle, using the washbasin opposite the bed. (She assumed the water would be safe to drink once it was boiled.)

The strange girl nodded appreciatively as Megan brought out a box of Sainsbury's Red Label teabags then shuddered in horror at the sight of a jar of Coffee Mate. "You can't put *that* in a cup of tea!" she protested with outrage. (She had, Megan noticed, suddenly dropped her pretentious use of the third person indefinite pronoun.)

"I'm sorry," Megan began, fleetingly speculating why she was apologising to an unknown girl who had gatecrashed her room and demanded a hot beverage.

"I've got some milk in the fridge." Now it was Sally's turn to vanish, leaving Megan wondering despairingly if she would ever see either of her new friends again.

"Will your sister want a cup of tea too?" she asked tentatively, inwardly cursing her mother for having instilled her with such inconvenient good manners.

The girl shook her head. "Cordelia doesn't do tea. My parents have brought cans of fizzy drink for them all to quaff once they've finished unloading. My baby sister Portia's helping too, but she's only eleven so she tends to be more hindrance than help." She gave a wry half smile. "You probably think I'm very spoilt, making my family do all the heavy work while I just sit back and sip tea."

"I didn't …" Megan stuttered, but the girl wasn't listening.

"I'm just getting over a back injury," she confided, her honesty making Megan warm to her. "I fell off a horse in the Easter holidays and one of my discs slipped out of place. I spent most of the summer term sleeping on the floor." She noticed Megan's quizzical look. "The mattresses in here aren't exactly orthopaedic, you know!"

"Do you do a lot of riding? When your back's okay, I mean?" Megan was realising that this girl wasn't so terrible after all.

Before the stranger could answer, Jen and Sally breezed back in, respectively carrying biscuits and milk. Megan regarded them gratefully.

"Thanks, both of you." She started to make an introduction - "This is Jen and this is Sally …" – then paused.

"Sue," the unknown girl said obligingly.

Jen laughed. "Really? I thought if your sister was called Cordelia, you'd be something equally literary."

"Like Regan or Goneril?" Sue enquired drily. She shrugged. "My parents named me Susanna, after Shakespeare's eldest child, but I've always been Sue." She took a proffered biscuit gratefully. "Thanks. I'm second year French and German. What are all of you studying?"

One by one, the other girls gave their details. Sue nodded approvingly when Sally said she was doing German, and again when Megan mentioned French. "I'll probably bump into you both in the Muirhead Tower, then. There's a nice coffee lounge on the first floor – better than the one in the Arts Faculty. *We* have filter coffee; the tea lady in the Mason Lounge uses instant."

"Mason Lounge?" Megan queried, thinking the name seemed familiar.

Jen nudged her. "That's where the Cheese and Wine is tomorrow. We talked about it earlier, remember?"

Over the next ten minutes, tea was drunk, biscuits were crunched, and friendship began to evolve. It was with a certain sense of regret that Megan watched the others disappear – Sue to wave off her departing family and Jen and Sally to start organising their room – and realised that she now had her longed for five minutes to herself. She had been here for – she checked her watch – one hour and seven minutes and already she had found some friends.

Chapter Three

Jen tapped on Megan's door impatiently. "Aren't you ready yet?"

Megan gazed at her reflection in the full length mirror that graced the wardrobe door and sighed. Never confident when it came to her own appearance, she somehow knew she looked wrong but couldn't explain why. The letter she'd received a few weeks ago from the Hall of Residence had promised a 'Formal Dinner and Barn Dance' this first evening and she had consequently used some of the money she'd earned from her waitressing job to buy herself a new dress. In retrospect, she wasn't sure she'd made the right choice.

Opening the door to her friend, she pulled a face. "I look awful, don't I?"

Jen snorted. "Are you kidding? I'd kill to look like you!" Noting Megan's disbelief she added, "Long blonde hair, big blue eyes, killer legs … If you were taller, you'd be the perfect woman!"

At five foot nothing, Megan certainly wasn't tall, but she was perfectly in proportion with a tiny frame (so tiny that she constantly bemoaned what she imagined to be a non-existent chest) and legs that were surprisingly long for her height. Add to that huge eyes framed by long dark lashes, generously curved lips and a cloud of naturally wavy flaxen hair and you could see that she was definitely pretty – and totally oblivious to the fact.

This lack of confidence wasn't exactly something new. Dave had been her first and only boyfriend. He wasn't among the best-looking boys in the sixth form, but she had been so grateful to think anyone found her attractive that she had reciprocated his advances, even if she had wondered sometimes whether he were only going out with her to prove something to himself and Joe.

And even though Dave had seemed to want her physically, Anita had told her once that men weren't really that interested in how a girl looked: it was her availability that was important. Unaware that her friend had been generalising, Megan had taken Anita's words to heart and had interpreted them to mean that Dave had only found her desirable because she was unattached and female. Anita had expounded further on the subject by claiming it was all a question of hormones: both Dave and Joe, she claimed, were like any other testosterone fuelled teenagers and would happily sleep with "anything that had a pulse". No wonder, then, that Megan was unaware of her own allure.

Now hearing Jen's words, Megan found herself automatically assuming her friend was making fun of her.

"I've got eyes, haven't I?" she snapped defensively. "I might have the right ingredients, as you put it, but they're just not put together properly. This dress is wrong, and I don't know why."

Jen's eyes widened in surprise. "You mean you really have no idea how good you look?"

"The dress is wrong," insisted Megan, tugging at it half-heartedly.

"No ..." Jen eyed her thoughtfully. "It's the right sort of dress for you: you're just not wearing it properly."

Stepping over to Megan, she adjusted the material. "You've pulled it all the way down when it should be sitting on your hips like this ..." Deftly she showed her friend how the dress was supposed to be worn, exposing several inches of thigh as she did so. "What were you doing, pulling it down to your knees?" she asked wonderingly. "You've got great legs – why hide them?"

Megan regarded her altered image. The black, stretchy material now fell in short folds from her hips to mid-thigh. It was the sort of outfit she had never imagined herself wearing, a million miles away from her usual conservative garb and – dare she say it? – somewhat sexy.

"I look different," she said at last.

Jen shot her an amused glance. "You don't have a clue, do you? Have you got heels? And make up?"

"I don't normally wear makeup," Megan confessed. (Her mother had always been violently opposed to teenage girls "plastering their faces with muck.")

"Shoes?"

"I've got the pair I used for waitressing," Megan conceded. "I don't know how practical they are for barn dancing though."

The heels must have been all of an inch in height, Jen thought, examining the shoes that Megan thrust at her for inspection. Still, at least they were black, and Megan had had the sense to wear black tights.

"I've got a new lipstick I haven't used yet," she told her, taking pity on this gauche eighteen year old. "It's too pale for me but it should look just right on you."

An hour and a half later, the formal dinner was well underway. Megan had been disappointed to discover that there was a seating plan and that she was nowhere near Jen, Sally or Sue; she was, however, by some strange coincidence directly opposite Big Ron (she recognised him as being one of the boys who had helped with her trunk earlier), who spent most of the evening telling her about his passion for fantasy role playing games, even offering to show her his axe. (It wasn't until years later that she realised this had been a clumsy chat up line.)

"You should try it some time," he slurred at her, already on his fifth glass of wine. "You'd make a really good elf."

"Why?" Megan wanted to know.

Ron regarded her thoughtfully. "Well, elves are usually tall and very beautiful," he said solemnly, "and you're not tall but you're quite beautiful, so you're halfway there."

Ron thought she was quite beautiful? Megan was momentarily flattered until she remembered another of Anita's warnings: "Watch out for beer goggles," her friend had told her once. "Joe says a woman's attractiveness is in direct correlation to how much a man's drunk." Then, as Megan still appeared clueless, her friend had elucidated, "The more he drinks, the better looking you get."

She had no time to ponder this further. Waitresses were circulating with tea and coffee and after dinner mints. Megan accepted a coffee then wished she hadn't as the strong bitter liquid assaulted her tastebuds. Hastily stirring in several sachets of sugar to hide the taste, she tried to focus on the activity at the top table, where an angular faced woman in a black tuxedo was rising to her feet.

Amidst drunken drumming of tables and some misguided wolf whistles, the woman introduced herself as Ann Taylor, the President of Ridge's SCR. The Senior Common Room, she explained, was made up of several post graduates and lecturers who had pastoral responsibility for the students in their hall of residence. "What that entails," she continued in a flat American drawl, "is that if you go down with mono …" - someone at her side whispered to her – "sorry, *glandular fever* in the middle of your Finals, I'm your first port of call. But if your significant other chucks you, or you drink too much and pass out in the middle of the bar, you're on your own."

Surrounded by inebriated laughter, Megan found herself hoping fervently that she would never be in need of pastoral care from this unfeeling woman.

"You may also notice," Ms Taylor continued, "that the Gideon Bible Society has placed a bible in every room in the hall." She paused for effect. "The next stage is to place a box of condoms in every room."

More raucous laughter and wild cheering. Megan was secretly horrified. *Condoms? In every room?* Was this a Hall of Residence or a brothel?

The speech from the President of High's SCR, a silver haired gentleman who looked sixty if a day, was much more sedate and far less inflammatory. Megan wasn't entirely sure who had decided to enliven the proceedings by throwing a leftover bread roll at the top table, but it seemed only minutes until the speeches had degenerated into a full-on food fight, causing the meal to end suddenly as chairs were pushed back and numerous people leaped to their feet.

This, thought Megan grimly, would not be happening in an entirely female setting. She scanned the crowd anxiously, searching for her three friends and sighing with relief as she saw Jen making her way towards her.

Megan was hoping that they would return to the safety of the Ground Floor corridor but, to her surprise, Jen grabbed her arm and steered her to the edge of the room. "Come on! You're getting in the way."

Blinking foolishly, Megan swivelled her gaze, realising that the people who had leaped to their feet were busy pushing tables to the High Hall end of the room to clear a space for the promised barn dance. So it wasn't a riot after all!

As if reading her mind, Jen remarked cheerily, "For a moment I thought everything was going to kick off, especially when so many people started throwing bread rolls. Luckily Sue was on my table and she told me that it's a High Hall tradition."

"Tradition?" Megan felt confused.

"Throwing bread rolls when you've had enough of the speeches," Jen explained airily. "Apparently Professor Jenkins is a bit deaf and it's the only way to get his attention!"

Megan's relief at the non-existence of a violent riot was swiftly replaced with a sense of horror as she realised that the barn dance was about to begin and that she, Jen and Sally were in serious danger of attracting male attention. Wildly she looked round for some way of escape. Sue was nowhere to be seen: that meant that there must be some sort of safe haven somewhere.

But she needn't have worried. High's occupants seemed just as reluctant to ask anyone to dance as the inhabitants of Ridge were to accept such an invitation. In the end it was a girl Megan thought she recognised from further down her corridor who made the first move, approaching one of the smartly dressed males and more or less dragging him onto the dance floor.

Whether the watching men felt shamed by this act of female aggression or whether it just lent them confidence, Megan wasn't sure: all she knew was that suddenly several men were walking towards her, each with a hopeful yet hungry look in his eye. She turned to flee, but Jen pushed her forward. "Go on! Barn dances are a great way to meet people! You swap partners every other minute so you'll get to know loads of men."

Which was just what she didn't want to do! Megan thought savagely as she let herself be steered unwillingly onto the dance floor by an earnest looking young man with neatly brushed hair and a tweed jacket.

He smiled at her apologetically. "I'm Andrew and you are ...?"

"Megan," she supplied abruptly, then relented. He was, after all, a polite young man, much more respectable than the majority of males she could see on the dance floor.

"So, Megan," Andrew continued, walking her through what seemed to be an incredibly complicated dance step, "are you a First Year?"

She nodded. "English and French. And you?"

Third Year Chem Eng." Noticing her mystified expression, he added, "Chemical Engineering."

"Oh." Megan wasn't sure how to respond but she needn't have worried: at a word from the caller, all the men simultaneously took a step to the right, leaving all the girls facing a new partner. This time her opposite number was a Physics student called Dan who was nowhere near as much of a gentleman as Andrew had been. His eyes lingered lasciviously on Megan's legs and chest and his hands were several inches lower than they should have been when the men were told to hold their partners round the waist.

"Fancy sitting the next one out and getting a drink?" He winked as he said it.

"No, thank you. I've already got a boyfriend," Megan said primly, removing Dan's hands from her posterior.

He grinned lazily. "I was offering you a drink, not a permanent relationship. Mind you, there could have been some snogging ..."

Luckily, the men moved on again at this point, meaning that Megan didn't have to respond. Secretly she felt rather flattered that this stranger had flirted with her. Perhaps Jen was right and she wasn't really as plain as she thought.

With each new partner, Megan's ordeal began again. Whether tall or short, well-groomed or raffish, all these young men – apart from Andrew - seemed to have one thing in common: they were all desperate to buy her a drink and get to know her better.

Sally offered an explanation when the dance ended and Megan fled to the side of the room for safety. "There are three hundred and sixty-seven men in High Hall," she declared, "and only a hundred and forty-seven girls in Ridge, so you see, there aren't enough of us to go round. There's one girl to every two and a half men." She paused. "Even I might get a look in at this rate."

Megan studied the other girl carefully. Sally had a pleasant face, but she wasn't beautiful. And whereas the majority of the girls here tonight were in party dresses of varying styles and lengths, Sally was wearing black trousers and a sparkly tee shirt. She looked presentable but next to Jen, who was poured into peacock blue satin with more than a hint of cleavage showing, or even Megan herself, her outfit was decidedly uninspiring.

"Have you ever had a boyfriend?" Megan asked carefully.

Sally nodded. "My German penpal. He came over on an exchange visit after O levels and we sort of got together."

"What happened?"

Sally shrugged. "He went back to Germany. We still carried on writing, but after a while that fizzled out. So it's not like I've never been kissed, just that it's a long time since it happened – two and a bit years now, actually."

"What's two and a bit years?" Jen appeared beside them, clutching a drink. "The bar's heaving at the moment. I think there are more people up there than down on the dance floor. It's standing room only."

"We were just discussing old boyfriends," Megan said lightly. "Speaking of which …" - she glanced at her watch: was it really half nine already? – "I must go and give *my* boyfriend a call. I promised him I'd ring tonight."

She hurried off before the others could stop her, glad of the excuse to leave the dancefloor.

Fumbling in the pocket of her dress for her room key – and silently congratulating herself for having had the foresight to buy a dress with pockets – Megan stole through the deserted foyer of Ridge and made her way to her room. She had left her money in there, securely locked in her wardrobe, naturally, and would need to use some of her supply of fifty pences for the payphone.

Slowly she unlocked the door and made her way to the wardrobe, catching sight of her face in the mirror above the washbasin as she did so. She almost didn't recognise the girl who stared back at her: cheeks flushed from dancing, combined with Jen's borrowed lipstick, lent her an almost sultry look. Was *that* why those men had tried chatting her up? Had she been subconsciously presenting herself as a *femme fatale*?

There was no time for introspection. She hastily grabbed her precious coins, remembering to lock the doors of both the wardrobe and the room as she exited, and hurried to the payphones in reception.

There was no one about. Good. The last thing she wanted was anyone listening in on her private conversation. With trembling fingers, she dialled Dave's number – his parents' number, she corrected herself – and waited for him to reply.

Chapter Four

The phone rang several times before it was answered. Megan was disappointed to hear Dave's mother's voice – not that she'd expected him to sit by the phone waiting for her call, she told herself crossly; still, it would have been nice to be connected to Dave straight away and not be forced to spend her precious pennies on enforced small talk with his mother.

"Can I speak to Dave, Mrs Price?" she asked eventually, cutting off his mother in the midst of yet another enquiry about the Hall of Residence.

"He's at a party, Love. Didn't he tell you?" Mrs Price seemed genuinely surprised. "He said he was meeting up with a whole crowd of people from school: Jarvis, was it? And Rachel and Paula."

The ones who would be going to Rochdale College instead of travelling further afield to go to University, Megan thought, suddenly wishing that she too were still back home instead of here. At least there she'd known the rules whereas much of student life in Birmingham was still an unknown quantity.

"Please tell him I rang," she said at last, aware that her money was about to run out. "I'll try to call again tomorrow evening."

It would have been all too easy to have disappeared into her room for an early night. If anyone asked the following morning, she could always say her phone call to Dave had lasted much longer than anticipated. However, Megan prided herself on being truthful and she didn't want to start her new friendships by being dishonest. Besides, leaving aside the unwanted barn dancing, she'd been quite enjoying herself getting to know Jen and Sally a little better.

When she arrived, there seemed to be even fewer people on the dance floor than there had been previously. The caller carried on regardless, blithely exhorting everyone to "doh-si-doh" and swing their partners despite the fact that there were only about twenty people making the effort.

Megan looked round a trifle uneasily, frantically searching for a face she knew.

"Hello again." Dan loomed in front of her, clutching a can. "Changed your mind about that drink yet?"

Pushing past him, Megan stumbled in her unfamiliar heels and almost slipped. Dan caught her gallantly and set her back on her feet. "Looks like you've had one too many already," he observed wryly.

Megan gazed at him, instantaneously aware of how good looking this complete stranger was. Her heart skipped involuntarily, the air between them suddenly thick with tension. Time seemed to slow.

"Have you any idea how sexy you look in that dress?" Dan's voice was a throaty murmur in her ear, his breath warm against her skin.

Desperately Megan tried to think of Dave, to imagine the hurt, the horror he would feel if he could see her now; yet even so her mouth moved towards Dan's in slow motion, almost as if she were compelled to let him kiss her.

"Megan!" Jen's voice broke the spell, causing Megan to recoil from Dan in embarrassment. Thank goodness her friend had rescued her! A minute later and she might have totally compromised herself.

Without stopping to offer Dan a word of explanation, she turned aside and followed Jen's voice to safety.

*

"So," Jen's voice was deliberately casual, "how was your boyfriend?"

Megan's cheeks flamed with embarrassment: she was certain Jen had called her name in an attempt to stop anything happening with Dan. What must her friend think of her?

"Hey," Jen gave her a reassuring smile. "You wouldn't be the first person to get off with someone at university when you've got a boyfriend back home."

"Nothing happened." Megan was aware she sounded tense. "I was coming to look for you, actually. Dave wasn't in, so I thought I'd come back to the barn dance, only I tripped and Dan caught me. That's all."

"Well he looked like he was enjoying rescuing a damsel in distress," Jen commented lightly. "And you seemed pretty keen on letting him know how grateful you were."

Megan groaned and covered her face with her hands. "I don't know what came over me. Nothing happened – but it could have done."

"Well, it didn't – and even if it had, one kiss hardly constitutes being unfaithful," Jen said reasonably. "Lighten up, Megan. Don't take it so seriously."

The problem was, Megan reflected, as she pulled off her dress a little later and popped her nightshirt over her head, ready for bed, that she *did* take things seriously. She'd always been proud of herself for working hard at her A levels instead of partying away at the local nightclub like so many of her contemporaries; now, however, she wondered if she'd overdosed on being sensible. She would have to see if Jen and Sally – and Sue – could help her lighten up.

*

The next morning arrived with a fanfare of shrieks and giggles as fourteen girls attempted to simultaneously use three shower rooms and two bathrooms. Megan lay in bed, trying to block out the unwelcome cacophony and luxuriate in her cocoon of sheets and blankets a little while longer. She and the others had agreed the previous evening to go for breakfast at nine, and this was only seven thirty. Since she didn't wash her hair every day – she had no need to – she could conceivably lie in until eight thirty, take a five minute shower and still be ready on time.

Now that she was awake, though, she found it impossible to drift back to sleep. Besides, she had a kettle in her room and a pint of milk in the fridge down the corridor (there was a Hall Shop which opened between 7 and 7.15 pm every evening and which she and Sally had discovered quite by chance when exploring the Lower Ground floor yesterday), so she could make herself a cup of tea and drink it leisurely while she decided what to wear for the day's shenanigans.

Hauling herself out of bed, she thrust her feet into her slippers and pulled her dressing gown around herself to protect her modesty. As she opened her door, she realised she needn't have bothered: half-clad females – some in ridiculously scanty underwear and others wearing only a towel the size of a face cloth – wandered brazenly in and out of their rooms, not caring how much flesh was on display.

Head down, averting her gaze, Megan hurried to the tiny kitchen and opened the fridge door. The space her milk should have occupied was empty.

For a moment, Megan was too stunned to speak. That milk had cost twenty eight pence and now it was gone! Even worse, the Hall Shop wouldn't open for almost another twelve hours. How was she to have a cup of tea now?

As she gazed round the room, trying hard not to let her frustration escape as tears, she suddenly spotted her milk, sitting on the worktop, next to the communal kettle. It was definitely *her* milk: the evening before, she had neatly printed her name and room number on the side of the carton before putting it in the fridge. *Someone else had opened it and used it!*

She hurriedly picked it up, noticing as she did so that it was still more than three quarters full. From now on she would keep her milk in her room, she decided. She could fill her wash basin with cold water before she left for campus and keep her milk cool that way. Leaving it in the fridge would be far too stressful.

As she indignantly made her way back to her room carrying the milk, she bumped into Sue, resplendent in a red silky dressing gown that made her somewhat resemble a beach ball.

"Morning, Sue," Megan said politely.

Sue blinked at her owlishly. "Megan!" she said at last. "It took a while for me to work out who you were – I haven't put my contact lenses in yet!" She gestured towards the kitchen. "I've just helped myself to some of your milk for a cup of tea – the shop had run out by the time I got there last night."

Instantly Megan felt ashamed of her earlier petulance. It seemed there was, after all, no sinister plot afoot to defraud the foresighted of their dairy products; and to begrudge one's own friend a splash of milk for a cup of tea would be both selfish and churlish.

She was thoughtful as she sipped her tea that morning. Milkgate had brought home to her just how much she needed to relax her uptight attitude. She had always been highly strung, but to turn a missing milk carton into such a melodrama was impressive even for her. Perhaps Jen and Sally would be able to help her unwind.

*

"So ..." Jen speared a sausage and bit into it hungrily, "what are the plans for today? I was thinking Freshers Fayre in the Student Union –"

"Guild," broke in Sue, busy shelling a hardboiled egg and slicing it onto a piece of toast. "It's called the Guild, not the Union – that's why everyone has a Guild card."

"Freshers Fayre at the Guild," Jen continued, "then hit the campus bookshop, find something for lunch, have a general explore and be ready for Cheese and Wine at four."

"Are we all invited to Cheese and Wine?" Sue sounded hopeful.

"Only if you're doing English," Jen told her. "*And* if you're a Fresher, like us."

"I want to check out the sports centre," Sally informed them, buttering a fourth piece of toast and spreading it liberally with marmalade. "I'll come to Freshers Fayre first, though: I think there's a running club and a women's hockey team."

Megan regarded Sally pensively. Her athletic physique suggested that she exercised regularly. She had also, apart from the marmalade, chosen a relatively healthy breakfast: porridge, followed by wholemeal toast, instead of emulating Jen's full English or Megan's and Sue's boiled eggs.

"You should try Popmo!" Sue was suddenly animated. Noting their puzzled expressions, she clarified, "Popmobility: keep fit exercises to music. I went every week last year before I hurt my back." She took a gulp of tea. "It used to be at lunch time on Fridays. We'll have to see what day it's on this term."

They were still chattering about the different activities potentially on offer as they set off for campus. Sue led the way, out of a different doorway than the one they'd arrived at from the carpark and down a gentle slope that skirted a lake of ducks and geese. It really was most idyllic.

The leaves were beginning to turn vibrant shades of russet and orange but the grass underfoot was still soft and springy. Sue pointed to a couple of buildings near the lake.

"That one's Lake – it's another men's hall – and the one next to it's Wyddrington – girls only. It's a lot bigger than Ridge: I think both halls have about four hundred and fifty residents. The monstrosity behind them is Mason – mixed."

Megan tried to take it all in, knowing that she would only remember half of what Sue was telling them. They turned out of The Vale and onto the main road, merging with the hundreds – or was it thousands? - of students who were marching ant-like towards campus.

Five minutes down the road, Sue motioned to them to stop. "That's the short cut," she announced importantly, gesturing off to her right. "It's the quickest way to the Health Centre or a few steps further to the Muirhead Tower and Arts Faculty. The library's next to the Arts Fac and the banks and bookshop are a minute or two's walk from there – on the way to the station and the Medical School. But if we're going to the Guild, we keep going straight on – it's at the bottom of this road."

"Which banks are they?" Sally wanted to know.

"The three big ones," Sue told them: "Midland, Lloyds and Barclays. They're always desperate for people to sign up for a student account because they want your money, so they offer incentives. Last year I got a free Railcard when I signed up with Midland, but I'm opening an account with Barclays this year because they promise to give you twenty pounds when you pay in your first term's grant cheque."

Megan listened in dismay. She hadn't thought of a student account, hadn't even been aware such things existed. She had been so excited to be earning money from her waitressing job that she had simply strolled into the nearest bank she saw, a Barclays, and opened a current account on the spot. She had then spent hours practising her signature so that no one could forge it if her chequebook were stolen.

They were now nearing the Guild. The imposing looking arched doorway at the front of the building sat underneath two heraldic shields which flanked a carved inscription: *'Per ardua ad alta.'* What did it mean? Megan wondered.

"Through hardship great heights are reached," Sally muttered, as if to herself.

She moved towards the entrance but Sue pulled her back. "If we're going to the Freshers Fayre, the quickest way is through that door there."

She pointed to a tiny quadrangle containing a stone fountain topped by a large mermaid. "That's the Mermaid Square. The door behind it goes to the Guild Shop and to Concourse. All the Freshers stalls will be set up in there." As she led them through the requisite doorway, she continued, "The shop does a DIY packed lunch for 25p: a bread roll, pat of butter, lump of cheese and an apple. It's a good way to make sure you stick to a budget."

Glancing at the shop as they passed, Megan spotted some Basildon Bond writing paper and envelopes. Perhaps she should splash out later and treat herself? After all, she and Dave would be writing to each other several times a week.

Dave. The thought of him reminded her of how nearly she'd misbehaved the previous evening. Should she tell him? she wondered. Maybe it was better not to mention it: after all, she wasn't likely to do anything like that again.

*

They had now reached the Concourse. Filled with what seemed like a million stalls and an equal number of students, it was the most claustrophobic environment Megan had ever found herself in. Her head whirled as she tried to take in the clubs on offer: Rock Soc (she later found out it was for aficionados of rock music, not geology), J Soc ("The Jewish Society," Sue told her obligingly.) and the Real Ale Society were definitely not for her; but Greenpeace, Amnesty International and the Jane Austen Appreciation Society were all distinct possibilities.

"What's Niteline?" she asked Sue, after spotting another stall.

"Sort of like a student version of the Samaritans," came the reply. "One of my friends is a volunteer. They counsel people over the phone. You have to be willing to sleep with a boy though."

"What?" Megan could hardly believe her ears. Since when had sex been a prerequisite for giving advice?

"In the same room as a boy," Sue elucidated. "My friend, Charley –" she broke off, noting Megan's expression: "her real name's Charlotte, but no one ever calls her that - says they have mattresses in the office so the people on duty can sleep if they get the chance. They always have at least one male and one female Niteliner on duty in case they have a caller who's fussy about who they speak to." She looked suddenly uncomfortable. "Don't repeat that to anyone. It's a bit like a secret society – everything's confidential. Charley would get into trouble if anyone knew she'd told me."

"What's the difference between Student Advice and Niteline?" Sally asked. She'd obviously been listening in.

"One's daytime and one's night time," Sue said promptly. "And Student Advice is just advice, but Niteline listens to your problems too." She grinned. "It's a free phone number, so most people ring them when they want a train timetable or the number for a pizza delivery place."

"So they're not really a counselling service then?" Megan felt confused.

Sue shook her head. "They get traumatic calls too – people with depression or problems with housemates; stuff like that – but Charley says they get more information calls than anything else. Anyway, while we've been talking, Jen's wandered off. Goodness knows what she might have signed up for without me to give her some friendly advice!"

Jen, as it turned out, had put her name down for Guild TV – or GTV as it was more snappily named on the banners. She turned to the others, her eyes shining. "If I want to go into journalism after I graduate, this will be perfect experience!"

Megan listened with half an ear, her attention already caught by a stall proclaiming 'University Choir'. What sort of music would it be? she wondered.

Turning back to Sue, who seemed to be an expert on each and every available club or society, Megan voiced her interest in the choir. As she had suspected, Sue was once again a fount of knowledge, not least because she was a member of the choir herself. Last year, she informed Megan, they had "done Bach's St John Passion" in the weeks leading up to Easter and carol sung around campus in early to mid-December.

"I wouldn't have to sing on my own, would I?" Megan asked tentatively. She had belonged to the school choir when she was younger and enjoyed singing; but the thought of having to perform a solo terrified her.

"Why don't you go and ask the people on the stall?" Jen sounded amused. "Every time you've wanted to know something, you've asked Sue. The people who run the societies don't bite, you know!"

Megan bit her lip. She felt reasonably confident with Jen, Sally and Sue - they were her friends after all – but these self-assured students on the stalls made her feel strangely shy. They seemed so effortlessly put together, for one thing, whereas she had spent twenty minutes this morning debating what to wear before deciding on the nondescript sweatshirt and jeans she normally hid behind. She knew full well that the men who had been so eager to talk to her little black dress the night before wouldn't have given her a second look the way she was dressed today.

How wonderful it must be to know instinctively what suited one and how to dress accordingly, she thought wistfully, mentally appraising one girl who wore a long patchwork skirt and Doc Marten boots and another clad head to toe in black with dark purple lipstick and dramatic eye makeup. (Well, maybe the latter was a little too extreme for her own taste, Megan conceded, but the Goth girl certainly looked striking.)

She touched Sue's arm. "Come on. Why don't you introduce me to the guy in charge?"

The rest of the day passed fairly uneventfully. The Three Musketeers ("There were *four* of them!" Sally protested when the others teased her over her choice of nickname for the group) worked through everything on Jen's itinerary. Megan loved the campus bookshop with its seemingly endless rows of classic literature but agreed with Jen that perhaps they should wait and find out exactly what they would be reading this term before they went mad and splurged half their grant on the tempting titles in front of them.

Five to four saw Sue and Sally scuttling off to the sports centre whilst Jen and Megan headed into the Arts Faculty for the dreaded cheese and wine – not that Jen would be dreading it, Megan thought sadly: by no stretch of the imagination could her friend be termed an alcoholic but she had certainly enjoyed a glass or two of wine at the previous evening's formal dinner.

The Mason Lounge was crowded with students of various shapes and sizes, mostly female. "We picked the wrong course!" Jen murmured. "There must be – what? seventy or so girls here? – but I can only see five men, no six."

One of these men was approaching them both. He grinned at Jen. "I saw you in the Guild earlier, didn't I? At the Freshers Fayre? I was helping to run the J Soc stall."

So he wasn't a Fresher then? Megan realised. In that case, why was he here?

As if reading her mind, the young man continued, "I'm doing English and Russian, Combined Honours, but because Russian's so difficult, they make you spend the whole of your first year doing nothing but Russian. So, I'm second year Russian but only first year English." He held out a hand. "My name's Elliot but everyone calls me Elly."

The next couple of hours sped by in a blur as faces introduced themselves and A level stories were swapped. Megan was relieved to find that soft drinks were on offer for the handful of people who didn't like alcohol and that grapes and strawberries accompanied the cheese. After a while she began to relax. She was never fully at ease in a social setting, but Jen was managing to talk enough for both of them. Megan found herself envying Jen's effortless conversational skills and the way in which she could move seamlessly from one topic of conversation to the next without having to consult an instruction manual.

Six o'clock and the party was breaking up. Jen and Megan trudged back up the hill to The Vale, accompanied by various people they'd met who were in Mason or Wyddrington. Megan found herself longing for a hot bath and a cup of tea and wondered whether she would find time for either before the second mandatory formal dinner began at seven thirty.

"You're so lucky!" One of their companions, Meryem, was a stunningly attractive Turkish girl from Mason who was also studying English and French. "We had a formal and a barn dance last night, like you, but there's nothing special laid on for tonight. I hear you've got Showaddywaddy performing."

"I hope they do *'Under the Moon of Love'*," Jen broke in eagerly. "We must have been – what? nine or ten when that came out. Do you remember it, Megan?"

Megan had a vague recollection of children at school singing the lyrics but she hadn't been allowed to watch 'Top of the Pops' or listen to Radio One like her peers. Her mother had the kitchen radio permanently tuned to Radio Two and so Megan had grown up listening to The Grumbleweeds when everyone else was humming music by Blondie or David Bowie. Once she'd turned fourteen and been allowed to sleep over at Anita's some weekends, she'd been introduced to the New Romantics and synth-pop and had acquired at least a working knowledge of Spandau Ballet, Duran Duran and The Human League. (*'Don't You Want Me'* was still one of her favourite songs.) Then, as Anita had 'got into' Adam and the Ants and Soft Cell, Megan had been exposed to their music too: Anita must have played *'Tainted Love'* to her well over a hundred times before she finally became disillusioned with Marc Almond and moved onto The Smiths.

For the time being, she just nodded politely and let Jen and Meryem carry the weight of the conversation. She had a feeling that, for her, a night of Showaddywaddy would prove just as stressful as the barn dance the previous evening.

Chapter Five

"You can't wear that!" Sue sounded outraged and Megan wasn't sure why. "You wore it last night," Sue told her patiently, "and a girl never wears the same outfit two days running. It just isn't done!"

Megan bit her lip worriedly. She didn't have anything else to wear to a formal dinner and said so immediately, but Sue wasn't taking no for an answer.

"Let me look in your wardrobe!" she ordered bossily, marching past Megan and yanking the wooden door open. Her fingers skimmed the rail. "Where are the rest of your clothes?"

"That's everything I've got," Megan said, a little defensively.

Sue pulled hangers out of the wardrobe, tossing the clothes on the bed. It was certainly a pitiful collection: apart from the black dress, which Megan was wearing, everything was conservative, outdated or both.

"What on earth is this?" Sue held up an embroidered blouse. "Cheesecloth may have been fashionable in the 1970s but it certainly isn't now!" Noticing Megan's expression she added kindly, "I was all set to go to college and study fashion, only my A level grades were too good for me to 'waste myself' on a non-academic degree. Trust me: I know what I'm talking about."

Megan surveyed Sue's outfit critically. They were of a similar height but Sue's ample proportions made her look much shorter. Her rounded figure put Megan in mind of Boule de Suif in the Maupassant short story she'd studied at A level.

Even so, Sue certainly knew how to dress with style. For campus she'd worn jeans teamed with a flowing smock that had "hidden her wobbly bits" as she'd put it, accessorised with a necklace of Victorian style beads and a chiffon scarf in her hair. She had managed to look at the same time casual yet artistic – no, Bohemian, that was the word. And she looked equally individual tonight in a floor length silk skirt topped with another flowing blouse and a fringed suede waistcoat; multiple silver bangles adorned each wrist and she wore her red hair in a loose bun with artfully escaping tendrils framing her face. She wasn't beautiful but she was certainly attractive.

Sue pulled a face as she examined the rest of Megan's clothing. "I'd ditch most of this and just buy yourself a whole new ensemble," she said finally, shuddering as she picked up a blouse with a pie frill collar. "I can't understand why someone with your potential to look good insists on dressing like a woman in her forties. Talk about lamb dressed as mutton!"

"I can't afford new clothes!" Megan exclaimed in alarm. She wouldn't put it past Sue to sneak into her room and get rid of everything she deemed dowdy or frumpy.

"Rubbish!" Sue's Received Pronunciation increased in tandem with her passion. "Most of my clothes are second hand. Selly Oak has several charity shops and there's a flea market every week in the Guild. One doesn't have to run up an overdraft to dress well!" She paused, her eyes taking in Megan's measurements. "I bought a shirt recently that should fit you. It's huge: I was going to wear it as a dress."

She disappeared into her own room, leaving Megan feeling vaguely alarmed. She and Sue were totally different sizes. She would have to think of a tactful way to turn down her friend's offer.

But when it came down to it, Sue knew exactly what she was doing. The oversized men's dress shirt she laid on the bed skimmed Megan's thigh at roughly the same length as her little black dress when cinched with a wide black belt worn low on the hips. Sue also produced a packet of thick black footless tights, explaining she had been going to use them for Popmobility but had another pair that would do just as well. Completing the outfit with Sue's Victorian beads and a pair of black lace fingerless gloves, Megan hardly recognised herself when she looked in the mirror. She could have easily been mistaken for a member of the audience on Top of the Pops.

"We still need to do something about your hair though," Sue said thoughtfully, removing Megan's scrunchie from her prim and proper ponytail. "Put your head down like this and shake your hair." She demonstrated.

Megan did as requested.

"That's much better!" Sue sounded approving. "Very Stevie Nicks."

Who?

"You could do with some eye make-up, though," her friend continued relentlessly. "I don't suppose you've got any black eyeliner?"

Megan hadn't.

"Well, not to worry." Sue remained cheerful. "You've got good skin so you don't need any foundation. I've got a free sample of mascara from the Avon Lady that I haven't used yet, so you can have that, and you can wear the lipstick you had on last night."

She vanished again, returning with not only the mascara but a turquoise eyeliner. "It's another freebie," she explained. "It wouldn't suit me but your eyes are a different shade of blue to mine. They were almost green yesterday when you were wearing that black dress."

It was true: Megan's eyes could take on any shade from grey to green to blue, depending on the colour that was closest to her face. Dave had called her a "Chameleon Girl" and started singing the song by Culture Club. Megan had found the whole thing highly embarrassing.

Now the eyeliner turned her eyes a startling aquamarine colour and the mascara defined her eyelashes so they stood out against her pale skin. Megan swallowed as she looked at her reflection. This wasn't her; then again, maybe it would be fun to be someone different, just for tonight …

Jen and Sally seemed equally impressed with Megan's transformation, joking that Sue must be a fairy godmother and asking if they could play Cinderella next. Jen was more casually attired tonight than she had been on the first evening, in a long yellow skirt with tassels and a black gypsy style top, whilst Sally was in trousers again, this time teamed with a different tee shirt. Megan wondered absently whether Sally actually possessed any skirts or dresses.

The meal took place as before with pre-allocated seating - which a lot of people seemed to be ignoring, thought Megan, glancing at the name card next to hers and deciding that the statuesque girl at her side definitely wasn't an Edward. She was pretty sure that the admiring crowd of men who surrounded this interloper were out of place themselves, particularly since Megan seemed to be the only other woman on the table.

"Over here!" Jen was gesturing to her frantically. "No one seems to be bothering with the seating plan tonight unless they're at the top table. We might as well all sit together."

Megan grabbed her room key and hurried over to the empty chair between Jen and Sally. Although the outfit Sue had picked for her was growing on her, she wished momentarily for last night's black dress with its handy pockets. Jen seemed to have a similar problem.

"Go on, Sally," she wheedled. "You're wearing trousers. You're the only one of us with pockets."

"I don't know why you even bothered bringing your room key when you know I've got mine," Sally snapped back, not unreasonably.

"What if one of us wants to go back earlier than the other one," Jen protested. "Please, Sally."

"I don't mind being the Key Lady." Sue made this surprising offer, holding out her hand for Jen's key. "I can take yours too, Megan." She patted her skirt conspiratorially. "I made this out of an old ball gown from a charity shop," she confessed. "I decided to make a couple of pockets with the material from the bodice. They're huge enough to hide half a canteen of cutlery so a few keys won't make much of a difference."

"You're a life saver," Megan began gratefully, but Jen cut her short.

"Just as well you're not into shoplifting, Sue. Just think what you could fit in there!"

This merry banter was stopped by the clinking of a fork on a glass from the top table. After everyone had quietened down, Ann Taylor rose to her feet.

"I just wanted to let you know that no other hall on The Vale has two formal dinners this Freshers," she drawled. "Ordinarily, this would just be a normal Saturday evening: find your own food and grab a drink or two at the bar later. Luckily for you, the JCR got their wires crossed when they were organising your Freshers events and double booked, which is why you had a meal and a barn dance last night and you get another meal and live music tonight."

This last remark prompted several cheers from High.

"So," Ms Taylor continued, "tonight there will be no more speeches after this one. Enjoy the food; enjoy the drink; enjoy the music. And if you end up with a hangover, don't come hammering on my door at some unearthly hour tomorrow morning expecting aspirins and sympathy – because I'll be out of both."

She sat down to tumultuous applause and the meal began.

This time, there were fewer bread rolls thrown and everyone seemed eager to leave the table quickly once they had finished eating. Megan and her friends were just about to get up when a tall, broad shouldered hunk waved at Sally from across the room then made his way to their table and stood there expectantly.

"Girls, this is Ged." Sally's cheeks flushed as she made the introduction. "Ged, this is Jen, my room mate. And that's Megan, and this is Sue."

Ged nodded politely to the other girls as he slid into the seat next to Sally.

"Are we still on for tomorrow morning?" His voice was deep but unexpectedly gentle.

"I met Ged at the sports centre earlier today," Sally explained. "We were both looking for the running club, and then we thought, why not go running together?"

"You must be a rugby player too," Jen broke in, gazing admiringly at Ged's physique.

He nodded shyly. "First fifteen at school. I don't know if I'll keep it up here though."

Ged was good looking, Megan thought critically, but he was a little *too* good looking for her. His dark hair and well-groomed appearance made him seem as if he belonged on a knitting pattern and she said as much to Jen, whispering to avoid hurting Ged's feelings.

"Seriously?" Jen seemed amused. "I would have thought that a nice, clean cut guy like that was exactly what you would go for. Don't tell me you have a secret fetish for bad boys!"

Megan was silent. Before Dave, she had experienced a totally unsuitable crush on a chain smoking, cider drinking boy a couple of years above her at school. That had fizzled out when she realised he rode a Vespa and not a Harley Davidson. At the time though, he had seemed the epitome of glamour in black drainpipe jeans and a battered leather jacket. Dave hadn't exactly channelled that sort of edginess himself, although he had gained a sort of reputation by stealing a plastic tray from the school canteen for a dare.

Dave. With a start she realised she had forgotten him again, despite telling his mother she would ring. She hadn't written to him either, being too busy unpacking yesterday and socialising today to put pen to paper.

"Sorry," she muttered, finding her feet, "I just need to go and make a phone call."

"Megan can't survive longer than five minutes without calling her boyfriend back home," Jen explained to Ged, a little unnecessarily, Megan thought.

Was she mistaken, or did a look of regret cross Ged's features?

Hurrying out of the dining room, Megan repeated her quest from the previous evening. This time, however, she was in luck: Dave answered the phone himself but sounded slightly surprised to hear her voice.

"Didn't your mum tell you I'd be ringing tonight?" Megan asked.

"Maybe. I don't know." Dave's tone was guarded. "Did she say where I was last night?"

"She told me you'd gone to a party with people from school." Megan was puzzled. She had been expecting Dave to sound slightly more enthusiastic after not seeing her for a few days.

He seemed to relax then. "Yeah, it was a good night. What have you been up to?"

Megan hesitated. Should she mention Dan? Better not to: after all, nothing had actually happened.

"I miss you," she said honestly.

"Yeah, me too." His response was just a little too quick. She wondered what she'd done wrong.

"I was thinking I might come home next weekend," she tried next.

Dave let out a sigh. "Next weekend's no good. I've been invited to another party."

"Can't we go together?" Why was he trying to push her away?

"Look, you wouldn't know anyone, okay? It's people from college. You wouldn't fit in." Although she said nothing, he must have realised his words had hurt her because his next suggestion burst out of nowhere: "But I could come and stay with you the following weekend. At least that way we'd get some privacy …"

He left the suggestion dangling in mid-air, but she knew exactly what he meant: he would be coming to Birmingham to sleep with her and she couldn't think of a single reason to put him off.

For some reason the phone call with Dave had unsettled her, so much so that she felt in a strange mood when she finally rejoined the others. By now the room had been transformed into a concert venue. A stage had been set up at the end nearest Ridge and a disco ball was shedding coloured shapes on the floor. Sue and Sally were standing chatting to Ged but Jen was nowhere to be seen.

"Where's Jen?" Megan asked as she joined the others.

Sally shrugged. "Went to get a drink twenty minutes ago and hasn't come back yet. Either there's a massive queue at the bar or she's got lucky."

And Megan had been so sure that Jen had been eying up Ged with a view to a possible relationship! Just then she caught sight of her friend: Jen was leaning against the bar in the corridor overhead, one hand clutching a drink and the other touching the arm of someone who looked suspiciously like Dan.

"I think she's busy," Megan heard herself saying. Deep down she felt a little hurt. Dan had acted as if he liked her, Megan, and now he was chatting up Jen. The situation made her feel somewhat foolish.

"Where have you been all my life?" A voice at her side made her jump. Megan looked up to see a tallish blond haired boy gazing at her with undisguised admiration.

"Sorry," she apologised, "do I know you?"

"Not yet ..." His chat up line was unbelievably corny. "... But we've got the rest of our lives to rectify that. I'm Ross. First year Geography. And you must be Stevie Nicks."

Megan hesitated, well aware that this Ross character had fallen for the girl he thought she was, not the real Megan at all. A sense of bedevilment entered her: tonight she could be anyone she wanted and hang the consequences! Peering up at him seductively from her mascara-ed eyelashes, she smiled. "My name's Esmerelda and I'm here to have a good time ..."

*

Only, because deep down she was still Megan, "a good time" consisted merely of letting Ross buy her two or three orange juices and allowing him to drool over her whilst she fluttered her eyelashes and managed to avoid letting him kiss her. Ross had already told her that he lived in Mason but was a huge Showaddywaddy fan, hence his reason for gatecrashing the High/Ridge event tonight. That meant he was quite safe to flirt with: she wasn't likely to bump into him again any time soon.

Out of the corner of her eye, she could see Jen and Dan, still talking to each other but now on the dance floor. Ross wasn't in Dan's league looks-wise or even in Ged's, but he was pleasant enough company and she found his enthusiasm for the band infectious. As the set came to a close, she thanked him again for the drinks and said she had better be making a move.

"I can walk you home," Ross said, just a little too eagerly.

Megan shook her head. "There's no need: I live here. Besides," she hated to burst his bubble, "I have a boyfriend already."

His face fell. "Of course you do. I should have realised that someone like you …" His voice tailed off in embarrassment.

"It's been a lovely evening," Megan told him sincerely.

"Just not with the right person," he finished for her. He kissed her cheek softly and slipped out of the room.

Chapter Six

It was only as they reached her end of the Ground Floor corridor – no, Megan corrected herself, their end – that she registered that Ged was still with them whilst Jen was not.

They paused as a group, looking from one to the other hesitantly. Sally spoke first. "Who wants to come in for a coffee? My room's the biggest."

Megan yawned. "If you'd said a mug of bedtime cocoa, I would have taken you up on the offer, but it's far too late for me to be drinking coffee." She placed her hand on the door handle of her room, then remembered that Sue had the key.

"Do you have decaff?" Ged asked hopefully.

Sally shook her head. "Just the normal kind."

"I've got decaff," Sue broke in, handing Megan her key. "My room's not as big as Sally and Jen's, but you can all fit on the bed."

Megan hesitated. "Thanks anyway, but no. I'm not used to being up late and it's been two nights in a row."

"Just the three of us then," Sue said matter-of-factly. "Unless you're expecting Jen to join us, Sally?"

The other girl frowned. "Perhaps I'd better go and look for her," she said quietly. "She hasn't got her key."

Sally was right: Jen had given her key to Sue and not asked for it back before she disappeared. Sue offered it to Sally but the latter shook her head. "You keep it – just in case I can't find her and she gets back here before I do. I'll leave a note on the door telling her to get the key from you if I'm not in."

It was a complicated business sharing a room with someone else, Megan thought drowsily as she unlocked her door and turned to say goodnight. She watched Ged disappearing into Sue's room, wondering if she should have accepted a decaff coffee after all, just to be sociable. After all, she hadn't visited anyone else's room yet and it would be interesting to see how Sue had arranged her own furnishings.

There was always tomorrow, she decided as she slipped under the sheets fully clothed, too tired to do anything else but take off her belt and turn out the light.

*

The next morning Megan was awoken by a light but frantic tapping on her door. She looked blurrily at her alarm clock, waiting for the numbers to swim into focus, and realised it was only just gone six. Who on earth could be wanting to speak to her at this time?

Sally stood outside, wearing a worried expression. "Jen didn't come back last night." She looked as if she had stayed up all night waiting for her.

"Might she have crashed at Sue's instead?" Megan suggested. "She might have come back late and not wanted to wake you up."

"Then why wake Sue instead?" Sally wanted to know. "Anyway, Sue still had her key. If she'd knocked on our door and there was no reply, she would have got her key from Sue and let herself in."

"Unless she couldn't wake Sue either," Megan suggested.

"But then she wouldn't have crashed out on Sue's floor," Sally argued. Her shoulders slumped. "Do you think I should tell Ann Taylor?"

"She probably just got chatting to someone and lost track of time," Megan said consolingly, although at the back of her mind a nagging voice reminded her that she had last seen Jen getting very friendly with Dan.

There was no time for further speculation as the door next to hers opened quietly and a sheepish looking Ged began creeping out.

"Morning, Ged." Sally said sweetly. "Were you asking Sue to come running with us?"

The poor man blushed. It was quite obvious that Sally thought he'd had another reason for being in Sue's room.

"You didn't see Jen last night after I went to look for her, did you?" Sally continued, trying to keep the concern out of her voice.

Ged shook his head. "We sat up for most of the night ... *talking*. We must have both dozed off at around four or five this morning. I'm just heading back to High now."

"Jen probably did the same thing," Megan said reassuringly as she and Sally watched Ged stride along the corridor in the direction of the foyer.

Sally nodded. "I'm sure you're right. I wish she'd warned me, though: I've felt really worried not knowing where she is."

Speak of the devil ... Here came Jen now, creeping through the corridor like the negative to Ged's photo. She started guiltily when she saw Sally and Megan waiting for her.

"I am *so* sorry," she began, looking from one to the other.

"Where were you?" This was Sally.

Jen reddened. "I can explain everything, but not out here in the corridor. Let's go inside."

Sally beckoned to Megan to join them. She grabbed her dressing gown then realised she was still in her outfit from the night before, Was she really turning into a slattern after just two nights away from home?

Sally and Jen's room was a cosy L-shape, half of it similar to Megan's in layout and the other half a rotated version of that. Sally filled an electric kettle at the single washbasin the room possessed and flicked the switch. While she waited for it to boil, she fussed about with mugs and a coffee jar, noticeably avoiding looking at Jen.

Eventually Jen broke the silence. "I know you're annoyed with me," she began, a little uncertainly.

Sally snorted.

"And yes, I probably should have let you know where I was, but I didn't think I'd be back late, and you're my roommate, not my mother." The words tumbled out in a rush. Megan and Sally looked at each other.

"So, where were you, then?" Sally asked casually.

Jen sighed.

"Last night in the bar I got talking to a guy called Dan – you remember, Megan: I interrupted you both the night before …" She paused meaningfully.

"Nothing happened," Megan said defensively.

Jen nodded. "I know. Dan was very quick to tell me the same thing himself. He's got quite a thing for you, Meg. When he came up and started talking to me last night, I thought I was onto something …"

Sally looked at her quizzically.

"He *is* very good looking," Megan said quickly.

"… Only it turned out he remembered me dragging you away and so he thought we were friends and I could put in a good word for him," Jen finished, looking slightly put out. "Anyway, we carried on talking and then he said did I want to go back to High …" She paused again. "It's not what you think. There was quite a group of them. He's on the eleventh floor, next to a double room which is twice the size of this one, and they had a sort of party going on in there so I thought, Why not? I was only going to stay for half an hour or so and then come back to Ridge. Only …" She swallowed. "… Only I got talking to this guy called Phil and we really hit it off … and he seemed to like me as much as I liked him … and so I went back to his room and we talked … and then we kissed … and we spent most of the night like that, cuddled up, talking and kissing …"

She gave Sally a pleading look. "I know you think I slept with him, but I didn't. Believe it or not, I *do* have morals. I happen to think you should be in love with someone, not just fall into bed with them because you fancy each other."

"It's none of my business." Sally sounded as uncomfortable as Megan felt.

"No, it is," Jen insisted, looking on the verge of tears. "If we're sharing a room, we have to trust each other."

"Maybe you need to set some ground rules," Megan suggested tentatively.

The other two looked at her.

"I don't know." She began to feel flustered. "Both of you make sure you've got your room key. And set a deadline for when you come back – if one of you isn't in by midnight, that means she's not coming back until next morning and the other one doesn't need to worry."

"Do you know," Sally said thoughtfully, "she might have a point. Although I can't see me ever being the one to act like a dirty stop-out …"

She caught Jen's eye as she said it and they both grinned.

"You've forgotten something, though," Sally continued after a moment.

"What?"

"When are you going to see Phil again?"

Megan excused herself a few moments later and returned to her own room. What with Jen and Phil and Sue and Ged, everyone seemed to be pairing off – and it was only Sunday! *Sue and Ged!* She suddenly realised that she and Sally had omitted to fill Jen in on the latest gossip.

No, that would have to wait until later. It was now a quarter past seven and Sunday breakfast didn't finish until ten. She would put on her nightshirt and grab another hour's sleep before she had to get up properly. Pulling off her borrowed attire, she crawled under the sheets, too tired to finish the job. Within seconds she was fast asleep.

*

"So," Jen began, buttering toast, "how was the boyfriend last night?"

Megan blinked. In all the other excitement she'd completely forgotten her own news.

"Oh," she tried to sound detached in spite of her rapidly beating heart, "Dave's coming over in a fortnight's time."

"We get to meet him then?" Jen sounded interested but Sally just grunted.

Megan nodded. "I was thinking maybe we could all go out for food together on the Saturday evening. We don't normally get fed in Hall then, do we?"

"Oh great!" Sally muttered. "That's all I need: a night playing gooseberry to you and Dave, and Jen and Phil, and Sue and Ged!"

"Phil and I aren't exactly a proper couple yet," Jen began. Then, as the full impact of Sally's words dawned on her, "Hang on! Did you say *Sue and Ged*?"

Megan and Sally both nodded.

"When did all this happen?" Jen demanded. "And why didn't you say something before?"

Briefly Sally described what they had seen that morning: how Ged had tiptoed out of Sue's room only minutes before Jen had returned from High Hall.

"He claimed they were only talking," she reported, "but I thought he looked guilty. What did you think, Megan?"

Before Megan could reply, Jen nudged her in the ribs. "Look out! She's coming over."

It was a very disgruntled Sue who plonked her tray down at the empty space on their table. "You could have called for me to go to breakfast!" she complained indignantly.

"We thought you'd want to sleep in," Sally said slily. "You know, after sitting up all night *talking* with Ged."

Sue blushed, her face almost matching her hair.

"We saw him leaving at six this morning," Megan told her, wondering if they would all now be uninvited to take tea in Sue's room.

Sue let out a sigh. "You've probably realised we weren't discussing French and German literature." She stirred her cornflakes listlessly. "Girls who look like me don't get chatted up by men who look like Ged. I was flattered. And I liked him too: he's a gentle soul who's never had any luck with women. I think he thought I was a safe person to confide in."

"And then you tripped and landed with your tongue in his mouth," suggested Jen, winking at Sally.

Sue started to stand up. "If you're not going to take this seriously …"

"Sit down," Megan told her, shooting Jen an angry look. Was she the only one who had noticed Sue seemed close to tears?

"When he kissed me," Sue continued, her voice wobbling a little, "I kissed him back. I thought I might never get the chance again. And then this morning … This morning …" Her voice cracked. "This morning he couldn't wait to leave. He's probably embarrassed in case his friends find out he kissed a fat girl."

There was an awkward silence whilst the others tried to think of something to say.

"And the worst of it is," Sue went on after a moment had ticked by, "I'll have to see him every morning when he goes running with Sally."

"No you won't!" broke in Jen quickly. "You're never up before eight and Sally's going to go running at seven. Anyway," she checked her watch, "I need to go. I still haven't finished unpacking, let alone decided what to wear for my first day of lectures tomorrow. Come on, Sal!"

They disappeared, leaving Megan alone with Sue. Life was beginning to get complicated.

Chapter Seven

The rest of the day passed rather uneventfully. Megan took Sue's advice to heart and put a few items of clothing aside for the charity shops. Would they consider part exchange? she wondered. It would certainly save her some money if she could take away a new outfit for each one she donated.

She also sat down and penned a long letter to Dave, telling him about her new friends and the Hall of Residence. "I'm looking forward to your visit," she wrote, "so you can see how gorgeous The Vale looks with all the autumnal colours – and so my friends can see how gorgeous *you* look!"

Perhaps she should take that last bit out? Dave was distinctly average looking compared to a lot of the men she'd met so far. That was another point to consider: it probably wasn't tactful to tell him that so many men had expressed an interest in her, or that she was living next door to a Hall that housed enough men for her to have a different one for every day of the year.

She screwed the letter up and was about to begin again when she thought she heard a tapping on her door. Opening it carefully, she realised that it was Sue who had a visitor, not her: there stood Ged outside the room next door, carrying a bunch of carnations and wearing a nervous expression.

Megan began to shut the door quietly, not wanting to pry; even so, she couldn't miss seeing Sue's door open and Ged stepping inside. Perhaps he was keener on her than Sue had thought?

A few hours later, the knocking was definitely for her. Jen bounced excitedly in the corridor. "We're going out for food. Are you coming?"

"What sort of food?" Megan was cuisinally cautious: her mother's repertoire consisted of meat and two veg or, if she was feeling adventurous, a shop bought quiche with green salad.

"There's a place in the centre of town called The American Food Factory." Jen's eyes were shining. "Phil and some other people are going and they've asked if we want to join them."

Other people? Did that mean Dan would be there too?

"Who else is going?" Megan asked slowly.

"Sal, Sue, Ged, Phil, a friend of his called Matt, me – and you. If it's any good, we can go again when your boyfriend's over."

Still Megan hesitated. She had realised that the names Jen had mentioned added up to a total of seven. Presumably Matt had been called upon to sit with Sally so she didn't feel like a gooseberry again, but that meant Megan would be the spare part. On the other hand, it would be nice to go out in a group – and to talk to a few men who didn't have a hidden agenda.

"Okay," she said, making her mind up, "but the food had better be good!"

The food was good. In fact, it was a perfect outing: from the camaraderie as they walked to Fiveways Station to catch the train into town ("Only a few minutes' journey from here!" said Phil, looking pleased.) to the excitement of trying food she'd never experienced before (whoever had invented lasagna was a genius, Megan decided), nothing could have been improved upon. It had been fun getting to know Phil and Ged better too, Megan reflected, secretly envying her friends for having met such genuinely nice guys.

Not that Dave was unpleasant, she reminded herself hastily, but Phil and Ged were still at the best behaviour stage where they wanted their girlfriends' friends to like them and so acted accordingly. She certainly couldn't remember Dave ever buying her flowers – although he'd once tried to give her a shoplifted packet of jelly babies, when they were fifteen, before they'd started going out.

Phil's friend Matt was nice too, she thought, if a little highly strung. Shorter than Phil and Ged, he was about five foot six and handsome in a clean cut public school way – like so many of the men she'd encountered so far. (She was beginning to realise that few of the students here had been to a comprehensive, like she had; then again, wasn't it only around thirteen per cent of the population that actually made it into higher education these days and even fewer who got to go to a 'real' university?)

Matt was a Combined Honours student like her, taking French and Drama. She had told him she would look out for him in French lectures and he had seemed pleased. He was also surprisingly nervous for someone taking Drama: he had been unable to speak to her without stammering and had struggled to make eye contact. Perhaps he was always shy around women, having gone to an all-boys school? Still, he had been pleasant enough company.

And now they were all strolling back to Hall, Sally in front of her with Matt; Sue and Ged lagging behind; Jen and Phil bringing up the rear. Tonight would be the first of the weekly Sunday discos organised by the JCR, Sue had warned, wrinkling her nose as she said it. When pressed, she had admitted that the discos were generally regarded as the low point of the week and that hardly anyone ever made it onto the dance floor.

*

Sue had been right. Against her better judgement Megan had agreed to accompany her three friends to the Hall bar that evening and, as they walked through the empty dining room, its flashing coloured bulbs highlighting people's absence, she was struck by how forlorn it all seemed.

By way of contrast the corridor-bar was heaving. "Standing room only, I think," gasped Jen as they squeezed their way to the counter to order drinks. "What are you having, Megan?"

"Just an orange juice, thanks," Megan replied promptly. She hadn't realised that university life would revolve around such an alcohol-fuelled culture: what she had mistaken for a toothbrush holder in her room was actually the half pint glass every girl was supposed to take to the bar. (The boys' rooms were equipped with pint glasses, which Jen claimed was pure sex discrimination. "I know girls your size who can drink every man I know under the table!" she'd protested when Megan had foolishly suggested that maybe women drank less than men.)

"Why do we have to bring our own glasses?" Sally complained. "They don't have to in the other halls – I asked some of the people who gatecrashed Showaddywaddy last night and they were surprised we have to."

"That's because they have proper bar facilities and we don't," Sue explained. "There isn't anywhere to wash glasses, so we either bring our own or pay a penny for a disposable plastic glass."

"Ah," Jen said with sudden understanding, "so *that's* what a 'flimsy' is!" She pointed to a notice affixed to the counter which proclaimed that students without their own glass would be "charged extra for a flimsy."

"I'd say I've forgotten my glass tonight but that would be a flimsy excuse!" Sally quipped, making them all groan.

Later they were joined by their male counterparts – or Miles Per Gallon as Sally insisted on calling them. "MPG," she explained when the other girls looked puzzled: "Matt, Phil and Ged."

"I'm not surprised you're still single, making jokes like that," Jen muttered darkly.

As they continued chatting, it transpired that Matt had also signed up for the University Choir. Megan wasn't surprised: he looked like the sort of young man who would be more into madrigals than heavy metal. Meanwhile, Sue was busy making plans for the three of them to keep each other company on the walk to the School of Music that Tuesday evening.

"What about Ged?" Megan asked. "Doesn't he want to join us?"

Sue shuddered. "The poor boy's tone deaf. He tried singing along to Phil Collins last night and it was not a pleasant experience."

It was, however, a pleasant experience to wake up the following morning and know that this was the first proper day of term. Each of the Freshers had discovered a letter in her pigeonhole containing a timetable for lectures and tutorials. Megan would be 'free' until her two o'clock 17th Century French Drama lecture and then had English lectures at ten on Tuesday and Thursday, more French with Phonetics at nine and a Language tutorial at eleven on Wednesday, followed by her English tutorial at twelve, and a French Lit tutorial and lecture at eleven and two respectively on Thursday.

"I don't seem to be doing anything at all on Fridays!" she said in surprise. She had envisaged her days being mostly full with perhaps the odd 'Private Study' session, like in Sixth Form, but she only seemed to have seven or eight hours actually accounted for.

"Lucky you!" said Jen with feeling. "I've got Anglo Saxon at nine on Fridays. Mind you, it's the only early one I've got. What about you, Sal?"

Sally shrugged. "Probably similar to the two of you. One or two hours every day. I wish they weren't so spread out though: on Tuesdays I have a ten o'clock and a five!"

"Don't let any of the engineers or scientists hear you complain," broke in Sue, who was waiting for them to join her for breakfast. "They're on from nine till five every day!" She turned to the girl behind her and Megan recognised her from the car park on Saturday. "Ali, what's that joke everyone makes about Arts students?"

Ali grinned. "Why don't Arts students look out of the window in the mornings?"

The others looked at her expectantly.

"Because then they'd have nothing to do in the afternoons!" Ali explained triumphantly.

Perhaps university life wasn't going to be as challenging as Megan had first thought.

Chapter Eight

The first week went quickly. For French Literature this term Megan would be studying Corneille, Racine and Molière – the first two, Sue explained knowledgeably, would be like reading Shakespearean tragedies in French – and her set book for English tutorials was 'Joseph Andrews' by Henry Fielding, to be read in conjunction with a critical work entitled 'The Rise of the Novel'.

Despite there being so few timetabled hours, Megan realised she would have to work at least as hard as she had for A levels: then she had read four French texts over two years, with the teachers translating most of what was studied; now she would have to read a French play every week, write and deliver a mini lecture for one of her weekly tutorials and produce a 5,000 word essay for assessment before the end of term. In addition to this, she would be given an extract from an English classic every Wednesday and be expected to hand in a perfect French translation of it by midday on the Friday – and this wasn't counting her workload for English, which also required her to write and deliver a seminar paper at least once a term as well as reading all the extra books which would aid her understanding of 'Joseph Andrews'.

Megan's work ethic now stood her in good stead. Rather than idle away the hours she had free between lectures, she would take herself off to the library where she could hide in one of the stacks and read or write in privacy. She knew it would be only too easy to walk back to her room in Hall, intending to work, and be sidetracked by one of her friends 'popping in for a coffee,' so she resolutely made herself do as much as possible between the hours of nine and five.

She did make an exception after Tuesday's ten o'clock English lecture, though, allowing herself a 'coffee break' with Jen in the Mason Lounge. There she encountered the tea lady Sue had mentioned previously: an older lady whose hair was an interesting shade of yellow. She dispensed shop bought biscuits along with tea from a giant urn and milky coffee in polystyrene cups. Megan enjoyed the coffee but found the service exceptionally slow. One came here for convenience and ambience rather than competence, she thought.

As the first week elapsed, everything seemed to hurtle past Megan in a blur. She soon got into a routine: up at seven, breakfast at eight, on campus by nine. Everyone in Hall was allocated two slices of bread and a roll with their evening meal, so Megan and her friends saved their pennies by keeping the bread for sandwiches for the next day's lunch. It was often possible to snaffle hard boiled eggs or sausages from breakfast too. There was a strict 'No Food' policy in the library, but Megan soon perfected the art of surreptitiously eating in a quiet corner where she could remain undetected.

It was with a shock that she realised her first week of lectures was at an end. She was surprised how much she had fitted into the week along with her academic studies: choir with Sue and Matt on the Tuesday evening; Popmobility with Sue on the Friday, after she'd handed in her first French translation homework; and an hour or so in the Hall Bar every night with Jen, Sue and Sally – and the MPG boys. Considering that the highlight of her week when she was still living at home in the past year had been a break from revision to watch Coronation Street with her mother, this newly rediscovered art of socialising was most welcome: it reminded her of the Lower Sixth and how she and Anita had hung out in a group with Joe and Dave before romance had blossomed.

Dave would be visiting in another week. She wondered how he would get on with her new friends. She had written to him twice this week, lengthy letters telling him about Hall and lectures, but been careful only to mention the girls she had met: she didn't want him jumping to conclusions about any of her male friendships. For his part, he had sent her a postcard of Littleborough with the inscription "Weather crap – wish you were here?" Although it wasn't a romantic message, at least he'd made the effort.

The second week of term was unsurprisingly like the first: from the poorly attended Sunday disco in Hall to the sausage, bacon and beans for breakfast on Wednesday, nothing changed in the daily routine – except for her Wednesday morning Phonetics lecture which initially had seen a full turn out of seventy but by Week Two had dropped alarmingly to only fifteen or twenty students. This was partly due to Professor Burns, their lecturer and the Head of Department, who epitomised the absent minded academic, dropping his notes, tripping over his board pointer and obliviously beginning to eat his chalk whilst he contemplated the room vaguely. "Oh dear!" he spluttered when he finally came to his senses, "I do hope it's not poisonous!" He then proceeded to study the chalk packet, searching for the words 'non-toxic', before declaring, "All it says is *'blanche'*!"

"How on earth is he in charge of the department?" Megan whispered to Matt as this fiasco unfolded.

He smiled shyly back at her. "I expect he's very clever – just not in touch with the real world." A moment's pause; then, "Do you like jazz?" he asked next.

She was flummoxed by this random question. "It's okay. Why?"

"There's an open air jazz festival in Cannon Hill Park this Saturday. That's not far from here? Do you want to go?"

It sounded like both an excellent day out and the ideal opportunity for Dave to meet her friends in a fairly casual setting; but when she rang him the following evening, Dave flatly refused to spend the day in the park, commenting that he'd thought they could spend some time exploring the city centre.

"I thought I'd arrive at lunch time," he told her. "There must be loads of places we can eat near the station."

Her friends wouldn't meet him until later then. Megan tried not to feel disappointed; was secretly rather relieved. After a fortnight apart, she was struggling to remember what it was that she liked about Dave. Would they have got together at all, she wondered now, had his best friend not been going out with hers?

Even so, her heart fluttered when she woke up on Saturday morning. Should she ask Jen if she could borrow something to wear? Dave had already seen everything in her rather limited wardrobe and she felt suddenly anxious to make a good impression.

Luckily she had succumbed to Sue's insistence the day before that they hit the Guild after PopMo to check out the flea market. She now possessed a set of thin, silver bangles like Sue's and had chosen (with her friend's help) two silk scarves for her hair: one patterned in pinks and blues, the other plain black.

In the end, she found herself knocking on Sue's door in her nightie, asking to borrow the oversized men's shirt again. She would wear it with her jeans this time, she decided, and tie back her hair with the black silk scarf.

Sue was happy to give her not only the shirt but some advice as well. "If you're meeting him at New Street, you should take him to the Art Gallery," she suggested. "You can have as much or as little culture as you want and then have lunch in the Edwardian tea room."

That sounded like a splendid plan. A light lunch for two in a period setting would be the ideal counterbalance to a group meal later at a more modern venue. Megan set off to meet her boyfriend with a heart full of anticipation for what would surely be the perfect date.

Only it wasn't. Instead of greeting her like she'd hoped, with a heartfelt embrace and a lingering kiss, Dave stared at the scarf in her hair. "What on earth are you wearing? You look ridiculous!" He then proceeded to veto the Art Gallery idea, including the tea room: "That sounds far too pretentious. Isn't there a McDonald's?"

Megan acquiesced but inside she was fuming. Why was Dave being so awkward? As they sat eating fries and burgers, sipping milkshake (her) and root beer (him), she mentioned the planned group outing to the American Food Factory that evening.

"I don't think so." He was unexpectedly brusque. "I've come to see you, not your friends. Anyway," – he actually leered at her – "this is our chance to be alone together, remember? I've been looking forward to this ever since you went away."

For a moment Megan was too stunned to speak. Was *that* the only reason why he'd come to see her? If she'd had any doubts before about sleeping with him, these now increased tenfold as she gazed at the stranger in front of her and admitted to herself that he simply wasn't what she wanted anymore.

There was no way she could tell him that, of course: not when he'd come so far to see her and especially not in McDonald's, of all places. No, she would have to ride out this weekend and then tell him as kindly as possible when he left that it was all over.

Dave adamantly refused to walk back to Hall from Fiveways, despite Megan's protestations that it was only twenty minutes. In the end they compromised, taking the train to the University and walking the half mile from there. She couldn't help comparing his attitude to the easy-going natures of her new male friends.

Nothing she said or did was right that day, it seemed. Her room was poky; The Vale boring; and he was outraged that the Hall Bar was a corridor. "Aren't there any proper pubs around here?" he complained.

Feeling close to throttling him, Megan tapped on Jen and Sally's door, hoping to find at least one of them in. To her surprise, the whole crowd was in there, including Matt.

"How was the jazz?" Megan asked.

"Wonderful." His enthusiasm was in stark contrast to her boyfriend's apathy. "Are you coming out to dinner with us?"

"Dave doesn't want to socialise," Megan said shortly. "He said he wants to go to a proper pub tonight – I don't suppose any of you know where I can find one?"

"If you go down past the Guild and onto the Bristol Road, there are three or four of them pretty close together," Sue said, looking up from the neck massage Ged appeared to be giving her. She began to reel off names. "The Brook's on the other side of the road – that's normally packed with students; then on this side you've got The Gunbarrels and another one – I think it's called The Goose."

"Thanks." Megan wished irrationally that she were spending the evening with her friends instead of Dave. And then she reminded herself that Dave would soon be history and felt slightly ashamed of herself. She would make his last evening with her a pleasant one: it was the least she could do.

*

It was nine thirty and Dave was extremely drunk. She'd followed Sue's advice and taken him down to The Gunbarrels, where he'd rapidly drunk six pints of something (she was hazy about the difference between lager and bitter) and then demanded that she take him for a curry. Never having tried that type of cuisine herself, she would have been clueless had it not been for the helpful young man who'd overheard her asking the barmaid for assistance. (He'd looked slightly put out a moment later once he realised she had a boyfriend.)

So now here they were, sitting in The Dilshad on the Bristol Road. Dave had ordered some sort of ridiculously hot dish which he hadn't been able to eat and looked ready to pass out in the mango chutney. Megan had been too anxious to order a main meal or even a starter so had made do with nibbling a poppadom, which seemed to be rather like a large crisp.

"Come on!" She tugged at Dave's sleeve. "We need to start heading back to Hall."

Dave opened one eye and regarded her blearily. "I'm too tired to walk back. Can't you order a taxi?"

"Have you got money for a taxi?"

Megan felt like crying. This wasn't how she'd wanted her evening to end.

After some futile fumbling in his jeans pocket, Dave suddenly remembered that he'd put his wallet in his jacket for safekeeping. Megan extracted a ten pound note to pay for his meal and wondered how one went about ordering a cab.

Eventually she remembered that her Guild card displayed several numbers of taxi firms and one of the waiters took pity on her and let her use the restaurant's phone to make the call. It wasn't long after that until the car arrived and she somehow managed to squeeze Dave into the back of it, hoping desperately that he wouldn't be sick on the journey home.

The taxi pulled up outside Ridge a few minutes later. Megan found that she could just about scrape together enough coins for the fare. (The driver wasn't impressed with the array of small change, but it was all she and Dave had between them.)

Dave looked indignant as she led him into the foyer. "What am I doing here?" he protested, his voice far too loud. "This is a girls' hall!"

Trying to keep him quiet, Megan pushed him along the Ground Floor corridor towards her room, praying that no one would notice him. He collapsed onto her bed the moment he entered.

Megan was in a quandary: she had borrowed a sleeping bag from Sally, thinking that Dave could sleep on her floor whilst she kept the bed. She doubted Dave would go along with this in his inebriated condition but resented the idea of him taking her bed after he had behaved so badly.

"Come here and give us a kiss." He was slurring his words and his breath reeked of alcohol. At this moment she found him totally resistable.

"I'm not going to sleep with you." The words popped out before she had time to think what she was saying.

"Who said anything about sleeping?" He raised his arm and made a half-hearted lunge at her.

"I don't want to have sex with you."

She had finally said it but his reaction surprised her. Instead of sounding angry or even dejected, Dave let out a hollow laugh. "Just as well I'm getting it somewhere else then."

"You don't mean that," she said automatically. He was just trying to save face, to pretend he was seeing someone else to salvage his own dignity.

He rolled over, addressing his comments to the wall. "Two weeks ago, when you rang and I wasn't in, and my mum told you I'd gone to a party ..."

A sick feeling started to form in the pit of her stomach. Even so, she let him continue.

"I went with a few other people, in a group. It was me and Jarvis and Paula and Rachel. I could tell Paula fancied me and I felt the same way. When she asked me if we were still together, I said yes, and then she said it didn't matter because you were so far away …"

Megan swallowed. "Did you sleep with her?"

"It wasn't really cheating on you." His voice was harsh. "It's not like we were having a normal relationship."

"You could have waited," she said softly. Waited until he saw her again to tell her it was over before sleeping with someone else. Waited for her as long as it took.

"I'm eighteen," he said abruptly. "Everyone else was having sex. I wanted to know what I was missing out on." He paused. "I came here thinking I'd give you one last chance."

"That's very big of you!" she said sarcastically.

"I thought I'd see how it went this weekend … whether we could make it work. But I could tell straight away it wasn't right: you want art galleries and jazz festivals and I want …" His voice tailed off.

"What do you want?" She was aware she sounded brittle.

"I want a girl I can get drunk with and then get laid with," he said simply. "Paula just wants a good time – and so do I."

"So that's it then?"

Pain squeezed her heart. She wondered why it hurt so much when she'd been going to end it anyway.

Chapter Nine

Megan spent a tortured night on the floor, tossing and turning as much from her inner turmoil as from her uncomfortable sleeping position. Although a part of her felt she should have kicked Dave out of not only her bed but her room as well, she had been brought up to be a well-mannered hostess. Dave was her guest, ergo he had to have the bed. She drew the line at taking him along to the Hall breakfast though.

Unable to bear her friends' company this morning – they were bound to ask how things had gone the previous evening and she was still too raw to want to talk about it – she decided to go to breakfast early and thus avoid having to sit with anyone. Better still, she would fill her pockets with hardboiled eggs and toast which she could take outside and eat by the lake. Dave was still fast asleep in her room so she couldn't eat there; the lake seemed a perfect alternative.

She was so early that she had to wait a few moments for the catering staff to unlock the door to the dining room. No one else was about. She would be able to accomplish her mission.

Just as she was about to leave, a familiar face swam into her vision. "Megan! You're up early."

"Just getting a breakfast picnic together." She gestured at her contraband.

"Ah, I see. For you and Dave." With his typical bumbling gaucheness, Matt put two and two together and made forty-seven.

It was far too complicated for her to attempt an explanation now, so Megan merely nodded and made her goodbye, fleeing to the sanctuary of the lake where she sat in silence for a good forty minutes, soaking in the atmosphere, trying to heal her broken heart.

Early morning sunlight dappled the water with golden ripples. Everything around was still, apart from the occasional splashing of ducks or the indignant honk of a goose. In the distance she could see students in running gear and wondered whether Ged and Sally would be out jogging this morning.

Reluctantly she looked at her watch, cognisant that Dave would be waking soon and that she should be getting back. Not for *his* benefit, she told herself sternly: no, she wanted to check that he hadn't damaged anything in her room – and to ensure that he left as soon as possible.

One day, she promised herself, she would have the sort of boyfriend who would enjoy the same sort of things she did: a man who would not only like art galleries and jazz festivals but lakeside picnics too. That was an aspiration for the future; her priority now was to put Dave on the first train back to Manchester.

An hour later and it was all over. Megan breathed a sigh of relief as the train doors closed and her ex-boyfriend left campus – and her life – for good. She was aware that at some point she would have to tell the others what had happened. For now, though, she could hit the library and hide in her usual fourth floor sanctuary. Annotating 'Joseph Andrews' wouldn't exactly make her feel better, but it least it would take her mind off Dave. And in the stacks there were no awkward questions …

It was approaching six when Megan finally put down her pen, having worked hard on *'Le Cid'* as well as Fielding's classic. Her stomach rumbled suddenly, reminding her that she had eaten nothing since her early morning eggs and toast. She had possessed the foresight to bring a bottle of water with her to the library, but that was long since drunk. There would be no food in Hall this evening; she had better find something to eat here on campus – and fast.

The Guild was busy, despite it being a Sunday evening. Although the Guild Shop was closed, along with some of the food venues, the first floor fast food outlet seemed to be doing a roaring trade. Gazing at the menu on the wall – What on earth was a McDocherty burger? Megan wondered – she realised that this must be the university's answer to McDonald's. Didn't they have anything healthy? she conjectured crossly.

A voice behind her made her jump. "I didn't have you down as a closet burger-fiend."

Dan stood there, a half-eaten greasy mound of beef clutched in his hand.

"I'm not." Megan struggled to collect her thoughts, distracted by the sight of Dan's long legs in their close-fitting jeans and the way his studded boots tapered to a point. She had forgotten how good looking he was.

"On your own then?" He took another bite of the revolting looking burger. Megan watched, fascinated, as a dribble of juice rolled slowly down his jaw.

"I've been working in the library," she explained, knowing how feeble this must sound.

He nodded. "I'd already noticed you're not the party animal type."

He grinned and Megan felt her stomach flip, the memory of their almost-kiss flooding her body with an unwelcome chemical reaction.

"What are you doing here?" she asked stiltedly.

He pushed the rest of his burger into his mouth and chewed thoughtfully before making a reply.

"Waiting for The Mermaid to open. You know how it is with Sundays: the four hours from three to seven seem to last forever."

Since Megan wasn't the type to frequent pubs on any day of the week, she was ignorant of Sunday licensing laws so just nodded at his words.

"I'd better let you go then ..." She turned back to the menu but Dan caught her arm. "Fancy a coffee? I'm having one."

She nodded dumbly, too surprised to speak. "Okay," she stuttered finally.

He counted a couple of coins into her hand. "I'll find a table. See you in a minute."

By the time she reached him, carrying a tray with the coffees and a fishburger, he had lit a cigarette. Megan wrinkled her nose distastefully. She had never understood people who liked smoking in restaurants.

"Thanks." He took it gratefully and helped himself to sugar. "This stuff's not great but it's better than nothing."

Megan tasted the coffee and wasn't sure she agreed. It was the bitterest liquid she had ever experienced. Was it really coffee, or had the girl at the counter handed her a cup of cleaning fluid by mistake?

Dan stubbed out his cigarette on the aluminium ash tray provided and deftly lit another. "Not a smoker either?"

She shook her head.

"Sensible girl. It's a dreadful habit."

Was he laughing at her?

Slowly he reached out his hand and stroked her cheek. "You're just a little girl, aren't you? How long do I have to wait for you to grow up enough for me to seduce you?"

Megan choked on her last mouthful of burger.

"Hey!" He sounded alarmed. "I was only joking!"

She pushed her unfinished coffee aside and stood up. "I've got to get back to Hall. Thanks for my drink."

"Any time." He still seemed amused by her. She had only ever been a diversion. "See you around some time."

"Yes," she said softly. "See you around."

*

Megan returned to Hall, walking slowly as if to put off the inevitable moment when she would have to tell her friends that she was now without a boyfriend. Maybe she wouldn't have to say anything, she reasoned: there were, after all, other topics of conversation to be had.

And then the shame of it hit her afresh. Dave had cheated on her. With Paula, a girl she had always regarded as a friend. How many other people from school knew? she wondered. Were they already laughing at her behind her back?

It didn't matter how many times she told herself she was better off without him: she was now Megan Jackson: The Girl Whose Boyfriend Slept With Someone Else. If only she'd rung him earlier in the week and finished things then, instead of trying to protect his feelings and wait until she saw him face to face!

She had fully intended to stay in her room that night, not knowing whether she could trust herself to be around her friends without bursting into tears; but when first Jen and then Sue came and practically begged her to join them for a quick drink in the bar, she found herself unable to refuse.

So now she sat here, sipping her habitual orange juice and trying to pretend that her heart wasn't shattered into a thousand tiny pieces. It wasn't the loss of Dave she mourned so much as the loss of her self-esteem.

"It must have been a good weekend with Dave," Sally began, oblivious to Megan's mood. "We didn't see either of you at all."

"They must have had a lot of catching up to do," grinned Jen. "Did you manage to reignite the passion, Megan?"

It was too much. Megan sprang to her feet and rushed out of the bar, leaving the others staring after her in shock.

"Was it something I said?" Jen muttered, bewildered.

"Go after her!" Sue hissed at Ged.

He looked slightly uncomfortable. "Shouldn't it be you? Or one of the other girls?"

"What she needs," Sue told him bossily, "is a bit of male support. She's obviously broken up with him – or he's dumped her: it amounts to the same thing. She just needs someone who can give her a manly perspective on why it went wrong."

"But I don't know what's gone wrong," Ged protested.

"It doesn't matter." Sue looked wearily at Jen and Sally. "Back me up on this one: Megan needs a 'safe' male i.e. one who's already happily attached – that's why you'd be no good, Matt: she might think you were trying to chat her up – to tell her she's an attractive woman and Dave must have been mad to let her go."

In the end, Ged did as he was told - although he didn't look very happy about it.

"Are you sure that's a good idea?" Sally asked hesitantly as they watched his back retreating down the corridor. "If Dave *has* dumped her, she probably won't want to speak to another guy for weeks."

"Which is why Ged needs to talk to her now," Sue explained patiently, "so she can see that there *are* still some nice men out there and that they're not all scumbags like her ex."

Megan wasn't difficult to find. She was sitting in the empty foyer, gazing listlessly through the plate glass windows at the darkened Vale. Ged marvelled at how tiny she looked, curled up on one of the mustard vinyl chairs, like a child waiting for a parent to come and make everything better.

She looked as if she had been crying.

Wordlessly he sat down next to her. People thought him the 'strong silent type' whereas the truth was that he was actually quite shy. He was also feeling very confused: he'd been attracted to Megan upon first meeting her, but she'd had a boyfriend so he'd held back. Now she was single – and he was with Sue. It might only be a fortnight into their relationship, but Sue had already stolen his heart with her sense of humour and her incredibly generous nature. She was a good listener too. He thought he might be falling for her.

No, Megan was definitely off limits. If only she didn't look so attractive with her tear stained face and those huge eyes.

"Dave cheated on me." The words came out in a whisper, almost as if they were too painful to say aloud.

She looked up at him, eyes over-brimming with liquid emotion, and something stirred inside him. "You bewitching creature!" he murmured as he bent to kiss her.

Megan was momentarily too stunned to do anything but kiss him back. Then her brain started to function again. No! This was Ged, Sue's boyfriend: it was wrong! At the same time, a part of her wondered, Did he *really* call me a bewitching creature?

Pushing him away hastily, she struggled to her feet, attempting to put some distance between them. For a moment they stared at each other in horror, then Ged covered his face with his hands.

"Megan, I'm sorry ..."

He couldn't look at her; didn't know what had come over him.

Without waiting to hear the rest of his apology, she turned and fled for the sanctuary of her room.

*

"Well, did you find her?"

Sue fired the question at him as he returned to the bar. He nodded.

"And?"

"He cheated on her." Ged held out his hand. "Let's go to your room."

"So ...?" She was obviously wanting more information. Ged sat down on the bed next to her, then thought better of it and stood up again.

"There's something I need to tell you," he began.

"I'm listening." Sue thought she knew already what the 'something' was: she hadn't failed to notice Ged's initial interest in Megan: in fact, that was one of the reasons she'd sent him after her, to see whether he'd try anything on now that Megan was unattached.

"I ... She ... She was upset ... crying ... so I kissed her." Noticing Sue's expression, he added unnecessarily, "I just wanted to make her feel better."

"I'm sorry. I didn't realise snogging was a valid counselling technique." Sarcasm dripped from Sue's lips like rain from a leaky gutter.

Ged tried again. "I didn't plan it: it just happened."

"That makes me feel so much better!" Sue took a breath. "Why do you think I sent you after her? I've seen the way you look at her when you think no one's watching."

"Yes, she's pretty," Ged argued, "but she's like a little doll. She's so tiny she makes me feel as if I could break her by mistake. She's not a real woman ... like you." He ran his hand slowly over her curves. "It's you I want, not her."

"Hmmph." She still sounded unconvinced. "And how would you feel if I told you that you're not the only man in my life?" she challenged.

"Seriously?" Ged looked momentarily worried. Surely he wasn't going to lose her now?

By way of answer, Sue drew back the covers, revealing a battered looking teddy bear wearing red shorts.

"Last year Ted used to sit at my desk every day when I was on campus, working on my seminar papers for me," she explained. "He's had to keep a bit of a low profile this year: I wasn't sure how Megan and the others would react to him." She picked him up and caressed him lovingly. "I've had him since I was a baby and he's slept with me every night."

"Lucky Ted!" Ged said feelingly.

"So you be careful, Ged Masters," Sue said in a warning tone, "because any nonsense from you and I'll get Ted to beat you up!"

"I promise I'll behave."

"That's a pity," Sue murmured back at him, "because I was rather hoping we could misbehave together …"

And after that there was no more talking.

Chapter Ten

Megan quickly adjusted to Life Without A Boyfriend. Really, she thought, it was no different than before, apart from the time she saved not having to write Dave letters or try to ring him. And, since within hours of being dumped she had been bought coffee by one attractive man and kissed by another, she had no reason to let it knock her self-confidence.

She realised that Ged had mentioned something to Sue when the latter appeared at her door the following day and asked for a quick word.

"Ged's told me everything," she declared with no preamble.

"I see." Megan wondered what she was supposed to say. 'Sorry I let your boyfriend kiss me'? 'Sorry I didn't beat him off with a stick'? In the end she settled for, "I didn't come onto him."

"No," Sue sighed, "you were just you. Ged's like most men: he can't resist a damsel in distress."

Megan didn't know whether to feel relieved or offended: Sue didn't seem to be blaming her for what had happened; but she wasn't sure she liked being labelled a helpless female.

"Next time," Sue tried to sound stern, "I'll send Matt after you instead. No one else will mind if he tries to kiss you."

Sally might, Megan reflected. She'd noticed how Sally sparkled when Matt was around. He seemed oblivious though, which was hardly surprising given his inexperience with women. Maybe she should drop him a hint when Sally wasn't around: at the next Choir practice, for example.

Only things didn't quite turn out as she'd expected. Sue woke up with a sore throat the next day and told Megan that she wouldn't be going to Choir that evening.

"I daren't risk it," she told her friend. "I lost my voice completely for a few days in the summer term because I carried on singing when I should have given it a rest. You and Matt will have to go without me."

So now Megan strode through The Vale with Matt, enjoying the early evening sunset and wondering how to broach the subject of Sally.

"That's a lovely smell," Matt said suddenly. "Have you just washed your hair?"

His puppy-dog expression told her that it definitely wasn't Sally he was interested in. Megan panicked.

"It's probably the autumn leaves!" she said crossly, not knowing how to take this compliment from her friend. She could handle Dan's flirting because she knew it wasn't serious – he probably said those things to all the girls – but Matt was so earnest, so sincere. It was very off-putting.

Things were made even worse later on as they were leaving the Music School to return to Hall. Alex, a girl in Mason, had asked to walk with them; now, as they set off, she remarked casually, "You two get on really well. Do you ever think about going out together?"

Megan's cheeks flamed as much as Matt's. Why did people always think they should start matchmaking when there were two unattached people?

"We're just friends," she said stiffly.

She avoided looking at the hurt in Matt's eyes.

She confided in Jen the following morning as they queued for sausages and beans.

"I don't see what the problem is." Jen looked puzzled. "He's single; you're single; why don't you give it a go?"

Megan sighed. How could she explain this?

"Matt's lovely," she said carefully, "and I really like him as a friend; but ..."

"But you don't fancy him," Jen finished.

Megan nodded. "I know he's good looking, but I just don't feel attracted to him. I don't think he's my type."

"So, what is your type then?" Jen was curious.

Megan was silent, thinking of Dan with his floppy hair and too tight trousers – and the way he smoked and drank. He was so wrong for her: was that what attracted her so much?

"I don't know," she said at last. "Someone ... not as clean cut as Matt. Someone with a bit of edge."

"Like Dan, you mean?" Jen asked perceptively. She shook her head. "I don't think he's looking for a relationship, Meg. Bad boys never do."

"I'll just gaze at him from afar then," Megan grinned back, "and daydream about what might have been."

She kept Matt at arm's length for the rest of the week, choosing a seat next to one of the others in the bar, sitting with other people in their French lectures – apart from Phonetics, which now numbered twelve students. She wondered how many would be left by the end of term.

Sitting with other people had its advantages, one of them being the new friend she made: a girl from Edinburgh named Heather. Since Heather now resided in Wyddrington, she proved an ideal companion on the early Wednesday walk. (Jen never went in until much later on Wednesdays: the twelve o'clock tutorial was the first class she had.) Heather was a gregarious soul with a mine of amusing stories, the only disadvantage being that Megan found herself subconsciously imitating Heather's Scottish burr after spending more than ten minutes listening to her.

Friday evening came round: the end of their third week. Megan felt as if she had been a student forever; was amazed to think that there were only seven weeks left of term.

The Hall Bar was always much quieter on a Friday evening, most people preferring to hit the city centre and see what the various nightclubs had on offer. Megan gazed at the drink in Jen's hand. "What's that?"

"It's called a Coral." Jen sipped it appreciatively. "You might like it: it's peach flavoured."

Megan hesitated. A lifetime of abstinence due to her teetotal upbringing made her wary of anything even vaguely alcoholic.

"I asked for a Babycham," Jen continued, "but they didn't have any left, and then the barman said why didn't I try this." She offered it to Megan. "Have a taste."

Throwing caution to the wind, Megan sampled the proffered drink. It *was* nice! Perhaps she should have one herself?

It was while she was paying for her third Coral that Dan appeared at her side. "Long time no see." Then, as his gaze took in her glass, "Good grief, Woman! That's the girliest drink I've ever seen!"

A pleasant warmth suffused Megan's body and her mind was just slightly fuzzy – *not*, she told herself, because she'd been drinking: this was only a tiny glass, for heaven's sake, not a huge pint pot like the one in Dan's hand.

"It's the girliest drink I've ever drunk," she told him with dignity. "In fact, it's the only drink I've ever drunk, but it's not really alcoholic."

"And you're not really pissed! How many of those have you had?"

Despite her senses being somewhat dulled, Megan could definitely feel her body tingling when Dan was around. Subconsciously she moved closer to him, put a hand on his arm. "This is my third, but you can buy me another."

He stroked her hair back from her face. "Do you want to come and see my room?"

She had never been in a boy's room in High – or anywhere else for that matter. When they went out as a group, they always congregated in Jen and Sally's afterwards – it made sense to utilise the extra space of the double room.

Tonight, though, she felt reckless. It was amazing how even a tiny bit of alcohol made one lose one's inhibitions.

"Okay." She surprised herself as much as she did Dan.

They exited the bar at the opposite end to normal, walking into a foyer with a huge lift.

"We don't have one of those!" Megan felt indignant.

"That's because Ridge doesn't have seventeen floors. Don't spill your drink."

Dan pushed a button to open the lift door and ushered her inside the metal box. It smelled awful.

"Going up," he murmured, punching in the eleventh floor. Megan's stomach moved with the lift and she wondered if she was going to be sick.

The corridor, once Dan opened the lift door, was totally different to Ridge. Megan wasn't sure if the smell emanated from unwashed male bodies, alcohol or despair; whatever it was, it was most unpleasant.

There were only six doors in front of her. Dan fished a key out of his pocket and unlocked 1103. The room was similar in size to hers but there any comparison ended. Empty beer cans were lined up on the window sill and an ashtray overflowing with cigarette ends stood on the table. The bookcase housed a few Physics textbooks and a lot of beer.

Dan gestured to her to sit down on the bed. He placed himself next to her and studied her face intently. As his lips moved towards hers, Megan pondered fleetingly if this were a good idea, and then his mouth met hers and she decided it was too late to back out now.

She had only been kissed by two other people before: Dave and Ged – and you couldn't really count Ged since it was a kiss that had been over almost before it had begun. Kissing Dan was a totally different experience to the other two: he tasted of cigarettes and danger, and the combination was addictive. All her life Megan had been a good girl; now she was finally letting her wild side escape. Who knew that acting this way could be so much fun?

Yet despite the alcohol, she still retained some caution. Dan's kisses were pleasurable, but when his hand started moving down her body, in the way Dave's used to, she thrust him aside. "I don't do any of that."

He looked at her in surprise. "I'm not going to make you do anything you don't want to."

Reassured, she crept back into his arms. The kissing recommenced. After a while she found that they were lying on top of his bed and, ten minutes or so later, Dan's fingers started wandering again. This time she let him as far as her thigh before removing his hand in a very definite way.

"No?" He looked up at her, smiling lazily.

She shook her head. "No bed till I'm wed," she said flippantly.

"I guess we'll both have to wait then." He rolled over and sat up, wincing slightly. "Let's get you back to Ridge.

Megan woke early the next morning, trying to work out whether she had a hangover. She could remember having three drinks of Coral – damn Jen for introducing her to alcohol! – and going back with Dan to his room, but what had happened next?

And then it all started coming back to her: the insalubrious lift and corridor; the seedy room; the kissing. Dan had been a gentleman, despite his bad boy appearance: he had been far less insistent than Dave; had returned her to her room and tucked her into bed with a chaste kiss on her forehead. Far from trying to talk her into sex, he had acted in an almost fatherly fashion.

She said as much to Sue later on when her friend tapped on her door, full of concern over what Megan had potentially got up to the night before.

"You were very lucky!" Sue thought Megan had acted somewhat naively. "You should never go back to a strange man's room. Anything could have happened!"

"But it didn't."

"No," Sue wasn't convinced, "but it could have done."

Jen's reaction was slightly different. "It probably did you good to get off with someone," was her opinion. "After the crap Dave put you through, you needed to know you were still attractive." Then, "Are you going to see him again?"

"I don't know." Megan felt bewildered. What *did* one do in these circumstances? She had no frame of reference.

"I wouldn't tell Matt, though," Jen continued. "If he's got a crush on you, that's the last thing he'll want to hear."

"If Matt looked like Dan, I probably *would* go out with him." Megan was thoughtful. "There's definitely a strong physical attraction with Dan, but I could never be his girlfriend. He smokes, for one thing, and his bookcase was full of beer cans. I can't imagine us ever having an intelligent conversation."

"Do you and Matt have intelligent conversations?"

"Well," Megan tried to be honest, "we do talk about the French plays we're studying, although it sometimes feels like he's looking at them from more of a Drama perspective. And he did English Lit A level so we've talked about 'Hamlet' a bit too."

"The problem is," Jen said lightly, "that you're doing the wrong course. We outnumber the men ten to one in English, so your chances of finding an available, well-read, literate man – let alone a good looking one – are pretty slim."

"I can't suddenly switch to Engineering just to get a boyfriend!" Megan protested.

"No," Jen agreed, "because from what I've seen of Phil's Engineering friends, they don't read anything unless it's their course textbooks or the graffiti on the toilet wall."

"That's a bit harsh!" Megan couldn't help smiling at the thought.

"Harsh but true," Jen commented. "So, young lady, you'll just have to decide what's more important: your head or your heart. Either you find a nice boy you can read poetry with, or you go for someone like Dan who's sex on legs – you can't have both."

Neither of them realised at the time that Megan would spend most of the First Year making up her mind.

Chapter Eleven

As one week bled into another, Sue finally hosted her long-promised tea-party and invited Megan, Jen and Sally to a very ladylike repast in her room one Sunday afternoon. Throwing caution to the wind, she placed Ted, resplendent in a red bow tie to match his shorts, in pride of place on her sole armchair. This would be her chance to introduce the others to the real man in her life.

All three girls were suitably smitten with Ted, especially when Sue explained that he was as old as she was.

"It must be wonderful to own something with such sentimental value," Megan sighed feelingly; whereas Jen was more interested to discover why they hadn't met him before now.

He had been rather busy, Sue explained, working on an essay for her: a discussion of the works of Al-bear Camus.

Everyone groaned at this, even Sally.

"Just as well he's not a scientist," she quipped back, "or he'd be writing about Thomas Ted-ison."

"If that's going to be the level of conversation in here, I'll be better off talking to the stuffed toy," Jen said severely.

Sally pulled a face. "Don't say you weren't trying to think of a witty comment yourself," she warned. "I've lived with you for four weeks now, Jen Mitchell: I know what you're like."

"Okay!" Jen conceded with a sigh. "I *was* toying with the idea of Marco Polar Bear, but I thought even you wouldn't find that funny. Anyway," she glanced at Sue, "shouldn't we be making the most of this now we've finally made it past your door?"

Her eyes slid round the room, taking in Sue's homely yet artistic touches, and Megan followed suit. A patchwork quilt was draped over the bed and a bowl of fruit stood on the table, flanked by a large blue and white striped teapot and a doily-bedecked plate of French Fancies. A tall vase of scarlet carnations on the windowsill added another splash of colour, and Sue had collected an assortment of fir cones and acorns from outside and arranged these artfully around the base of the vase, completing her autumnal theme with a tiny pottery hedgehog. All of the girls were enchanted.

"You should be doing Interior Design, not French and German!" Megan said feelingly, and the others echoed her sentiment.

Sue blushed, obviously pleased by the compliment. "One does one's best," she murmured modestly.

"Watch out! Madame Pretension's back!" Jen whispered to Megan.

"I heard that," Sue said with dignity, "and I beg to differ. One should always strive to use correct English, in any and all circumstances."

"Even with Ged?" Sally sounded curious. "That must make your intimate moments interesting," she continued chattily. "One greatly appreciates how one's boyfriend is using his …" she began in an affected tone – until Sue threw a cushion at her and shut her up.

Tea was done and the talk had turned, as usual, to men – or, to be more specific, to Matt and Dan. Jen was still of the opinion that Megan should throw caution to the wind and "give Matt a whirl", as she put it; Sally wasn't so sure.

"Why ruin a perfectly good friendship?" she argued. "You and Matt get on at the moment; but what would happen if you tried going out and then found it didn't work? It would be too awkward for you to carry on being friends afterwards, so then Matt would have to stop hanging around with us and that means Phil probably wouldn't want to spend time with us either …"

Jen shot her a look.

"So Jen and Phil would go off on their own together," Sally continued, ignoring her room-mate's eye signals, "and then …"

"I'm not going to go out with him!" Megan felt annoyed – not with Sally but with Jen, for failing to realise that Sally was interested in Matt herself. "And I'm not going to go out with Dan either," she added, noticing Sue's mouth opening as if she, too, wanted to voice an opinion. "Just because you're all cosy with Phil, Jen, and Sue's happy with Ged …"

"*And* Ted!" Sally murmured.

"… Doesn't mean that Sally and I think we're missing out because we're single," Megan finished firmly. "So, no more matchmaking from either of you, please!"

Only, later on in the bar, as she and the others sat sipping drinks to the strains of an American singer called Madonna, whose song 'Like A Virgin' seemed to be having the most unlikely effect of actually getting people onto the dance floor – unheard of for the Sunday night disco – Megan found herself wondering if Dan would be making an appearance tonight.

Not that she was remotely interested in him, she told herself sternly. He was good- looking and he seemed to like her, but she wasn't about to fool herself that he had any genuine feeling for her, nor she for him.

Nevertheless, when he suddenly appeared at her side, proffering her an unexpected but welcome Coral, she couldn't prevent the shiver of anticipation that immediately ran down her spine.

"Thought you might like one of your girlie drinks." He rolled his eyes at her. "Have you any idea how much it's ruined my street cred asking for one of those?"

"Thanks." Megan was too surprised to say anything else. "These are my friends," she heard herself say next. "That's Jen, and her room-mate, Sally; and this is Sue."

Sue was regarding Dan somewhat disapprovingly, although that could have been due as much to the lit cigarette in his hand as to the lascivious look he was giving Megan.

Feeling suddenly nervous, she downed her drink far faster than she'd intended and felt her head spin. Maybe it was more alcoholic than she'd thought?

"Fancy another?" He was a hungry wolf and she was the lamb.

"I think maybe I'd better get some air," she stuttered in a voice that wasn't her own.

He pulled her to her feet and began to steer her deftly towards the nearest exit.

"We'll look after her." Jen's voice.

Dan batted her friends away. "I can manage. It won't be the first time."

His hand at the base of her spine, gently propelling her forward. Bile began to rise in her throat. *Please, God,* she prayed, *don't let me throw up – not in front of everyone!* (Not in front of Dan.)

This time the door to Ridge. Dan's fingers, closing around hers; his voice a soft whisper in her ear. "Let's get you some air."

Gently he led her to the fire door and pushed it open. The abrupt coolness of the night air brought her to her senses and she gulped at it gratefully, feeling the nausea subside.

"Better?"

She nodded, and then his mouth was on hers, the smoky taste of his cigarette at once strange and familiar, his fingers cupping her face, his tongue probing deeper. Instinctively she began to respond to his touch, needing to be loved, knowing she was only wanted.

How different he was to Dave! Bizarrely, her ex-boyfriend had always seemed to have too many teeth, so that kissing him had always felt like an obstacle course. Dan's mouth was a perfect size; his expert kisses hinted at years of practice. He knew just where to find the pulse at the side of her neck; understood how to caress her earlobe in such a way that her defences began to melt under his touch.

She pushed him away suddenly, realising her mistake. Dan was a good-looking boy, but he wasn't interested in *her*: she could have been any one of the one hundred and forty-seven girls in Hall and he would have still kissed her in the same way, would have run through the tried and tested formula he'd used so many times before.

It wasn't enough. Megan wanted to feel special, not be treated like the latest in a long line of conquests. *Besides,* her brain argued stubbornly as her body tried to recover, *kissing him's okay, but there aren't any fireworks.*

Did such a thing actually exist? she wondered absently as Dan regarded her coolly, lighting another cigarette. Her mother's Mills and Boon novels had certainly suggested that physical passion should be accompanied by trembling knees and a palpitating heart (better not let anyone on her English course know she'd read such drivel!), but the closest she'd ever come to that with Dave had been an attack of cramp when her foot went to sleep after lying in a field for too long.

Kissing Dan was definitely a step up from Dave with his attempted clumsy fumbling, but it wasn't earth shattering. Perhaps that was the best she could hope for?

Dan's eyes, still watching her. How far did he think she would let him go this time? It was time to disillusion him.

"I'd better get back to my friends," she said awkwardly. "Thanks for my drink."

He leaned in to kiss her goodbye. "It's not going to happen, is it? You and me, I mean." He didn't sound particularly regretful.

"No," she agreed, wondering why she didn't feel more dejected herself.

"Look after yourself." He kissed her once more and was gone, leaving her to return to the bar alone, wondering if she would ever attract such a good-looking boy again.

*

The others looked relieved to see her return. Phil and Matt had now joined them, the former regaling the group with the account of a prank he and his friends had played on one of the occupants of his floor. "So then he opened the lift door," he was explaining as Megan arrived, "and instead of the foyer, he saw his whole room laid out in front of him: bed, table, bookcase … The only thing we couldn't move was the washbasin!"

The girls shrieked with laughter whilst Matt smiled shyly at Megan. She slid into the seat beside him, grateful for his safe male presence. It was a relief to sit and chat with a man who didn't confuse her emotions and confound her hormones. As for his crush on her, she was sure that would disappear once Matt found himself a girlfriend: surely there must be plenty of women out there who wanted a 'nice', clean-cut boy? But while they were still both unattached, they could at least keep each other company.

Turning towards him, she began to chat about their most recent French lecture.

Chapter Twelve

She didn't bump into Dan in the Hall bar again, but she did encounter him about a week later in the Mermaid Bar when, uncharacteristically, she found herself going for a lunchtime drink to celebrate Heather's birthday.

By this time, Reading Week had come and gone. Megan had debated returning home briefly on the train, but the thought of even a few days with her mother had been enough to convince her to wait until the Christmas holiday. Since she would then be forced to spend four whole weeks under the family roof, she reckoned she deserved some time off for good behaviour now. Besides, she was aware that she was not the Megan Jackson who had arrived at University some five or six weeks ago: she was pretty sure that her mother wouldn't approve of the more interesting sense of fashion Megan had adopted this term; and she would be horrified to learn her daughter had been drinking alcohol and frequenting the pub at lunchtime!

Not that she was doing anything wrong, she told herself hastily. Mindful of her impending two o'clock lecture, she was playing it safe with an orange juice, sipping it slowly as she listened to Heather and the two other people who'd joined them: a mature student of twenty six named Beverley, who was married to an Egyptian and had a little boy with dark curly hair and huge brown eyes (she'd shown Megan a photo), and a boy their age named Simon who, she suspected, had been invited along because Heather rather fancied him. Alas, it seemed Simon was already taken: he spent most of his time talking about his girlfriend back home and waxing lyrical about his plans for the Christmas holiday, when they would go skating and Christmas shopping along with a whole host of other equally nauseating couple-y activities.

Poor Heather! Megan thought as she watched her friend's eyes glaze over. It was bad enough having to smile politely whilst Simon fondly remembered meeting this unknown girl (Gillian? Or was it Rebecca?) at the school Christmas disco a year ago; but it must be agonising to spend your birthday with a boy you liked who was so obviously in love with someone else.

She was interrupted from her reverie by a nudge in the ribs from Beverley. "Look at that couple over there! I must be getting old: there's no way I'd go out dressed like that!"

Megan swivelled her gaze and saw a familiar figure standing at the pinball machine. Dan's legs were as long as ever, his brown hair just as floppy, but his hand was resting proprietorially on the shoulder of a leggy female whose head to toe black clothing matched not only her hair but the dramatic rings around her eyes. For a brief moment she wondered if it was the same Goth girl she'd spotted at the Freshers Fayre so many weeks ago; and then Dan turned and kissed his girlfriend long and hard on the mouth before offering her a drag on his cigarette, and Megan felt an unexpected pang for what might have been.

He looked up and caught her eye, nodded briefly, then turned back to the game, punching the buttons as expertly as he had kissed her in the past. Megan's emotions ricocheted like the rapidly whizzing ball bearing, flinging her from loss to relief and back to sadness again. It would never have worked out long term with Dan, she knew that; but it had been wonderful to be wanted by someone so good looking.

Beverley was still talking. Megan drifted in and out of the conversation, her mind preoccupied with thoughts of Dan. Maybe she should make more of an effort to find a boyfriend, she mused vaguely. After all, it would be convenient to have a partner when they all went out together as a group, and then Matt could pair up with Sally, and who knew where that might lead?

*

She gave the matter some more thought in her French Drama lecture that afternoon. Racine's play, *'Phèdre'*, bristled with unrequited longing as the eponymous tragic heroine realised she was consumed by an illicit but overpowering passion for her stepson, Hippolyte. Megan sat enthralled, Matt on one side and Heather on the other, as Dr Banks painted a vivid picture of Phèdre's overwhelming desire, her reckless confession to Hippolyte and her jealous fury upon discovering he loved another.

"It's like East Enders set in Ancient Greece!" Heather murmured as the lecturer finally drew his synopsis to a close.

Megan nodded breathlessly, wondering how it would feel to desire someone as intensely as Phèdre had done. She'd felt physically attracted to Dan, but she hadn't yearned for him the way Phèdre had for Hippolyte.

"Have you ever felt that way about anyone?" she asked Heather as they streamed out of the lecture theatre with the rest of their year group.

"What? Do you mean forbidden love?" Heather's eyes gleamed and her Scottish accent became more pronounced. "*I* haven't, but a friend of mine at school had a massive crush on one of the teachers. She kept taking him little presents – chocolate bars and things like that: nothing major – and he seemed to quite like it. She managed to get him to dance with her at the school disco too – you should have seen how thrilled she was afterwards." She chuckled. "She would have been okay if it had stopped there, but she got over-excited and sent him a Valentine's card, absolutely covered with rhymes and poems – some of them were a bit racy! You know the sort of thing: 'I wish I were a bar of soap/All slippery in your hand/And if you dropped me in the bath/I'd see your Promised Land!' And some that were a bit naughtier than that too!"

"So what happened?" Megan was fascinated.

"She got into a lot of trouble." Heather was suddenly serious. "She tried to claim she hadn't sent it, but it was her handwriting on the envelope and inside the card, and we'd all seen her write it and helped her out with the rhymes."

Megan was silent, contemplating Heather's story. Although this unknown girl had technically not been as bad as Phèdre (who had lied to her husband, Theseus, and then sent Hippolyte off to his death), she had still allowed unrequited passion to prompt her into doing something foolish. And then she thought once more of Dan and of their brief encounters together, and she knew with absolute certainty that he was not and never had been 'the One'.

Recognising that she and Dan were definitely over – not that two snogging sessions actually constituted anything resembling a relationship – freshened Megan's resolve to find a replacement boyfriend. Not Matt – she liked him but it was with fondness more than anything else - and not any of the six men on the English course: the attractive ones were already taken and the others were single for a reason. Maybe she should ignore the intellectual side of things and concentrate on finding someone who made her knees buckle instead? After all, Jen was happy with Phil and he was a Geography student! And Sue seemed equally contented with Ged, despite the fact that he was a physicist (like Dan, her inner voice reminded her).

*

And so it was with some anticipation, mixed with more than a little trepidation, that she surveyed the Hall Bar this evening in a way she hadn't done before, wondering if she would spot a potential partner. High's inhabitants might significantly outnumber those of Ridge; even so, the girls around her were stiff competition she thought now, suddenly conscious of how young and inexperienced she must appear in comparison to the group of impossibly confident women who had just entered the room.

She nudged Jen. "Do you know any of those girls?"

Jen shook her head. "They're out of our league. They're the ones who's be the cheerleaders in an American High School."

Everything about them was right, Megan thought wistfully: from their long, flowing hair to their perfect, well-toned bodies, they had the effect of turning every man's head, even Matt's. Amazonian in stature, they stalked the bar with a predatory air, tossing back their tawny manes with an air of insouciance that proclaimed their innate superiority to the rest of Ridge. They ruled these Halls – and everyone knew it.

"The one in the middle does Chemistry," Ged broke in. "She's another Sally. My lab partner has a crush on her."

"And the one next to her's called Helen Appleyard," Phil added. He grinned. "The rest of my corridor calls her 'Horny Helen'!"

Helen could have been a model, Megan decided. She had endless legs, perfect cheekbones and long, naturally light brown curly hair that only just escaped being golden. Megan felt decidedly average just looking at her. And it wasn't just her height or her willowy figure that made every man's eyes swivel in her direction: the girl had an undeniable sex appeal that seemed to leak out of her as she passed.

Their unidentified companion was another matter: plumper than the others, she was, nevertheless, indisputably attractive with tumbling dark locks and the same confidence that hallmarked her friends. Megan watched as she casually strode over to a table of beer-swilling boys and somehow made them all move to accommodate the girls with just a smile and a flirtatious wink.

"We'll never be like that, will we?" Sally voiced what they were all thinking.

"No," Jen replied honestly, "but I'm not sure I'd want to be." She gestured at the three goddesses who were now lighting up cigarettes before matching the men pint for pint. "They look like they know how to have a good time; but I doubt they have as much fun as we do when they're sober. Anyway," she finished her white wine spritzer with a final sip, "didn't you say there was a party on the sixth floor, Phil? Let's pop along and see if we can find someone for Megan and Sally."

*

The party turned out to be in Matt's room. Megan had known he was on the sixth floor – he'd mentioned it during one of their early conversations – but not that he shared a room. She wondered now why he'd waited until they arrived to tell her it was his party.

"It isn't actually anything to do with me." Matt blushed as he spoke to her and she realised he was still infatuated. "My room-mate Doug and his friend Gio were supposed to be having a party in Gio's room – he shares with someone else at the other end of the floor – but the other room-mate's having a CU meeting in there so Doug said we'd use our room instead. I think it's going to be mainly Rock Soc people because that's what Doug and Gio are into."

He was right: the room was dominated by denim-clad young men with long hair and a dubious taste in tee shirts. The choice of music seemed pretty unconventional too: Megan found it disturbingly discordant, although Phil seemed to be enjoying it.

"I've always liked AC/DC," he explained when Jen complained about the noise. "I just don't put it on when you're around."

Megan didn't think it appealed to Matt's musical taste either, judging by the pained expression on his face. "What do *you* like listening to?" she asked him, thinking she should at least make the effort to be sociable.

Matt's face lit up. "I like Phil Collins," he said eagerly. "And have you heard of a singer called Alison Moyet? I've been listening to some of her songs recently on my Walkman." He gestured at the record player in the untidier half of the room. "Doug's heavy metal's a bit loud for me and I don't own any records, but if I turn the volume up on the Walkman I can just about hear the music I want to listen to."

"I've only got a Walkman too," Megan told him in an attempt to make him feel better. Perhaps they were the only students without a proper stereo system?

"Can I get you a drink?" Matt's manners were impeccable.

"Just orange juice, thanks." Boxes of wine and cans of beer (or was it lager? She still didn't know the difference) covered both the tables, along with some family sized bags of Ready Salted crisps and several tubs of peanuts, almost hiding the solitary carton of Sainsbury's own brand juice.

She noticed that Matt poured himself a glass of red wine before bringing her drink over. Since he normally stuck to soft drinks in the bar, she had assumed he was teetotal; now she wondered if he were trying to give himself Dutch courage to hint once more how he felt about her.

Before she had time to discover what Matt's intentions were, a voice sounded behind her: "You hang around with Phil and his girlfriend, don't you?"

The stranger had a Scouse accent and curly hair. He wasn't particularly good looking, but he seemed friendly. Megan gratefully seized the opportunity to put off a possible declaration of love from Matt.

"I'm Megan," she told him, her gaze taking in hazel eyes and a slightly bent nose. Was he a rugby player? He wasn't overly tall and had a wiry frame rather than being solidly built, like Ged; but he looked as if he knew how to look after himself.

He toasted her with his can. "Steve. First Year Accountancy – and yeh, it *is* as boring as it sounds, but I need a decent career to fall back on while I wait to hit the big time with my band."

"You're in a band?" Megan was impressed. She'd never met a *bona fide* musician before.

"Well, it's just a group of us who got together in the sixth form, but we've played a few gigs and the crowds seem to like us." He was casually dismissive, although Megan sensed he would like to tell her more.

Matt was here with the drinks. Megan took her orange juice and wondered if she should introduce the two men. Steve looked at Matt then began to apologise. "Sorry, mate, I didn't realise she had a boyfriend."

"He's not my boyfriend," Megan cut in, ignoring Matt's disappointed expression. "Matt, this is Steve. Matt's on my French course and this is his room."

"Great party!" Steve told Matt; then, turning his attention back to Megan, he continued, "I've got some tapes of the band in my room, if you want a listen?"

Megan hesitated, Sue's warning of weeks ago ringing in her ears: *You should never go back to a strange man's room. Anything could happen!* But this was different: she was going to listen to music, rather than responding to an invitation to 'get to know someone better.' Besides, Matt knew where she was going and could step in and rescue her if necessary.

"Where's your room?" she heard herself ask.

"Fifth floor – just under this one. My room mate's out at the Guild."

Again she hesitated. Then, "Come and find me when the others are ready to go back to Ridge," she ordered Matt, pretending not to notice how his eyes clouded at her departure. Looking Steve in the eye, she told him, "Okay, then: impress me with your music."

*

Steve's room was a carbon copy of the one she'd just left, apart from the absence of people and the distinct lack of alcohol.

"Do you want a coffee?" He was crossing the room, opening the window and retrieving something from the windowsill. She was expecting it to be a pint of milk; was surprised to discover he was clutching a can of beer. "I'd offer you one of these, but I noticed you weren't drinking at that party."

It was a bit late for coffee. "Have you got any teabags?" she asked hopefully.

He gestured at a box of Tetley on the floor. "They're Jack's, but he won't mind."

Looking around her, Megan wondered where the kettle was. Steve had produced a bizarre looking piece of twisted metal. He now filled a chipped mug with water from the washbasin and proceeded to place the contraption inside it, plugging the other end into an empty socket. Megan watched, fascinated.

After about a minute and a half, the water began to bubble. Steve dropped the teabag inside the mug and began to poke around under the bed. Megan's heart sank as he resurfaced with a jar of Coffee Mate: although she'd optimistically brought a jar of the powered milk substitute with her to University herself, one drink had been enough to convince her that it had been a waste of money. For her it was cow juice or nothing.

"Is that your guitar?" she asked, attempting to divert him from his substandard hospitality.

Steve nodded, plucking it from the floor where it leaned half drunkenly against the wardrobe. He ran his fingers expertly across the strings. "What do you want me to play? And don't say 'Stairway to Heaven' because I'm fed up with girls asking me to play that."

She had no idea what he was on about; had never heard of Led Zeppelin or any of the other bands that adorned the walls in poster form.

"Why don't you play me something your band does," she suggested at length, knowing instinctively that 'Don't You Want Me Baby' probably wouldn't be part of his usual repertoire, even if it was the only song she could think of at this moment.

A look of annoyance crossed his face. "I can't sing – and the songs wouldn't make sense without the words."

Throwing the guitar down on the opposite bed, he joined her on his own, sitting just fractionally too close to her so that Megan shifted imperceptibly. "We both know that's not the real reason you're here ..."

His breath told her he'd drunk more than just a couple of cans this evening; his hand was reaching for her in a way that suggested he wouldn't take no for an answer.

Megan stood up abruptly. "Thanks for the tea," (she hadn't drunk any of it) "but I must be getting back to Matt's room before my friends wonder where I am."

As if on cue, a knock sounded at the door. There stood Matt, a curious expression on his face. "Jen and Sally want to leave now. I said I'd fetch you."

"Thanks again," Megan said hurriedly, reaching the door in a few quick steps. Pulling the door shut behind her, she left Steve alone with his guitar.

Chapter Thirteen

To Megan's surprise, Jen and Sally were nowhere to be seen. "I thought you said the others were ready to leave ..." she began.

Matt looked sheepish. "I thought you might need rescuing sooner rather than later," he confessed, not meeting her eyes. "I didn't like the way that Steve was looking at you ..." His voice tailed off in embarrassment.

Secretly, Megan was rather relieved that Matt had come to her aid – in addition to feeling guilty that her desire to escape from Matt had caused this situation in the first place. Her guilt was further compounded when Matt added that he had come to find her after overhearing some of Doug's friends expressing amusement that yet another girl had fallen for Steve's hackneyed chat up line. Apparently he wasn't in a band at all but kept the guitar to impress women.

Megan groaned inwardly, berating herself for being such a terrible judge of character.

"I couldn't bear the thought of anything bad happening to you, Megan," Matt was saying now, his eyes luminescent with unrequited love. "I ... you ... I value our friendship," he finished lamely.

Megan sighed. Much as she disliked being the object of Matt's affection – was irritated by it, even – she knew she owed him something for chivalrously defending her honour. In the end she settled for, "I'm glad we're friends too," and left it at that.

And now, she thought wearily, she would have to go back to the party and make small talk against the raucous cacophony that masqueraded as music. She could only hope that Jen and Sally wouldn't want to stay too late ...

*

Feeling slightly shaken by her near miss with Steve, Megan spent the next week studiously avoiding any man who seemed to want to talk to her. It was only after Jen told her off for blanking Elly, who normally sat next to them in the Tuesday and Thursday lectures, that she realised she was being slightly paranoid.

"He only asked you if you wanted a ticket for the English panto," Jen complained crossly, "and you looked at him as though he'd just pinched your bottom!" Without changing the subject, she added, "I told him you had a headache and said to put us down for two tickets. We could both do with a man-free night out."

"When is it?" Megan asked, her curiosity piqued.

"December ninth," Jen told her. "That's the last Monday of term."

Megan's face fell. She had a French grammar exam the following morning at 9 a.m.

"You might have to take Sue or Sally instead," she said carefully. "I've got a massive grammar test on the tenth and I'll probably need to spend the whole night revising."

"Rubbish!" Jen's tone was brisk. "It'll do you far more good to have a couple of hours off. Anyway, it will all be over by nine, so you can still get in an hour or two once you get back to Hall."

Eventually Megan acquiesced. Jen was right: a night without men was just what they both needed.

*

Only, in the end, Jen cancelled their evening at the last minute. Phil had managed to acquire tickets for a concert - a band Megan had never heard of – and decided to take his girlfriend so he could "introduce her to some of his music."

"You'd think listening to some of his heavy metal albums with him would be enough!" Jen sighed as she pulled on the band tee shirt that Phil had assured her was a requisite for the concert. Secretly she was quite flattered that Phil liked her enough to take her to the gig – especially when Doug had been desperate to go himself and had offered Phil a ridiculous sum of money for one of his tickets.

All this left Megan with a dilemma: should she ask one of the others to accompany her to the pantomime; or should she stay in and revise instead?

After some consideration, she decided not to miss the show. She knew several people who had small parts in it, and rumour had it that several of the lecturers were also involved. Sally was her first port of call: she declined, claiming that she had an essay to finish; Megan wondered if Sally was hoping to have a better chance with Matt in the bar if she, Megan, were not there. Sue also turned down the invitation, as did Ged: it wasn't fair for her to abandon the poor boy two nights in a row, Sue told her, and since she and Megan would be out at Choir the following evening, she should really spend some time with her man now, while she could.

That left only Matt. Megan was loath to ask him – what if he thought this were a date? – but knew she couldn't *not* ask him after she'd invited the rest of their group. "It's just as friends, Matt," she told him sternly, noticing how his eyes had lit up at the suggestion. Even so, he seemed pathetically grateful.

*

Sitting next to him an hour later, Megan was glad she had asked Matt after all. Things like this were always so much more fun when one had someone to share it with; and although Matt didn't know any of the English lecturers, meaning he didn't understand any of the lines that cunningly alluded to their teaching styles, he dutifully laughed in all the right places.

For a brief moment she wondered whether this was enough: Matt was pleasant company (when he wasn't gazing her like a lovestruck calf) and he was certainly attentive, listening to everything she said and being quite willing to discuss literary topics instead of insisting on talking about football. Could she overlook her complete lack of sexual attraction to him if, in all other respects, he were the perfect boyfriend?

A faint stirring within as she thought briefly of Dan. They had never been right for each other, despite the obvious chemistry; nevertheless, he had ignited a spark of longing, made her aware that she was capable of feeling far more physical interest than she ever had with Dave.

No, Matt was a lovely friend, but she couldn't see herself falling for him: not now; not ever. She needed some sort of hybrid boyfriend with Dan's looks and Matt's personality; she didn't know if such a creature existed, but she would do her best to find out.

*

The performance was over and the cast had taken their final bow, amidst heartfelt applause. Megan clapped extra hard for Elly, who had played the part of Beowulf, and for her Wednesday tutor, Russell Welch, who had made a convincing Shakespeare.

Matt turned to her with a shy smile. "Would you like to go for a drink? We could go to the Mermaid – or back to the bar in Hall if you'd prefer that."

She shook her head. "Better not if we've got that French test tomorrow."

He pulled a face.

*

They walked back to Hall slowly, each seemingly lost in thought. Matt gallantly escorted her to her room and waited while she fumbled for her key.

"Thanks for going with me," Megan said a little awkwardly, wondering if he was expecting her to invite him in. She hesitated with her key still in the lock. "We'd better both get an early night, then, if we want to be fresh for Dr Brown's test in the morning."

Matt leant forward and brushed her cheek lightly with his lips. "I've had a lovely evening. Perhaps we can do it again sometime?"

"Maybe," she said guardedly. "Good night, Matt. I'll probably see you at breakfast."

She hurried inside her room and shut the door before he could kiss her again.

*

Ten minutes later, Megan had cleaned her teeth and begun to undress when she realised she was still wearing Sue's Victorian necklace which she had borrowed for the evening. She bit her lip. Sue had lent it to her on the understanding that Megan would return it when she arrived home. She looked at her alarm clock: nine thirty. Pulling her jeans back on, she decided to go and knock on Sue's door now, just in case she missed her in the morning.

Sue wasn't in. The note on the dry wipe board blutacked to her door simply said "Bar." It wouldn't take long to track her down in such a small venue, so Megan fetched her key and pulled her door shut, hurrying through the corridor on her mission. If she was quick, she could still be tucked up in bed with the light off by ten.

Sue was pleased to see her and the necklace, reassuring Megan that the next day would have been fine and asking her if she was stopping for a drink with her, Ged and Sally. (Matt must have gone straight back to his room then.)

Megan declined politely, reminding Sue about the imminent grammar test. Although she knew she had worked hard all term, she wanted to prove to herself that she was as good as everyone else when it came to the Language side of French: at school she had always been far stronger in Literature.

Walking past the bar counter on her way out, still lost in thought, she bumped against a figure coming the other way. "I'm sorry," she began, looking up.

As her eyes met the stranger's, a sudden jolt ran through her. This man was certainly good looking: brown eyes set in in a face with impeccably chiselled cheekbones were offset by dark spiky hair and legs wrapped in the tightest jeans Megan had ever seen, tighter even than Dan's. He was good looking, but he was so much more than that: his whole being exuded sex appeal and Megan felt herself melting instantly at this first glance.

He, for his part, seemed equally struck, his eyes taking in her face, her hair; his gaze travelling appreciatively over the entire length of her body. In that instant, something indefinable passed between them, leaving Megan feeling weak at the knees. So was *this* what it was like to be hit with a *coup de foudre*? she wondered clumsily.

His voice was a husky murmur. "I'm Mike. What are you drinking?"

A half-formed thought at the back of her mind tried to tell her to walk away, reminded her of the upcoming French test; instead, she smiled up at him. "I'll have a white wine spritzer, thanks."

*

Twenty minutes later, she was still sitting with Mike and his friends, all male, enjoying being the centre of attention and pretending she didn't notice the disapproving looks emanating from Sue, Ged and Sally. It must be easily past ten o'clock, but Megan didn't care. Perhaps there was more wine than she'd thought in her spritzer (she'd actually wanted a Coral but hadn't wanted Mike to think her too girly), or less lemonade; whatever it was, she was feeling decidedly drunk, so much so that when one of Mike's friends pushed his half empty tankard towards her, she actually took a sip.

Instantly, she wished she hadn't. The concoction tasted disgusting. It was like drinking despair and desolation, distilled into a pint pot of dark, bitter liquid. Then again, the terrible taste could have had something to do with the extinguished cigarette she found floating at the bottom of the glass once she had drained it to its dregs.

Mike looked angrily at his friends as they hooted with laughter. "Sorry," he told her, removing the glass from her hands. "They play that trick all the time." He looked at her searchingly. "Want to come back to my room for a coffee?"

It was far too late for coffee, but Megan felt reckless. More than anything, she wanted to keep on talking to Mike – even if she was feeling incapable of coherent conversation right now. So far, everything they had said had been on a fairly superficial level: along with his friends, they had kept to the safe topics of moaning about Hall food and discussing recent football scores. Megan had been able to contribute to the former but was entirely clueless about the latter.

Now as she rose to her feet at the same time as Mike, one of his cronies let out a suggestive comment that made her blush. It seemed that 'coffee' didn't always mean coffee but was actually a euphemism for something else.

So why on earth was she following Mike out of the bar and into the High Hall foyer? Why was she waiting with him for the lift and watching as he pressed the buttons to take them to the tenth floor?

She knew the answer to that one: there was something visceral that urged her forwards: a cocktail of longing and desire that had left her feeling shaken and stirred.

The sexual tension between them filled the lift, enveloping them both. Even so, he made no attempt to kiss her, not yet. As the lift shuddered to a halt and the door opened, he took her hand and led her to his room: 1006. For a moment, her brain wondered fuzzily why there were now a thousand floors in High and then it registered: ten-o-six.

Unlocking the door, Mike ushered her inside. His single room was so different to Dan's. An overflowing ashtray that looked suspiciously like the one she had seen in the campus burger place stood on his bedside chest of drawers – did he lie in bed smoking then? – but that was the only similarity. Mike's bookcase was bursting with volumes: a fat Collins Robert French dictionary rubbed shoulders with its German counterpart (so he must be doing French and German, then; they hadn't even asked each other about courses yet) and there were books she recognised from her recent A levels: Lenz's *'Das Wrack'*, Goethe's *'Urfaust'*, Maupassant's *'Boule de Suif et Autres Contes de la Guerre'*. More exciting still, there were novels in English: a couple of Graham Greene titles, ditto Evelyn Waugh, and Kurt Vonnegut's *'Slaughterhouse 5'* which she had just finished reading. (One of the girls in her tutorial group had delivered a seminar paper the week before, comparing Billy Pilgrim to Joseph Andrews.)

Dragging her eyes away from the bookcase – who would have thought that a man who looked like that would be so well read? – Megan took in the rest of the room. A couple of posters of modern art flanked a facsimile of the original advertisement for Hitchcock's *'The Birds'*. Mike obviously had depth. And what was that on top of his wardrobe?

Climbing onto his chair to take a closer look, she found herself staring at a Tyrolean hat. It seemed oddly incongruous with Mike's tight trousers and spiky hair.

Turning back to him, she realised her lips were on a level with his. It seemed only natural to let him kiss her, despite the fact that she was beginning to experience mild vertigo. His mouth touched hers and the effect was electrifying: Megan could have sworn she saw blue sparks. (Years later, someone would tell her that this was the result of standing on a nylon carpet, but she wouldn't believe him.)

Mike wrapped his arms around her and lifted her off the chair, half-carrying, half-dragging her over to the bed. Aware that this was happening far too quickly, Megan began babbling aimlessly, some part of her brain mistakenly thinking that if her mouth was busy talking, he wouldn't be able to kiss her again.

This time she realised his kiss tasted of cigarettes and lager. (One of his friends had kindly explained what they had all been drinking.) She must like him, then, if she was prepared to let him kiss her despite the acrid taste.

He pulled her into him, almost crushing her against his chest. "I've noticed you before – in French lectures."

Why had she never spotted him?

Without waiting for her to reply, he continued, "And I know that girl who was giving you evil looks – we do German together. What's *her* problem?"

"You mean Sally?" Megan felt compelled to defend her friend. "I think she's just looking out for me," she said lamely. "She knows I've got a big French test tomorrow – I told her and my other friends that was why I couldn't stop for a drink."

"And then she saw you having a drink with me," Mike finished. He gave her a wry look. "No doubt tomorrow she'll be regaling you with horror stories about me!"

"*Are* there any horror stories?" Megan sat up, feeling slightly worried.

Mike gave her a lazy grin. "Not especially – unless you count the fact that she overheard me talking to someone else when we were ranking all the girls in the lecture theatre in the order we'd like to sleep with them. She's probably annoyed that she was near the bottom of the list!"

Megan's eyes widened in shock. Did boys *really* do that sort of thing?

Misreading her expression, Mike hurried to reassure her. "We ranked the girls in French too, and you were number one."

She didn't know whether to feel appalled by his sexist attitude or thrilled that he wanted her more than anyone else.

Mike's hand was stroking her shoulder, sending little thrills of pleasure throughout her entire body. She closed her eyes fleetingly, focusing on the sensuality of his touch. When he pulled her back down beside him, she abandoned herself to the moment.

*

Some time later, she was aware of his hands travelling down her body. Despite the intensity of his kisses, she pulled away. No matter how drunk she felt – on alcohol or desire – she still had standards. There was no way she was going to have sex with someone she had only just met – even if he *was* having such a devastating effect on her.

Mike watched her narrowly. "What's wrong?"

She shrugged helplessly. "It's just moving a little fast, that's all. I only met you a few hours ago."

He rolled over and plucked his cigarette packet from the bedside cabinet where he'd placed it earlier. Opening it up, he offered it to her but she shook her head. "No thanks. I don't smoke."

"Do you mind if I do?"

She was surprised by the question. Dan had never bothered to consider her feelings like that.

"It's your room."

He sighed and closed the box again without taking one out. "I can wait till later." Then, "So how long do you normally wait before sleeping with someone?"

Embarrassment suffused Megan's face. "I'm not in the habit of sleeping with anyone," she said stiffly.

Mike whistled softly. "I didn't think girls like you existed anymore – even in Ridge!"

Megan stared at her fingernails. Was she really so unusual?

Sensing her discomfort, Mike stroked her face. "Don't look so worried. We don't have to do anything you don't want to."

The problem was, she *did* want to – at least, she wanted the kissing and the holding, was remarkably hazy about what happened next, only that she was afraid it might hurt – or that she would end up getting pregnant. But it wasn't just that: a lifetime of sensible behaviour made Megan want to say no and yes at the same time: no to a casual encounter, which she was pretty sure this was; yes to acting out of character and letting herself fall for this dangerous yet exciting boy who looked like every mother's worst nightmare but was well read and intelligent.

She looked up at him, vulnerability spilling from her eyes, and Mike was taken aback. Something instinctive told him she needed looking after, but he knew he wasn't the right person to do that.

"I'd better get you back to Ridge," he said, a little roughly. "They close the connecting door at midnight and it's about quarter to now."

Silently Megan acquiesced, wondering what she had done wrong. She had thought Mike was enjoying kissing her: was she no good at it?

As if reading her mind, he said, "It's not you: it's me ..." then stopped abruptly. "Look," he tried again, "we've both got this French grammar thing tomorrow. If I could, I'd lie and hold you all night, but we both know that's not a good idea." He held the door open for her. "I'll walk you back to Ridge, okay? We both need to get some sleep before the test."

The lift was already there when they reached the foyer. They were both silent as it descended, tension this time pushing them apart instead of drawing them closer together. As the doors opened, Mike strode out without a backward glance so that Megan almost had to run to keep up with him.

They reached the connecting door and he finally looked at her. "Let's do this properly another time – when we haven't both got an exam the next day."

What did he mean by 'do this properly'? Megan wondered.

As she pushed open the door, Mike wedged his foot in the gap and bent towards her, his face close to hers. "Sweet dreams, Goldilocks. Don't lie awake all night thinking about me!" He kissed her briefly on the lips, a strangely touching gesture, then turned and was gone, leaving Megan wondering if she would ever see him again.

Chapter Fourteen

Once he had escorted Megan to the High/Ridge door, Mike retraced his steps to the foyer and slipped out of the front door. Fumbling for the battered cardboard box he had slipped into his pocket just before leaving his room, he withdrew a cigarette and lit it, idly playing with his lighter as he stood and dragged on the dose of nicotine.

Despite having a girlfriend back home – or rather, a girlfriend at Bristol University – he knew he wanted to see Megan again: not necessarily for anything physical, he told himself, wanting it to be true, but to get to know her properly. They'd hardly talked this evening and yet already he felt a connection with her.

He dropped his cigarette butt on the ground, extinguishing it fully underfoot. Reaching for another, he contemplated his complicated love life. Megan wasn't the first girl he'd kissed since arriving at university; then again, he had a feeling Amanda wasn't exactly being an angel in Bristol. The long, intense phone calls of the first few weeks of term had quickly fizzled out, *I love you*s being replaced by *See you soon*s. If she suspected that he hadn't been entirely faithful, she hadn't voiced any doubts; that, in itself, was enough to make him surmise that the relationship was decidedly shaky and that she might be just as relieved as he, should they decide to call it a day.

Gazing up at the clear midnight sky, he tried to remind himself of how he'd felt the first time he'd kissed Amanda. He'd known her for years, ever since the start of secondary school, but had always thought she was out of his league. She was one of the 'cool' kids: the ones who had bottle parties at the age of fourteen and spent her break times smoking behind the science labs. She, for her part, had ignored him – until sixth form started and they were two of only three people sitting History A level.

They had danced on the edge of a relationship for months before he finally asked her out, at the time sufficiently unsure and uncertain not to know whether she laughed at his jokes and sat next to him in the sixth form canteen because she liked him or because she was just being friendly. After tentatively inviting her to a friend's eighteenth – well, not exactly inviting: more a case of asking her if she was going – they had spent most of the evening trying to talk over the unfeasibly loud music of the nightclub before he'd dared to suggest going outside for a breath of fresh air. She could have slapped his face but instead she'd kissed the living daylights out of him. He'd been surprised by her forward attitude – and immensely turned on by it.

The next morning at school, everyone knew she had claimed him. Boys his own age who had previously ignored him now sought him out to slap him on the back or nod approvingly in his direction. After a lifetime of being a nobody, he had suddenly become popular by default of being Amanda's boyfriend. He was part of a crowd he'd never imagined belonging to.

Now that he hung out in Smoker's Corner, he took up the habit himself, trying to look as though he'd been doing it for years. He joined them too after school as they sat swigging cans of cider in the park. His enhanced cool factor was well worth his parents' disapprobation.

It came as a shock to him to realise that Amanda was as inexperienced as he was. He'd assumed naïvely that the whole crowd of them would have the same casual approach to sex as they did to drink and cigarettes. Amanda enlightened him the first time he tried to take it too far, pushing his hands away as they canoodled in the back row of the local cinema. "Not here. I want the first time to be special."

When she finally let him make love to her, some months later in her parents' bedroom when they were out for the evening, he felt an overwhelming sense of relief that he had proved his manhood. That was when she told him that he'd succeeded where others had failed. "The rest of them talk big," she'd declared, puffing a post-coital cigarette, "but it's just talk. None of them has actually scored yet."

How did she know? he wondered.

Later on she would confide that it was his seeming diffidence that had won her over. "You were always so aloof," she told him wryly. "It was driving me crazy wondering why you weren't chasing me like every other boy in the sixth form. If you hadn't asked me to go outside at that party, I would have dragged you there myself!"

Gradually they began to relax with each other, growing into a mutual comfortableness so that their coupling became more of a habit, less of a novelty. He was pretty sure her parents knew what she was up to since they started leaving boxes of condoms in the bathroom cabinet, a subtle reminder for her to be careful.

As the summer holidays between Lower and Upper Sixth arrived, they became more adventurous, finding a secluded spot in the woods a bus ride away and indulging in uninterrupted carnal pleasure - which came to a sudden halt when they rolled over into a patch of nettles. The resulting rash they both experienced afterwards was enough to put them off any further *al fresco* antics.

Upper Sixth began and the academic workload increased. Amanda was just as determined as he was to go to a good university, so their snog-fests evolved into revision sessions instead. They still fancied each other, but they knew A level grades were the priority.

Mike noticed they were arguing more now they were kissing less. He knew Amanda was stressed: she was taking Maths and Further Maths along with her History, and she was worried she wouldn't achieve the grades she needed for Bristol, her first choice university. When he unwisely suggested that it might be quite enjoyable if they ended up at their second choice university together (Leeds was asking for lower grades than either Bristol or Birmingham), she had exploded into a violent diatribe against him, accusing him of being possessive and not trusting her to go off to Bristol without him. It had taken him almost an hour to calm her down.

They had agreed then to let things cool off for a while until their exams were over. Perhaps it was just as well, he reflected now, or he might not have managed the two Bs and a C that Birmingham had asked for. His homework had certainly suffered in the early days as a result of having a girlfriend: even when he wasn't with her, he spent most of his 'study time' daydreaming about her.

Once A levels were finished, they had resumed 'going out', but even then Mike thought he detected a distance that hadn't been there before. Amanda seemed to be somewhere else: it was as if she had already gone off to university, leaving only a shell of her former self behind.

The day before their results came out, she confessed that she'd cheated on him, letting her hair down at a post-exam party he hadn't been invited to and ending up having a drunken fumble with one of the others in their group. She told him defiantly, as if daring him to break up with her; but he thought he detected fear in her eyes.

As it turned out, he was more hurt than angry. He'd always been afraid it wouldn't last; thought it was only a matter of time before she realised he wasn't good enough for her. She swore blind it "hadn't meant anything"; even so, he felt betrayed.

Back then (was it really only four months ago?), he couldn't distinguish what was worse: knowing she'd been unfaithful or losing her entirely. In the end, they patched things up, but it was an uneasy truce. He couldn't trust her fully after that, and she knew it.

Perhaps that was why he'd slipped up himself once or twice since arriving in Birmingham, he mused now. Was he trying to punish Amanda somehow, to even the score?

The chill of the night air sent a sudden shiver down his spine. Grinding his last cigarette under his heel, he turned and re-entered High, going straight to his room and bed, where he tossed fitfully for several hours, his mind still busily juxtaposing the events of the evening with those of his past.

Sleep eluded him and it was gone four by the time he finally dozed off.

*

Megan awoke the next morning with a headache, wincing as morning sunlight hit her eyes. The sun had no business being up this early in December! she thought crossly, trying to focus her vision on the numbers on her alarm clock. Good heavens! Was that really five to eight? How had she managed to oversleep like that? And then fragments of the previous evening came back to her with sickening clarity and she groaned. What had she been thinking, sitting in the bar so late the night before a test? And why on earth had she been drinking lager?

Lager. The taste of Mike's lips on hers, his tongue in her mouth. Her mind scrambled for the memory of his room: the books, the posters.

She would have indulged herself further, lying in her bed, trying to recapture the moment, but a cannon fire of knocking erupted against her door, making any additional attempt at reverie impossible.

Staggering towards the unwelcome sound, she opened the door to an irate Sue and Sally.

"We're going to breakfast without you," Sally told her firmly, looking at Megan's nightshirt with disapproval. "If you want to join us when you're dressed, you can; but we're not happy with you."

Sue chimed in with her own reprimand: "I *was* going to give you today's advent calendar chocolate, but I don't think you deserve it!"

Megan watched their retreating backs, aware that she had some serious apologising to do.

*

By skipping breakfast (for the first time ever in Hall: she didn't like the idea of not getting her money's worth), Megan managed to meet Heather in time for their habitual morning walk to campus. For the first five minutes, she let her friend chatter on, listening with only half an ear to a saga involving one of Wyddrington's bathrooms being hogged by a male guest in a pink frilly shower cap.

"You look tired," Heather said unexpectedly.

Megan nodded. "I was supposed to be having an early night yesterday evening, but it didn't work out like that."

Waiting for Heather to ask why, she felt a sudden need to divulge. "I was up until midnight 'revising genders' with Mike."

"But gender's not on the test," Heather began, puzzled. Then, "Oh! You mean ..."

Megan nodded.

"And Mike, as in Mike Hurst? You lucky thing: he's gorgeous!" Heather's eyes were shining in admiration. Megan felt suitably gratified.

"I was just saying to Helen the other day how Mike's the most improved male on the French course this term," Heather continued. "Don't you remember what he looked like at the start of term, before he'd got his contacts and when his hair was just flat?"

Was *that* why Megan hadn't noticed him before?

"Mind you," Heather added thoughtfully, "I do think he wears his trousers too tight."

Megan thought fleetingly of Mike's long legs and neatly defined bottom. She'd never really noticed a man's backside before; now here she was casually wondering what Mike looked like without his trousers. She blushed. This wasn't like her at all!

They had reached the Muirhead Tower. Slowly Megan slipped into the lecture theatre with Heather, gazing round to see if Mike had arrived yet. Would he want to sit with her? The room was still quite empty: she could choose seats for herself and Heather in an empty row near the aisle and keep a space free for Mike, just in case.

Even as she was debating this in her mind, Mike walked in, chatting to a girl she'd seen before. By the way they sauntered past her and took the last two available seats on the back row, she could tell they were more than casual acquaintances.

*

She left the lecture theatre an hour later, knowing she'd failed the test. Lack of sleep combined with an overwhelming sense of rejection had addled her brain, making it almost impossible for her to recall any of the grammar she'd revised so carefully over the past weeks. She had thrown away her chance of a decent grade – and for what? An hour or so of drunken kissing with a boy who hadn't even acknowledged her presence as he'd entered the room this morning.

There was no time to waste over post-mortems: she had an English lecture to go to. She hurried down the stone steps that led from the Muirhead Tower to the Arts Faculty, wondering what Mike and his female companion would be doing now the test was over.

*

A stern faced Jen was waiting for her inside the lecture theatre. She must have talked to Sue and Sally because her expression now mirrored the one they had worn earlier this morning.

"I hope you were careful last night," she began brusquely. When Megan looked blank, Jen elucidated: "Sue and Sally said you went off with a guy who makes Dan look like a Boy Scout! What is it with you and bad boys, Meg?"

For a moment Megan was silent, remembering Mike's arms around her, the fiery sensation when his lips had touched hers.

Jen scrutinised her closely. Megan's eyes had a faraway look. She was lost.

"Megan!"

"Nothing happened," Megan said defensively. But it could have done, had she wanted it to.

"I hope you know what you're getting into," Jen said eventually. "Sal says he does German and he's horrendously sexist about the girls on the course."

But he had ranked her, Megan, number one on his list – or did he say that to all the girls?

She was still contemplating this conundrum when their lecturer arrived.

*

Sue and Sally were decidedly frosty at dinner that evening. Megan poked listlessly at her cheese and onion flan, wondering how long it would be before they forgave her for daring to have a good time without them.

The arrival of Matt at their table didn't make things any better. As he sat down shyly next to Megan, she couldn't help comparing him to Mike and wishing that the latter were engaging her in conversation instead.

Matt, meanwhile, was feeling torn: he had been hopelessly in love with Megan ever since the first time he saw her, on the magical evening at the American Food Factory when she'd stolen his heart with her gentle manner and her huge blue eyes. He'd been so overcome that he'd been unable to do anything but stammer like an idiot whenever she addressed him. His longing for her was so strong that it hurt: more than anything, he wanted to tell her how he felt but he was afraid of rejection. She was so beautiful that she had dozens of men chasing after her; and how could he compete with that tall guy, Dan, on Ged's Physics course or any of the other confident, cocksure youths that she seemed to draw to her like moths to a flame?

He had a secret fantasy in which he swaggered up to her in the bar, looked at her knowingly and then led her off to his room where he would throw her roughly onto the bed. His daydream always stopped there: never having had a girlfriend, he was sufficiently hazy about what came next. He thought that kissing would be involved at some stage but wasn't sure whether this was before or after 'the other stuff'. He grew hot and bothered any time he tried to think about it.

Now, sitting next to Megan, he found his shyness returning. It was all as hopeless as the crush he'd had back in the sixth form when his school and the nearby Girls' Grammar School had joined forces for a production of A Midsummer Night's Dream. He had been cast as Bottom, opposite Louise, a golden haired goddess playing Titania. She had been the object of his fantasies throughout rehearsal time although she hadn't been as pretty as Megan.

A memory stirred inside him: Louise as Titania, cradling his head in her lap whilst her fingers stroked his scalp and caressed his hairy donkey's ears. At the time he'd been disappointed that the script hadn't called for him to kiss her; now he was relieved: he wanted Megan to be the first.

"I love you!" he wanted to blurt out recklessly; instead, he stifled his longing and asked her how she'd found the French test.

*

Later that evening, as they occupied their usual spot in the bar, Sue and Sally began to thaw towards Megan.

"We wouldn't mind if we thought he had any genuine feelings for you," Sally explained earnestly, "but he's obviously only got one thing on his mind."

Megan sighed. She was beginning to reach the same conclusion herself. Still …

She looked up and caught a glimpse of Mike's spiky hair at the bar. Had the others seen him?

Gulping down the last vestiges of her drink, she stood up. "I'm getting another. Does anyone else want one?"

No one did. Good. She hurried to the counter, casually sidling in beside him as if she were unaware of his presence.

His voice in her ear surprised her. "So you've finally seen me! I've been standing here for ten minutes waiting for you!"

Just standing beside him was doing funny things to her solar plexus, tying her stomach in knots and then untying them again. She wondered if she was having a similar effect on him.

His voice again, low and urgent: "My room. Five minutes."

What would her friends say?

As if reading her mind, he continued, "Go back to Ridge. If you go out of the main front door, you can walk round to the High entrance and come in through the foyer. I'll wait for you outside the lift."

Then, within seconds, he was gone.

Megan hurriedly ordered and paid for an orange juice. Carrying it back to the table and the others, she felt a sudden thrill at the thought of being in Mike's arms again. It didn't occur to her not to go. Something primeval was calling her to him so that she was as helpless as a rat hearing the Pied Piper's tune.

"I'm just popping to the loo," she heard herself say, putting her drink down on the table and turning to leave.

No one challenged her. She quickly made her way through the bar, back into Ridge. Once there, she hesitated. If she didn't return, the others would worry. Better leave a note.

She walked briskly to her room and let herself in. Grabbing a pen from her desk, she wrote a brief Post It note for her door: "Gone to bed. Was feeling sick." That should cover her.

Now she was here, she wondered if she should clean her teeth; but Mike was waiting, and if he smoked and drank, he probably wouldn't care what her own mouth tasted of. Nevertheless ... She compromised by squeezing a small amount of toothpaste onto her toothbrush and hastily brushing for ten seconds. She'd made an effort of sorts.

Fixing her note to the door, she locked it and headed for the main exit. She had never used High's outside door before, only having accessed the men's hall through the corridor bar, but it didn't take long to reach it.

The foyer was deserted except for Mike. His face broke into relief when he saw her. "That felt like the longest five minutes of my life!"

Checking her watch, she saw it was fifteen minutes since he had told her to meet him. He must like her, then, if he's been prepared to wait.

Without a word, she followed him into the lift.

*

Back at the bar, Jen was growing impatient. "How long does it take to 'pop to the loo'? Megan's been gone for over ten minutes!"

"Tummy trouble?" Sue suggested.

"Mmm." Jen wasn't sure. "Maybe I'd better check. I think she felt a bit got at, the way we all told her off for getting involved with that Mike character. I just want to make sure she's not crying in her room."

*

When she returned, five minutes later, Jen looked thoughtful. "There's a note on her door that says she's gone to bed," she reported.

"Sulking?" Sal asked.

"She said she felt sick …" Jen let the sentence dangle.

Matt felt awkward. He'd taken advantage of Megan's absence by having a bathroom break of his own, trotting back to High and the safety of the men's toilets. Entering the foyer, he was sure he'd caught a glimpse of Megan disappearing into the lift with a tall, dark stranger. It couldn't be Dan: the hair was wrong. Should he say something now?

Jealousy choked him, making it impossible to get the words out. Was this unknown man doing what he, Matt, wanted to do himself: was he throwing Megan roughly onto the bed, holding her down and kissing her into submission?

He was feeling hot and bothered again. He pulled his thoughts together, trying to blot Megan's image from his mind.

*

Once she was safely inside Mike's room, Megan felt she could relax. Mike pointed to the bed. "It's comfier than the chair. Do you want a coffee?"

"Have you got real milk?" she asked, stalling for time.

He shook his head. "Only Coffee Mate. I drink mine black."

"Just hot water then, thanks."

He pulled a face at her. "Seriously?"

It was preferable to black coffee.

Handing her the drink she'd asked for, Mike sat down next to her. The air still hummed between them, but it seemed less intense than the previous evening. He gave her a lopsided grin.

"We're doing this the wrong way round. If I'd had any manners yesterday, I would have talked to you first, got to know you before I started snogging your brains out."

Did that mean he regretted kissing her?

Before she could continue torturing herself with any further questions, Mike continued, "Let's pretend I met you at Freshers when everyone starts their conversations by saying where they're from and what they did for A level." He took a breath. "I'm Mike. I live in London and I did French, German and History A level. Your turn."

"Why History?" Megan wanted to know.

Mike shook his head. "You have to answer my question first before I can answer one of yours."

"Okay." She felt slightly embarrassed. "I'm Megan. I come from a little place about fifteen miles away from Manchester, and I did French, German and English A level – and General Studies. Now tell me why you did History. And why you didn't choose it for your degree."

Mike reached for his cigarette packet, then looked at Megan, sighed and put it down again.

"I've always loved History," he said contemplatively. "The O level stuff was okay …"

Megan nodded. She had done History herself: it had focused on the Industrial Revolution and Transport rather than the kings and queens she'd hoped for. Still, she had managed a 'B' grade.

"… But there wasn't much post-1900 and I knew that if I did A level it would be World Wars One and Two and the Cold War, so I picked that."

"You weren't tempted to do English?" Megan felt puzzled. Mike was obviously a reader - the well thumbed volumes in his bookcase were testament to that – so how could he not have wanted to take A level English Literature?

"I like reading," Mike was wishing he'd had that cigarette after all, "but I wouldn't like to ruin a book by analysing it to death the way you have to for A level. All the books on there are things I've read because I wanted to, not because I had to."

She picked up *Slaughterhouse 5*. "I wouldn't have looked at this if I hadn't been told to read it for an English seminar last week."

Mike's eyes shone. "I love that book. What did you think?"

She had been surprised by how much she'd relished it herself, never imagining from the title that the tale would be so quirky, chronicling the adventures of Billy Pilgrim, a time traveller, as he zipped between not only World War Two and his present but also between earth and the planet Tralfamadore, where he had ended up as an exhibit in a zoo!

"I enjoyed it," she said honestly. "I liked the way I didn't know what to expect from one page to the next."

He nodded in agreement. "That book's got everything: you've got the historical side of things with the bombing of Dresden, but then you've got the fantasy and sci-fi element with the time travel and the scenes with Billy Pilgrim and Montana Wildhack in the alien zoo."

"She was a sensational invitation to make babies," Megan quoted.

"That seems like a pretty accurate description of *you*," Mike told her. Removing the book from her hand, he pulled her towards him. "I think we've done enough talking for the time being ..."

*

They must have drifted off, lying there in each other's arms, still fully clothed, because Megan woke suddenly, alerted by Mike shifting his body weight.

"What time is it?"

"About half one. I've got to pee."

He gently extricated himself from her embrace and stood up, secretly berating himself for having fallen asleep with her. He would have to walk her back to Ridge, but only after he'd visited the bathroom. He was bursting.

As he disappeared out of the door, Megan sat up, unsure of the correct protocol in this situation. Was she supposed to stay here until morning? And, if she did, would Mike expect more than just kissing?

She needed to blow her nose. Perhaps Mike had tissues in the top drawer of his bedside chest, the way she did. She pulled open the drawer and then stopped. Gazing up at her was a photograph of Mike with his arm around an attractive dark haired girl. There were several more snapshots of the same girl: she was obviously Mike's girlfriend.

She was still staring at the photos when he returned. "Why didn't you tell me you had a girlfriend?" Her voice was flat, emotionless.

Mike sat down next to her. He needed to tell her the truth.

"That's Amanda." He took the photos from her. "We started going out in sixth form. She's in her first year at Bristol University, doing Maths."

So she, Megan, had just been his 'bit on the side', then? She felt suddenly cheap, worthless. And then she remembered the other girl, the one from French that morning. Just how vast was Mike's harem? she wondered.

"Who was that girl I saw you with this morning?" she asked bluntly.

Mike looked confused.

"You sat with her for the French test."

His face cleared. "You mean Rose?"

"Are you sleeping with her?" She tried to keep the hurt, the insecurity out of her voice.

Again Mike tried to be honest. "I met Rose at Freshers. We got drunk together the second or third night and one thing led to another, but it was a one-off. We've been friends ever since, but that's all. She's got a boyfriend back home in Ireland."

"So how serious is it with your girlfriend if you cheated on her as soon as you got here?" Megan knew she had no right to ask the question but she needed reassurance.

"It's complicated with Amanda and me." He was avoiding her gaze. "We've been together for a year and a half but I've cheated three times since I came to Birmingham: Rose; someone else on the French course called Tracie – she was upset about something and I was trying to make her feel better; and you."

He was lumping her in with his one-night stands: she was just another notch on his bedpost, nothing special at all.

"Is it really cheating with me if we've not slept together?" she wanted to know, clutching at straws, desperate to redeem herself, no matter how slightly.

"I'd mind if Amanda was doing it to me."

Silence.

"So why are we doing this then?" she asked at last, still keeping her distance. Two nights of holding, kissing; but he had never been hers to hold or kiss.

Mike placed his hands on her shoulders, pulling her into him almost roughly, looking intently into her eyes. "Because when you're in my arms, I forget about everything else."

At that moment, her heart melted and, for the briefest of seconds, she was tempted in a way she never had been before to stay in his arms all night and see whether this intensity of desire she felt for him was something deeper.

Perhaps he felt it too, for pulling her even closer, he murmured, "You don't have to leave …"

The air grew thick between them, their longing for each other almost palpable. It would be so easy to stay; so hard to walk away.

"It wouldn't mean anything though, would it?" Wanting him to contradict her; fearing what his response would be.

He could have told her what she wanted to hear; instead his answer was painfully honest: "Maybe not in the long run, but it would be pretty special at the time."

A sharp stab of regret – for both of them.

"I'd better go then." Not wanting to move; knowing she had to.

He stroked her cheek gently, brushing her hair away from her face. "Or you could stay and just let me hold you …"

The temptation tugged at her heart. The idea of lying in his arms all night, feeling loved, feeling wanted, answered a need she hadn't realised she possessed. Yet still …

"Would you be wearing anything?" she asked cautiously.

Mike grinned at her, his face suddenly full of mischief. "I always sleep in the nude."

He left the information dangling suggestively and she pulled away reluctantly, knowing that if she stayed she would be playing with fire. She wasn't prepared to risk the consequences, aware of how easily she could be burned.

"Maybe another time," she said, as lightly as she could.

She began to leave but he rose from the bed and followed her to the door. "I'll walk you back."

Silently they left his room, waiting in the foyer for the lift, suddenly awkward with each other again. It was, she thought, as if his room always cast some spell upon her: an enchantment easily broken by the prosaic solidity of the tired lift with its faint odour of stale testosterone.

He took her hand as the lift door opened - a curiously intimate gesture - and led her out of the front door and around the back of the building. "They lock the internal door at midnight," he reminded her. Then, "Have you got a front door key for Ridge?"

She only possessed her room key. A slight panic overtook her: would she be able to access the building?

They had arrived. Mike peered through the large plate glass window, spotting the night porter at his desk. He hadn't previously encountered Gordon the Warden (as he was affectionately known) but he knew of him: countless residents of High Hall had returned from Ridge at some unearthly hour in the morning, their eyes glazed over from being forced to listen to Gordon's anecdotes before he would allow them to leave.

Now Mike tapped on the window, attracting Gordon's attention. The latter showed no sign of surprise at seeing Megan return home at this hour in the morning, unlocking the door without a single question.

They paused as they reached the doorway, both suddenly shy. Mike bent and kissed her slowly, passionately; then, wordlessly, he was gone.

"I thought 'e was coming in with yer." Gordon's thick Brummie accent made the words sound matter of fact. Perhaps he was used to girls turning up with overnight guests?

As Megan made her way through Ridge's foyer, he remarked chattily, "Not 'ungry, are yer?"

Whilst she contemplated why he was asking her such a strange question at two a.m., he produced a ham sandwich, compounding the absurdity of the situation by commenting, "They gave me this for me supper, but I've gorra bit o' cake as well and I'd rather 'ave the cake."

In the end she took the proffered sandwich, muttering her thanks. It would probably end up in her bin, but she appreciated the gesture.

*

Back in the safety of her room, she examined her face in the mirror, wanting to see if she looked like a wanton woman. Her eyes were dark with desire; her lips bruised by love. She knew then that she had fallen irrevocably for Mike, despite his girlfriend, despite everything else that should have kept them apart.

She stepped to the edge of the precipice and let herself plummet.

Chapter Fifteen

When Megan opened the door to Jen's insistent knocking the following morning, she looked dreadful. Dark shadows ringed her eyes: she looked as if she hadn't slept in weeks.

"How are you feeling?" Jen sounded sympathetic.

Letting her enter, Megan decided to confess everything.

"Last night, I didn't come back to my room when you thought I did. I went to Mike's room again ..." she paused.

"Go on." Jen's tone was now less gentle.

Megan swallowed. "We talked. He likes books and we talked about some of our favourite authors." Lying in his arms, she had told him about her passion for Hardy and the Brontë sisters; he, in turn, had waxed lyrical about Graham Greene's *Dr Fischer of Geneva* and *The End of the Affair*.

"And?"

"And we kissed – and that was wonderful too." Megan's voice had taken on a dreamy quality; her eyes had a faraway look.

"And?" Jen repeated her question.

"And then I found out he has a girlfriend," Megan said in a small voice. Saying it out loud made her feel worse. She was The Other Woman.

"So, are you going to see him again?" The question was casual. Jen wasn't judging her.

Megan shrugged miserably. "I don't know. When I'm with him, everything seems so right; and then I think about his girlfriend and how I'm making him cheat on her, and I feel confused. I know I shouldn't want him like this, but I can't stop myself." She looked at Jen helplessly. "I feel like I'm drowning."

"If he really cared about you, then he wouldn't be cheating," Jen said severely. "He'd finish things with his girlfriend first and then ask you out."

Jen was right, of course: Megan knew that, deep inside; nevertheless, it was galling to be told.

"I won't see him again," she said suddenly, wondering if she would be able to keep her promise.

"Good girl!" Jen sounded approving. "Make sure you stick to it," she added as she turned to leave. "We'll be keeping an eye on you tonight to check you behave!"

*

Once Jen had gone, Megan checked her alarm clock. Eight fifteen and the last Phonetics lecture of term was at nine. Would she make it? She felt torn between staying in Hall for sausages and beans or skipping breakfast and arriving at her lecture on time.

Eventually, her conscience got the better of her and Megan missed breakfast for the second day in a row. Illicit love came at a price! she thought crossly as she pulled on her jeans and hunted for a clean top. Wonderful though Mike's kisses had been, they were no substitute for a hearty meal.

She was so late by the time she reached Wyddrington that Heather had already left without her. Megan was forced to half-run, half-walk the rest of the way to campus on her own. It should have been the ideal time to reflect on her misadventures with Mike, but jogging along at breakneck speed was not conducive to serious soul searching.

*

She entered the back of the lecture theatre just as Professor Burns was striding to the front. Flopping down into the nearest available seat, she realised she was sitting next to Matt. He gave her a strange look.

For the next twenty minutes, Megan scribbled busily, writing down everything Professor Burns said, no matter how ludicrous it was. Needing something to take her mind off Mike, she filled page after page with examples of fricatives, lateral approximants and semi-vowels; whether or not she understood more than a tenth of what she was writing was unclear.

After a while, Matt whispered, "Where did you disappear to last night?"

Megan hesitated. She knew Matt had feelings for her; would it crush him if she told him the truth?

In the end she compromised, telling him she'd bumped into someone she knew at the bar and gone back to his room to talk about books. It wasn't *really* fibbing – unless you counted lying by omission.

Matt's relief was tangible. "Thank goodness for that," he said simply. "I saw you going into the lift with him and I thought you were going to say you and he ..." His voice tailed off in embarrassment.

Megan felt guilty. Matt was so sweet, so innocent. He reminded her of a puppy, looking up at her with adoring eyes, desperate for a pat on the head or an affectionate word. And then the thought hit her: *was that how Mike saw her?*

No, she had told Jen she wouldn't see Mike again. She would file those two magical evenings away in her memory, only taking them out when she was well and truly over him.

Sitting beside Matt, she strengthened her resolve, oblivious to her own inability to keep her promise.

*

"This is our next to last evening here before we all go home for Christmas." Sally's statement sounded wistful.

Megan looked from one face to the other: Jen and Phil were sitting together, she on his knee, he with one hand stroking her leg; Matt was sipping a glass of red wine thoughtfully; Sue, for once without Ged, was working her way through a packet of Smoky Bacon crisps. She felt a sudden rush of affection for this disparate group of people, all so different, all now friends.

Across the bar, she could see Mike sitting with his usual male coterie. She had watched him for half a minute before he glanced up and caught her eye. Beside her, Jen muttered, "Forbidden fruit, remember?" She looked away again, but not before something indefinable had passed between them. She knew then that she would see him again tonight, no matter what Jen thought.

A slight scuffle broke out at the table next to theirs. Phil's arms tightened around Jen; Matt looked worried.

"Let's move this party somewhere else," Sally declared, standing up. She looked at Jen. "Our room?"

Jen nodded, sliding off Phil's lap with reluctance. "Come on, Megan. Sue, are you coming?"

The redhead declined. "I'm expecting a wee Geddy," she began.

"Congratulations!" Sally broke in, winking at Jen. "When's the happy date?"

"I'm expecting Ged to join me in the bar in about ten minutes," Sue continued with dignity. "He had an end of term Physics shindig to go to, but he said he'd be back by nine thirty."

"We may as well wait with you then," Jen remarked, reclaiming her place on Phil's knee. "Anyone else fancy another drink?"

"I'll go." Megan got up slowly. She needed to distance herself from the rest of them. "Another Coral, Jen? Matt, do you want anything?"

She noticed that Sally followed her. Had Jen charged her with keeping an eye on Megan's virtue?

Standing at the counter, having paid for the drinks, Megan felt a sudden jolt of electricity. Without turning round, she knew that Mike stood behind her. As the bartender handed over two Corals, she pushed them towards Sally. "Do you want to take these and I'll wait for Matt's wine?"

Mike's voice, low in her ear. "My room." Again, a spark.

Not caring what the others thought, she slipped her hand into his and let him lead her through the bar.

*

Jen watched Megan leave, feeling any number of mixed emotions. Although she thought her friend was foolish to get involved with someone like Mike, she herself knew what it was like to want someone so much you felt compelled to be with them. She hadn't told the others, but Phil hadn't been unattached when she met him. He'd been up front, though, telling her about Debbie straight away, giving her the option to walk away before anything started or to take a chance that he would choose her, Jen, instead.

After their first night together, when they'd talked for hours, covering both Primary and Secondary school, family and friends, favourite music and the best TV shows from their childhoods, they both knew this was something special. He'd written to Debbie the following morning, telling her he'd met someone else and apologising for breaking it off by letter. This Mike, though, seemed different: happy to have two girls on the go at the same time. She hoped Megan wasn't going to get hurt.

Matt, meanwhile, was wildly jealous. He had recognised the man with Megan and realised that she probably wouldn't just be talking about books tonight. She obviously had feelings for this stranger, but Matt didn't trust him an inch. Neither, as it transpired, did Sue and Sally.

"What on earth is she playing at?" Sue hissed at Sally, watching as Megan's back retreated into High.

Sally rolled her eyes. "What did you expect? She was just as bad over Dan. If you ask me, she's looking for a father figure."

Matt's mind whirled. What were they on about?

"Ged said something similar," Sue mused thoughtfully. "He said Megan gives off this vibe about needing to be looked after."

"She's hardly an advert for feminism," Sally agreed. "She just breezes in, looking small and helpless, and the next thing you know, she's got half a dozen men drooling over her."

Was there a touch of rancour in her voice? Matt wondered.

"What about you, Matt?" Sue turned to him suddenly. "Do you think Megan knows what she's doing; or is it subconscious?"

"I ... umm ..." Matt was at a loss to know what to say. "I don't think she's a flirt," he suggested timidly.

Sally groaned. "It's no good asking Matt: he's obviously fallen for the helpless female act too."

"It isn't an act!" Matt felt indignant. "Megan's a sweet girl. She can't help being so beautiful!"

"See what I mean?" Sally was relentless. "She's got you wrapped around her little finger!" she said in disgust, before draining Megan's untouched Coral and stomping back to her room without the others.

"What did I say?" Matt was genuinely puzzled. He obviously had no idea that Sally liked him, Jen thought. She sighed inwardly. Life was rapidly becoming something akin to a Shakespearean comedy as far as her friends were concerned: Sally liked Matt, who liked Megan, who liked Mike. It was like *A Midsummer Night's Dream*, except with no meddling fairies or useful love potion.

"Come on," she said, spotting Ged wending his way towards them. "Let's go back to my room and see if we can cheer up Sally."

*

Megan was feeling intoxicated, despite the fact that she'd only had one alcoholic drink this evening. Mike's kisses had a dizzying effect on her, making her light headed. When they finally broke apart, she found herself breathless, gasping for air.

For his part, Mike felt totally confused. No matter how many times he told himself to leave Megan alone, he couldn't resist her. One look across a crowded bar had been all it had taken to convince him to take her to his room, against his better judgement, and stockpile enough time with her to sustain him through the Christmas holiday.

He wasn't sure what he would tell Amanda. It was one thing to confess to having slept with someone under the influence of alcohol; another to admit to having fallen for another girl. He must feel something for Megan if he could hold her and kiss her for three nights in a row without trying to take things further. Mind you, if she'd offered sex, he wouldn't have refused …

She looked up at him now, her eyes clouded by passion. "My friends will never speak to me again after seeing me leave the bar with you tonight."

He kissed the top of her head. "Who cares? We're having fun."

Was that all it was? She shrank from him slightly, almost imperceptibly. She wasn't expecting Mike to fall in love with her – bad boys didn't do things like that – but she would have liked to think that their time together constituted more than mere 'fun'.

Mike sensed her reaction and almost kicked himself for hurting her like that. *Isn't it better this way?* a part of him argued stubbornly. *You're no good for her and you know it.*

He didn't belong in her world just as she wasn't part of his. Megan needed a 'nice', gentle boyfriend, like that public schoolboy type she sometimes hung out with in the bar: the one who looked at her as if he wanted to worship her. He pushed her away and sat up. "I need a cigarette." He didn't normally smoke in front of her, but maybe it was time he reminded her how different they were.

Megan watched as Mike put the cigarette in his mouth and flicked his lighter. Smoking fascinated and repelled her at the same time. She thought it a disgusting habit; nevertheless, there was something indescribably cool about the way he dragged on the cylinder, eyes half closed, and then blew the smoke across the room, away from her.

"What happens when we come back after Christmas?" she asked suddenly.

Mike lit another cigarette. "What do you mean?" He wasn't looking at her.

"You and me. Us." She swallowed. "Are you going to keep on cheating on Amanda?"

"It's none of your business!" he said rudely. He knew she would be hurt; would it be enough to make her walk away from him for good?

Megan felt tears pricking at the back of her eyes. She mustn't cry in front of him, couldn't let him know how miserable she felt.

"It looks like it's come to an end, then," she said stiffly, hoping he would contradict her. Moving over to the door, she paused, expecting him to escort her back to Ridge as he had on the previous two occasions. Instead, he remained where he was, the half-finished cigarette still dangling from his mouth.

She had never meant anything to him, she saw that now. Whereas he ... He had unlocked the door to her heart and left it wide open, an invitation for anyone else to break in and vandalise what he found.

With trembling legs, she left the room, walking away from the only man in High with whom she could have visualised a future.

*

Matt left Sally's room after forty minutes. Having made a half-hearted attempt to party with the others, he realised it wasn't the same without Megan. Giving the excuse of an early Drama lecture (when in truth he didn't have anything until his French Lit tutorial at eleven), he hurried through Ridge and the bar, making his way towards the High foyer.

The lift doors opened and Megan stumbled out, looking as if she'd been crying. She was alone.

"Megan!" Matt couldn't keep the concern from his voice. What had that scoundrel done to her?

She lifted her tear-stained face, wiping her eyes. "I'm sorry. I didn't see you there."

"Are you okay?" Matt thought his heart would break, seeing her like this.

She nodded listlessly. "I'll live."

He wanted more than anything to take her back to his room and look after her: dry her tears, kiss her pain away. He couldn't. If Doug wasn't there already, he was liable to return at any moment. Matt needed somewhere private to be alone with Megan so he could rescue her properly, be the knight in shining armour he was sure she needed.

"Shall I walk you back to Ridge?" he asked tentatively.

She shook her head. "Thanks, but I don't want to go back to my room. I think I just want to go for a bit of a walk, clear my head."

"You might not be safe on your own." Matt's head was spinning. "Let me come with you, just to make sure," he pressed, secretly amazed that he was being so forward.

Wordlessly she nodded, leading the way out of High's huge double doors, walking away from the building and down towards the lake. He trailed after her, his mind forming half a dozen declarations of friendship, rejecting them all as either too strong or too half-hearted. He had to tell her how he felt, to make her see that he wasn't like Mike or Dan or any of the other men who'd made her cry.

A cool breeze ruffled the surface of the lake, making the stars reflected there skip and jump. Overhead the moon was a silvery orb. Under any other circumstances, it would have been a romantic evening.

Megan paused at a bench near the water, standing quite still before she finally sighed and sat down. Matt perched at a slight distance, unsure of how close she wanted him.

They sat in silence for several minutes before Matt dared to speak. Even then, all he could manage was an awkward "I think that's the Big Dipper over there. Can you see it?" He pointed it out, but Megan wasn't interested. She seemed locked inside herself, tolerating his presence rather than finding comfort in it.

Another five minutes and Matt tried again. "What time's your last lecture on Friday? Mine's at eleven so I'll probably travel home straight after that and avoid the weekend rush later."

Still no answer.

"Megan?" He was beginning to feel worried. She wasn't normally this quiet.

She turned her face towards him, moisture glistening in her eyes. "I've been so stupid …"

Misery emanated from her as a large tear began to roll slowly down her cheek. Almost instinctively, Matt put his arm around her, at first patting her shoulder clumsily, then throwing caution to the wind and enfolding her in a hug. She felt so small and vulnerable in his arms.

She also felt disturbingly soft and curvy. It would be so easy to stroke her hair, to kiss away the tears; but being a well brought up public schoolboy, he merely held her close, trying not to let his raging hormones get the better of him. He was a gentleman, not an animal!

He wasn't sure how long she cried on his shoulder. He was aware that his shirt was beginning to feel damp and that his left arm was going to sleep, trapped as it was between Megan and the bench. When she finally pulled away, he wasn't sure whether to feel relief or regret.

"I'm sorry." Her words escaped in a whisper. "I didn't mean to cry all over you like that."

"Did he hurt you?" At this moment in time, Matt felt capable of inflicting physical violence on anyone who upset Megan.

"Only my heart." Her voice wobbled as she said it. "It's my fault. I knew he had a girlfriend, but I still went back to see him again."

Matt had a brief but very satisfying image of slamming his fist into Mike's perfectly chiselled face.

"I … we …" She was fumbling for the words. "I kissed him, but I knew he wasn't mine to kiss. Does that make me a bad person?" Before he could reply, she rushed on, "I won't be seeing him again. I thought he cared about me, but he was just using me. I see that now."

She sounded so sad when she said it.

I *wouldn't* treat you like that, Matt wanted to say, and, *If you were* my *girlfriend, I'd treat you with respect.* The words died on his lips: it was too soon to tell her any of this.

"We'd better get back." She was drying her eyes, blowing her nose. Matt looked away tactfully.

Unexpectedly he felt her arms stealing around him for a brief hug. "Thanks for tonight," she said simply, releasing him almost immediately. "You're a good friend, Matt."

He wanted to be so much more, but that would have to wait for another time.

Chapter Sixteen

Thursday: her last day of lectures this term. For the third night in a row she had slept badly, her mind too full of Mike to embrace sleep. Despite knowing she was better off without him, she couldn't help replaying the memories, wondering as she did so whether she should have done anything differently. Had she made a mistake in walking away just because he'd referred to their time together as 'fun'? Should she try to see him again tonight and see if there was anything worth hanging onto?

She said as much to Jen over her toast that morning (there was no way she was going to miss three breakfasts in a row). Jen, however, was sceptical.

"I think you should let it lie," she advised, slicing a banana into her Bran Flakes. "It's not as if he's made much effort with you, is it? He hasn't sat with you in any of your French lectures or bought you a coffee. Does he even know where your room is in Hall?"

He didn't. They had always gone back to his place in High.

"I'm sorry, Meg," Jen continued, as gently as she could, "but it looks as though you were a lot more serious about him than he was about you. If he's already got a girlfriend ..." She let her voice trail off tactfully.

A mixture of guilt and vulnerability overwhelmed Megan. She had known Mike was attached, but that hadn't prevented her from kissing him, hadn't acted as a deterrent to make her stop seeing him. And it didn't end the hurt she felt now: the pain of rejection, the agony of unrequited love.

She sharply slammed the brakes on her train of thought. She wasn't 'in love' with Mike, she told herself sternly. What she felt for him was attraction, no more. She tried hard to forget the longing she'd felt to stay in his room, in his arms all night.

"You've got to let go of him," Jen repeated.
Deep down inside, Megan knew she was right.

*

The day's classes had passed quickly and it was now nine p.m. and her final evening in the bar with Jen, Sue and Sally. Megan was surprised to realise that she had spent almost an entire term socialising in a place she would have previously regarded as a den of iniquity: her mother had always led her to believe that alcoholic establishments were the haunts of the devil.

"What are you going to do over Christmas, Sue?" Sally asked as the redhead slid into a seat next to them.

Sue beamed. "One will be introducing Ged to one's parents," she informed them importantly, with more than a touch of the pretension she'd adopted for Freshers. Megan thought that Ged looked significantly underwhelmed.

"What about you?" This time Sally addressed her question to Megan.

"Well," Megan began shyly, "it's my birthday next week ..."

The other four emitted protesting noises. "Why didn't you tell us?" Jen demanded. "We could have gone out for dinner."

"I thought we'd be having a formal dinner in hall for the end of term," Megan confessed, "and then there was the pantomime ..." *And Mike,* her mind added silently.

"Why haven't we had a Christmas formal?" broke in Sally, looking at Sue, who usually knew about such things. "All the other Halls have had one this week."

"So did we last year." Sue sounded somewhat annoyed. "I think it's because the JCR double booked Freshers and spent the Christmas budget on Showaddywaddy," she added. "We're supposed to have one formal a term, plus the Freshers' Formal, so we've still had two this term but just not had them spaced out."

"Where've Phil and Matt got to?" Sally asked next, scanning the corridor to see if she could spot them anywhere.

Ged coloured slightly. "They went to a JCR Events meeting," he mumbled.

"Whatever for?" Jen was mystified. "Phil's always saying the Hall events are rubbish. The discos are terrible, for a start and whenever they do a film night, it's always *'Nightmare on Elm Street'*!"

"Well, maybe he's trying to suggest something a little less naff," Sally suggested. "Did they say what time they'd be finished, Ged?"

Before he could reply, Matt and Phil strode into view, both looking remarkably pleased with themselves.

"You're looking at High's newly appointed Video Rep," Phil told them. "And Matt's the new Music Rep – which means he chooses the records for the High/Ridge discos."

Matt was watching Megan, wondering if she would be impressed by his new role. She had seemed to like that Steve character when she had thought he was in a band; and although being a glorified DJ wasn't quite in the same league, it might still make her think Matt was now possible boyfriend material. Maybe he could dedicate some songs to her? He didn't actually know much about music, apart from Alison Moyet and Phil Collins, but he was willing to learn.

"Well done, both of you!" This was Sally. "I'll be having words with you about Sunday's discos," she added to Matt. (Any excuse to get the chance to talk to him.)

"Hmmm," Jen said thoughtfully, regarding her boyfriend, "does that mean better films on a Wednesday night, then? Because I might start coming along to film night every week now you're in charge. I've got a list of things I want to see …"

"And I get to keep the VCR in my room for the rest of the week." Phil looked at Jen meaningfully. The previous Video Rep had abused his position by showing blue movies in his room and charging an entrance fee, but Phil was looking forward to romantic evenings in with Jen: he was sure that a soppy film or two would put her in the mood. And if he let Jen choose the videos they watched together, he would be able to show action/adventure and horror on a Wednesday evening, which should keep the rest of High happy.

Megan was only vaguely aware of the conversation. Across the bar she could see Mike, surrounded by his usual crowd of friends and totally oblivious to her presence.

Jen caught her eye. "You do know he's off limits now?" she said gently.

Megan nodded, desolation a stone in the pit of her stomach. She still wanted him, but she knew she might as well wish for the moon. Mike would never be hers.

Pushing her disappointment aside, she turned to Matt and began to ask him about his plans for Christmas.

*

The following morning, a deputation arrived at Megan's door to escort her to breakfast. The three girls handed Megan a large, handmade birthday card bearing cleverly drawn caricatures of each of them.

"We didn't know Sally was such an artist," Sue explained, "until we started talking about finding you a card, after you'd gone to bed last night, and she told us she could make one."

"Although if you'd mentioned it sooner," Jen broke in, "we would have bought you flowers and a cake. It was too late for any of that by the time you said anything last night."

Megan was touched. She examined the card carefully. Each of the four friends was instantly recognisable: Sally had drawn herself in running gear, looking ridiculously sporty; Sue was a voluptuous vamp, displaying her generous cleavage whilst clutching Ted – no! She looked closer and realised the teddy bear in the picture had Ged's face!; Jen was dark and sultry, carrying an enormous wine glass full of something pink (presumably Coral); and Megan herself was half the size of everyone else, with a cloud of blonde hair and a tiny black dress. (She wasn't quite sure what to make of the three scrawny youths staring at her with eyes literally popping out of their heads.)

"It's the best birthday card I've ever had," she said truthfully.

Her friends grinned.

"We'll still go out for your birthday," Jen promised, as they began walking to breakfast, "but we'll have to wait until the start of term." She sighed. "I would have suggested the first night back, but it's the High/Ridge disco and we ought to support Phil and Matt now they're involved with it."

"*And* we have to dress up," Sally added. "I hope it wasn't Phil's idea to make it fancy dress, Jen, because, if it was, I'll throttle him!"

Phil and Matt had dropped this bombshell towards the end of the previous evening, casually pointing out that the first disco of the year would be a belated New Year's Eve party (*very* belated, thought Megan, since they weren't returning until the thirteenth of January!) and that there would be a prize for the best fancy dress.

"Hardly anyone will bother," Sue said knowingly. "Last year there was a 'Tarts and Vicars' disco and only three people made the effort."

"We should though." Jen looked worried. "How will Phil and Matt feel if we don't join in? I've got a French maid's outfit at home: I'll bring it back in January."

"Exactly *why* do you have a French maid costume?" Sue asked severely as they reached the dining hall and approached the serving hatch.

"I was in 'The Importance of Being Ernest' last year at school," Jen explained, "and I played the maid. The school didn't have a maid's outfit, so I bought my own. I thought it would come in handy if I ever went to Rocky Horror."

Megan looked mystified.

"It's a film from the seventies," Sally explained kindly, helping herself to toast. "Every so often, they reshow it at the cinema and people dress up as characters from the film when they go to see it."

It sounded most bizarre.

"We should all meet up for lunch before we go home," Sue said suddenly. "There's no PopMo today, so why don't we all go out for food? We could make it Megan's birthday celebration"

The others seemed to think this was a good idea. Immediately they began debating whether it should be on- or off-campus, eventually settling on the salad bar in The Cellar because, as Sue pointed out, it was the end of term, their grants had run out and it was nearly Christmas – "So we can save our money and have a plate of salad for a pound each," she declared.

Megan didn't think that salad sounded particularly festive, but Sue reassured her that the choice on offer included jacket potatoes and pasta as well, so that was decided upon.

"What are you going to do for the rest of the morning?" Jen asked her. Since she was Single Honours English, she had Anglo Saxon this morning, but Megan's Fridays were always free.

Megan hesitated. They all had an extended essay to do over the Christmas holidays. She could start planning that now, but she knew she would work better if she sat down for a whole day at home and concentrated until it was finished.

"It'll probably take me all morning to pack," she said honestly. She would be leaving her monstrous trunk in the box room, stuffed full of everything that was too heavy to take home on the train and too bulky to lock inside her wardrobe.

"We'll see you at twelve then," Jen told her, rising from the table. "I'll have to go: my lecture's at nine."

Sue and Sally also rose to their feet. It transpired they both had ten o'clocks, but were walking to campus earlier than necessary so they could return Short Loan library books on time. Megan watched them leave, idly contemplating the day ahead as she sipped her tea.

"Oh good! You're still here." Matt plonked his plate down on the table and took the seat opposite her. "I wanted to catch you before you left."

Megan felt a growing tension inside her stomach. This wasn't going to be another attempted declaration of love, was it? She began to feel nauseous.

Matt was taking a small leather-bound book from his jeans pocket and producing a pen. "I wanted your address – so I can write to you over Christmas."

He actually had a little black book! Megan thought in amazement; although, unlike the cliché, she knew that this book would not be full of women's phone numbers and vital statistics.

Matt was pushing it over to her. She picked it up and began to flick through the pages, searching for 'M'. Noting 'Auntie Mary', 'Gran' and 'Leisure Centre', she felt a sudden rush of affection for him. Matt was so earnest, so innocent. She could picture him now, visiting his granny every week, playing Rummy with her, weeding her garden. He was such a *nice* boy: why couldn't she fall for someone like that?

"I'm getting addresses off the others too," Matt said hurriedly. He had seen Megan hesitate briefly: was she deciding not to give him her contact details after all?

Megan hastily scribbled at the top of the 'M' page. She had already given her mother's address and phone number to the other girls – they had exchanged Christmas cards at the start of December – and was looking forward to having the monotony of four weeks at home broken by the arrival of letters.

"Have a good holiday, Matt," she said now, getting up from her chair.

He rose too. "I'll miss you." It was the closest he dared get to telling her how he felt.

He kissed her awkwardly on the cheek. Maybe next time he saw her he would feel more confident, but he doubted it: no matter how many times he rehearsed what he was going to say, what he was going to do, her presence always reduced him to a tongue-tied idiot.

"I'll miss you too." She surprised both of them by giving him a quick hug. "I'll have to go, Matt. I've got loads of packing to do."

He watched her leave, holding the memory of her fleeting embrace and wrapping it around his heart.

*

Inside her room, Megan packed quickly, putting aside the books she needed to take home with her – she had a 5,000 word essay to write on a modern novel she disliked, *'The Tenants'*; a critical work called *'Metafiction'* to read and refer to in her essay; and the whole of Milton's *'Paradise Lost'* to read and annotate in preparation for the following term.

She thought she heard a noise outside. Was someone coming to visit her? Sighing with annoyance, she went to investigate. The corridor was empty, but there was a Penguin paperback that looked vaguely familiar, lying on the floor beside her door.

She picked it up and examined it closely. It wasn't new: the broken spine and dogeared pages suggested that it had been read several times before. As she flicked through it, a piece of paper fluttered to the floor. It was a note in handwriting she didn't recognise.

'*Megan, I'm sorry about the other night. After you'd gone, I reread 'The End of the Affair': it's one of my all-time favourite Graham Greene novels. If you get time, read it over Christmas. Mike. PS Don't lose it – I want it back! I was going to buy you your own copy, but the campus bookshop didn't have it in stock.*'

She turned the book over and studied the title. Was it a coded message, Mike's way of saying that whatever had been between them was now over?

Nevertheless, no boy had given her a book before. For Megan this was an immensely romantic gesture: the equivalent to anyone else being given flowers or chocolates. Did this mean that Mike liked her after all? But he had totally rejected her thirty-six hours ago. And he had a girlfriend, wasn't going to leave her for anyone else. It was all very confusing.

*

She was still feeling perplexed when she arrived at the Cellar Bar to meet the others for lunch. Should she mention Mike's gift? She had a feeling that Sally and Sue would be disparaging: they didn't like Mike. (She often felt that Sally didn't really approve of her, Megan, either – despite being her friend.)

Jen was there already but the other two weren't. Good: Megan had a chance to ask for advice. Joining her friend in the line for food and ignoring the dirty looks from the people she queue-jumped, she told her about the book Mike had left for her. "It must mean something, mustn't it?"

Jen observed Megan critically. Megan's eyes were bright with hopefulness; her face wore a pleading look. She had all the hallmarks of a woman in love.

It was time to be brutal. For Megan's own good, she needed to hear the truth.

"Don't you think you're reading too much into it?" Jen began carefully. "It's only a book: it's not as if he gave you jewellery or something expensive. And it's not even new."

"But that's the point," Megan argued, wondering why Jen was being so obtuse. "It's a book he likes and he wants me to read it too. A jacket potato, please," she added, reaching the counter and addressing the woman in charge.

"If he was really serious," Jen said slowly – "Quiche and salad, please – don't you think he would have knocked on your door to see if you were in? Or left an address or a phone number so you could get in touch over the holidays?"

Megan was silent, thinking of Matt and how he'd sought her out to ask for her address. Mike had been all the way to her room but not tried to speak to her. Maybe Jen was right after all.

"Anyway," Jen nudged her in the direction of an empty table, "we'd better grab some seats. This place is filling up fast and Sue and Sally have just walked in."

*

Some time later, as Megan sat on the train to Manchester, her suitcase safely stowed out of the way of the other passengers but where she could still reach it when she needed to, she pulled Mike's book out of her rucksack. She hadn't read any Graham Greene before and wasn't sure what to expect.

It wasn't long before she was caught up in the tale of Maurice Bendrix and Sarah Miles and their illicit relationship. She read quickly, trying to find hidden meanings in characters' thoughts and actions. Did Mike see himself as Sarah, trapped in a marriage he was unable or unwilling to leave?

No, she was overthinking everything: Mike wasn't married to Amanda, nor was she, Megan, as jealous and possessive as Bendrix. Maybe he just thought it was a good story and that she'd like it because she was studying English?

By the time the train pulled into Manchester Piccadilly, she had devoured half the book. She had always been a fast reader but she found the narrative so compelling that she didn't want to put it down.

The streets around the station thronged with busy-ness. She had mistimed her journey, not leaving New Street until almost three and arriving in Manchester bang in the middle of rush hour. Somehow she would have to find her way to Victoria, along with her baggage, to catch the train that would take her back to Littleborough. It would be at least six by the time she arrived. She could ring her mother from the station and ask for a lift home.

She managed to lose her way almost immediately, finding herself walking in the opposite direction to the arrow on the sign for Victoria Station. Placing her suitcase on the pavement for a while, she wondered what to do. She had taken a taxi to Fiveways earlier on, aware that whilst she could probably lug her suitcase between platforms at New Street, carrying it a mile to the station was overambitious. She'd been able to share with Jen and Sally, though – both going in opposite directions to her own at New Street – so the cost hadn't been prohibitive. Now with only enough for the phone box and a couple of pounds 'for an emergency', she found herself sadly lacking in the funds needed for another cab.

"Need a hand?"

A strange voice interrupted her reverie. Startled, Megan looked up. A young man stood in front of her. His face seemed vaguely familiar but she wasn't sure why.

He was extending a hand towards her. "Justin. I'm on your English course. We met at the cheese and wine at Freshers."

Megan hastily searched her memory, trying to locate any information about this stranger. It was no use: she had encountered so many people over her first few days in Birmingham that she couldn't place him at all.

"I thought I recognised you when you were on the platform at New Street," Justin went on. "I was going to say hello, but then you got on the train a few carriages up from where I was standing, and I wasn't sure I'd get a seat if I followed you." He grinned suddenly. "I did have a wander later, to see if I could spot you, but you had your nose in a book so I left you to it."

Megan wasn't sure how to respond to any of this. It was flattering that Justin had remembered her from a brief meeting over ten weeks ago but slightly unnerving to think that he had been hunting for her on the train.

"You've got a good memory," she said at last. "I wouldn't have known who you were if you hadn't told me."

Justin smiled again. He wasn't good looking, but he had a pleasant, honest face. "You're not easy to forget," he told her, his gaze sweeping across her. "All that blonde hair is very distinctive." *Was he flirting with her?*

Megan blushed. She still hadn't learned how to receive a compliment.

"We've nicknamed you 'The Pocket Venus'," Justin went on, colouring slightly. "We used to call you 'The Blonde Bombshell', but that's too much of a cliché."

"Who's 'we'?" Megan asked curiously. She was somewhat stunned to discover that people on her degree course had invested her with a moniker.

Justin looked sheepish. "Just me and a couple of other guys. That dark haired girl you sit with, she's 'The Latin Lovely'. Because she looks like she might be Spanish or Italian."

Jen was from Devon.

"Well," he was staring at his feet now, "I just wanted to say Hi, that's all." He turned to go.

"Wait!" Megan wasn't sure why she'd been bold enough to call him back. "Where do you live?" Without waiting for a reply, she rushed on, "I need to get to Victoria station with my luggage, but I've managed to get lost. Can you point me in the right direction?"

By way of response, Justin gallantly picked up her suitcase. "I'm going that way myself. I'll walk with you."

Megan trotted along at Justin's side, admiring the way he strode forward so confidently. It was a pity he wasn't better looking, she thought absently, then checked herself, feeling ashamed. Was she really so shallow that she couldn't contemplate going out with someone unless he looked like Dan or Mike?

"So, where do you live, Megan?" Justin's long legs easily covered the distance to the station.

"A town about three miles away from Rochdale: Littleborough. Do you know it?"

Justin shook his head. "Is it anywhere near Hebden Bridge? I've got relatives there."

Hebden Bridge was only about ten miles away from Megan's mother's. She had been taken there several times as a child but couldn't remember much about it.

"Where are *you* from, Justin?" she asked curiously.

"Bolton. Can't you tell from the accent?"

She couldn't: it was too similar to those she'd grown up with, although she didn't have a northern accent herself, thanks to a mother who hailed from the Home Counties and had passed her own exquisitely rounded vowels onto Megan.

"I can't place your accent, though." Justin was regarding her thoughtfully. "You don't sound like you come from round here but then the odd Lancashire word creeps in."

Megan's accent – or lack of one – had been the bane of her existence. From the time she started school at the age of four, she had been labelled 'posh' for the simple reason that she pronounced the word 'bath' as if it had an 'r' in the middle. After being constantly mocked by her peers for her 'newscaster's voice', she stopped using certain words altogether by the time she was fourteen or fifteen, replacing 'bath' with 'shower' and 'grass' with 'lawn'. It had been a relief to arrive at university and discover that no one made fun of the way she spoke any more.

"My mum's a southerner," she said lightly, hoping that would be enough of an explanation.

Justin nodded. "That explains it then."

They had reached the station. Justin put Megan's suitcase down on the ground. "Will you be okay at the other end?"

"I've got a lift, thanks." Her mother would be expecting a call.

"I'll see you then." Justin was suddenly shy. "Now we've broken the ice," he began hesitantly, "perhaps we could go for a drink or something when we get back to Birmingham in January?"

She smiled at him. "I'd like that. Thanks, Justin. Have a good Christmas."

"You too." He hesitated again. "I'd best be off. I've got a bit of a journey to get back to Bolton.

It was on the tip of his tongue to ask her out, but he decided not to. Girls like Megan didn't go out with guys like him. He was glad he'd talked to her though: got to know the person behind the fantasy.

"See you in January, then." And with that, he was gone.

*

Megan was thoughtful on the thirty minutes' train ride back to Littleborough. The world, it seemed, was full of pleasant, unattached men, so why on earth did she keep falling for boys she couldn't have?

Perhaps Anita would be able to shed light on the matter? She was looking forward to seeing her best friend again after almost three months apart. They had kept in touch by letter, writing to each other every few weeks, but it wasn't the same. She had been hoping that Anita would visit her in Birmingham or invite her to stay with her in Hull, but so far they hadn't been able to find a weekend where both of them were free. (Although, to be honest, it was Anita who always seemed to be booked up weeks in advance.)

Should she tell Anita about Mike? She was aware that there wasn't really much to tell: *I met a boy in the bar, we snogged for a couple of nights, then he said he was breaking it off because he already had a girlfriend. But he gave me a book as a consolation prize.*

Put like that, it did sound rather pathetic.

Megan started concentrating on her journey, not wanting to miss her stop and end up in Clitheroe (wherever Clitheroe was). Smithy Bridge already: that meant she was only four minutes away. She grabbed her suitcase and yanked it over to the door.

As she stepped down onto the platform, Megan was struck by a wave of sentimentality. She liked living in Birmingham, but there was no place like home. She hadn't realised how much she had missed Littleborough until just now. The quaint northern village was embedded in her soul.

Dragging her suitcase out of the tiny station and towards the nearby phone kiosk, she surveyed her surroundings. The Pennines towered above her on every side, their bleak presence strangely comforting to someone who had grown up with them. To her left, the Parish Church was a familiar landmark: several of her friends had gone to the attached school; whilst ahead of her, Kelsall's Antiquarian Books and the Roundhouse Newsagent's both held happy memories: she had spent many a happy hour browsing in the former and been friendly with the daughter of the latter.

Pushing her ten pence piece into the slot by the telephone, she lifted the receiver and dialled her mother's number. The call was answered on the third ring and Megan heard the familiar tone, not without trepidation.

It was settled. Her mother would be there within five minutes. Megan exited the phone box and looked for somewhere to sit. A chill breeze made her fasten her jacket; moths circled the streetlight overhead.

Perching on the low wall that separated the 'public gardens' (five flower beds) from the road, Megan waited. Twilight had started to filter through before four o'clock and by now the sky was almost the colour of midnight. She was glad that Justin had bumped into her when he did and that she hadn't been forced to cross Manchester alone in the dark.

Approaching headlights announced her mother's arrival. Megan picked up her suitcase and prepared for a difficult four weeks.

Chapter Seventeen

Mrs Jackson seemed somewhat on edge as her daughter hauled her suitcase into the boot and then climbed into the front passenger seat. "How was your journey?" she asked, a little stiffly.

"Fine, thanks." Megan was wondering why her mother had switched off the engine.

An uncomfortable aura filled the car. Her mother spoke again.

"Before we go home, there's something I need to tell you. There's a visitor waiting to see you. I told him to come with me to meet you, but he declined. He said you should see me on your own first, to … to explain things."

He? Megan's mind was awhirl. Did her mother have a boyfriend? She sat up straight in shock.

"As you know, I don't really talk about your father …" Megan pondered where this conversation was going. "But you're old enough now to know the truth," her mother continued, her voice shaking a little.

"All I know is that he died suddenly." Megan felt suddenly wary. "What did he die of? Did he have some incurable disease, something he passed onto me?"

"Oh, don't be ridiculous, Megan!" Mrs Jackson snapped at her. "Your father …" She paused. "Your father was an alcoholic," she continued at length. "I didn't realise that when we met each other, or even when we got married. I knew he drank from time to time, but I did too: a glass of wine at a party; a night out at the pub with friends. By the time I noticed he had a problem, it was too late: you were on the way and I couldn't have managed on my own."

"So what happened?" Megan felt numb. She'd always idolised her unknown father, had imagined a kind and clever man who would have read her bedtime stories and taken her to the park at weekends. He would have been easy to talk to, unlike her outwardly cold and distant mother.

For a moment, her mother was silent. She appeared to be searching for the right words. Finally, "It got to the point where he wasn't safe anymore," she said slowly. She seemed relieved to be telling the truth at last.

"What do you mean, 'not safe'?"

"Several times," Mrs Jackson began, trying to make eye contact with her daughter, "your father was so drunk that he passed out in the living room, with a lit cigarette in his hand. On one of those occasions, he set fire to the sofa ..."

She paused. Megan's thoughts flew to the battered sofa in their living room. Her mother had always kept it covered with a blanket: was that the reason why?

"Another time," her mother continued, "he set fire to himself. Luckily, I walked into the room just as his trousers had become alight and I was able to beat out the flames. I took him to the local hospital and they treated his burns, which were very mild. If I hadn't been there ..." She shuddered.

Megan felt sick.

"So, is that how he died, then?" she asked her mother now. "Did he set fire to himself again, or walk in front of a car or something?"

It made sense now why her mother was so violently opposed to alcohol.

"I tried to get help." Mrs Jackson was speaking quickly. "He was a danger to himself and to us. Several times, he went out to the pub and forgot his key. He was so drunk when he came home that he broke the door down because he couldn't open it."

"Why didn't you let him in?" Megan cried.

"I was frightened," her mother said with dignity. "You were only a few months old, and he was out on the street, shouting through the letterbox and causing a scene. I thought if I pretended I wasn't in, he might go away again and come back when he'd sobered up."

"But he didn't, did he?" Megan felt indignant on her absent parent's behalf. "What did you do when he broke the door down?" she challenged.

"I called the police." The simple statement sent a chill through Megan. "I called the police, but they wouldn't do anything because they said it was a 'domestic disagreement'. The only way they would intervene was if I divorced him."

"Is that what you did?" Megan whispered. "You divorced him and told me he was dead?"

"Not exactly." Mrs Jackson looked uncomfortable. "I told him I was going to divorce him, and I explained why, and he disappeared overnight. For a time, I was worried: I thought he might have done something stupid. Then, after a while, I began to relax. It was so much easier without John around. After five years, I could have gone to a solicitor and filed for a divorce on the grounds of desertion, but I never got round to it. Besides," she looked embarrassed now rather than uncomfortable, "we'd moved away to make a fresh start, somewhere where no one had known your father. It was easier to tell everyone I was a widow. It meant that no one would ask awkward questions, including you. If I'd told you your father was still alive, you might have wanted to see him, and I didn't know where he was or whether he'd be in any fit state to see you anyway."

"So you just ran away?" Megan's voice was harsh with disgust. How dare her mother lie to her for all these years! How dare she!

"I did what I thought was right at the time." Mrs Jackson sounded weary. "I can't expect you to understand. You're still only a child yourself."

"I'm nineteen next week!" Megan blazed back at her. "And you've let me grow up believing my dad was dead! How could you?"

She stopped suddenly, a suspicion forming in her mind. "He wants to see me, doesn't he? Is that why you're suddenly telling me the truth after so many years?"

Her mother said nothing. Megan's misgivings were instantly confirmed.

"Is *that* the visitor you mentioned when I got in the car?" she demanded, her voice shaking with emotion.

Her mother nodded.

Megan opened the car door.

"Where are you going?" Her mother sounded frightened.

"I can't do this," Megan said simply. "Not when you've just sprung it on me like this. My dad was dead and now he's not: I've got to get used to the idea before I can meet him."

At that moment, she would have been glad of Anita's company – or Jen's or Sue's – even Matt's. Instead, she had to face this dilemma alone. She would meet her father, but not today: she would get to know him on her own terms, at a time *she* chose, in a venue *she* decided.

"Megan!" Her mother's plea was almost a wail.

"I'll see you later." Megan slammed the car door shut. She needed a walk to clear her head and Anita's house was only fifteen minutes away. Grimly she set off, ignoring her mother's cries floating after her. She would never forgive her mum for this: never!

A tear rolled down her cheek as she crossed the road and carried on walking.

*

By the time she reached Anita's, Megan had had ample time to reflect on her mother's shocking revelation. Her father wasn't dead! She wasn't sure whether to feel elated that he was alive, or angry that he had let her reach the age of almost nineteen before trying to contact her.

Would it have made a difference had she known he was out there somewhere? she asked herself now, still trying to process her mother's words. Would she, for example, have spent every birthday waiting for a card or telephone call that didn't materialise? Would she have spent the whole of her conscious life wondering where he was, what he was doing, and why he didn't want to see her?

As she rang Anita's doorbell, she wondered, briefly, why her mother had decided to confess everything now. Surely she must have realised that Megan would be furious at having had a secret kept from her for so long?

Anita's mother opened the door, her familiar, comforting face a panacea for all Megan's woes.

"Megan!" Mrs Clarke seemed genuinely delighted to see her daughter's friend. "How are you, Petal? How's university life been treating you?"

She enfolded Megan in a warm, motherly hug, so different to Mrs Jackson's stiff, formal embraces. Megan relaxed into the reassuring arms, her face pressed against Mrs Clarke's ample bosom, and debated whether to confide in her friend's mother.

No, she would talk to Anita first (she would no doubt pass the gossip on to her mother anyway) and try to gain a little perspective from someone her own age.

Wriggling free with some reluctance, Megan squared her jaw and looked Mrs Clarke in the face. "Is Anita in? I really need to see her."

Mrs Clarke's face fell. "She's not back until tomorrow, Love. She's got a party or something tonight - didn't she tell you?"

Anita *had* mentioned a party in her Hall of Residence, but Megan hadn't realised it was tonight.

"We're driving to Hull to collect her once Tony finishes work at lunchtime," Mrs Clarke continued. "You can come with us if you like – we're taking Claire –" (this was Anita's younger sister) "- but there's still room for a little one."

Megan ached at the woman's kindness, knowing she couldn't accept the offer. She couldn't discuss such personal family details in the back of a car with three other people eavesdropping! No, she would have to wait until Anita was home and they could go out for a walk and have some privacy.

"It's very kind of you, Mrs Clarke," she said hesitantly, "but I'm already doing something tomorrow afternoon. Perhaps I could come over and see Anita in the evening though? There's something I need to talk to her about."

"You know you're welcome here any time, Megan, Love." Mrs Clarke hugged her again and Megan felt like crying. Anita and her family were all so demonstrative! It was no wonder she'd spent so many weekends here on sleepovers before going to university: the Clarke household was a positive joyfest compared to the sterile atmosphere of Megan's own home.

*

Trudging slowly back to her mother's house, Megan contemplated her immediate course of action. She knew she would have to meet her father at some stage – in fact, she was quite looking forward to it – but she needed time to get used to the idea. She would ask her mother if they could get her birthday and Christmas out of the way first.

As she neared her home, Megan drew in her breath sharply. There was a strange car on the drive. She knew instinctively whose it was.

Her mother opened the front door, her face lined with worry. "Thank goodness you've come home! I didn't know where you were!"

Behind her, a grey-haired man hovered expectantly. Megan's gaze took in twinkling eyes, much bluer than her own, a casual shirt and trousers, and a slight paunch. Her father looked totally inoffensive; nevertheless, she didn't trust him – not yet.

"Megan ..." Her mother sounded nervous. "Come in and meet your father."

"He's not my dad!" Pushing past her parents rudely, Megan stopped and looked at them both. "He may be my biological father, but he doesn't know anything about me!"

Rushing up the stairs, she slammed her bedroom door shut, threw herself on the bed and began to cry.

*

Some time later, a cautious tapping on the door alerted her that someone was there. Megan sat up slowly, her tears abated for the time being. What was that Alison Moyet song Matt liked? *'All Cried Out'*: that was how she felt right now.

The door opened slowly and her mother entered.

"Is he gone?" Megan asked abruptly.

Her mother nodded. "You were very rude ..." she began, but Megan cut her short.

"*I* was rude? What about you? You lied to me for nearly nineteen years and then you suddenly produce a father, like a magician pulling a rabbit out of a hat, and expect me to talk to him! Don't you think I need time to get my head around all this?"

Mrs Jackson sat down on the bed and tried to put an arm around her daughter but Megan shrugged it away.

"Why didn't you tell me sooner?" Megan demanded.

Her mother looked embarrassed. "For years I didn't know where he was. I could have hired someone to track him down, but it was easier to leave things as they were. I didn't know how much he was drinking and whether he'd be in any fit state to see you."

"So you decided to live in denial for nineteen years instead," Megan said scornfully. "Are you sure you weren't an ostrich in a previous life, Mother?"

Mrs Jackson winced. "I was trying to protect you," she said evenly. "When you started secondary school, John wrote to me and said he'd like to know how you were getting on, so I sent photos - one every three or four months - and copies of your school reports."

Megan gazed at her mother in disbelief. "You mean he was in contact with you from the time I was eleven or twelve? Why didn't you say something then?"

"I didn't want to let him back into our lives until I knew he'd stopped drinking." Her mother's cheeks had become abnormally pink. "He said he'd joined Alcoholics Anonymous, but I wanted to make sure. When he'd gone a year without a drink, I arranged to meet him for a coffee. I think you were about fourteen at the time. The meeting was a success, so we agreed to meet once a term – not just to talk about you: I wanted to know if there was anything still there between us." A tear formed in her eye. "You have no idea how lonely it's been living as a single parent all these years."

"So you were dating him? Behind my back?" Megan couldn't believe what she was hearing. "You chucked him out and then you decided to take him back again? Don't you think you should have said something to me then?"

"You had O levels to think about," her mother replied. "I didn't want to upset you when you were doing your exams. And anyway, it was … a little more complicated than that. Your father was involved with someone else when we started meeting up."

This was getting worse and worse. Megan began to feel as if her life had suddenly become an episode of East Enders.

"So why did you keep on seeing him if you knew he already had a girlfriend?" she asked at last, then gasped as she was struck by *déjà vu*. What was it she had said to Matt when she had told him about Mike? *'I knew he had a girlfriend, but I still went back to see him again.'*

"Because he was my husband," Mrs Jackson said simply, "and even though he was living with another woman, he was still mine. I just needed to remind him why he fell in love with me in the first place and help him to see that he was better off with *me* – with us."

At that moment, Megan saw with sudden clarity why her mother had refused to divorce her father: she had never stopped loving him, despite the alcohol addiction, despite the other women (she was sure there had been more than one), despite everything. Who would have imagined that her mother was capable of such passion and loyalty? Megan was beginning to realise that she didn't know this woman at all.

"How long did it take for him to fall in love with you again?" she requested, still trying to come to terms with this new, unexpected side to her mother.

Mrs Jackson smiled. "He ended it with Helen in March and moved out into a flat of his own." She coloured slightly. "I don't know if you remember that I suddenly started going out 'to the theatre' every week? Well, I was actually visiting your father."

Her mother had been acting like a teenager, sneaking off behind Megan's back to go and have sex with her boyfriend! Megan didn't know whether to feel shocked or impressed.

"You could have at least told me then, though," she argued.

"Not with your A levels only a few weeks away," her mother countered. "And then you were working over the summer and off to university. I wanted you to have a chance to settle in properly before I broke the news." She paused. "I'm not moving him back in here straightaway if that's what you're bothered about. We've been coping for the best part of a year without being under the same roof. But I would like you to try to get to know him and so he'll be popping round every other day – to see you, not me."

"What if we don't get on?" Megan struggled to keep her voice from wobbling.

Her mother stroked her hair. It reminded Megan of how, when she was little, her mother used to lie down next to her and stroke her hair to send her off to sleep. "You'll get on," she said reassuringly. "You're a lot more like him than me."

She carried on stroking Megan's hair until the girl fell asleep.

Chapter Eighteen

Megan woke the next morning feeling momentarily disorientated. Nothing in her room was where it should be, and what had happened to her colourful throws?

She gazed blearily at her alarm clock then stiffened in horror. Half nine! She had missed breakfast. Why had none of the others come to wake her?

Then, as she began to wake up fully, she remembered that she was back at home for the Christmas holidays – although the mother she had left behind in September was not the woman she had been talking to the previous evening. "We're not in Kansas anymore, Toto," she whispered to herself.

Replaying her mother's revelations in her mind, she thought briefly of the father she'd never known and wondered how they would get along. More importantly, what should she call him? 'Dad' seemed too intimate for a stranger who had seen her school reports and her photographs but never spent time with her. Would she be allowed to call him John?

"Megan?" Her mother's voice intruded on her reverie. "Are you awake? Your dad said he might come over later this morning."

She supposed she should get it over and done with as soon as possible. Maybe she would feel better once she had taken a shower and washed her hair?

*

By the time her father turned up on the doorstep, clutching a bunch of flowers Megan presumed were for her mother but were actually for her, she had run the entire gamut of emotions from 'A for anxiety' to 'Y for You must be joking' – and yet she still had no idea how she was supposed to feel when presented with this virtual stranger.

Mrs Jackson made them both a cup of tea then withdrew tactfully to the sanctuary of the kitchen and the washing up. Megan thought wistfully of the dirty dishes and wished that she too was scrubbing saucepans instead of making forced conversation with a man she didn't know.

"So, Megan," John was trying to be jovial, "how's university life treating you? Your mum says you're studying English and French."

Megan nodded dumbly, suddenly shy.

John tried again. "Look, I know this must be awkward for you – it's awkward for me too – but this is important to your mum. She knows she should have told you about me before, but we can't turn the clock back so why don't we try to get to know each other a little?"

"Are you still an alcoholic?" Megan burst out.

Her father looked uncomfortable. "Yes, but I haven't had a drink for over five years. Does that make you feel any better?"

"I've been drinking at university." Megan felt a sudden need to confide in this man. She was sure he wouldn't judge her, not when he had demons of his own.

"Go on." He was watching her narrowly.

"There's a bar in my Hall of Residence," Megan explained. "Well, it's not really a bar – more a corridor – but people go there every night. My friends do too, so I go with them. I started off just drinking orange juice, then Jen – she's one of my friends – got me to try a drink she had called a Coral, and I found I liked it." She raised worried eyes to his. "Am I more likely to become an alcoholic myself if it runs in the family?"

"What?" John was puzzled. He had been expecting to talk about music or films or whatever else Megan was into, not be treated like some counsellor at an AA meeting.

"Am I going to become an alcoholic like you?" Megan repeated.

"How much do you drink?" John asked cautiously. He wasn't sure what a Coral was, but it didn't sound particularly threatening.

Megan looked thoughtful. "Jen says it's similar to a Babycham – that was what she wanted the first time she had one, only the barman didn't have any Babycham in stock so he gave her a Coral instead. I normally drink one or two – I get a bit giggly if I have more than that. I don't drink them every night, though: sometimes I stick to orange juice."

John heaved a sigh of relief. "You don't sound like you've got a drink problem."

"Mum doesn't know," Megan said in a small voice. She sounded guilty. "She's always made such a huge thing about the evils of alcohol, I didn't dare tell her I'd tried it for myself."

He felt a sudden rush of affection for his daughter. He could imagine how it must have felt for Megan to be away from home for the first time and how thrilling it must have been to rebel against her strict upbringing by drinking alcohol behind her mother's back.

"Any other secrets you want to share with me?" he asked casually.

Megan shook her head. Mike was something too painful, too personal to talk about. Perhaps she would tell Anita later.

*

After a while, Mrs Jackson rejoined her daughter and husband. They *seemed* to be getting on all right. John was reminiscing about their courtship, a dreamy expression in his eyes as he recounted their first date for Megan's benefit.

"So there she was, standing on the platform," he was saying as Julia re-entered the room, "and I thought she looked stunning. Then I realised that she was getting on the same train as me, so I pushed past a few people and sat down in the empty seat next to hers, and that's how it all started."

He turned to Julia. "Do you remember? I said I thought I recognised you from somewhere, and then you said you sat in front of me every week, in our Friday lecture ..." He broke off, turning to Megan. "We met at teacher training college, you know. I was training to teach Maths and your mum was going to teach English ..."

Megan tried to imagine her mum as a teacher and couldn't. She wondered what had happened to make her mother choose a different career.

"And then we got together and things moved a lot more quickly than we expected them to," Julia finished, her face softening. "So we got married and I dropped out of my course and had you, Megan."

"*When* did you get married." Megan was suspicious. Had she been the cause of her parents' hasty wedding after all?

"It was the Easter holidays," John supplied. "March 1966. We were both in the second year at the time." He paused. "I'd only known your mother for a month when I asked her to marry me – crazy, isn't it? She was going to finish her course before we thought about children, but you surprised us both ..." He grinned at her, his blue eyes full of mischief.

"And I was mortified in case anyone thought it was a shotgun wedding," Mrs Jackson finished. "That was the end of studying for me. I had to wait until you were at school and then sign up with the Open University so I could get my degree."

She hadn't been much older than Megan was now, and the world had been a different place. Sometimes she wondered how different life might have been had she turned John down when he asked her out.

She smiled as she replayed the memory: John's surprise and embarrassment when she told him they had lectures together, then the way he'd rescued the situation by inviting her out for dinner the following evening by way of apology. They'd both been so poor back then ... All he could afford was a greasy spoon sort of place near the college. The food had been terrible, but it hadn't mattered: they were both too busy devouring each other with their eyes. He had walked her back to her hostel afterwards and kissed her chastely on the cheek before leaving. That was when she knew she wanted to marry him.

They could have got engaged straight away and married after they'd both qualified as teachers, but they couldn't wait – or, rather, she couldn't. She'd been engaged before, to a boy back home in Berkshire, who rode a motorbike and earned her parents' disapproval. Ian had proposed just before she left for London: he didn't produce a ring but he'd put a daisy chain bracelet on her wrist and a crown of them in her hair, calling her his fairy princess and promising to wait for her. Now that she knew he loved her, she gave in to his demands, lying with him under the stars when her mother thought she was tucked up safely in her own bed at home. At the time, he was tender, romantic, and she thought she had never been so happy; but only weeks after starting her course, she received a letter breaking it all off. He'd never loved her at all: had only proposed to get what he wanted.

Older and wiser by the time she met John, she determined not to make the same mistake again. This time she would make him wait until they got married. To be honest, they couldn't have got up to anything even if they'd wanted to, not with him in digs and her in a hostel, surrounded by twenty-nine other girls.

Once they were married, she moved into his room with him: the landlady didn't mind as long as there was a ring on her finger. It was a respectable establishment, she'd said, and she intended to keep it that way.

It was odd how the so-called 'permissive Sixties' had been so prim and proper compared to today. She wondered briefly whether Megan was behaving herself at university. Perhaps John could find out: Megan might find it less embarrassing talking to him.

She came back to the present with a start. Megan and John were both looking at her expectantly. "I'm sorry," she apologised, "I was miles away."

"John was just asking …" Megan began. She paused, feeling confused. John was her dad, but that word didn't feel right on her tongue yet. It would take time to adjust to having a father. "He was just asking what we're doing for my birthday next Tuesday. I said I didn't know whether you'd planned anything or not."

"I …" Mrs Jackson seemed at a loss for words. "What would *you* like to do?" she asked, stalling for time.

Megan hadn't really thought about her birthday. It was so close to Christmas that it always ended up being a bit of an anti-climax. She would see Anita at some point, she supposed, but apart from that she had planned nothing herself.

"Why don't we go out for dinner?" she suggested, surprising herself. It might be a good way to get to know her father a little better. Despite this morning's meeting, he still felt like a stranger. Her conversation with him had been fairly superficial until her mother walked in and the two of them had started reminiscing about the old days, but listening to her parents talking about their own college life had been fun. Megan had found herself warming to both of them as they talked about their courtship. They had obviously once been very much in love.

"You'll struggle to find anywhere that's not fully booked this close to Christmas," warned Julia.

"Leave it to me." John smiled encouragingly at Megan. "I'll sort something out. A friend of mine runs a restaurant near here, the Bella Vista. Do you know it?"

It was an Italian restaurant about two miles away. Megan had been driven past it every day on the bus that took her and Anita to the school where they went to sixth form, and one of the girls in her A level French class had worked there as a waitress.

"The Bella Vista's fine, thanks," she said gratefully. Mrs Jackson looked relieved.

John got to his feet awkwardly. "I'd better be off. I know it must be overwhelming meeting me for the first time, Megan. Is it okay if I pop round again tomorrow?"

He looked first to her and then to her mother for approval. Megan nodded. Twenty-four hours ago she hadn't known she had a father; now he was taking her out to dinner and telling her about his past. In all of the excitement, she had hardly thought at all about her disappointment over Mike.

Chapter Nineteen

"You're kidding me!" Anita looked at her friend in disbelief.

"It's true," Megan insisted. "My dad's alive and he came round to see me earlier today."

They were both in Anita's room, Anita sprawled upon her bed and Megan sitting cross legged on the floor, and the bombshell had been well and truly dropped.

"I can't believe it!" Anita repeated. Then, "You must have been furious with your mum for lying to you like that!"

Megan shrugged. She *had* been furious the night before – when she'd called round to see Anita only to find she wasn't there; but a good night's sleep, coupled with the visit from her father, had made her mellow somewhat. She still felt slightly uncomfortable with John: you couldn't switch on family closeness or instantly create nineteen years' worth of father/daughter intimacy; but at least things were moving in the right direction. She had a father and she was getting to know him. She said as much to Anita.

"Well, if you're sure …" Anita still sounded doubtful. "Maybe you and your mum should slow things down a bit, though: you know, start with a coffee and work your way up to dinner in a few weeks' time."

Megan pointed out that her mother had been having coffee with her father for a number of years now. (She thought it best not to mention what else they might have been getting up to.)

"Do you think they'll get back together again, then?" Anita wanted to know. Her eyes shone. "You could end up with a baby brother or sister! Imagine that!"

That was the last thing Megan wanted to imagine. Having only just discovered her father, she didn't like the idea of him diverting all his attention away from her to a baby.

Anita rattled on. "And you'd be the glamorous big sister, away at university, wafting in every so often with presents for your little sibling ..."

"Shut up!" Megan said uncomfortably. "I don't want to talk about it anymore, okay?" She chewed listlessly at a hangnail. "Why don't you tell me about life in Hull," she suggested eventually, knowing that Anita would talk for hours once she got going. She leaned back against Anita's bed and made herself comfortable.

*

Anita, it transpired, had been making the most of student life. She had partied hard all term and had several boyfriends, although none of it seemed serious. "Oh, for goodness' sake, Megan!" she'd snapped when Megan tentatively asked if the most recent boyfriend had been 'the One', "I'm eighteen, not twenty-eight! I'm just trying to have a bit of fun!"

With a pang, Megan thought of Mike. He'd only regarded *her* as fun. Perhaps Anita had the right attitude, not taking any of her relationships seriously. She might be able to tell Megan how to lighten up.

"So, what about you?" Anita regarded her friend quizzically. She knew that Megan and Dave were no longer an item – she'd had a lengthy missive from Megan, detailing the breakup soon after it had happened – but there had been no hint of a replacement for him. It was odd because Megan was an attractive girl; she must have hordes of men falling over themselves to go out with her.

Megan blushed. "Well, there was a guy called Dan ... He was really sexy and we got off with each other a few times, but it wasn't really going anywhere."

Anita whistled. "Megan Jackson! You little minx! Don't tell me you've finally done the deed!"

If Megan's cheeks had been pink before, they now positively flamed with embarrassment. "Of course I didn't! We kissed: that's all."

"Oh." Anita was visibly disappointed. She was also slightly confused. "Well, if he was so sexy, then why didn't you sleep with him?" she wanted to know.

"Because I wasn't in love with him," Megan explained patiently. "He was a gorgeous looking guy, but we didn't really have anything in common. His bookcase was full of beer. I liked kissing him, but it was just sexual attraction."

Anita was shaking her head. "So you fancied the pants off each other, but you wouldn't sleep with him because he didn't like books!" she uttered in disgust. "What am I going to do with you, Meg? You'll never get laid with an attitude like that!"

"Perhaps I don't want to get laid!" Megan flashed back. "From what I can see, sex is over-rated anyway."

"Only because you've never done it!" Anita told her. "Wait until you meet someone that you're *really* attracted to: you won't be able to keep your hands off each other."

Mike kissing her for the first time as she stood on the chair in his room. The electricity that had sparked between them. The way he'd made her feel.

"There *was* someone ..." she said reflectively.

His body pressed against hers, his lips on her own. 'When you're in my arms, I can't think about anything else,' he'd said.

"Well?" Anita was agog with excitement.

And suddenly it all spilled out: the overwhelming attraction on both sides; the girlfriend back home; the way Mike had ended it all.

"You should have slept with him while you had the chance," Anita said softly. "It's what *I* would have done."

It was on the tip of Megan's tongue to protest that she wasn't like that; but, deep down, a part of her wondered if Anita was right.

*

John didn't come round to see her the following day. Instead, he kept a tactful distance, giving Megan time to process her feelings.

It was hard to know how she should feel. Growing up without a father, without even any memories of him, meant that she had learnt how to live without him from an early age. She hadn't missed him because she couldn't remember a time when he'd been part of her life.

Now that she unexpectedly had him back again, it felt strange, artificial – as if she had suddenly started wearing contact lenses or a hearing aid. The world seemed out of focus somehow, like a poorly tuned TV channel. No doubt a little fine tuning would restore everything to its proper setting – maybe even enhance it; but all this would take time. She thought of her mother and wondered how long it had taken *her* to adjust.

The Bella Vista had been booked for the seventeenth, but for lunch, not dinner. There were no slots available in the evening, John explained. Megan didn't really mind, as long as they went out somewhere. It was very inconvenient having a birthday so close to Christmas and feeling as if her own celebrations were always being eclipsed by a much more important occasion.

"So, Megan," John began, his mouth full of garlic bread, "is there a boyfriend on the scene at the moment?"

Megan shook her head, aware that her ears were flaming.

"So you're not still seeing Dave?" Mrs Jackson sounded surprised. "I can't say I'm sorry," she added. "He never seemed right for you."

Since her mother had met Dave three times in total in the past fourteen months, Megan didn't really think it qualified her to comment.

"It was a mutual decision," she said carefully.

John grinned at his daughter. "Too young to settle down yet, eh? Don't make the same mistakes your mother and I did."

"John!" His estranged wife sounded indignant. She wasn't noted for her sense of humour.

Megan surveyed her parents carefully. Although it had been a shock to learn of her dad's existence only days ago, she was actually relieved that she wouldn't be spending the festive season with only her mother for company. She had spent too many Christmas holidays suffering in uncomfortable silence as she and her mother sat round the turkey, unable to carry on a conversation. At least when John was around there was someone else to talk to – and he certainly seemed to have a positive effect on Julia: she positively sparkled when he was around.

For a moment she envied them both. It must be wonderful to love someone who loved you back. She'd never had that – not even with Dave. She'd managed to convince herself that she was in love, while they were together; but after some months without him, she now recognised that what they had shared had been friendship with a soupçon of physical attraction, nothing more. She wondered vaguely if he were still with Paula; found she hadn't the slightest interest in him anymore.

As the waitress arrived to collect their finished starter plates, John remarked casually, "I've got something for you."

Ignoring Julia's protests, he handed Megan an envelope. Inside, along with a card that proclaimed 'To a special daughter on her birhday', was a cheque for £190.

Megan was momentarily stunned. Apart from her grant cheque (and most of that went on her Hall fees), she'd never had such a huge amount of money at once before: it was as much as she'd earned in the café over the entire summer.

"John!" Her mother looked scandalised at the amount of money she was being given. "It's far too much!"

"It's only ten pounds for every birthday she's had so far," John remonstrated mildly. "Every birthday I've missed," he added pointedly.

It seemed like untold riches to Megan. What would she do with such a fortune? She could buy a proper radio cassette player instead of relying on her Walkman; better still, she could afford some new clothes, meaning she could actually afford to replace her frumpy, outdated wardrobe, the way Sue had advised her to over the Freshers' weekend.

Her mother still looked unconvinced. "It's too much money for her to have all at once," she repeated.

Megan sighed. She knew things had been tough financially for her mum over the years – life as a single parent hadn't been easy and Mrs Jackson had scrimped and saved since Megan was tiny, making thrift an art form. But penury had taken its toll on Megan too: she still felt embarrassed when she remembered the shame of wearing clothes that weren't like everyone else's but had been on offer for a pound in the Bargain Bin at Woolworth's. It had felt like a dream come true to buy even the smallest accessories for herself at University: scarves and bangles were fripperies that didn't register on her mother's radar.

"Can't she save some of it and spend the rest?" her father suggested, winking at Megan.

At that point, she could have kissed him. She was beginning to realise that there were unanticipated benefits to having a father, not the least of these being that she now had someone else on her side against her mother.

Eventually Mrs Jackson conceded that Megan should pay £100 into her Post Office Savings account and keep the remaining £90 for a shopping spree. "At least that way you'll have a bit of money put by for emergencies," she told her daughter.

Megan tried not to feel guilty at these words. There had been £70 in her Post Office account when her mother had finally handed the book over on Megan's sixteenth birthday. The amount represented the five pounds her grandmother had sent her every year for her birthday, minus the two years when she couldn't afford it and sent a Jackie Annual instead. Anita's mum had a catalogue and Megan had ordered a rugby top for £4.99 so she wouldn't look out of place at a school disco. Her two pairs of stretch jeans (Rhino wasn't a well-known brand name but the jeans were a good fit, even on her skinny legs) had cost £9.99 each at RifRaf, the village's only clothes shop; and she'd spent a further £7.97 on a shopping trip to Rochdale with Anita, just before they started sixth form, when she'd splurged £7.97 on two satiny bras from Littlewoods and a blue eyeliner which she'd lost almost immediately before they even reached the bus stop to return home. If she factored in sundries such as the odd trip to the cinema, or one or two milkshakes in MacDonald's, it was easy to see how she had squandered over half her life savings in a few short years. She was dreading what would happen if her mother asked to see the Post Office book.

The rest of the meal passed relatively uneventfully. Remembering how much she'd enjoyed her lasagna at The American Food Factory, Megan ordered it again and followed it with a lemon mousse dessert. She and Mum never usually ate out together – her mother regarded it as an unnecessary extravagance – but having her father around lent the occasion an air of merriment that she could easily get used to.

She still didn't feel she knew John, of course: it was too soon to have formed anything deeper than a superficial impression of his character based on his clothes and conversation. She thought wistfully of Anita's family and how they had so many in-jokes and familiar puns. That kind of closeness took a lifetime to build: she couldn't artificially construct it in the space of a few meetings.

Her mother invited her father to join them for coffee back at the house, but he declined. Megan had a feeling he was trying to take things slowly, which was fine with her: she had reading to do.

Back home, the morning's post had finally arrived. Several envelopes addressed to her sat on the mat by the door. She picked them up, recognising Sue's surprisingly untidy scrawl, Jen's confident copperplate and a missive bearing small, neat handwriting that looked vaguely familiar. She opened the unknown card first, half expecting it to be from Sally. Matt had sent her a card from the Birmingham Art Gallery: a print of Millais' *'Death of Ophelia'*. She had seen it recently when she and Sue had visited the gallery and tea room together, a treat to make up for missing it with Dave. Had she mentioned it to Matt; or had he unknowingly chosen one of her all-time favourite paintings as a birthday card?

As she turned the envelope over, a sheet of writing paper fluttered to the floor. *"Dear Megan,"* Matt had written, *"I'm sorry you were upset last night –"* Had he penned this letter last week, then, after their lakeside vigil? – *"and I hope you are feeling happier this morning. I don't think you should see Mike again: he doesn't care about you; and love shouldn't be abused –"* Megan broke off in confusion. What did that last part mean? Was Matt talking about her and Mike, or himself and Megan? She put the letter aside for later.

She turned next to the envelope with Jen's writing on it. It felt slightly bulky and, when she opened it, she discovered why: Jen had sent her a tape, one she'd recorded herself. Megan hadn't heard of the artist before: perhaps Anita would know who Sadie was? She was scheduled to go round to Anita's house later on – it felt much more welcoming than her own home – so she would ask her friend what she thought.

Sue's card had a picture of two teddy bears on the front and was signed 'Sue and Ted'. Megan wasn't sure whether the second signature was deliberate or a misspelling. Sue's teddy bear had taken on a life of his own in the last few weeks of term: popping up in unexpected places, often with items that had gone missing earlier, and generally making his presence felt. He was rapidly becoming the mascot for their friendship group.

Anita had a gift for her when she arrived: a pretty butterfly brooch which Megan pinned to her jacket straight away.

"You look different." Anita was surveying her critically, trying to gauge what was unusual. Then, "Your hair! It suits you, tying it back with a scarf." Her gaze lingered on Megan a moment longer. "You're wearing bangles too – *and* flowery baseball boots! University's obviously having a positive effect on you!"

Megan blushed. She had always admired Anita's effortless ability to put an outfit together: to have her sounding appreciative of Megan's own attempts was high praise indeed.

"Actually, I was hoping you'd come shopping with me some time in the next few weeks," she confided. "My dad's given me some money" – how strange that sounded: *'my dad'* - "and I want to revamp my wardrobe."

"About time too!" Anita nodded enthusiastically. "There's no point shopping now though: wait for the January sales and you'll get lots more for your money."

As Anita busied herself, making them both a coffee, Megan took the tape out of her bag. "Do you know who this Sadie is?" she asked.

"You idiot! It's Sade (she pronounced it Shar-day), not Sadie!" Anita took the tape from Megan's outstretched hand. "It's not really my sort of thing, but I can see why you'd like it."

"I haven't listened to it yet," Megan told her.

Anita thrust the tape into the stereo system in the living room and turned up the volume. "See what you think."

As the singer's sultry tones filled the room, Megan closed her eyes and tried to make out the lyrics. The first song caught her attention straight away: "Is it a crime/That I still want you/And I want you to want me too ..." It summed up everything she had thought about Mike during those heady few days when he had deigned to spend time with her.

Had Jen done this deliberately? she wondered. Every song seemed loaded with significance. Titles like 'The Sweetest Taboo' and 'You're Not The Man' were just as meaningful as the first one had been, and their lyrics as equally poignant.

Anita was watching her closely. "You're miles away. What were you thinking about?"

Megan coloured. "It made me think about Mike," she said at last.

"Oh, for goodness' sake, Megan!" Anita was aware that her friend had a hopeless crush on a boy she'd snogged a couple of times, but did she have to be so pathetically gooey-eyed every time she thought about him? "You need a good night out," she said thoughtfully. "A group of people from sixth form are meeting up in the pub tonight and I think we should join them. No," as Megan began to look panic-stricken, "not to get drunk - you can stick to orange juice if you like – but it would be good for you to take your mind off Mike by kissing someone else."

Megan didn't like to point out that she hadn't liked anyone else in the sixth form enough to kiss them – unless you counted Dave, and he was very much ancient history now. Nor had any of the sixth form boys ever shown any interest in her (again, Dave excepted); but when she said as much to Anita, her friend hooted with derision.

"Don't be so obtuse! Of course people fancied you, but there wasn't much point them telling you when everyone knew you and Dave were an item."

Megan was sure Anita was wrong.

"No," Anita insisted, ""wasn't there a guy who used to try to sit next to you all the time in the sixth form common room, even after you and Dave got together, and ask you about the books you were reading? You know, the one with the boots and the cravat."

Megan tried to locate the memory. There *had* been a boy, now she came to think of it - but she'd thought he was just trying to wind Dave up by sitting next to her. She certainly hadn't done anything to encourage him. As for him talking to her about books, at the time she'd assumed the boy in question was a fellow bibliophile, so it was gratifying - and a little alarming – to think he had been interested in her.

"I didn't know he liked me," she said now, "and I didn't lead him on."

"You never do," Anita said matter-of-factly. "Men see you as a challenge because you *don't* flirt. They think you're mysterious whereas I know you're just apathetic!"

"Perhaps I shouldn't be going out with you tonight then," Megan said, a little huffily. Deep down she was rather hurt by what Anita had said. Besides, she was sure her mother wouldn't approve of her going out drinking: Megan still hadn't mentioned the Hall bar – or the fact that she'd discovered alcohol.

"Oh, just relax, Meg!" Anita told her, grabbing an apple from the fruit bowl on the table and biting into it. "Come on, it'll be fun! Besides," she added with a wink, "you can tell everyone it's your birthday and they'll all buy you drinks!"

Megan still hesitated. "My mum won't like the idea of me going out to the pub," she said at last.

"She doesn't need to know. Give her a call now and ask if you can stay for tea and a sleepover. My parents will be happier if they know I'm not going out on my own. Please."

It was obviously important to Anita, so Megan acquiesced, although, "I haven't got anything to wear," she said, looking worried.

Anita surveyed her friend thoughtfully. "Your jeans are okay," she said at last: "at least they're pretty tight, but I'd lose the rugby shirt if I were you. You can borrow one of my tops." She stared sadly at Megan's trainers: they had been the sensible option for Megan to wear whilst walking the mile between her own home and her friend's but they definitely wouldn't do for an evening out. "I wish your feet weren't so ridiculously small!" she said crossly. "What are you: a size two? I can't lend you anything of mine because I'm a six." She frowned, pondering what to do to make her friend more acceptable. "Got it!" she exclaimed at last. "Claire's a three and she's got some new stilettos. I'll see if she'll lend them to you."

Anita disappeared upstairs for a few minutes. While she was gone, Megan looked around the living room, counting the Christmas cards on display and admiring the tree. Anita's family always had a proper tree whereas her own mother brought the same tired artificial offering (a three foot affair made from silver tinsel) out of retirement every year and placed a few jaded baubles at random intervals along its twigs.

When Anita returned, she was clutching a pair of black suede stilettos that didn't look wildly huge. "Claire's out at the moment," she explained, "and what she doesn't know won't hurt her. Try them on."

It was really quite embarrassing to be wearing a twelve year old's shoes; nevertheless, Megan placed them on her feet and surveyed the result. They *looked* all right, despite being a size too big.

"I'll never manage to walk all the way to the pub in them, though," she grumbled.

"My dad can give us a lift." It seemed Anita had thought of everything.

Mum would have a fit if she could see me now! Megan thought as she sat in the back of Anita's dad's car later on. Mr Clarke had been persuaded to give them both a lift to the pub and collect them at the end of the evening, which was just as well since Megan could hardly walk in the black suede shoes she'd borrowed from Anita's little sister. The way she was tottering about, people would think she was drunk already. It was most embarrassing.

Since Anita was bigger busted than Megan, the top she'd lent her hung in despondent folds as if bemoaning the lack of curves to fill it. Megan wasn't sure it was an improvement on the rugby shirt she'd been wearing earlier. Anita had also persuaded Megan to release her hair from its customary ponytail and let it fall in loose waves down her back. "*Very* Stevie Nicks," she'd said approvingly. (Megan really would have to find out who this character was: it was the third time in recent months she'd been compared to her.)

Anita was dressed in her customary flamboyant style: a denim mini skirt teamed with a close fitting black top which accentuated her generous bosom, thick black tights and red Doc Marten boots. Her ears sported large silver hoop earrings and her eye makeup was dramatic. Megan felt positively underdressed by comparison.

The two girls entered the pub and Megan took a swift look at her surroundings. It wasn't wildly different to the Hall bar, apart from being a lot larger. Some people stood at the bar, chatting to each other whilst they sipped drinks, whilst others sat at tables festooned with beer mats. A jukebox stood in one corner of the room, blaring out songs of yesteryear. Megan wondered if she would hear 'Don't You Want Me?' Around them, the air was thick with smoke: it was too cold for most people to want to go outside. It wasn't the venue she would have chosen to spend an evening in, but it was passable.

She scanned the room quickly, looking for anyone she and Anita might know, catching sight of Dave as she did so. Megan's ex-boyfriend was propping up the bar, his hand wrapped around a bottle of beer. She looked at him and wondered what she'd ever seen in him.

Anita must have spotted Dave at the same time she did because she turned to Megan, her mouth forming a hasty apology. "I'm sorry, Meg. I had no idea …"

"It doesn't matter," Megan said quickly, and it really didn't. Dave was in the past now: she had already lost her heart to someone else.

It didn't stop him sauntering over to chat to her though. Megan watched Dave's self-confident swagger as he approached her and Anita and wondered what on earth they could find to talk about.

"How's it going?" He addressed the question to Anita's chest, his eyes travelling appreciatively over the expanse of leg he could see beneath her mini skirt.

"Fine, thanks," Anita said coldly. Then, turning towards Megan, "We're just going to the lav. Come on, Meg!"

Once inside the Ladies' cloakroom, Anita exploded with outrage. "Did you see that? He was eying me up! His best friend's ex!"

Megan wondered if she should feel insulted that her ex-boyfriend had been drooling over her best friend instead of her.

"I never liked him," Anita continued, shaking with rage.

"You never said!" Megan protested, surprised.

"No, well I didn't like to when you seemed so wrapped up in him, but that guy's just an ego on legs. Who does he think he is?" Noticing Megan's expression, Anita coloured. "I'm furious about the way he treated you too, obviously," she added. "He didn't even say hi to you."

Megan shrugged. Her last encounter with Dave, when he'd come to visit her in Birmingham, had left her in no doubt regarding his inadequacies as both a boyfriend and a human being. "I'm really not bothered by it," she said now.

Anita pulled a lipstick from her bag and stared at the mirror, reapplying a colour that didn't seem to need it, as far as Megan could tell. "Sorry, Meg, but your ex-boyfriend's a total slimeball. Anyway," she replaced the lipstick in her bag, "we don't need to talk to him: there are plenty of other people here. Let's see if we can get you fixed up with someone."

Megan followed her friend back into the main lounge area. It was on the tip of her tongue to tell Anita *not* to try to find her a boyfriend, but she knew from experience that Anita never listened to her. Maybe she could find some girls to talk to instead?

A group of ex-sixth formers had found a table and were swapping stories about college and university. Anita slid into the conversation seamlessly whilst Megan listened, interested to hear who was where, doing what.

After about ten minutes, a familiar face swam into view. "Joe!" Anita said with pleasure. To Megan's surprise, the other girl stood up and hugged her ex-boyfriend, keeping hold of him for just fractionally too long. "Come and sit with us and tell us what you're up to."

Joe grabbed a vacant chair from another table and eased himself in between Megan and Anita. "Good to see you, Megan," he said, turning to her briefly before returning all his attention to Anita. Megan watched the couple's body language with a mixture of fascination and horror as they caught up with each other's news. Yes, Joe had a girlfriend, Sam: she lived in Essex but might visit Littleborough over Easter – "If we're still together then. It feels quite serious at the moment, but things change."

Joe looked meaningfully at Anita when he said this. She, for her part, looked back for longer than was strictly necessary, holding the eye contact for so long that Megan felt nervous. Both seemed equally captivated by each other, Anita touching him lightly on the arm when she spoke to him; Joe letting his gaze slide over the entirety of Anita's body in a way that suggested he wasn't thinking about Sam at the moment.

"Meg, do you want to go and see if there's anything decent in the jukebox?" Anita was holding out a couple of fifty pences.

Megan acquiesced, glad of the excuse to remove herself from the pair of them. She was beginning to feel quite uncomfortable. She scanned the playlist rapidly. She chose The Smiths' *'Heaven Knows I'm Miserable Now'*, knowing how much Anita liked it, as well as Soft Cell's *'Tainted Love'*, another of Anita's favourites.

Turning to walk back to their table, she realised that Anita and Joe were locked in a passionate embrace, in a kiss that lasted for several minutes. They came up briefly for air, only to dive back into each other's mouths again. Megan didn't know where to look: it was all highly embarrassing.

At last Joe tore himself away for long enough to ask if anyone wanted a drink. Anita ordered a rum and coke and Megan an orange juice. As soon as Joe reached the bar, Megan hissed at Anita, "I thought you said it was a 'one-off' when you slept with Joe after breaking up with him."

"It was," Anita answered off-handedly. "And anything that happens tonight is a one-off too. Anyway," her gaze became hostile, "I don't see what business it is of yours."

She was right: it wasn't any of Megan's business what her friend decided to do; but it didn't stop her worrying on her friend's behalf.

"Didn't Joe mention something about having a girlfriend?" she asked hesitantly. "Someone he met at University?"

Anita regarded her coolly. "So?"

When Megan didn't reply, Anita sighed. "I'm not trying to break them up. I don't want him back, you know; but we still fancy each other and old habits are hard to break."

Megan was stunned to realise that her friend was on the verge of tears. She gave her an awkward hug then pulled away as Joe returned with their drinks.

A quarter of an hour later, the place was filling up with people of all shapes and sizes. The noise of assorted chatter was loud enough to make it hard for Megan to hear anyone's conversation.

"Megan!" No, she had definitely heard her name. She span round, searching for the person who wanted her. A good-looking youth stood before her, clutching a glass of something that could have been lager. "I thought it was you," he continued, smiling at her. "What have you been up to for the past six months?"

Megan desperately ransacked her brain, trying to place this unknown stranger. Then her mind cleared and she remembered: Tom Denton. He hadn't been in any of her A level classes but he'd hung around in her friendship group at the start of the sixth form, before they'd all paired off into couples.

"I've been away at University in Birmingham," she told him now. "Doing English and French."

Tom grinned. "You were always one of the brainy ones."

"What about you?" she asked, trying to remember exactly what it was that he'd studied for A level.

He shrugged. "I wanted to go to University and train to be a vet, but I didn't get the grades. I'm resitting my A level Maths and Chemistry at Rochdale College. I've reapplied and hopefully I'll be able to go to University next September.

Megan nodded politely but was having trouble hearing Tom properly over the background noise. He must have been thinking the same thing because a moment later he leaned towards her and asked, "Do you want to go outside?"

She followed him gratefully out of the smoky, noisy atmosphere and into the cool of the night. The fresh breeze was a welcome sensation on her overheated cheeks. (*Why* did she always start blushing when she was talking to a good-looking boy? she wondered.)

"So," Tom seemed oddly unsure of himself now that they were alone together, "what are your plans for the next few weeks, Megan?"

The question flummoxed her. Somehow she knew that Tom didn't want to hear about essays and reading lists.

"Oh, you know ..." She was deliberately vague. "I'll probably hang out with Anita: go shopping; other girly stuff ..."

"And what about the rest of your time?" He had put his drink down on a nearby table and was edging closer. He *was* good-looking, but she found she didn't feel the least bit attracted to him.

Megan panicked. "I'm sort of seeing someone at University," she blurted out. It wasn't *really* a lie: Mike's book could have been a goodbye present or an apology.

"That's a pity ..." He was still moving nearer. "...Because I was hoping to get to know you a bit better. You must have known how much I fancied you in the sixth form."

Tom had 'fancied' her? Megan felt dumbfounded. She had never tried to encourage him; was doing her best to put him off her now.

Tom's face, looming closer. She sidestepped neatly, making for the safety of the pub. "I'm really flattered, Tom, but ..." But what? *'But I'm in love with someone I know I can't have'*? *'But I don't want to go out with anyone who doesn't enjoy reading'*? She reached the door and slipped inside, wondering whether she had done the right thing turning him down.

Anita grabbed her as soon as she entered. "Where have you been? My dad'll be here in ten minutes."

Megan decided not to tell her about the non-event of her encounter with Tom. She was sure that Anita would tell her off for not kissing him.

*

She was thoughtful on the drive back to Anita's house. It seemed that most people had looser moral boundaries than she did herself. A number of their former classmates had ended up kissing and cuddling at the end of the evening, even the ones who were already spoken for.

She would have been grateful to return to her own bed instead of going back to her friend's house, but it was too late to change their plans now. Her mother had sounded suspiciously pleased when Megan had rung to ask if she could stay at Anita's: was she planning another romantic assignation with John? If so, Julia might not be going home herself tonight.

Anita was in a talkative mood as they got ready for bed. Joe had looked all right tonight, hadn't he? she asked Megan, not waiting for an answer. And had Megan noticed that Katie and Robin seemed to be an item?

Megan let her rattle on, wondering if she should mention Tom's attempted seduction. She decided against it: after all, nothing had happened. She closed her eyes and let the sound wash over her.

She must have drifted off whilst Anita was still gossiping because, when she opened her eyes again, it was morning.

*

Megan spent the next few days in the run-up to Christmas reading *'Paradise Lost'*. It seemed preferable to writing her essay on *'The Tenants'*. She also made a solo voyage into Rochdale to buy gifts for both her parents and something small for Anita.

A Christmas card arrived from Matt. She scanned it carefully for any signs of unrequited longing, but Matt had simply written, "Have a good break. See you in January." and added a single kiss after signing his name.

It must have been around ten o'clock on the Friday morning, three days after their night out, when Anita rang Megan, full of indignation.

"Why didn't you tell me you got off with Tom the other evening?"

"I didn't," Megan began, then stopped suddenly. *Had she kissed Tom on Tuesday evening? Was it possible that someone had spiked her drink, causing her to act out of character and remember nothing about it afterwards?* (And was it *really* out of character when she'd originally kissed both Dan and Mike under the influence of alcohol?)

"I don't *think* I got off with him," she said carefully.

At the other end of the phone, Anita snorted. "That's not what he told Joe. Besides, loads of people saw you going outside together. I wondered where you were and now I know!"

Megan's heart stood still. She was now utterly convinced that nothing had happened between her and Tom, so why had he lied about it?

"He's making it up," she said shortly. "We *did* go outside but nothing happened. He wanted to kiss me, but I wouldn't let him." She felt suddenly annoyed with her friend. "And I can't believe that you fell for a story like that. You ought to know me better."

"I suppose so," Anita sounded regretful. "Only, it seems odd that someone would make up something like that about *you* ..." She broke off instantly, as if realising how tactless this must sound.

"It's okay." Megan felt suddenly wearied by this conversation. "Look," she lied, desperate to return to the safety of *'Paradise Lost'*, "I'll have to go: my mum wants to use the phone."

She put the receiver down without even saying goodbye.

*

She continued to feel annoyed with Anita for the next few days. It wasn't just because Anita had accused Megan of secretly getting intimate with Tom. Her friend had always been far more confident with boys but, even so, Megan had thought of them as sharing similar values. Now though ... She couldn't forget that Anita had been kissing Joe, even though she knew he had a girlfriend.

And then she thought of Mike and Amanda and realised she didn't hold the moral high ground herself.

*

Christmas Eve. Since John would be spending Christmas Day with them, Julia was pulling out all the stops to impress him. Not only had she bought a proper tree this year – well, a new artificial one that looked more realistic than its predecessor - she had also made a trifle and was busy icing a shop bought fruitcake in an attempt to pass it off as a homemade Christmas cake.

Megan wondered if perhaps her mother was trying too hard. After all, John must like her if he'd ditched his previous girlfriend so he could be reunited with Julia. And then she thought how odd it felt to be a spectator for her parents' courtship. It was also somewhat unsettling: one didn't really like to think of one's parents having urges.

*

Megan awoke on Christmas morning, full of expectancy. Her mother had never gone in for stockings or pillow cases so there was nothing at the end of her bed for her to open. There *were* presents under the tree when she peeped into the living room a little later, *en route* to the kitchen to make a cup of tea. She was tempted to pick up one of the ones with her name on and feel it, to see if she could ascertain what was inside, but she managed to restrain herself. She had had plenty of practice doing that with Mike, she thought sadly.

Mr Jackson arrived just after ten o'clock, wearing a Santa hat and carrying gifts. He kissed first his wife and then his daughter. Everyone felt vaguely ill at ease.

"So," her father tried in what was obviously an attempt to be jovial, "what did Father Christmas bring you, Megan?"

"We haven't opened anything yet," Mrs Jackson said quietly. "We were waiting for you."

Megan didn't like to point out that they usually waited until after lunch for presents.

"Well, let's make a start!" John dived under the tree and started pulling out presents at random. "This one's for you, Megan, and this one here's got your mum's name on it ..."

Megan looked at her mother, checking that this was okay. Julia gave an almost imperceptible nod. Carefully removing the sellotape a piece at a time – she had never been one for tearing off the paper – Megan unwrapped a box of liquorice allsorts and a packet of American Tan tights. She sighed. Her mother's Auntie Violet had sent Megan the same gift every year since she was twelve (before then there had been socks instead of tights). Megan always wrote a dutiful note, thanking her great-auntie for her kindness – even though she hated liquorice and only ever wore black tights.

The next package she opened was slightly better. Her mother had given her a bottle of bubble bath – "To take back to University." Megan deemed it tactful not to mention that she only took showers in the Hall of Residence. However, she was delighted with her father's gift: a large bottle of Anaïs Anaïs perfume. She had never been able to afford anything like that herself, thinking it profligate to splash out £2.99 on one of the cheap perfume sprays from the bargain shop in the village. Now she would be able to waft confidently into the Hall bar, knowing she smelled of something more upmarket than 'Tweed' or 'Tramp' (the only aromas stocked in the local shop).

It was time for her parents to open the presents she had chosen for them. She had thought long and hard before purchasing a new pair of fluffy slippers and a small box of Milk Tray for her mother and some Bugs Bunny socks for her father. (He had mentioned a few days ago that the rabbit was his favourite cartoon character.) Julia appeared pleased with the slippers - her old ones were worn through, which was why Megan had decided to replace them. She knew from experience that her mother preferred 'useful' gifts.

Only one present remained under the tree. John gave Julia an enquiring glance. She nodded, taking the large, gift wrapped box and handing it to Megan. "This is a joint present from your father and me," she said, a little awkwardly.

Megan hadn't expected anything else on top of a ten pounds record token from her mother and the perfume from her dad. With trembling fingers she peeled back the sellotape, spinning out the moment, just in case the contents turned out to be a disappointment. When she finally revealed a radio cassette player, she was speechless. It was only a cheap one, probably worth forty five or fifty pounds, but it was entirely unexpected. It also meant that she could spend more of her money on clothes now that her in-room entertainment was catered for.

"Thank you so much!" Eyes shining, she hugged her father. Instinctively she knew that this was his idea.

"It's from your mum too." But they both knew her involvement was negligible.

Later on, as they sat round the table enjoying a 'proper' family Christmas dinner, Megan thought her heart would burst. Her dad had carved the turkey; her mum (who was actually incredibly good at traditional dinners, especially the gravy) had piled everyone's plate high with crispy roast potatoes, seven types of vegetables and succulent slices of meat; and there was a general air of contentment exuding from everyone.

Would she appreciate this as much if she had grown up with it? she wondered. She was aware that many of her friends found their parents' company challenging, but for her it was still a novelty. The conversation was less strained than it tended to be with just her mother and Mr Jackson was proving to be quite witty in his casual remarks. He even managed to make the cracker jokes seem funny.

It was a very relaxed and happy Megan who finally crawled into bed at eleven that night after sitting with both her parents to watch the Christmas Day film. Chocolates had been eaten; Christmas Specials had been watched; and, best of all, her mum and dad had snuggled up together on the sofa, looking for all the world like a couple in love. She was beginning to feel very positive about the future.

Chapter Twenty

Megan looked doubtfully at her friend. "It's not really me."

The two friends were in Top Shop, fighting their way through the hordes of excited females desperate to find a bargain in the January sales. Anita had grabbed a handful of outfits she thought Megan should try on, but some of them were obviously more the sort of thing Anita would wear herself.

"Well, what do you want then?" Anita asked, a little crossly.

Megan hesitated. She knew that the purple jumpsuit Anita was brandishing would look ridiculous on someone who was only five feet tall; ditto the wide legged stripy trousers. And she just didn't have the chest for the slinky red dress with its plunging neckline.

Just then her eye fell on something she *could* wear: a short, shocking pink skirt in stretchy material. If she teamed it with those thick footless tights in a matching shade, she would look perfectly respectable, and she could wear them with her floral baseball boots, which Anita had definitely approved of when she'd seen them.

There was a similar skirt in black underneath the pink one. Megan seized that too. She was already beginning to form an idea of what she wanted her new image to look like. She would buy a couple of large men's shirts from a charity shop and layer one on top of the other: maybe a black one, worn open but knotted at the waist, over a white one that was properly done up? If the shirts were long enough, she might not even need the mini skirt: the footless tights she had chosen were easily thick enough to pass for trousers.

"You do know that's a child's skirt?" Anita was reading the label on the black one. "It says 'Age 9-1'0. And the pink one's 'Age 12-13'."

Megan didn't care. She'd never been particularly interested in wearing something just because everyone else was wearing the same thing (just as well, since her mother hadn't believed in spending much on clothes); and, despite Anita's efforts, she wasn't going to spend her birthday money on clothes she knew wouldn't suit her. Besides, the practical part of her brain argued, these skirts were only £1.99 each, so who cared if they were supposed to be for children? They were the right size for Megan and that was all that mattered.

She did, however, let Anita give her some advice over which skirt to buy if she wanted to project a more sophisticated look. "You can't go wrong with a long, tight black skirt," Anita counselled. "If you ever need to dress up for an interview with your bank manager or look smart for anything at all, a black skirt's the way to go."

The one Megan liked best was figure hugging tight to a couple of inches below her knee but had a useful slit at the back to enable movement. She found a black cardigan embellished with a cable design in grey and white that came down to her hips: when worn, buttoned up, with the black skirt it was very stylish. Even Anita approved.

"Afflecks next," Anita announced. "If you want quirky, that's the best place to go."

Megan wasn't sure that she would find anything suitable in Afflecks Palace – not if those tight trousers covered in skulls and crossbones were anything to go by. Anita dragged her towards the stairs to the next floor. "Come on! I bet we find something you like."

The something turned out to be a man's trilby from the 1950s in a soft brown nap. Megan was instantly enchanted, trying the hat on and posing in front of the mirror.

"It's a pity it's not black," Anita commented, "but it's still very 'you' somehow."

They also found the oversized men's shirts Megan had been looking for, along with a long girl's shirt in a thin sunshine yellow cotton which fell almost to her knees but had huge slits up both sides. If she wore it with a belt, over the footless tights, it would be another decent outfit.

"We'd better find you a belt, then," Anita said practically. The wide black belt with the huge buckle cost more than both the mini skirts combined, but Megan didn't care. She had still spent less than half of the £90 she'd put aside for clothes out of her father's birthday money. Perhaps she could splash out on some makeup too? She would ask Anita's advice about eyeliner and mascara.

"Maybe you should save some of your money for when you go back to University," Anita suggested after a while in Boots. She had steered Megan towards an eyeshadow palette in browns that would bring out the blue in her eyes and some black mascara to complete the look. "Didn't you say there was a really good flea market in the Student Union?"

Megan pouted. She was having fun spending her father's money. Nevertheless, she knew Anita was right. She'd spotted some Indian style dresses and skirts at the last Guild flea market and had regretted not having the funds to buy one. If she was careful now, she would be able to shop again in a few weeks' time.

"There's one thing you haven't thought of though." Anita deftly steered Megan into Chelsea Girl and towards the lingerie section at the back. "You need some decent underwear, just in case you get lucky!"

Megan stared at her friend, stupefied. What did she mean?

"You need something sexy," Anita supplied helpfully. "Do you really want things to get interesting with a boy and then for him to be put off because you're wearing Minnie Mouse knickers?"

Megan hadn't been planning on anyone seeing her underwear, least of all a boy. She was still sufficiently hazy about the idea of sex to assume that it always happened with the light off, but Anita seemed to think that all girls paraded about in skimpy garments as a prelude to the act.

In the end, she compromised by buying some pretty black lacy knickers and a camisole. She still wasn't convinced anyone else would see it, but she would certainly feel sexier knowing she was clad in satin and lace. She would have to hide the garments from her mother though: Julia was sure to think that interesting underwear meant that Megan was indulging in a promiscuous lifestyle.

*

That evening, Megan sat down and wrote to her university friends. She had already received a missive from Sue, detailing Ged's visit to her parents' house. They had taken him out to a Toby Inn for a meal. "Immensely stuffed, we all squeezed back into one's carriage," she had written, "and proceeded to visit Granny. (I thought she would like to meet Ged before she becomes too senile to remember who he is.) Imagine the shock when we received a call from the police to say that our house had been burgled in our absence!"

Goodness! That sounded serious. Megan read on.

"Arriving home, we found the kitchen window had been broken and the burglars had eaten our crackers and drunk our Ribena," Sue continued, adding indignantly, "One was most put out to realise they hadn't taken any of my designer clothes!"

Megan smiled as she stuffed the letter back in its envelope. The damage had probably been caused by bored teenagers with nothing better to do, but it made entertaining reading. She found her writing paper and began to reply, detailing her shopping trip and the clothes she'd bought.

After a while she stopped, aware that her letter read like an inventory. Bother! She'd wanted to tell Sue about the clothes because it was partly due to her that she'd revamped her wardrobe, but the list she'd penned now seemed self-indulgent and shallow. She sighed and began again.

*

All too soon, it was the end of the holidays. Megan wondered where the time had gone. Even New Year's Eve seemed to have sneaked by without her noticing it. Four weeks had seemed like a huge amount of time back in mid-December; now it was Friday evening and she had only just finished the dreaded essay in time for the start of the new term. At least her copy of *'Paradise Lost'* was well-annotated. She was looking forward to studying that over the next few months.

Anita rang just as she was contemplating making a start on her packing. "Do you fancy a night out? It'll give you a chance to show off your new clothes."

"What were you thinking of doing?" Megan asked cautiously.

There was a pause, then, "Joe's brother's just bought a car," Anita said at last. "He's offered to take us all to a pub he knows about ten miles away."

"Who's 'us all'?" Megan didn't want to find herself forced to spend the evening with Tom.

"Just you, me, Joe and his brother." Anita sounded slightly guilty and Megan thought she knew why.

"Have you seen Joe again since the time we all went to the pub?" she challenged.

"Maybe." Anita was being evasive.

Megan didn't probe any further. She had a feeling she wouldn't like the answer if she did.

In the end, she let Anita talk her into going, aware that she had seen far less of her friend that she'd intended these holidays. She would much rather have had a girly night in with Anita and a video, but at least they were doing something together. She hoped that Joe wouldn't monopolise her friend too much.

Joe's brother turned out to be tall and rather dangerous looking. Megan felt her heart flutter with anticipation. Was *that* why Anita had invited her along? Her best friend had often teased her about her predilection for 'bad boys'.

They sped through the Lancashire countryside in Andy's new car. Anita had opted to sit in the back with Joe, leaving Megan the front passenger seat. From time to time she tried to catch a glimpse of the other two in the rear view mirror, to see if they were canoodling, at the same time answering questions Andy was firing at her about life in Birmingham.

It transpired that Joe's brother was studying Maths at Hatfield Polytechnic. When Megan looked puzzled, Andy explained that Hatfield was in Hertfordshire. "It's a dump," he said, grinning at her sideways whilst he kept his eye on the road, "but the beer's incredibly cheap, so I guess I made a good choice."

They finally arrived at the pub Andy had been aiming for and tumbled out of the car. Megan examined it critically: the car might be new to Andy, but it had certainly seen better days. She had been in such a rush to get in before her mother could ask too many questions that she hadn't paid it much attention earlier on: now she was aware of the tired looking paintwork, the multitudinous scratches and the rather alarming dent in one of the passenger doors.

"That wasn't me," Andy said hurriedly, noticing her consternation. "I got it cheaper because of that."

The car was an 'R' reg Datsun in a startling lime green. Megan thought that maybe the dent hadn't been the only reason the car had been cheap.

As they walked inside, she noticed that Joe and Anita had their fingers intertwined. They were still dallying with each other then. She hoped Anita wouldn't get hurt.

The pub was a tiny village affair, full of olde worlde charm. One wall was covered in horse brasses and a roaring log fire burned in an inglenook fireplace. A large golden Labrador snoozed in front of the fire. It really was most idyllic.

For a moment, Megan wondered why they had come to such an out of the way place, charming though it was. Then her eye caught sight of a crudely drawn poster tacked to the wall: "Grand Quiz Night January 10th. £50 prize for winning team."

"*That's* why you invited me!" she said reproachfully, turning to Anita.

Her friend had the grace to blush. "Sorry, Meg, but we needed someone who was good at literature questions. Joe's good at science, and his brother's good at sport and politics, but they're neither of them very arty. If we win, we split the prize four ways," she added generously.

Megan supposed she should be flattered that Anita had so much confidence in her; nevertheless, it would have been nice to have been asked. She felt as if she had been lured here under false pretences.

Andy disappeared to get a round of drinks whilst the other three set up at an empty table. Quiz Night must have been popular because the venue started filling up quickly. Megan noticed that they seemed to be the youngest competitors: everyone else appeared to have at least ten years on them.

Round One began with Current Affairs. Having spent three months in Hall without access to a newspaper or television, Megan felt totally clueless. It was just as well that the rest of her team were better informed than she was. Geography was the focus of Round Two. Andy proved surprisingly knowledgeable, explaining that his grasp of cities and counties had improved remarkably since becoming a student because he travelled all over the country supporting his favourite football team at away matches. "I spend far too much of my grant on travel," he laughed. "Just as well the Student Union's bars are so cheap or I'd never manage!"

The Science round followed next. Megan knew a few of the Biology questions but was totally stumped by anything relating to Physics or Chemistry. Luckily, Joe managed to answer all but two of the questions correctly, putting them in third place overall.

"It's all up to you now, Megan," Andy told her solemnly as Round Four, Art and Literature, began. Megan wished he hadn't said that: she hated feeling under pressure.

The first few questions were easy: name four novels by Jane Austen (she chose *'Pride and Prejudice', 'Sense and Sensibility', 'Persuasion'* and *'Mansfield Park'*), write down the artist who painted the 'Mona Lisa' (she would be surprised if anyone got that wrong), and identify four Shakespeare plays beginning with the letter 'M'. (Megan *picked 'Measure for Measure', '(The) Merchant of Venice', '(A) Midsummer Night's Dream'* and *'(The) Merry Wives of Windsor'*.) After that, though, it became a little trickier. Megan *thought* that Ernest Hemingway had written *'The Old Man and the Sea'* but wasn't entirely sure. And was the writer of *'Rip van Winkle'* called Washington Irving or Irving Washington?

At the end of the round, they were in second place. Only one more subject remained: Sport and Leisure. Megan hoped the others knew something about this category because she was clueless.

As the final scores were added up, Megan realised, to her surprise, that she'd had a good time. And she hadn't touched a drop of alcohol!

That was more than could be said for Anita and Joe, who had matched each other pint for pint, both taking an additional swig whenever their team got a question right. They were now sufficiently intoxicated to ignore everyone else in the room and indulge in a very public display, wrapping themselves around each other and kissing passionately. Megan was uncomfortably reminded of the group session in the pub on her birthday.

Andy caught her eye. "They'll regret it in the morning. At least, Joe will: he's going back to London on Sunday and his girlfriend will be waiting for him." He sounded non-judgemental.

Megan thought for a second of Mike and Amanda. Had he told his girlfriend of his indiscretions this last term; or would he be returning to Birmingham, ready to carry on as before with her none the wiser? Whatever the situation, Megan wouldn't be seeing him again. Watching Joe and Anita made her feel sad: it was all too close to her own situation with Mike. No matter what Anita thought herself, Megan didn't want to be someone's 'bit on the side': she wanted the full fairytale. Better to have no relationship than only half a relationship, she thought now, determining that the Megan who went back to Birmingham in two days' time would be a very different girl to the one in September.

Part Two: Spring Term

*Let me not to the marriage of true minds
Admit impediments.*
Shakespeare, Sonnet CXVI

Chapter Twenty-One

Megan had been intending to take the train back to University: she had the return ticket after all; but she soon realised that all her new clothes wouldn't fit in the single suitcase she'd brought home with her. John unexpectedly came to the rescue, producing an enormous case twice the size of Megan's and offering to drive her back to Birmingham.

Megan hesitated. On the one hand, she liked the idea of getting to know her father better; on the other, she wasn't sure she could stomach a two hours' drive with her mother. However, Julia had already made plans for the Sunday, it seemed, and so Megan accepted John's offer gratefully, relieved that this time she wouldn't be getting lost as she tried to navigate her way from Victoria to Piccadilly.

It was only as they left the M62 and merged onto the M6 that Megan understood why her mother had been so keen to send her off on her own with her father. As he pulled into the correct lane of the motorway, John cleared his throat nervously and asked Megan if she had formed any close relationships in her first term.

To begin with, Megan thought her father meant friends. It was only when she began to talk about Jen, Sue and Sally that he stopped her and corrected himself: "I meant boyfriends. Yes," he continued as she wondered how to reply, "I know you had a thing going with a boy at school, and there doesn't seem to be anyone on the scene right now, but your mother … I mean, she and I … that is, we …" He floundered hopelessly for a moment until Megan took pity on him.

"You mean, have I been sleeping with anyone at university," she said drily, amazed by how easily she could say words to her father that would never have escaped her lips had her mother been present. Before he could reply, she went on, "I suppose Mum asked you to find out? She was always suspicious about me and Dave, even though I told her we weren't getting up to anything."

"I'm not judging," John said hastily. "I remember what it was like being a student, that's all. And these days, people your age seem a lot more free and easy in their relationships."

Megan sighed. "I haven't had sex with anyone. I don't intend to either – not unless I know I'm in a solid relationship."

Mike's lips on hers, his breath warm in her ear. 'It might not mean anything in the long run, but it would be pretty special at the time.'

She tried again. "I did meet someone I like a lot, but he's got a girlfriend already, so it's never going to go anywhere."

"I see." John seemed embarrassed. "I just ... Well, your mother ... She just wanted to be sure you were being careful, that's all."

She hadn't been careful with her heart, but all that would change. No matter how many times she caught sight of Mike in the bar or on campus, she wouldn't run back to him.

"It's all right, Dad," she said gently, the word sounding alien on her lips. "I know all about safe sex, but it's not necessary, not at the moment."

At the time she said it, she meant every word.

*

Her father managed to find the Hall of Residence without any of the problems experienced by Mrs Jackson. He was suitably impressed with The Vale and with Ridge and declared Megan's room to be "small but cosy". It was a much more positive response than her mother's had been.

"Do you get fed tonight?" he asked her. It was now almost four.

Megan shook her head. "Only on weekdays. We get breakfast at the weekends, and ratburger and chips for lunch on Saturday ..." -John's eyebrows shot up at that one – "... but in the evening, we have to fend for ourselves."

"Why don't I take you out somewhere?" John suggested. "There must be a pub somewhere that serves decent food."

She hesitated. Tonight was the Hall disco – the fancy dress one that Phil had organised – but that wouldn't start until seven thirty (and no one would bother turning up until nine). She still needed to unpack, including taking all her books and throws out of the trunk she'd left in Hall over Christmas, but that shouldn't take long.

"Okay." She smiled at her father. "Why don't you sit down in my chair while I unpack and then we can go and find something to eat."

*

By the time Megan's father dropped her back in Hall after a very pleasant meal at The White Swan (christened The Dirty Duck by students who thought they were being funny), everyone else had arrived and was fully unpacked.

Jen tapped on Megan's door. "Have you got a costume for tonight? I brought my French maid's outfit back with me, only I made the mistake of washing it and it's shrunk. It should still fit you though."

Even on Megan the black dress was decidedly skimpy, leaving little to the imagination.

"Mmm." Jen sounded thoughtful. "Maybe not." If Megan dressed like that, she would give Matt a heart attack. Better leave it for Rocky Horror instead: at least everyone would be looking sexually provocative then.

"What are you going as instead?" Sue stood behind Jen, addressing her question to both of them.

Jen pulled a face. "Phil's talked me into dressing up as a Heavy Metal groupie. It's only because he wanted to be Ozzy Osbourne and he thought we should go as a couple. What about you?"

Sue blushed. "I didn't have time to make anything, so I'm wearing one of my bedsheets as a toga. Ged's keeping me company." Turning to Megan, she added severely, "I hope you're *not* wearing that excuse for a dress. It makes you look like a streetwalker!"

Megan's cheeks flamed. "Actually," she said with dignity, "I did remember I needed a costume." It was true; she had remembered, but not until yesterday. She'd rung Anita in a panic, desperate to know if her friend had any suggestions.

"That's easy," Anita had said without thinking. "Wear your black mini skirt with an old school shirt and your school tie and you can go as a St Trinian's."

It seemed rather raunchy in Megan's opinion, but she had no other options – unless you counted Jen's offered French maid's outfit and she was sure the skirt of that was even shorter than the one she had intended to wear.

"What's Sally wearing?" she asked Jen.

The dark-haired girl broke into a grin. "Sally's Elvis," she said matter-of-factly. "Her costume's pretty good too."

"What time are we hitting the disco?" Sue asked next. "Do we really need to be there for seven thirty just because Phil's in charge?"

"Maybe just this once," Jen told her, avoiding Sue's outraged look. "I told Phil that he and Matt could come and call for us so we can all arrive in costume together. I think he's worried that no one else will bother."

Since it was now a quarter to seven, everyone drifted back to her own room to get changed, leaving Megan in peace. She would plait her hair, she decided; that would make her costume more authentic. Deftly she parted her hair down the middle at the back and set to work. Five minutes later she had two identical plaits, tied with black ribbon. Her schoolgirl transformation had begun.

Megan was the last to arrive at Jen and Sally's room. She entered nervously, hoping that no one would laugh at her costume.

Phil was the first to speak. He had always thought Megan pretty, but tonight she was a disturbing mixture of sexuality and innocence. With her hair in plaits, she looked about twelve; but then his gaze travelled down the rest of her body, taking in the short skirt and the long legs clad in black tights – or were they stockings? He came to his senses, aware that Jen was looking daggers at him.

"You'll have every guy in High wanting to take you to bed," he said slowly. "Half of them will want to have their wicked way with you; and the other half will want to tuck you up with a mug of warm milk and a bedtime story!"

Jen glared at him. Megan felt highly embarrassed.

Matt, meanwhile, was feeling hot and bothered again. Seeing Megan in her uniform made him realise he was lucky to have gone to an all-boys school. He was aware that he wouldn't have got any work done if Megan had been sitting next to him in lessons dressed like that.

Sally read Matt's expression and felt angry with Megan. Why did that girl have to make everything about her? Sally had chosen her own costume carefully, knowing that Matt quite liked Elvis: he'd told her once that his favourite song was 'Always on my mind'. The problem was that Sally wasn't the person on Matt's mind: Megan was.

Sue was watching Ged closely. It was all very well for him to tell her he preferred a woman with curves but his eyes had almost popped out of his head when Megan entered the room. The worst of it was that Megan seemed totally oblivious to the effect she had on men. In Sue's opinion, that made her more dangerous than an outright flirt. How did you compete with someone who wasn't even aware she was a gold medallist at stealing hearts?

Megan gazed round the room, noticing that Matt was fittingly dressed as a Victorian gentleman, complete with top hat. She suddenly felt out of place in her home-made costume: she probably looked as if she hadn't made much effort at all.

Phil cleared his throat. "It's twenty past already," he said. "Let's go and show High and Ridge how this is done!"

By eight o'clock the hall was still almost completely empty. Megan felt sorry for Phil and Matt and the rest of the Events committee. It must be disheartening to see so few people wanting to attend a free disco. However, ten minutes later, people started arriving in ones and twos, so that by nine o'clock there was quite an assortment of people on the dance floor, a few of them in fancy dress. Megan counted a pirate, a Robin Hood and a rather thin looking Father Christmas as well as a couple of other people who had come in bedsheet togas like Sue and Ged. There were still more people up in the bar corridor than down here at the disco, but at least it was a start.

Matt was panicking slightly about his new role as Music Rep. He'd dutifully spent several days of the holiday in his local library, researching bands and solo artists and trying to develop a feel for modern music. He still felt more comfortable with Classical stuff, or with artists he knew; but he'd also talked to some old school friends who'd assured him that the secret to a successful disco was just to play catchy songs that everyone would want to dance to – or at least sing along to. He hadn't heard of half the names they mentioned, but he wrote them down, determined to impress Megan with his choice of song titles.

Whilst Jen and Phil, Sue and Ged, and Sally bopped along to David Bowie and Mick Jagger's *'Dancing in the Street'* and the *'Ghostbusters'* theme, Megan stood at the side of the dancefloor, feeling conspicuous. She never danced at discos – she didn't know how – but usually she could blend into the background: not so tonight in her school uniform with its tiny skirt. She had a constant stream of High Hallers approaching her, either to ask her to dance or to offer to buy her a drink. There were so many of them that, after a while, she couldn't remember any names or faces. She had been stared at so much that she was beginning to empathise with Billy Pilgrim and Montana Wildhack in the Tralfamadorian zoo.

Busy at his turntable, Matt looked up every now and then to keep an eye on Megan. He didn't like the way that so many men were looking at her as if she were a piece of meat they were about to devour. She looked so sweet and innocent – irresistably so with her hair like that. He tried not to dwell on the disturbing amount of leg that was visible beneath the little black skirt she was wearing, or the fact that her school shirt was semi-transparent under the disco lights.

The time was approaching ten o'clock. Phil dragged himself away from Jen and the dance floor and made his way over to Matt. "Happy New Year High and Ridge!" His voice echoed through the sound system. The crowd, by now well and truly oiled with alcohol, went wild. "Thanks for joining us at our first disco of 1986," Phil continued. More cheering. "We're going to end the evening by asking Jez Harrison to present the prize for the best fancy dress costume."

Jez, aka Jeremy and the President of the High JCR, bounded up. "Happy New Year!" he echoed. "This has been a great turn out tonight – let's keep it that way for the rest of term." There were a few 'Boo!'s from the assembled crowd. "So," Jez went on, ignoring the heckling, "the prize for the best costume goes to …" He paused dramatically. "…The sexy schoolgirl!"

Megan stood rooted to the spot as the men on the dance floor broke into cheers and wolf whistles. *Why* had she listened to Anita? she asked herself bitterly. She should have just made a toga out of one of her sheets like Sue and Ged and about five other people, and then she could have avoided a scene like this.

All eyes were on her as she stumbled towards Jez who handed her a bottle of something alcoholic and then kissed her unexpectedly on the mouth.

"Go on, Jez!" someone yelled excitedly.

Her cheeks burning, Megan staggered out of the limelight, towards the sanctuary of the door that would take her back to her room. In her hurry, she walked straight into a tall figure coming the other way. Glancing up to apologise, she found herself looking into the eyes of Mike.

*

The room stood still as they looked at each other.

"I read your book," Megan said at last.

"What did you think?" His eyes bored into her own.

"It was very sad." Poor Bendrix and Sarah, so much in love but kept apart for so long by jealousy and superstition.

"I need to see you." His voice was low, urgent.

She had given him up, just as Sarah made herself give up Bendrix; but, like Sarah, she felt her resolve weakening and knew she had to do this – even if it was only for one last time.

Without another word, she followed him out of the dance hall and into the foyer of High.

He didn't head towards the lift this time. Instead, he led her towards some stairs she hadn't noticed before, grabbing her hand and hurrying her down, down into some sort of basement area containing a couple of abandoned table tennis tables along with various chairs and a few low cabinets.

For a moment she wondered what they were doing down here.

"It's a good place to talk," Mike told her, reading her mind. "No one ever comes down here." He looked searchingly at her. "I'd take you to my room, but we'd only end up kissing on the bed."

Irrationally, she found she wanted to be in his arms, on his bed.

She was still clutching the bottle she'd won. Mike gently detached it from her fingers and set it down on one of the ping pong tables. Perching on top of one of the low cabinets, he gestured to her to sit. She sank down next to him, her mind trying to work him out.

"Amanda and I did a lot of talking over Christmas." No preamble: he rushed straight into what he needed to say.

Megan said nothing.

"I told her about you and the others." That wasn't strictly true: he'd confessed to sleeping with two other women and said there had been someone else but it hadn't got that far. He hadn't told Amanda about falling asleep with Megan in his arms or mentioned the sexual chemistry that had sizzled between them.

"What did she say?" Megan kept her voice dull and lifeless.

"She cheated too." He said it matter of factly, no point in telling Megan how surprised he'd been when it hurt, or how Amanda had cried when she admitted that she'd slept with another man – not as a one off, but on a regular basis over four or five weeks before coming back home.

"I'm so sorry," she'd whispered, her mascara making streaks down her face as she cried out her guilt. "I don't want us to split up. Not after everything else we've been through."

She'd been so contrite and so needy, he hadn't had the heart to tell her it was over. Besides, he had bigger things to worry about: his parents had just announced that they were getting divorced and he was in a state of shock about it. It had never been a happy marriage, but he'd thought they were joined for life after surviving almost twenty years together.

"Does that mean you've split up then?"

He came back to the present, realising that Megan was asking him about Amanda. He shook his head. "We worked it out."

They'd agreed to stay together for now – but if either or both of them cheated again, the relationship would be over. He had a feeling Amanda would cave first, which was fine by him. He was too preoccupied with his parents' disintegrating lives to feel like investing time in reviving what was dying with Amanda.

"Why are we here then?" Megan asked softly.

Mike paused. He needed to unburden his heart to someone – Amanda had been too fixated on the two of them to pay any attention when he'd hinted he had problems of his own – but that would mean making himself vulnerable. He liked Megan, but he wasn't sure he was ready to give so much of himself away.

"How was *your* break?" he asked her, ignoring the question. He wasn't expecting the answer that followed.

"My dad died when I was a baby," Megan began.

Instinctively, Mike put his arm around her.

"At least, my mum told me he died." She looked up at him. "She let me grow up thinking he was dead – and then, at the start of the holidays, she suddenly told me he wasn't dead at all. She left him because he was an alcoholic."

She was angry. Mike could feel the tension in her neck and shoulders as he continued to hold her.

"And she didn't mention any of this before?" he asked in disbelief.

Megan shook her head.

"She picked me up from the station when I went home," she said in a small voice, "and told me there was a visitor waiting to see me. That was when she dropped the bombshell that my dad was alive." She swallowed. "My mum had been meeting up with him for years, letting him know how I was, doing it all behind my back. She should have told me earlier on, when she started seeing him. She should have given me the chance to get to know him then."

And her dad should have wanted to see her, she conceded unwillingly. He should have put his foot down with her mother and insisted that he was allowed to see Megan. She felt betrayed by both of them despite the effort they'd all made over Christmas. She could see now that every encounter with John, including the drive to Birmingham today, had just been papering over the cracks: it would take a lot to repair her crumbling relationship with her mother or build a solid foundation with her father. A lot.

"My mum and dad are splitting up." The words came out abruptly. She could hear his pain.

"Was it unexpected?" she asked hesitantly. "Or had they been arguing for a while?"

Mike delved into his pocket for his cigarettes. He'd given up for New Year – before his parents had broken the news - and he'd felt sufficiently stressed to start again. He lit one now, looking away from her.

"They've always had a lousy relationship," he said shortly. "My mum got pregnant when she was seventeen and my grandparents made them get married. My dad was only a couple of years older." He laughed bitterly. "If I'd been conceived a year or two later, I wouldn't be here now." Seeing the incomprehension in her face, he added, "The 1967 Abortion Act."

"No!" Megan was shocked.

"As it was," Mike continued, his voice tight, "she tried to get rid of me by sitting in a hot bath and drinking gin. When that didn't work, she had to tell her parents and they rushed her and my dad into a registry office straightaway. They didn't want me being a bastard."

He took a soothing drag on his cigarette and continued.

"I should be grateful she didn't try anything worse. In Victorian times, backstreet abortionists used knitting needles. Most of the women died."

Megan listened, horrified.

"She smoked throughout the entire pregnancy: that's probably one of the reasons why I find it so hard to give up. The nicotine must have entered my bloodstream when I was in the womb. At least it wasn't heroin."

He sounded so raw that Megan's heart broke. No one should grow up feeling so unwanted. No one.

"My dad was at naval training college when they met. He wanted to be a sailor. They were really hard up, so Mum got a job in a nearby office. She didn't tell them she was pregnant or they wouldn't have taken her on. She had to leave when they realised she was about to pop."

He had never told Amanda any of this, but somehow he felt safe with Megan.

"What happened after that?" she asked gently.

"Mum had a breakdown – I think it was severe post-natal depression, but people didn't talk about it then. You were just supposed to get on with things. My dad had recently joined the Merchant Navy, so he went off on a ship and Mum moved in with her parents. They more or less brought me up for the first couple of years when she wasn't functioning."

"How long was your dad away?"

Mike's face hardened. "He came back every three to six months, but he wasn't faithful. That old saying about sailors having a girl in every port, well, that was my dad. For all I know, I've got any number of half-brothers and sisters scattered all over the world. When he *did* come back, he and my mum argued all the time: she resented being stuck at home while he was off gallivanting. I'm pretty sure she knew about the other women, but she pretended it wasn't happening."

"So what changed?" Megan's mind was awhirl.

"She met someone else. One of my dad's friends who used to pop round to 'keep an eye on her' when he was away. He was always coming round to fix the plumbing or mow the lawn, but I didn't think anything of it when I was younger. He was married too. I think most of my parents' friends were at it with each other."

He lit another cigarette. These were secrets he'd kept hidden for years, ever since he'd come home from school early one day when he was thirteen or fourteen – he'd been hit on the head by a cricket ball earlier and had a headache – and heard his mum and Gerry in the shower. He'd gone out again quietly and then entered noisily, trying to alert his mother to his presence. A moment later she'd appeared at the top of the stairs, clad in a towel, claiming she'd been feeling hot and sweaty at work and had popped home for a quick shower. He hadn't challenged her, going straight to his room and closing the door. She must have managed to smuggle Gerry out quietly, because when Mike went downstairs to the kitchen five minutes later, his mother was the only other person in the house.

"So, why did they decide to split now? It sounds like they've both been leading separate lives for years."

"Because of me," Mike said simply. "They got married because of me; they stayed together because of me; and now I've left home, they don't need to pretend anymore."

He was angry that they'd waited until after Christmas to tell him. He was also far more upset than he was letting on. If your parents were still together when you were nineteen, you assumed their relationship was safe. It had come as a complete shock when they'd sat him down on New Year's Day and told him they were going their separate ways. Mum was moving in with Gerry, whose wife had finally given him a divorce; Dad was staying in the house. He didn't mention whether anyone else would be moving in with him, and Mike didn't particularly want to know.

He wished now they'd gone to his room after all. Megan's arms were round him; she was cradling his head, stroking his hair. More than anything, he wanted to fall asleep with her again, to wake up and find she was still there, a constant amid the chaos.

The cabinet they were sitting on was far too uncomfortable, but it would have to do. He burrowed into Megan, letting her embrace blot out the pain.

*

It was almost midnight by the time they left the basement. They hadn't kissed at all, beyond a brief peck on the lips as Mike unfolded his cramped limbs from the position they'd been in for far too long. For once, this wasn't about desire: they had shared something far deeper, far more raw.

It would only be the next morning, when a number of the men on his floor gave him knowing looks or else made suggestive comments about him disappearing with 'the sexy schoolgirl' that Mike registered that Megan had been wearing a somewhat disturbing outfit. His parents' divorce must have affected him far more deeply than he'd realised if he hadn't noticed how she looked: that was the only rational explanation for him spending an evening talking to her without once trying anything on.

As for Megan, she found herself on the wrong end of her friends' anger when she surfaced for breakfast on the Monday morning. It seemed disappearing for hours with a good-looking boy could only mean one thing. In vain she protested that nothing had happened: no one believed her.

"Just what were you 'talking' about then if it took you so long?" Sally demanded crossly.

Megan bit her lip. She couldn't betray Mike's confidence; nor did she want to talk about her own tangled family life, particularly when she'd never told anyone about her dad being dead in the first place. Essentially, she was a private person, so it had surprised her that she'd trusted Mike enough to tell him part of her story.

"You're like an addict, Megan!" Jen said witheringly. "You just can't keep away from him, can you? And how do you think poor Matt felt, watching you leave with Mike – again."

Megan stole a quick look at Sally, who was doing her best to pretend she hadn't heard Matt's name.

"I'll talk to him in French," Megan said miserably.

"That won't make it sound any better!" Jen snapped back, suddenly dissolving into giggles as she realised what Megan had meant. "Oh, you mean your French *lecture* …"

She was still laughing as Megan pushed her chair away and left the dining room.

*

Matt had already found a seat when she arrived for their two o'clock French poetry lecture. She slid into the space next to him. "Matt, I need to talk to you about last night."

His hurt expression told her that he'd already drawn his own conclusions.

"I wish you hadn't done it," he said at last. "You're too good for him, Megan. He's just using you – you must see that."

"Nothing happened." Her eyes were luminous grey pools of honesty. "He … I … We're both going through similar stuff with our families and we talked about it, that's all."

Matt felt instantly relieved. He had been torturing himself all day, imagining the worst. "So, you're not … seeing each other anymore?"

She shook her head. She and Mike had never really been 'seeing each other' in the first place and now last night had proved they could talk without it leading anywhere else.

"We're just friends," she said slowly. Being friends was better than nothing.

*

Mike and Rose had been sitting in the First Floor Coffee Bar, whiling away the time before their lecture.

"She didn't seem that bothered about you cheating, then?" Rose lit a cigarette, blowing the smoke away from them both.

Mike shrugged. He didn't want to tell Rose about his parents, but she'd known last term that things were rocky with him and Amanda – he wouldn't have slept with Rose otherwise – so he reckoned it wouldn't hurt to bring her up to speed.

"I think she felt worse about the fact she'd cheated on me again," he said drily, taking a swig of strong, black filter coffee, then lighting his own cigarette.

Rose stared at him. "I don't get you," she said at last. "You cheated on her, she cheated on you, but you're still together. Open relationships don't usually work. I should know: I was in one once."

Mike said nothing.

"An old boyfriend of mine decided we'd have an open relationship," Rose continued desperately, "only he didn't bother telling me about it." The joke had sounded so much better when she'd heard it on TV.

"It's *not* an open relationship!" Mike sounded annoyed. "If either of us cheats again, we're through."

"Why wait for that to happen?" Rose asked practically. "If you don't feel the same way anymore, why don't you just tell her it's over?"

Perhaps if his parents hadn't decided to split up, he could have done that; but he was too fragile right now to start messing with someone else's emotions. Not that he could tell Rose that, of course.

"You've still got a thing for that Megan girl, haven't you?" Rose said suddenly.

Mike wished his friend wasn't so perceptive.

"It's because she's the one who got away," Rose continued. "You only want her because you can't have her. If she slept with you, you'd move onto someone else."

He wanted to protest that he wasn't like that; and then he remembered his drunken encounter with Rose and how, after it had happened, he'd told her very firmly that nothing like that was going to happen again. He supposed he couldn't blame her for writing him off as a Lothario. She knew about Claire, too: the two of them often sat together, giggling whenever they looked in his direction. He wondered if they were swapping notes.

He and Rose sauntered into the lecture theatre. Megan was sitting with that public schoolboy type again: the one who was all floppy hair and beautiful manners. His body language suggested that he was more than a tad interested in Megan. Mike felt an irrational stab of jealousy. She wasn't attracted to *him*, though, despite the adoring way he looked at her.

Beside him, Rose whispered, "Competition?"

He could have throttled her.

Moodily he found a couple of seats on the back row, wondering if he was going to feel such turmoil every time he caught sight of Megan in lectures.

Chapter Twenty-Two

In the end, Jen and the others forgave Megan. It was hard not to when she was so ridiculously penitent. Sue even deigned to come and admire the new wardrobe, approving of the oversized shirts and the trilby but expressing reservations about both the mini-skirts.

"But I'm wearing them over really thick tights!" Megan protested. "You can't see anything, honest."

"Why can't you stick to skirts like this one?" Sue grumbled, pouncing on the 'smart' skirt Megan was saving for important occasions. Then, as her gaze fell upon some of Megan's carefully chosen accessories, her eyes widened in horror. "What *were* you thinking?"

In retrospect, the tights Megan had thought to team with the skirt – three pairs in shocking pink, jade green and Tango orange – had been a mistake, but she wasn't going to admit that to Sue. Instead, she made a mental note to donate the tights to the nearest charity shop as quickly as possible and stick to safe and reliable black from now on.

"I notice you haven't unleashed your mini-skirts on the general public yet," was Sue's next comment.

Megan blushed. She had been intending to wear the pink mini/pink footless tights combo for campus today but had chickened out at the last minute, wearing jeans instead – although since she'd teamed them with a long black jumper and her black suede cowboy boots (still going strong years after buying them from Anita's mum's catalogue), she had still managed to look rather alluring. (Sue was sure that was one of the reasons why Sally had been so cross with her this morning.)

"I thought maybe I'd try the pink one when we go to the bar," she said now, pretending not to notice Sue's disapproving expression. "I've got my flowery baseball boots and I found a white fluffy jumper in a charity shop in Rochdale."

Sue sighed and left her to it. She was pleased that Megan was developing her own sense of style, but she still thought some of her choices a little unwise. Or was she just jealous because Megan could wear things like that whereas she, Sue, couldn't?

It didn't really matter what her friends thought of her outfit, Megan decided later as she sat sipping her third Coral, because plenty of other people seemed to like the way she looked tonight. One of them, a boy from High she'd never met before named Piers, had shoehorned himself into their group and was telling her how nice he thought her legs were. Several other strange men had complimented her on her dress sense and offered to buy her drinks. It was a rather pleasant novelty to be the focus of so much attention.

"Don't you think you ought to slow down?" Jen asked gently. "That's your third alcoholic drink already and you know you can't handle it."

"It's all right," Megan declared grandly. "My dad's an alcoholic but he says I haven't got a drink problem!"

The others exchanged worried glances.

"You haven't mentioned this before," Sally began hesitantly.

Megan suddenly remembered her friends knew nothing about what had happened over Christmas. She wasn't sure she wanted them to.

"He's a recovering alcoholic," she admitted, a little more quietly this time. "He's not had a drink in over five years."

"That must have been difficult to grow up with." Jen sounded sympathetic.

"I didn't grow up with it." Megan said in a small voice. She was beginning to wish she hadn't mentioned John now. She stood up suddenly and the room blurred momentarily. "I think I'll go to bed now."

"I'll walk you to your door," Piers began eagerly, but Sally waved him away.

"We'll do it: we're her friends." Although she was genuinely concerned for Megan – what she'd said made sense of the way she seemed to be looking for a father figure all the time – she also wanted to make sure that this wasn't another excuse to sneak off to Mike's room. She and Jen had both agreed that they would be watching Megan closely from now on.

Megan stumbled fuzzily towards her room, aided by Sally. She wasn't sure why her head was spinning so much – or why Sally was being so nice to her.

"I didn't think you liked me much," she blurted out recklessly.

Sally stiffened. "I *do* like you," she said carefully. "I just think you need to be a bit more careful with the men you choose – and the clothes you wear."

Matt hadn't taken his eyes off Megan all evening. Sally should be used to it by now, but even so it was jolly annoying when the object of your affections only had eyes for someone else – and when *she* was hardly aware he existed.

They had reached Megan's door. After watching her friend struggle for a few minutes trying to turn the key, Sally took pity on her and opened the door herself. She watched Megan collapse on the bed, certain that there would be no late night trip to High tonight.

As Megan started snoring, Sally gently pulled the door closed behind her and went back to join their friends.

*

The next day, Megan threw caution to the wind and wore her black mini skirt to campus – over the black footless tights, of course. She topped her ensemble with a longish, bright blue shaggy jumper, making sure that her matching blue socks could be seen poking out of the tops of her baseball boots. Her hair was tied back with the blue Paisley scarf, giving her a definite Bohemian look.

Matt thought she looked adorable. He had liked the way she looked before, but since she had returned to Hall after the Christmas holidays, there was a new confidence in the way Megan dressed. He hoped she would continue to wear these exciting short skirts – even if their presence made it hard to concentrate on lectures.

Mike had also noticed Megan's revamped image. He thought it suited her. She had always had a touch of the Bohemian about her, but now she embraced it, ignoring what anyone else was wearing and choosing clothes that suited not just her personality but her body type as well. She was small but perfectly formed, he thought, catching sigh of her by the French pigeon holes and realising that he still wanted her. Maybe Rose was right and he only wanted what he couldn't have. He'd searched for her in the bar last night but hadn't seen her.

Megan was quite unaware of the effect she was having on her male acquaintances. It was only as she arrived in the Hall bar again that evening – this time she would be sticking to orange juice – to find another horde of male admirers desperate to sit with her or buy her drinks that she became aware that she was being regarded as a sex symbol. This was totally unprecedented but, at the same time, very exciting. She had hardly ever been noticed at school: in fact, when people realised she and Dave were an item, one girl had been heard to snort, "What do you want to go out with *her* for?" To which another had replied thoughtfully, "Well, I suppose she's not *bad* looking ..."

Sue, Jen and Sally, meanwhile, thought that Megan was becoming a little bigheaded. "It's not that your legs are nicer than everyone else's," Sue told her severely when Megan mentioned that she had received more compliments on her figure: "it's just that we can see a lot more of them. I could dress up like a bunny girl and parade through the High/Ridge bar," - Ged choked on his drink when she said that - "but I don't. I have too much self-respect!"

Megan felt crestfallen. It was very sad to have one's friends acting so pettily when all she was trying to do was have a bit of fun.

"Don't the two of you normally have Choir on a Tuesday night?" Sally asked suddenly.

"It doesn't start again until next week," Sue told her. "And then we'll be rehearsing round the clock for the St John Passion – it's only an eight week term so we don't have a lot of time."

Megan was looking round for Matt, aware that she hadn't seen him or Phil all evening.

"Events meeting," Jen told her. "I think they're pretty pleased with how the Fancy Dress disco worked out, even if it did look fixed when you won the prize."

Her prize. What had she done with it? She was unlikely to drink it herself unless it was Coral – and she had a feeling that didn't come in big bottles – but she could offer it to Jen and Sally by way of an apology for disappearing with Mike.

And then it all came back to her. She had put the bottle down in the basement room in High when she and Mike had started chatting. Would it still be there?

"I'm just going to get something," she murmured, getting up to leave.

Jen looked at Sally sharply. Mike hadn't been in the bar this evening – Sally thought he'd lost interest in Megan: she'd seen him with another girl in the Coffee Bar in the Muirhead Tower; but still ...

"Won't it do later?" she asked pointedly.

Megan hesitated. What if someone else found the bottle and took it? Better go and look for it now.

"If you must know," she said, turning to face Jen and Sally, "I'm only going to collect my prize from Sunday night. I put it down for a minute when I was talking to Mike ..." - the other two exchanged glances – "... and forgot to pick it up again. You can come with me if you like."

"You wouldn't be collecting it from Mike's room by any chance, would you?" Sally asked suspiciously.

"No," Megan said impatiently. "We didn't go to his room on Sunday evening: we just sat and chatted in the basement."

Matt and Phil chose that moment to turn up. Jen breathed a sigh of relief. "Take Matt with you," she ordered, ignoring Sally's thunderous expression. Megan wouldn't be getting up to anything she shouldn't with Matt in tow. She tugged Phil's arm. "Why don't you get me another white wine spritzer, and then you can tell me all about your meeting."

*

Matt was elated to be going somewhere with Megan. He was slightly surprised when she led him to the staircase in the High Hall foyer that led down to the basement. Surely she wasn't doing laundry at this time?

But instead of taking the route he knew to the room with the washing machines and the rather terrifying spin dryer that hopped off its pedestal if you didn't distribute your clothes properly, Megan opened a door he hadn't spotted before and led him into what looked like some sort of store room full of tired looking chairs and tables. She was looking about her, frowning, as if trying to locate something.

"I put my prize down somewhere the other evening," she explained, "only it looks like someone else found it and walked off with it." She paused. "I was going to give it to Jen and Sally: they're not very happy with me at the moment."

Matt felt a sudden protective urge. How dare the other girls upset Megan!

She turned towards him. "We'd better head back. Come on."

As they reached the foyer, Matt realised he needed the lavatory. There was probably a toilet on the ground floor somewhere, but he felt more comfortable using the one near his own room. He was used to that one.

"I ... erm ... I just need to do something," he murmured, feeling too embarrassed to say what he needed to do.

"Do you want me to come with you?" Megan asked innocently.

Matt choked. "No, I ... erm ... Why don't you wait here for me?" he suggested.

One of the lifts was in transit, but the other one stood ready for use. He stepped inside and pushed the button for the sixth floor, feeling flustered.

As Matt's lift moved away, the other one arrived in the lobby. The doors opened and Megan found herself staring at Mike.

For a moment, neither one spoke. Then, "Were you coming to see me?"

The air crackled between them, but Megan had told Sally that she wasn't going to Mike's room.

"I was looking for my prize from Sunday," she said lamely. "It was a bottle of something. I put it down in that room we were in, but it's gone."

"It's in my room. I realised you'd forgotten it about half an hour after you went back to Ridge, so I went back for it." He took another drag on the cigarette he'd lit in the lift. The sign said 'No Smoking', but he hadn't caused a fire yet.

She had told Sally she wasn't going to Mike's room ...

"You can come and get it now if you want," he offered.

... But if she just stood outside his room while he went in for the bottle, that would be okay, wouldn't it?

Her mind was made up. "Okay then." And she followed him into the lift.

Matt finished doing what he had to and hurried to the lift. When the doors opened again on the ground floor, Megan was nowhere in sight. Had she become tired of waiting for him. He checked his watch, realising he had been at least ten minutes. She had probably returned to the bar. Trotting along the corridor to rejoin her, he felt strangely optimistic about the probability of asking her out this term. She was no longer seeing Mike: that meant he, Matt, was in with a chance.

Mike opened the door of his room and motioned for Megan to enter. "Do you want a coffee while you're here?"

She was supposed to be waiting outside, so why was she walking into his room and sitting on the bed as if she had a right to be there?

"Not with CoffeeMate, thanks," she told him, leaning back against the wall.

Mike grinned. "I've got real milk!"

"You have?" Megan sat up straight in surprise. Had he bought it especially for her?

Mike didn't tell her it was stolen milk, purloined from someone else's carton in the kitchen. No, he corrected himself, 'borrowed': if he ever bought milk of his own, he would replace the tiny amount he'd taken just in case Megan came round. He sniffed the mug doubtfully: it had been sitting in his room since this morning, but he didn't think it had gone off.

Even with milk, Mike's coffee was terrible. Megan didn't care. She sipped it slowly, savouring the rightness of being back in Mike's room with its familiar books and posters.

What was that on the bookcase? She climbed off the bed and went for a closer look.

"I didn't know you liked Thomas Hardy," she said, startled to see *'Jude the Obscure'* nestling between *'Put Out More Flags'* and *'Our Man in Havana'*.

"You've made me a reformed character."

His fingers reached for the book at the same time as hers. A sudden jolt of electricity passed between them and Megan knew she was undone.

"Jude and Sue fell for each other because they had an intellectual connection." Megan knew she was gabbling.

"I think they had a pretty strong physical thing going on too. They had children together …"

His eyes met hers. The intense longing there mirrored her own.

"You're still with Amanda," she said at last, knowing that if he kissed her she would forget instantly about his girlfriend.

"Jude was still married to Arabella …"

Outside in the corridor, a door slammed and the sound of raucous laughter was heard. Within Mike's room, everything was silent. Megan was aware of her own breathing, fast and shallow, and the way her heartbeat seemed to echo oddly, as if it were trying to escape her ribs.

Without a word, Mike pulled her towards him, his eyes burning into her own. His lips met hers in an explosion of heat, need tugging them together. For a brief moment she let herself drown in the sheer intensity of desire, then pushed him away, guilt already driving a wedge between them.

"I can't." But she wanted to. Oh, how she wanted to.

He could have pulled her back into his arms, kissed her again until she forgot that it was wrong; instead, he forced himself to think of Amanda, then of his parents.

"You know I want you," he said at last.

"It wouldn't mean anything." She was avoiding his gaze.

She was wrong: it would mean everything. It would mean the end of his relationship with Amanda, for a start; and it would mean the loss of Megan's innocence; and it would mean giving away a part of his heart to someone who might not even want it. If he slept with Megan, it wouldn't be a one-off: he knew he would have to keep going back for more.

"Your bottle's on the table."

He stayed where he was as she picked up the whisky and left his room.

*

Megan wasn't in the bar when Matt arrived. He felt confused. Had he missed her in the foyer? Maybe she'd popped to the bathroom herself?

"Where's Megan?" Sally asked, a little sharply.

"I … er … we couldn't find what she was looking for." They were all looking at him expectantly. "So we started to come back here, but I needed the bathroom …" His voice tailed off.

"*Never* let her out of your sight!" Jen scolded him. She turned to Sally. "No prizes for guessing where she'll be."

There was an uncomfortable sensation in Matt's solar plexus. Megan wasn't seeing Mike anymore: she had told him that yesterday; so why did he feel so uneasy now?

"What do you think?" Sally was addressing Megan. "Should we go and look for her? Someone in High is bound to know where Mike's room is."

But here was Megan now, slightly pink cheeked, carrying a bottle of whisky. Matt sent up a silent prayer of thanks to a largely ignored God. She hadn't been with Mike after all.

"Where did you find it?" he asked her eagerly, relieved to think she hadn't abandoned him after all.

"Someone had moved it," was all she would say.

"Is that whisky?" Sue's eyes were bright with hope.

Megan nodded. "I know I didn't really do anything to win it, but I wanted to give it to the three of you ..." She swallowed. "... As a way of saying sorry for the other evening. Nothing happened, but I know you were all worried about me. I won't go off again without telling you what I'm doing."

Jen was touched by Megan's generosity – and her penitence; Sue decided that Megan couldn't be all bad if she was giving away an expensive bottle of whisky for free; and Sally felt rather put out. It was all very well for Megan to bat her eyelids and say she was sorry, she thought savagely, but you couldn't deny that she was acting very unwisely at the moment - not just by going off with Mike but by prancing about in skirts that were no bigger than belts. She wasn't jealous, she told herself fiercely: it just rankled to see Matt acting like an adoring slave with someone who couldn't care less about him.

Out of the corner of her eye, Megan saw Mike enter the bar and join his usual group of cronies. She deliberately looked away, aware that there was still unfinished business between them.

Mike was fully aware of Megan's presence but he, too, was doing his best to ignore whatever it was that was still flickering between them. He hoped Amanda would hurry up and commit another indiscretion because not being able to be with Megan properly was torture.

He lit another cigarette and tried to let the nicotine deaden his angst.

Chapter Twenty-Three

A fortnight later, Megan was leaving her French poetry lecture when Mike stopped her. Despite the crowds of people milling about them, she was aware only of his presence. Her stomach flipped involuntarily.

"I don't suppose you've got any elastic, have you?"

"What?" If this was a chat-up line, it wasn't a very good one.

Mike elaborated. "I'm in the German play and we're wearing masks …"

"Don't tell me: Brecht's *'Gute Mensch'*," she interrupted. (Her A level German teacher had taken her and Jules to see a production – in English, thankfully – of *'The Good Person of Szechwan'*.)

Mike grinned. "I've always seen myself as Yang Sun, but actually it's a play by Hauptmann, *'Die versunkene Glocke'* – do you know it?"

She had heard of neither playwright nor play, but Mike wasn't waiting for an answer.

"Anyway," he swept on, "we're wearing masks, but the elastic on mine has snapped, and I thought you might be the sort of person who would have some …"

Did he mean he thought she was so pathetic she would not only own a needlework basket but have brought it to University with her? Megan wondered. (As it turned out, she did, and she had.)

"I'll have a look," she said casually. "If I find some, I'll bring it round later."

She knew exactly where it was in her workbasket, but she wasn't going to tell him that.

His eyes held hers - only for a second, but that was enough.

"I'll see you later," he said softly, then turned and was gone.

Megan found it hard to concentrate on anything else for the rest of the day, her mind too busy rehearsing not only what she would say to Mike later on, when she took him the elastic, but how she would manage to escape the watchful eyes of her friends to do it.

In the end, she invented a seminar paper that she had to complete for the following day. Surely no one would tell her off if she claimed she couldn't join them in the bar because she had homework?

Jen looked slightly suspicious when Megan mentioned her paper. "Didn't you say you'd signed up for a session on Satan in three weeks' time?"

Megan mentally cursed her friend for having such a good memory before replying that she had been forced to swap with someone else who had gone down with glandular fever. The excuse sounded hollow in her own ears but the others seemed to accept it.

"Come and join us for the last drink of the evening if you finish in time," Sue called as the posse left for the bar.

Megan waved back at them, clutching a biro to aid verisimilitude and wondering if she would go to hell for lying to her friends again. A part of her wondered why she didn't just tell them where she was going, but she knew that at least one of them would insist on accompanying her and, whilst she had no intention of kissing Mike ever again, she wouldn't be able to talk to him properly with any sort of audience present.

Once she was sure they had really gone, Megan quickly brushed her teeth and ran her fingers through her hair. There was no point changing her clothes since she was only popping in briefly to deliver the elastic, not planning on stopping for any amount of time; nevertheless, she was gratified that she looked good today in the outfit she'd worn for campus: her black and white shirt combination with black leggings. (She'd thought they were footless tights but Sue had assured her otherwise.) She had teamed these with her newest acquisition: a pair of dainty Victorian style boots in black leather that laced up past her ankles. The boots were slightly too large for her, being a size three, but she had fallen in love with them at first sight and had known she had to have them, even if they did make a hefty dent in what was left of her father's money.

Briefly checking that the corridor was empty, she stole through the foyer and out of the outside door, circumnavigating the outside of the building until she had reached High's main entrance. The lobby was relatively empty. Good: there was less chance of her being seen. Slipping inside the empty lift, she pressed the button for the eleventh floor and waited for it to carry her to Mike.

Mike was lying on his bed, practising his lines for the play. He would have liked to have been cast as Heinrich but that role had gone to a Final Year student. It seemed the First Years were only allowed to be sprites. He had got involved because he thought it would be fun; but he was quite glad that none of his friends wanted to come and see him dancing about in tights. Even if they did, once he was safely behind his mask, no one would know who he was.

A quiet tapping on the door signalled Megan's arrival. "I've brought the elastic."

She could have handed it over and left – *should* have done that; but they both knew that wasn't the real reason why she was here.

"I'd better make you a coffee then," Mike began, but she pushed past him to the desk where his kettle and a mug stood waiting.

"Do you mind if I do it? The last one was a bit strong."

Mike watched, fascinated, as she poured the milk in first, followed by a quarter spoonful of Maxwell House. He didn't particularly like the coffee brand, but he wasn't buying any more Nescafé, not with the current student boycott over baby milk.

The liquid in Megan's mug, once she'd added hot water, resembled no coffee Mike had ever seen. "That looks like dishwater!" he said in horror.

Megan smiled, a gesture that lit the whole of her face. "It's the way I like it!"

"I'll stick to the way I normally have it."

Mike placed two heaped teaspoons of coffee in his only other mug and added the water. "Like me," he said smugly. "Hot and strong!"

"And black!" murmured Megan, catching his eye.

"Maybe not."

They both grinned at each other.

"So, Megan Jackson," Mike decided to take the bull by the horns, "why have you been avoiding me this term?" He took a sip from his coffee.

"I haven't noticed *you* beating my door down to try to see me; or wanting to acknowledge me on campus – apart from today," Megan flashed back. "Every time I see you in French lectures, you're sitting with Daisy …"

"Rose," Mike corrected her.

"So? I knew it was a flower. Anyway, you're either sitting with her or going for coffee with her."

"Jealous?"

By now the air was thick with longing. Mike put down his mug and stroked Megan's cheek. "I don't want anyone else," he said honestly. "It's you or nothing."

Taking Megan's own coffee away, he placed it on the table and led her to the bed.

Megan woke a while later, aware that she had dozed off in Mike's arms again. She opened her eyes lazily. Mike was breathing heavily, his chest rising and falling as he slept. She wondered if she could wriggle out from underneath him without waking him.

When she moved, he tightened his arms around her, as if begging her to stay. Megan felt torn. They were both still fully clothed but there had been a lot of kissing. It was strangely empowering to know someone wanted you so much. Then again, she was just as powerless to resist Mike's lips as he was to avoid hers. She doubted either of them had tried very hard.

Should she feel guilty about Amanda? Mike had refused to talk about his girlfriend but Megan couldn't pretend that she didn't exist. Did that make her a bad person? she wondered for the umpteenth time. How would she feel if the positions were reversed and she, Megan, was the one being cheated on?

"Mike." She whispered his name gently. "I have to go."

It was almost five thirty. The sun wouldn't be up for hours yet, but she would have to return to her room before her friends came to call her for breakfast.

"Mike." She tried again. "I have to get back to Hall."

This time he heard her. He sat up quickly. "What time is it?"

"Half five. It's time I was off."

"Do you realise that's the longest we've ever spent together?"

He'd never slept all night with Amanda in his arms like that; probably never would.

She gazed at him steadily, her eyes full of something he couldn't define. Hunger? Remorse? It was time to be honest with her. "For what it's worth," he said slowly, "that was incredibly special."

A look passed between them.

"It can't happen again, can it?" she said softly.

He shook his head.

"It's goodbye all over again, isn't it?"

This time, he nodded. "I'm sorry."

She would never know how sorry he was.

*

Megan slipped into her room ten minutes later, feeling a curious mixture of relief and regret. Mike had offered to walk her back to Ridge, but she had refused. Far better to walk away from him now, on her own terms, than to prolong the agony by pretending he was hers. He was someone else's boyfriend: she had to keep reminding herself of that. But she couldn't help a warm glow from stealing over her as she relived their kisses; nor could she blot out the memory of waking up in his arms. Physical pleasure was addictive; it was also wonderfully emancipating. Mike made her feel like a sexy, vibrant woman, one capable of achieving anything, including managing to persuade Gordon Warden to let her into Ridge without the Hall Card she'd inadvertently left on her desk.

She was too full of adrenaline to go back to sleep so she decided to run a bath and finally put her mother's Christmas present to good use. She had discovered an interesting book on Milton in the Short Loan section of the library yesterday and borrowed it, but it was due back before ten. Could she read it in the bath if she was careful? As long as she didn't drop it, it should be okay.

Megan was so engrossed in Lawrence Hyman's essay on 'Ambiguity in Paradise Lost' that she completely lost track of time, letting the water grow cold around her whilst she perused the pages. She only came to her senses when an irate fist hammered on the door, reminding her that "Other people want to use the bathroom too!"

She leaped out of the bath hurriedly, swaddling herself in a large towel and grabbing her armful of clothes. There was no time now to get dressed in here.

"Megan!" Sally's voice stopped her midway between bathroom and bedroom. "You don't normally have a bath in the mornings," she said suspiciously.

Megan indicated the book in her hand. "Catching up on reading," she said simply.

"Did you finish your paper?" Sally asked.

Megan blushed. She hated lying. "Almost." She hesitated. "Look, I'd better get dressed. I'll see you at breakfast."

"You'd better hurry then," Sally said drily. "It's nearly half seven."

Had Megan *really* managed to sit in the bath for over an hour? Sally must be wrong; but the alarm clock said twenty past seven. Bother!

She ended up dressing much more quickly than she'd intended, her jeans sticking to her still damp legs. Luckily she'd managed to coax her hair into a shower cap so it wasn't wet, but it was still a reasonably dishevelled Megan who made her way to breakfast ten minutes later.

"You look flustered," Jen commented, waiting for a reply.

"I just lost track of time in the bath." Megan began buttering some toast, searching for the Marmite.

"Only, Sally and I were wondering," Jen pursued relentlessly, "whether the reason you're so all over the place now is because you were up all night studying …" she paused for effect, "… or getting friendly with Mike all over again."

Megan's cheeks flamed. How did they know?

"One of Phil's friends saw you leaving Mike's room at some unearthly hour this morning," Sally told her. She looked at Megan severely. "Just how long has this been going on for?"

"It hasn't. I mean, that's the first time we've kissed since December." You couldn't really count the quick kiss in Mike's room when she'd gone there to collect the whisky.

"I don't know what we're going to do with you!" Jen looked at Megan in exasperation. "What were you doing, going to his room when you should have been in the bar with us?"

"He needed some elastic for a mask. For the German play." It sounded like a feeble excuse and she knew it. Sally rolled her eyes.

"Well, in that case, you should have handed over the elastic and then left straight away," Jen scolded her. Megan wondered if anyone else pronounced it 'elarstic', the same way Jen did.

"I didn't mean to kiss him." She looked up at the other two, her eyes pleading. "It just … happens … every time we see each other. And it makes me feel so … desirable. On my way back from High this morning, I felt like I was oozing sex!"

"That's disgusting!" Sally was shocked by Megan's confession, but Jen calmed her down.

"She's using a metaphor, Sally! At least, I hope she is."

Megan nodded. "No one ever wanted me before," she said quietly. "I know you two think I'm a trollop ..." - Jen hid a smile – "and that my skirts are too short, but at school I was always being teased because of my skinny legs and I just got carried away when people here started telling me I looked good."

"You're forgiven," Jen told her. There was something very endearing about Megan: one couldn't stay cross with her for long.

"It doesn't solve the Mike problem, though," Sally said grumpily.

Jen sighed. "What do you want to happen, Megan? Do you keep on going back to him because you think you'll make him change his mind about his girlfriend and get rid of her? Because, if you do, you're wasting your time. Men like Mike just aren't good boyfriend material."

"I know he's not going to leave her." Megan sounded despondent. "and I hate myself for going back to him time after time, even though I know he's just using me. But at least when I'm with him I feel wanted."

"Is that really so important to you?" Jen's tone was surprisingly gentle.

Megan felt a tear forming in her eye.

"My dad walked out on me when I was a baby," she said at last. "I grew up thinking he was dead."

Sally shot Jen a triumphant look. She had *known* her missing father theory was correct.

"I met him for the first time in the Christmas holidays," Megan continued in a wobbly voice, "and he's trying really hard to make up for lost time – with me *and* my mum. But I keep on thinking ..."

Jen put a sympathetic hand on her shoulder.

"I keep on wondering why he didn't try to see me sooner," Megan continued brokenly. "Why did he wait until I was nineteen before he tried to get to know me?"

"That's why you don't know how to relate to men," Sally broke in, looking from one to the other. "It's all in *'Families and How to Survive Them'* by Robin Skynner and John Cleese. I read it last summer."

"John Cleese as in *'Fawlty Towers'* and *'Monty Python and the Holy Grail'*?" Jen asked in disbelief.

Sally nodded. "Girls need to flirt with their fathers when they're toddlers," she explained. "It prepares them for flirting with boys their own age when they're teenagers. Megan didn't have any of that, so that's why she can't talk to boys properly now."

"Unless you count Matt," Jen said without thinking.

Sally's face clouded over. "Matt can't relate to girls," she said crisply. "That's why he and Megan get on so well: they're both as emotionally retarded as each other!"

"Sally!" Jen sad reprovingly, but Megan wasn't listening, her mind far away, thinking of her father – and Mike.

She came back to earth with a start as Sue and Ged crashed breakfast trays down onto their table, Sue remonstrating with Jen and Sally for not giving her a wake up knock this morning. "It's just as well Ged came to look for me," she was saying indignantly, "or I'd still be asleep now!"

"Didn't Ted bother to wake you?" Sally asked slily.

Sue sniffed. "He claims he has a headache this morning, but if you ask me, it's a hangover. I've left him tucked up in bed with a glass of water and a couple of paracetamol!"

Megan didn't wait to hear the rest of the story. Mike had just entered the dining hall. Grabbing her room key and leaving her dirty crockery on the table, she fled.

*

"We've got to help her, you know."

Sally stopped brushing her hair for long enough to give Jen a questioning look.

"I mean, we've got to help wean her off Mike," Jen explained. She hesitated. "Do you think it would help if we started hanging out in here in the evenings instead of going to the bar?"

"How would that help?" Sally was interested.

"Well ..." Jen paused from painting her toenails for long enough to give Sally her full attention. "If we're in here, she won't be able to see Mike – I mean, physically see him across the bar. If she doesn't see him, she won't think about him: 'out of sight, out of mind' and all that."

"Would we all fit in here?" Sally was doubtful.

"Two chairs of our own – four if you count the ones at our desks – and you can fit three people on each bed, sitting side by side." Jen's eyes sparkled as the idea began to take shape in her mind. "We can play music in the background and buy supplies from the off-licence. We can get cans of lager, and a box of white wine and some lemonade for spritzers. And when it's summer we can make Pimms!"

"Steady on!" Sally told her. "It's not even the end of January yet!"

"I'm not suggesting we do it forever," Jen broke in hastily. "But it would do Megan good to have a break from the bar without having a break from us. And we could invite other people too: men who might be more suitable than Mike."

"Ghengis Khan would be more suitable than Mike!" Sally said waspishly. But she liked the idea of Megan having someone other than Matt to talk to. Poor Sally! She still had a hopeless crush on Matt, despite the fact that he never noticed her if Megan was present.

It was all arranged. Tonight they would start off in the bar and then bring everyone back to their room to carry on the party. Tomorrow night they would come back half an hour earlier and continue to do this until everyone began meeting in G28 instead of the bar. It couldn't be simpler.

They had reckoned without Phil and Matt though. When Jen started explaining their idea to Phil, later that night in the bar, he objected straight away. "I don't mind coming back to your room at the end of a drinking session, but I'm not spending all evening in your room just to keep Megan's virtue intact." He paused. "If you ask me, you should let her and Mike get on with it. Let her sleep with him and get him out of her system! Anyway," he drew breath, "the Sunday discos have just started taking off. I'm not going to be anywhere else when they're going on. There's a big Valentine's disco on the fourteenth of February too."

Jen knew when she was beaten. But Phil hadn't ruled out the idea of a post-bar party in her room every night; nor had he said he wouldn't try to find a suitable date for Megan. Her plan wasn't working out exactly as she hoped, but at least it hadn't died a complete death.

Megan was surprised when Jen got to her feet at half nine that evening, closely followed by Sally, and announced she was going back to her room. "Why don't you all come?" Jen threw the invitation open to everyone at their table, including Howard, a friend of Phil's who had joined them for the first time tonight.

"Yes," urged Sally, looking at Matt, "come on! It'll be fun!"

Everyone grabbed their drinks and followed the two room-mates back to the party venue. Megan was surprised to see Howard joining them. She'd chatted to him a bit this evening and thought he was quite nice but very dull. He didn't read, for a start, and he seemed to have an overwhelming obsession with a TV show called *'Blake's Seven'*. She hadn't had a clue what he was talking about.

Beside her, Matt trotted along, carrying his glass of red wine. "This is the first time I've been invited to a party in Ridge," he told her, his cheeks pink with excitement.

"I don't think it's a real party," Megan said carefully. "I mean, we're the only ones who seem to have been invited."

She was beginning to feel suspicious about the whole thing. Was this a clever ploy by Sally and Jen to ensure she didn't end up running into Mike again?

The two girls had decorated their room with fairy lights and covered Sally's desk with an assortment of plastic cups and canned drinks. Megan could see Coca Cola as well as lager. Her heart sank: she didn't like either. Luckily there was a carton of Five Alive mixed fruit juice too, although she would have preferred the unlimited supply of Coral in the bar.

Phil was fiddling about with Jen's stereo system, a dinky little all-in-one ensemble which comprised record player, tape deck, amplifier and built in speakers. It seemed very grand compared to Megan's radio cassette player.

As Phil pressed the 'Play' button, music drifted round the room. "What's that?" Megan asked in surprise.

Jen looked pleased. "Phil's made me a tape of some of his favourite songs. Listen!"

Megan didn't know the first song at all ("Early Genesis," Jen said knowledgeably. "It's from an album called 'The Lamb Lies Down on Broadway'.") but she did know 'Bohemian Rhapsody' and she'd heard 'Somebody to Love' before as well. Howard was tapping his feet to all the songs. He was a big Queen fan, he explained. Megan tried to make her face look interested, but it wasn't easy.

As one song merged into another, with something that sounded alarmingly noisy ("That's 'Bat out of Hell'," Jen said, showing off) being replaced with something equally discordant ("It's Iron Maiden's 'Sanctuary'," Phil told her when Jen couldn't remember the band or the track title), Megan wondered if they would get into trouble for playing loud music late at night. "Turn the volume down," she mouthed at Jen.

Eventually, Howard turned to Megan with a hopeful expression. "Are you seeing anyone?" he asked her.

Before she could reply, Matt stepped in between them. "Time for us to make a move," he said, steering Megan towards the door.

Ignoring Howard's crestfallen look, Megan followed Matt to her own door opposite. Should she invite him in? Perhaps she'd better, just to convince Howard that they were an item. She felt slightly mean deceiving him like this, but surely it was better than just telling him outright that she didn't like him enough to go out with him?

Meanwhile, Matt couldn't believe that he was actually entering Megan's bedroom with her. Nervousness made him sweat slightly. Should he take this opportunity to ask her out himself?

Megan closed the door onto the corridor and they both sank down on the bed, giggling hysterically. "I'm sorry," she said after a while. "I was just so relieved that you rescued me when you did. Poor Howard!" She broke into laughter again.

Matt was close enough to Megan to smell the faint vestiges of perfume on her skin and the smell of her fruity shampoo. She must have washed her hair this evening, before going to the bar. He wanted to breathe in deeply, to enjoy the aroma of her, but he knew this wouldn't be appreciated. Instead, he pulled a face at her as he said, "I'm not sure I liked all of that music."

Mentioning music reminded Megan of something she'd been meaning to say to him for ages. "Can you listen to this some time?" she asked, pulling out the tape Jen had sent her for her birthday. "There are some songs on there that might be good for the Hall disco."

Matt hadn't heard of Sadie before and said so, apologetically.

"It's pronounced *Shar*-day," Megan corrected him, even though she'd made the same mistake herself before Anita had enlightened her.

Matt looked at the tape thoughtfully. "If you want to, you can give me a list of your favourite songs. I can't promise to play all of them every disco night, but I can play *some* of them."

"You're a good friend, Matt," Megan said, yawning. "Thanks again for everything you've done tonight."

She shepherded him towards the door. Soon after he left, she was asleep.

*

As one day followed on from another, Jen and Sally continued to host their select gatherings, inviting a succession of men they thought might be 'suitable' for Megan. None of them appealed to her at all.

She was, however, finding Matt slightly less annoying these days. He seemed content to be her friend rather than her boyfriend, so she began to relax more around him. Spending time with him was helping her keep her mind off Mike.

*

Matt positively bounced to the breakfast table a few days later. *"Charley's Aunt's* on at the Rep!" He addressed the words to Megan.

She looked at him quizzically.

"We put it on at school a few years ago," Matt explained. "It's a wonderful play: very funny." He hadn't been in it himself, but he had roared with laughter watching it.

"That sounds like a brilliant idea!" Sally was full of enthusiasm. "What are the dates?"

Matt felt confused. He hadn't meant to invite everyone: in fact, he'd envisaged just Megan and himself watching the play, laughing together, maybe going for food beforehand.

"It finishes on February the sixth," he said at last.

Sally beamed. "Let's go this Saturday – the first."

Before he knew what was going on, the whole crowd had agreed to join Matt at the theatre, Phil under duress from Jen. "I had to go to one of your heavy metal concerts," she said severely, "so you can jolly well do something cultural with me!"

At times Matt despaired of ever being properly alone with Megan.

*

Valentine's Day was approaching. The High/Ridge JCR had planned a themed disco for February the fourteenth but postponed it until the sixteenth instead when they realised that High Hall wouldn't be anyone's first choice for a romantic evening with their loved one.

Sally knocked on Megan's door at around seven o'clock on the Thursday evening, her eyes full of mischief. "Come to our room now!"

Megan wondered what was so important. They had only just returned from the evening meal: surely if it had been that critical, Sally would have mentioned something then?

Not, it seemed, in front of Sue. Sally almost dragged Megan into G28 then shut the door. Jen was sitting on her own bed, scribbling away on an A4 notepad, and Sally's desk was littered with plain paper and felt tipped pens.

"We're making Sue a Valentine's card from Ted," Sally explained in a whisper. "It's a surprise."

"Oh!" Megan said.

On the front of the card Sally had sketched a teddy bear wearing a black leather jacket and sunglasses. "We thought we could write some rhymes about Ted being really cool," Sally explained.

"She means, we thought *you* could write some rhymes," Jen broke in, without looking up from her notepad. "You know you're good at that sort of stuff."

It was true that Megan had always been able to write funny verses – doggerel, really – so she embraced the challenge eagerly. Valentine's Day might be only hours away, but she could scribble suitable rhymes in minutes.

"Have you thought of anything decent yet?" she asked, removing the pad from Jen's hands and scanning it rapidly. There were a few half-hearted attempts that fizzled out after only a line, but there was nothing she could work with. She ripped the page from the pad and started again.

"Okay," she said, after a minute, "what about this?
Violets are blue;
Roses are red.
I know a bear
And he is called Ted."

"That's perfect!" laughed Sally.

"Hang on!" Megan said, grinning. "There's more!
Roses are red;
Violets are blue.
What are you doing
Living with Sue?
And what about
Petrol's refined

*But oil is crude.
My loved one's from Wilmslow
And he's a real dude!"*

Jen was giggling too now. "How do you make things up so quickly?" she gasped.

Megan shrugged. She just could; that was all.

Half an hour later, the card was finished. Sally wrote Ted's name on the envelope, adding a 'care of Sue Green, Room G31,' and then she and Megan scampered over to the pigeon holes in Reception and placed it under 'G'.

Sally was a revelation tonight, Megan thought as they made their way back towards their own rooms. She often came across as disapproving – or, at least, disapproving of Megan, but this evening she had been fun. Sue had better appreciate her card after they'd been to all this trouble!

The following morning, Megan, Jen and Sally made a big deal out of stopping by the pigeon holes on their way to breakfast with Sue. "I need to see if Phil's sent me a card," Jen explained.

There was indeed a card in Jen's pigeonhole – and there were two in Megan's. She examined the envelopes cautiously. Would one be from Mike? She'd studiously avoided him ever since the 'Elastic Evening', as Sally had christened it; but had he been thinking of her? She thought she recognised Matt's handwriting on the fatter of the envelopes: she would open that later, in the sanctuary of her room. She didn't know who had sent the other one, but she didn't think it was Mike's writing.

"Hurry up!" Sue's voice echoed crossly across the hallway. "I don't want to miss the scrambled eggs!"

"Did I see you taking a card out of your pigeonhole?" Sally asked her, with a straight face.

Sue frowned. "It seems I've been ousted by my own teddy bear!" she said frostily. The others exchanged worried looks.

"I thought she'd see the funny side of it!" Jen hissed. "I hope Ged's got her a decent card, because otherwise his life won't be worth living!"

Alas, when Ged appeared at the breakfast table moments later, neither card nor present was visible. Irritation radiated from Sue: she was not happy.

"Who were your cards from?" Sally asked Megan, hoping to change the subject.

At the mention of cards, Sue looked thunderously at Ged, who hung his head in shame.

Megan hastily pushed Matt's card under her plate. It was the last thing she wanted to open in front of the others. She and Matt had been getting on so well ... Why did he have to spoil it by sending her a Valentine?

Instead, she carefully unsealed the flap on the unknown envelope. Inside was a fairly inoffensive card – no extreme declarations of love: just a cartoon drawing of a cat dressed as a medieval lady and another, wearing armour, presenting her with a posy of flowers. The unfamiliar handwriting declared, *"I've seen pretty maidens everywhere*

But never has been on so fair."

"Well, whoever it is, he can't spell for a start," Sue commented sniffily. "He's missed the 'e' off the end of 'one'."

"Definitely not an English student!" Jen agreed, winking at Sally.

Megan caught the wink and wondered whether the two of them were responsible for the card. She never did find out who had sent it, having forgotten totally about Big Ron and his clumsy chat up line at the Freshers Formal.

*

Back in her room, Megan opened the other card. As she had thought, it was from Matt. He hadn't bothered to disguise his handwriting.

The card was reasonably tasteful: rows and rows of small pink hearts, with one, much bigger, embossed in gold in the centre of the card. The caption read, "You're one in a million." Inside, Matt had printed neatly,
"*Did my heart love till now? Foreswear it, sight,*
For I ne'er saw true beauty till this night."
and enclosed a tiny hard backed copy of Shakespeare's sonnets.

Megan stared at the card and the gift. If only it had been Mike and not Matt who had written those words!

A tap on her door made her jump. She opened it to find Jen standing there, looking at her expectantly.

"Well?"

"Well what?" Megan asked foolishly.

"Who were your cards from?" Jen wanted to know.

Wordlessly, Megan pushed Matt's card towards Jen. The other girl read it, her eyes widening. "I wish I had someone to quote lines out of Romeo and Juliet to me! Phil wrote Genesis lyrics in my card – it's hardly the same thing."

"But at least it's a card from someone you love," Megan said softly. She looked up at Jen. "That's Matt's handwriting. And he sent me this." She showed her friend the book of sonnets.

Jen whistled softly. "Whatever you do, don't show either of those to Sally. She's still got a thing for Matt herself."

Megan felt a tightening around her chest. Why did so many people have to suffer unrequited love? She felt a genuine empathy for Sally: after all, both of them yearned for men whose affections were otherwise engaged.

"I haven't encouraged him," she said in a small voice.

But she hadn't discouraged him either, she thought now, remembering the conversations they'd shared before and after lectures, the beverages they'd been for in the Mason Lounge (so much nicer than the ones in the Muirhead Tower coffee bar), the couple of occasions where they'd shared a pizza for lunch.

"Have you told him it will never happen between the two of you?" Jen's gaze met hers, challenging. "Because if you haven't, you need to do it straight away. It's not fair to keep him dangling on a string while you make your mind up."

Again, that tight feeling in her chest. She didn't want to go out with Matt; but she didn't want to lose his friendship either. Was she just using him, until something better came along?

"I've got Anglo Saxon." Jen turned to go. "Phil's taking me out tonight, for a romantic meal, but I'll pop in and see you before I go. You need to do something about Matt before he ends up getting hurt."

She was gone before Megan could tell her that she was hurting too.

*

The number of people staying in Hall for the usual Friday fish and chips (or Vegetable Gratin if you'd signed up for the non-meat option) was seriously depleted thanks to Valentine's Day. Megan, Matt and Sally grabbed a table together, then cast around hopelessly for conversation. The atmosphere was definitely strained without the others.

"I'm assuming Sue forgave Ged in the end since they're not here now?" Sally addressed her question to Megan, fishing for gossip.

Megan grinned. "He turned up at her door earlier with seven Valentines cards and a box of cakes. She wasn't going to say no to éclairs and doughnuts!"

"She's got him wrapped around her little finger, hasn't she?" Sally commented. "What do you think, Matt?"

Matt was miles away, practising what he was going to say to Megan later on. He knew she must have received his card and present – he'd checked the pigeonholes to make sure – but so far she hadn't mentioned anything. He was planning on going to her room a little earlier than they usually left for the bar, so he could talk to her on his own and tell her how he felt.

"Matt!" Sally's voice interrupted his daydreams. "Don't you think Sue's got Ged under her thumb?"

"They seem very happy together," Matt said neutrally, debating what to do if Megan said yes. Maybe she would hold his hand when they walked to Choir, or let him put his arm round her in the bar. He took a forkful of Cod Mornay and chewed it speculatively.

Sally was multi-tasking, watching Matt taste his food whilst she ate her own. She knew he was still infatuated with Megan: you could read it all over his face, from the way his eyes never left her to the nervous subconscious gestures he made whenever she spoke to him.

It wasn't reciprocated though: in fact, she had a strong suspicion that Megan was still harbouring a crush on Mike. Their paths never crossed but unspoken longing followed Megan like a slug trail. She wouldn't look twice at Matt as long as that sexist pig was in her head.

For a while they ate in silence. The main course was followed by jam roly poly or fruit salad. Sally noticed that Megan had chosen the fruit option but was toying with it listlessly. There must be something on her mind.

*

At last all the plates and dishes were clear. Sally was the first to stand up. "Same time as usual for the bar tonight?" They both nodded. "I'll see you at nine then." She hurried off, wondering if she had time for a quick run round The Vale before socialising.

Matt and Megan looked at each other awkwardly. Both had something important to say, but the High/Ridge dining hall was not the place to say it.

Megan spoke first. "Do you want to come to my room for a coffee?"

Matt needed no second invitation. He followed her out of the dining room, rehearsing his speech every step of the way.

They reached G30 and Megan unlocked the door. Matt noticed that his card and present, both unwrapped, were on Megan's desk, along with another Valentine. The sight of the latter made his heart contract. Had Mike sent her a card as well?

Megan must have noticed his discomfort because she gestured at the rival card and laughed. "I don't know *who* sent me that!" she uttered, adding, a moment later, "It's not Mike's writing, if that's what you were wondering."

Since she had brought up Mike, Matt decided to be bold. "He doesn't love you. He's only after one thing."

The gaze she turned on him was devoid of self-pity. "I know that. And I haven't seen him for weeks – but that's because I've chosen not to. I've made myself avoid him."

She turned her back on him and fiddled with the kettle. "Tea or coffee?" It was amazing how calm her voice sounded in her own ears.

"Tea, please." He felt elated and nervous at the same time. If Mike were no longer a serious rival …

Megan found the teabags and placed one in each mug, She was aware that her hands were trembling slightly but she didn't think Matt would notice. "I'm just grabbing my milk." She hurried to the kitchen, glad of the excuse to postpone the fateful moment.

When she returned, Matt was holding the Sade tape she'd lent him. He startled guiltily. "I … this is yours. Thanks for lending it to me." His gaucherie was almost endearing.

"What did you think?"

Matt hesitated. "I really liked one of the songs. It made me think of you. Can I play it?"

She indicated her radio cassette player and he ejected the tape that was currently inside – one of Mahler's symphonies – and inserted Jen's home made one. As he pressed 'play', the familiar tones filled her room:

> "*Is it a crime*
> *That I still want you?*
> *And I want you to want me too* ..."

The irony pierced her soul.

The song was over. Matt touched the 'stop' button, his heart beating fast. She *must* know how he felt by now.

Megan handed him his cup of tea, indicating the easy chair. He sank down into it whilst she perched on the bed, staring into her mug as if expecting to find the words she needed floating on the surface.

"Why did you send me a Valentine's card? And a present?"

Her directness floored him.

"You must have realised I like you," he said at last.

"I like you too, Matt. You're one of my best friends at University."

She was choosing her words carefully, trying to let him down gently. He stared at his tea, a dull ache forming in the pit of his stomach.

He tried again. "I want us to be more than friends."

For a while she said nothing. He was aware of doors opening and closing in the corridor outside, of a cacophony of footsteps and voices forming a backing track to the beating of his heart.

"Where do you see this going, Matt?" She sounded weary.

He wasn't sure what she meant.

"What do you actually want? Because I think it's infatuation, not love." There, she had actually said it. "You don't really know me, do you? Only in a very superficial way."

"I …" Matt didn't know how to reply, never having got beyond the fantasy of declaring his love for her.

"I think about the two of us sharing our lives together," he said slowly. "Marriage. Children. Grandchildren."

It was true. He wanted all that with Megan. He pictured himself growing old with her, still as much in love with her when her hair had turned silver as he was now. He *needed* her. Why couldn't she see that?

The feeling of discomfort grew inside Megan. This intensity frightened her: it was too much.

"You've never even kissed me!" she burst out, a moment later. "You're talking about marrying me, but we're not even going out! That's not how it works, Matt."

More awkward and uncomfortable silence. In the minutes that followed, Megan thought, fleetingly, of Mike. She had to let go of him, she knew that now: her longing for him was as ridiculous as Matt's wanting to be with her.

Was Matt *really* being so ridiculous? she asked herself in a small voice. Would she have felt so discombobulated had it been Mike sending her a card and present for Valentine's Day, or Mike sitting in her room, telling her he wanted to spend the rest of his life with her?

Mentally, she weighed the two men against each other. They were both good looking, although Mike had the edge when it came to raw sexuality. Even now, her stomach flipped when she thought of him. In all other aspects, rationality told her that Matt was the better choice: there was a genuine friendship there, unlike Mike's casual attitude towards her. Matt constantly sat with her for lectures, went with her for lunch or coffee; whereas Mike never acknowledged her on campus, had only spoken to her once at the end of a French lecture when he wanted her to do something for him.

She continued her ruthless appraisal. Matt had sent her a birthday card, a Christmas card, a Valentine's card. He had written to her over the Christmas holiday. He had listened to her telling him about her A level English lessons and had bought her a copy of Shakespeare's sonnets because he knew how much she'd enjoyed studying them. Mike had written her one note, on a scrappy bit of paper that he'd shoved inside an old book of his own, not thinking she warranted a brand-new copy.

That's not fair, her heart whispered, remembering the note: *'I was going to buy you your own copy, but the campus bookshop didn't have it in stock.'*

But one note, one gift that was really a loan, couldn't tip the scales in Mike's favour. He would never be hers; whereas Matt …

Trying to ignore the pain her heart, she pushed away her memories of Mike, fixed a smile on her face and looked up at Matt.

"I'll think about it," she said.

Chapter Twenty-Four

With only three more weeks to go before the end of term, choir rehearsals were at a fever pitch. In addition to the usual Tuesday evening slots, there were extra practices on Wednesday and Friday lunchtimes too. Sue grumbled about having to miss Popmobility, but she still made every rehearsal.

"We haven't even got three whole weeks," she fussed when the new schedule was given out. "We're performing on the fifth of March, so that's three Tuesdays and two Wednesdays and Fridays."

Megan found the Wednesday rehearsal the most challenging, squeezing it in to a day already packed with lectures and tutorials at nine, eleven and twelve. Sue had a two o'clock but was free before rehearsal, so she and Ged ate a sandwich together at twelve whilst Matt kept Megan company over a late lunch after their practice.

"You and Matt seem to be getting on well these days," Jen remarked casually in the second week of full-on rehearsals. She and Megan had gone for a post-ten o'clock lecture coffee and were sitting in the Mason Lounge, eating Custard Creams and drinking milky coffee.

Megan sighed. "I'm trying to make myself fall for him, but he worships me so much: it's really off-putting."

"Courtly love," was Jen's instant reply.

"Pardon?"

"Didn't you ever read *'Morte d'Arthur'*?" Jen asked, amazed. "It's in Chaucer too, in *'The Knight's Tale'*. It's when a knight or another noble young man falls for a lady he knows he can never have and puts her on a pedestal, like Matt seems to have done with you."

Now Jen mentioned it, it was beginning to seem familiar to Megan. She was sure one of her A level English teachers had talked about courtly love in relation to Shakespeare's sonnets. It was meant to be an idealised, unrequited love, in which the man fell for an unattainable lady, expressed his attraction for her in ballads or poems, was rejected by her - so far, this all sounded suspiciously like Matt – renewed his protestations of faithfulness, threatened to die from unsatisfied love, and finally won the lady's heart with his heroic acts. She couldn't imagine Matt in the latter role and said so to Jen.

"Hmmm. Well, it doesn't quite fit, but it's close enough. Technically, you should be married to someone else to make you completely out of reach, but I don't think we need to go that far!" Jen quipped.

"Do the *'carpe diem'* poems link in with this?" Megan asked next.

Jen looked thoughtful. "Like Marvell's 'To His Coy Mistress'? You know the one:
"Had we but world enough and time
This coyness, Lady, were no crime."
Except, in your case, it's *'To Her Coy Matthew'*!"

"Coy's the right word where Matt's concerned," Megan agreed. "I think that's one of the reasons I don't feel attracted to him in that way: he's never tried anything on with me, despite being madly in love with me."

"Do you want him to leap on you, then?" Jen was puzzled.

"Not exactly. But I can't help thinking that if there was some sort of spark, I might give him a chance. For all I know, he could be an amazing kisser, but I'll never find out unless he gives it a go."

"You could always make the first move, you know," Jen said idly.

Megan paused. "I *could* ... But I'd far rather it was him." Her tone became wistful. "The first time Mike kissed me, I saw blue sparks. But we both knew there was some kind of attraction long before that: we just looked at each other and knew."

"I think you're romanticising it too much." Jen decided to be blunt. "What happened with you and Mike was ... well, chemistry, for want of a better word. But that's not enough to build a relationship on. You have to be friends too." She looked intently at Megan. "What you've got with Matt could turn into something else. But you'll never know unless you let go of Mike."

"I haven't seen him for ages," Megan muttered defiantly.

"Maybe not, but you still haven't let go of him." Jen wondered if she should pass on Phil's suggestion. "Do you think it would be easier to forget about him if you got him out of your system properly?"

Megan looked at her warily. "What do you mean?"

"If you slept with him." Jen's tone was deliberately casual, but her facial expression told Megan that her friend was aware she might have overstepped the mark.

For a moment neither of them said anything; then, "You know I'm not like that." Megan's cheeks flamed with embarrassment: not merely at Jen's proposal but because part of her thought that sounded like a very good idea.

"Well maybe you *should* be like that," Jen said softly, "because even the medieval ladies gave in to their desires eventually. What you've done is put sex on a pedestal so it becomes this unattainable thing you long for but can't have. You've put a whole new spin on courtly love, but it's not making anyone happy."

Megan rose to her feet. "I need to go," she said abruptly.

"Running away from it isn't going to solve anything."

"No," Megan agreed, "but it does give me time to think. Anyway," she gave a rueful grin, "I've got a book due back in Short Loan. While I'm at the library, I'll look up courtly love and see if any of the critics have an answer."

*

The University library did indeed have a number of volumes on the subject of love. Scanning through the card index, Megan discovered a copy of Denis de Rougement's *'L'Amour et l'Occident'* – she recognised the author's name but couldn't remember why - along with C S Lewis's *'The Four Loves'* and *'The Allegory of Love'*. There was an English translation of the de Rougement, but in the end she plumped for the C S Lewis because she'd enjoyed the Narnia stories as a child.

Sitting in one of the stacks, jotting down notes and relevant quotations, Megan found herself enjoying her self-imposed research. What fun it would be to do an MA specialising in all of this, she thought to herself, busily scribbling away. For a moment, she pictured herself three or four years into the future, sitting at her desk whilst she added the final touches to her Masters thesis, Mike standing behind her, massaging her neck and shoulders.

She came to herself with a jolt. She was supposed to be getting rid of her feelings for Mike, not indulging them. She returned to her studying, trying to concentrate on the academic aspect of love, not its physical expression, so intent on what she was doing that it was with a sense of annoyance that she had to pack away her pens and notepad so she could make it back to Hall in time for an early evening meal before Choir Practice.

*

Mindful of her conversation with Jen, Megan was trying extra hard to manoeuvre Matt into making a move on her, deliberately stumbling as they walked through the Vale on their way to the School of Music, in the hopes that some sort of spark would be ignited as he caught hold of her. When she only succeeded in pushing Matt into a tree (he seemed even less co-ordinated than she was), she realised she would have to be less subtle, so she tried dropping her sheet music in front of him, reaching for it at the same time he did. Their fingers touched but her knees remained decidedly unweak: her body just didn't respond to him, she thought sadly.

Walking back, later, she thought of another ploy. "Why don't you come in for a coffee when we get back," she suggested.

Matt's face lit up. An invitiation to Megan's room was always a treat as far as he was concerned. Ever since declaring his love for her on Valentine's Day, he'd tried hard to give her space, hoping she would appreciate his self-control in not pushing her for an answer. Tonight had been decidedly awkward when she'd clumsily fallen over and then dropped her music: it had been all he could do to stop himself catching her in his arms and gently kissing her before he set her on her feet again, like he so often did in his fantasies. (Although in reality he would probably have dropped her: his limbs seemed to stop working properly when Megan was around.)

Once they reached Ridge, Matt followed Megan along the Ground Floor corridor to her room. It was almost ten – too late to join the others in the bar, although Sue had shot off as soon as they were back so she could say goodnight to Ged. Megan closed the door behind them both and flashed Matt what she hoped was a sultry smile.

"It's much cosier without the others."

Matt nodded, his heartbeat quickening from the mere proximity of her. Would he ever be able to sit next to her without his palms sweating?

"What can I get you to drink? Tea? Coffee? Or would you prefer something stronger?" She produced a bottle of wine with a flourish.

Megan had never bought a bottle of wine before in her life – she'd had no reason to. Now, however, with Operation Seduction underway, she had popped into the off-licence near campus and purchased a cheap bottle of wine. (No point in wasting money on anything expensive.) She hoped Matt liked Lambrusco.

As a matter of fact, Matt only drank red wine, but he didn't have the heart to hurt Megan's feelings. Instead he smiled politely and accepted a mug of the sweet and fizzy white liquid. He drank it down quickly, trying to ignore the taste. Megan watched him nervously: would alcohol put him in the mood? Perhaps she should try some herself? She sat down next to him on the bed.

"Only a week to go." Matt's voice sounded nervous. She wondered why.

"Yes," she agreed hastily. "It doesn't seem real, does it? Performing for a massive crowd next week, I mean." She paused. "I'll miss our lunches together after rehearsals," she said in what she hoped was a flirtatious manner.

"We can still have lunch together …" Matt wasn't looking at her. It was almost as if he expected her to laugh at his proposal.

"Yes, I'd like that." She inched closer towards him, until her shoulder was touching his.

He made an almost imperceptible move away from her. She moved closer again.

292

"Megan ..." This time there was a definite note of panic in Matt's voice. She seemed to be pursuing him, but was he reading too much into it? What if he tried to kiss her and then she slapped his face?

She took another sip from her own mug, allowing the Lambrusco to blur her senses. She'd kissed Dan and Mike whilst under the influence; surely feeling tipsy now would help her to relax with Matt?

"Do you want to kiss me?"

No, he definitely *wasn't* reading too much into it.

He moved his mouth towards hers, clumsy with anxiety. Pressing his lips against her own, he pecked hastily, before she could change her mind.

Megan knew she was slightly drunk, but she was still sufficiently alert to feel profoundly disappointed by Matt's abysmal attempt at kissing. She knew he'd never had a girlfriend before, but surely kissing was something innate? After all, she'd had no experience before Dave, but her mouth had opened instinctively to his. Matt seemed to have no idea what he was doing.

Pushing him away, she stood up. "I'm sorry," she said with dignity. "I shouldn't have thrown myself at you like that."

Matt had never known such overwhelming despair. To think that he'd actually been kissing Megan, and now it was all over! Embarrassment flooded his body as he rose to his feet too. Was there a book somewhere, he wondered, which told one what to do in a situation such as this? Tongue-tied with mortification, all he could do was stammer, "I'm sorry too," before making a hasty exit back to High Hall.

*

After he had gone, Megan sat sipping her wine, wishing she could replay the evening. She liked Matt, wished she could fall in love with him, but that spark just wasn't there. It had been a mistake to try to force it.

She finished her mug of Lambrusco and reached for the bottle again. This stuff was rather nice. She might as well have some more.

By the time she reached her third mugful, she knew clearly what she had to do. She would go to see Matt in his room in High and show him how to kiss properly. The poor boy! she thought with affection. How would he ever learn unless someone showed him the right way?

She checked her alarm clock: it was either twenty to eleven or ten to eight. Either way, it wasn't too late for a visit. She swayed slightly as she stood up, but she didn't care. She would be able to sit down again once she reached Matt's room.

She decided to see if the internal doors in the bar were still unlocked. They were. Good. Her head felt a bit peculiar though.

Somehow she managed to stagger as far as the High foyer without passing out. She stared at the lift for several minutes, thinking it was taking a long time to arrive, before realising that she hadn't called it yet. Pressing the button on the wall, she sank down on the floor for a rest while she waited.

She was still sitting there when Mike came in ten minutes later from the pub. He had taken to avoiding the Hall Bar recently: it was the most effective way to stop thinking about Megan. Now, seeing her sitting beside an empty lift, he wondered if she was waiting for him. His resolve weakened.

"Mike." She gave him a crooked smile. "I don't feel very well."

"Were you looking for me?"

She shook her head slowly. "Matt kissed me tonight and it was terrible. But then, after he'd gone, I realised he doesn't know how to kiss girls. They only had boys at his school and I'm sure he didn't kiss any of them."

She was pissed, he thought with amusement: utterly and adorably pissed.

"What have you been drinking, Sweetheart?" He pulled her to her feet gently.

"Only white wine – the fizzy stuff in the bottle." She gave him a furtive look. "I was trying to seduce Matt, but it didn't really work."

"Matt?" Mike tried to keep his voice casual, telling himself he didn't care if Megan got off with someone else.

"You know, I sit with him in French." She giggled. "He's got a massive crush on me. I keep trying to fall in love with him, but it's not working."

"Let's get you back to your room." He began to steer her back towards the corridor and the empty bar. "Why are you trying to fall in love with Matt?" he asked her.

She stopped walking and looked up at him. "So I can stop being in love with you."

For a moment, everything stilled. Then, "You're not in love with me," Mike said automatically.

She looked at him petulantly. "That's what Jen says. She thinks it's just chemistry."

There was certainly plenty of that between them tonight. Despite Megan's inebriated condition and the fact he'd had five pints himself, she was still having a remarkable effect on him.

"That's because I told her and Sally how sexy I feel after I've been snogging you," she told him artlessly. "But it's not just physical: we've got an intellectual whatsit like Jude and Sue."

He was about to ask who Jude and Sue were when he remembered. He'd read that book over Christmas because of her.

"Whatever it is, you know it's not going anywhere," he said bluntly. He wasn't about to tell her how much he wished it *could* go somewhere. "Come on!" He made her start moving again. "We've got to get back to your room."

She was silent for the rest of the journey: brooding. From time to time, Mike stole a quick look at her out of the corner of his eye. Her hair was dishevelled and she was definitely the worse for alcohol, but she was still the sexiest girl he'd ever known.

They had reached the end of her corridor. Megan fumbled in her jeans pocket for her key. "Ssshhh!" she admonished him, putting a finger to her lips. He put the key in the lock and turned it for her.

"You'd better get some sleep," he told her, propelling her inside. "Don't you have a nine o'clock French lecture tomorrow morning?"

She gave him a withering look. "Phonetics finished in December. There was a test when we came back in January."

"Well, I only went to the first one or two lectures," Mike said cheerfully. "Nine's a bit early for me. What have I missed this term?"

"*I* have been having a class with the Lectrice," Megan told him. "What *you* should have been doing, I have no idea." She tried to look severe and failed.

Mike kissed her nose. "You can't do angry, can you? You just end up looking cute."

Without waiting for an answer, he kissed her on the mouth. It was everything that had been missing in her kiss with Matt. She closed her eyes and let the pleasurable sensation wash over her, then began to kiss him back, allowing his tongue to probe the inside of her mouth while her own teased his.

"You should give a seminar paper on French kissing," she heard herself say a moment later; followed by, "Is there such a thing as German kissing?"

He never got the chance to reply, suddenly finding the room full of other people: Megan's disapproving friend from his German lectures and the other two girls she hung about with were gazing at him with hostile looks.

"You left the door open," Sally said coldly.

"Just as well she did." That was Jen. "Megan!" She made her voice sound stern. "We've talked about this, remember?"

"I was just keeping an eye on her," Mike said hurriedly. "I found her in High about ten minutes ago, looking for that guy she sits with in French. She seemed a bit out of it, so I walked her back."

"And gave her mouth to mouth as well," Sue commented drily. "What an upstanding citizen you are!"

The other girls closed ranks around Megan, who felt decidedly put out. "I'm not drunk!" she muttered defiantly, and promptly passed out on the bed.

*

Megan awoke the next morning with a killer headache. When she knocked on Jen's and Sally's door to see if they had any paracetamol, she was met with a frosty reception.

"It's your own fault!" Sally was never one to mince words. "You drank too much wine and made a fool of yourself with Mike. I dread to think what would have happened if we hadn't heard the noise you were making and come to investigate!"

Megan was tempted to point out that the others hadn't actually done anything to protect her virtue. She had managed that very nicely herself, thank you very much, by collapsing in a drunken stupor before anything interesting could happen! However, she thought it wise to say nothing.

"I know you didn't go to High to look for Mike," Jen said, a little more gently, "but you shouldn't go wandering off like that on your own after you've been drinking. Anything could happen."

"I didn't drink a lot," Megan said in a small voice.

"No, but you don't have to." Jen sighed. "You're only little. You should know by now that it goes straight to your head.

Megan wondered privately if her father had been wrong and she was a closet alcoholic after all.

"Why were you looking for Matt anyway?" asked Sally suspiciously. "Didn't you spend most of the evening at Choir Practice together?"

It was a constant sorrow to Sally that she was tone deaf and thus unable to be in the choir with Matt.

Megan hesitated. "I was just returning a tape he'd lent me," she said at last. "He wanted me to listen to some songs and see if they were any good for the Hall discos."

It wasn't *really* a lie: Matt had recently given her a tape he'd made for her, although she hadn't listened to it yet. She had a feeling Phil Collins and Alison Moyet would both feature strongly in the compilation.

*

Eventually Jen took pity on Megan and gave her some headache tablets. At least Mike had walked Megan back to her room safely, she thought as she cleaned her teeth. Some men would have just had their wicked way with her in High and not bothered about what happened to her afterwards. She still didn't trust Mike – he was disturbingly attractive, for one thing – but she was beginning to accept that he might have been acting in Megan's best interests last night.

She still wasn't sure whether she should be trying to push Matt and Megan together, or whether she should back off and see what, if anything, developed naturally. Sally still liked Matt – she had a thing for boys with good teeth and nice manners; if Megan ever decided Matt was worth looking at, Sally would be crushed.

She'd thought that inviting an assortment of carefully vetted men back to their room might have resulted in a suitable partner for Megan – or Sally; but it hadn't worked. She might have carried on trying past the first week had Phil not taken her aside and told her that he had stood for Video Rep with the sole purpose of being able to spend nights in his room with his girlfriend, watching films together. She wasn't going to sacrifice her own love life for the sake of Megan's, so she and Sally had agreed that their party idea wasn't working and instead she'd started going back to Phil's room some nights after the bar. They never seemed to get beyond the first ten or fifteen minutes of the film before things started getting interesting between them …

Gritting her teeth before the tablets kicked in, Megan dragged herself to breakfast and managed to make it to her early morning French conversation class. She was glad that there were five of them who saw Fabienne at the same time because her brain wasn't up to speed this morning.
"Elle a une gueule de bois!" Heather told the lectrice.
Megan wondered what her friend was talking about – although saying she had a wooden mouth seemed a pretty accurate description of how she felt right now.

As she began to sober up gradually, bits and pieces of the previous evening danced before her. Had she *really* come on to Matt? And told Mike she was in love with him?
She wanted to bury her head in her hands in shame; instead, she forced herself to join in with a conversation about French cinema, feeling grateful that she'd once caught Truffaut's *'Jules et Jim'* on BBC2 and could falteringly string together a few sentences about that.

Heather was much more sympathetic than Jen and Sally had been. "The French for 'I've got a hangover' is one of the first things I learned to say in the autumn term!" she laughed once their lesson was over. "Come on – let's get a coffee and you'll feel much better."

This seemed like a good idea to Megan, conscious as she was that she had a Language tutorial in an hour. She didn't protest when Heather led the way to the First Floor Coffee Bar rather than the Mason Lounge in the Arts Faculty; and then she saw Mike, drinking coffee and smoking a cigarette, and her heart stopped.

He was on his own. She scanned the room for signs of Rose but couldn't see the other girl. He looked up and caught her eye. She turned away in embarrassment.

Heather, not always the most observant of people, had also spotted Mike. She had quite a crush on him herself and whatever had been going on with him and Megan before Christmas had obviously fizzled out (Megan never talked about him these days), so she grabbed her coffee and made a beeline for the table where he was sitting.

Megan followed, mentally cursing her friend. As they sat down, Mike grinned at her. "How's your head? You were well out of it last night!"

"Were the two of you out together?" Heather felt irrationally jealous.

Mike took another drag on his cigarette. "Nah. I bumped into her when I came back from the pub and walked her home."

He caught her eye again and Megan blushed.

Even Heather couldn't fail to notice a certain tension between these two. Had they slept together last night? Megan certainly seemed embarrassed about something.

An awkward silence; then, "How's your girlfriend?" Megan asked sweetly.

"She's okay." As a matter of fact, Mike had no idea how Amanda was at the moment. She hadn't written or rung for three weeks. He had a feeling she was seeing that bloke again, the one she'd slept with in the previous term.

As Heather got up to look for some sugar, Mike leaned across to Megan. "It's complicated with Amanda and me."

"Is that a variation on the old 'My wife doesn't understand me' line?"

She'd kissed him last night, but she wasn't going to do it again. She wouldn't steal another woman's boyfriend. Not anymore.

She stood up slowly. "Heather can keep you company. I'm going to the library."

*

She didn't go to the library. Instead, she walked around campus, breathing in the fresh air, trying to clear her head. Spending time with Matt wasn't having the desired effect: she still wanted Mike just as much as she had done the first time they kissed, before she knew she was poaching on another woman's territory.

And was it really fair on Matt to build his hopes up when it was never going to go anywhere? She'd tried so hard last night, but his kisses had left her cold.

Speak of the devil: there was Matt now, head down, hurrying out of the campus bookshop. He almost walked into her.

"Matt!" She couldn't pretend she hadn't seen him.

"Megan." His tone was guarded. Was he thinking about last night?

"I'm glad I've seen you." She decided to make the first move. "I wanted to apologise for my outrageous behaviour after Choir yesterday."

"I ... no ... you didn't do anything wrong," Matt blurted out. "I was very flattered," he added politely.

"If you don't want to go for lunch after the rehearsal today, I'll understand." She was giving him an opt out clause; would he take it.

Matt panicked slightly. Was she afraid he'd try to kiss her again?

"I promise I'll behave," he said solemnly.

They both began heading back to the Muirhead Tower. "French Language tutorial?" she asked.

He nodded. "I find the Language much easier than the Lit. I've been struggling with some of the poetry recently: what on earth are we supposed to write about it?"

Megan was at a loss for words. She had enjoyed Baudelaire's *'Les Fleurs du mal'*, even though some of the poems were somewhat erotic, and she loved Verlaine's poetry too, although she could take or leave Rimbaud. "It's all decadence and indolence, isn't it?" she said shyly. "Verlaine and Rimbaud were like Byron, only about fifty years later. It's all sensuality and drugs."

"I don't know anything about Byron," Matt confessed as they reached the steps that led up to the tower.

He must have been a bit like Mike, Megan mused as they waited for the lift. What was that quotation from Lady Caroline Lamb? *'Mad, bad and dangerous to know'*: it summed up Mike to a tee.

They had reached the fourth floor. "I'll see you at one, then," she said quickly as they parted to go to their respective seminars.

His gaze followed her as she disappeared. He wondered if he would ever have the courage to kiss her again.

Chapter Twenty-Five

All too soon it was the last week of term. The Saint John Passion would be performed on the Wednesday evening. It seemed a lot of rehearsing for one performance.

Megan wasn't looking forward to the Easter holiday: five weeks at home with her parents. Her mother had written her a brief letter, telling her that John was moving in so they could "try living as a family once more." She hadn't mentioned this to Megan in any of the strained telephone conversations they'd had while she'd been back in Birmingham. Mind you, her mother wasn't exactly a chatty person at the best of times, so Megan wasn't going to read anything sinister into this. It would have been nice to have been consulted, though.

She and Jen had already made plans to meet up over the break. Jen had an aunt in Leeds and was going to stay with her for a few days. If Jen could persuade her parents to let her borrow their car, she would drive over to Littleborough to see Megan; if not, Megan would take the train to Leeds and the two of them would have a day out together. Either way, it would provide a welcome relief from watching her parents rekindle their relationship.

Things were still slightly strained with Matt. Megan knew it was her fault: she'd set her standards too high, expecting his kisses to be so much more. Mike had ruined her for anyone else, she thought angrily.

Meanwhile, Matt wasn't sure where he stood with Megan any more. Did she want a relationship with him or not? She hadn't asked him to kiss her again: was she expecting *him* to be the one to make the next first move?

Sue was worrying about her future with Ged. They would only have one more term together before she went off to France and Germany for her year abroad. Would he be faithful in her absence, she wondered; or would he find his head turned by Megan again – or by any other pretty face that caught his eye?

There was another extra rehearsal on the Monday evening. "That's three nights in a row you're abandoning me!" Ged complained when Sue announced the news at the breakfast table that morning.

She fixed him with a steely gaze. "Only two. You're coming along on Wednesday to hear me sing."

"We'll come and find you all in the bar afterwards," Megan promised hastily. "It should end by nine thirty, so if we walk back quickly we'll still have time for a final drink." (Anything to prevent Matt asking if he could come back for a coffee again.)

To cheer herself up, Megan hit the Guild at lunchtime on her own. There was some sort of clothing fair going on. She wandered happily amidst racks of floaty scarves and Indian dresses, fingering necklaces and trying on various hats before something special caught her eye. It was a tiny purple skirt, made from layered triangles almost like something a pixie would wear, she thought wonderingly. At the point of each inverted triangle was a small purple bead. Megan had never seen anything so perfect in her life.

The skirt was £4.99. It seemed an unnecessary extravagance so close to the end of term, but she didn't care.

Wandering back towards the Muirhead Tower for the final poetry lecture of the term, she spotted Mike, chatting to Rose as usual. She envied the other girl's easy friendship with Mike, wished that she could enjoy something like that herself.

Rose couldn't believe what Mike was telling her. "What? You mean you and Megan still haven't done the deed?"

Mike looked uncomfortable. "It's a bit complicated with Amanda," he began, but Rose cut him short.

"Rubbish! You haven't heard from Amanda in weeks – you said so yourself the other day. That means she's shacked up with that musician guy from before," - how clichéd of Amanda to fall for someone who was the bass player in a student band! - "only she hasn't got the guts to tell you about it. Anyway," as Mike opened his mouth to protest, "having a girlfriend's never stopped you in the past." She stopped walking, turning to face him, trying to read the expression in his eyes. "You haven't made a move because you're scared she'll turn you down. Doesn't that kill you, to think there might be a girl out there who can actually resist your charms?"

She wasn't to know that, before Amanda, every girl he'd met had managed to resist him. He hadn't reinvented himself at university: he'd become someone else, someone cool, once Amanda started going out with him. Not that he would ever tell Rose any of that. He might tell Megan one day, though. He had a feeling he could trust her.

Rose reached up and stroked his cheek mockingly. "Poor little Mike! Can't get the girl he wants."

In the distance, Megan watched the two of them. She was unprepared for the stab of jealousy she felt when she saw Rose touch Mike's face. *He'll never be yours!* she told herself savagely. But it didn't make the pain any easier.

*

Although it was the beginning of March, it was still fairly cold outside in the evenings. Megan picked up her new skirt then put it back on the bed regretfully. Common sense told her it was not the most appropriate outfit for a choir practice that involved sacred music. Besides, she would ruin her dainty Victorian ankle boots if she trod in any mud in the dark.

In the end, she stuck to jeans with her black, baggy jumper and sensible flat boots, allowing comfort to triumph over style. She was only seeing Matt and Sue for goodness' sake! Mind you, she had a feeling that Matt would be attracted to her even if she were wearing a bin liner.

Walking through the Vale with her two partners-in-song, Megan felt unbearably sad. She loved having so many things to do at University and having friends to do them with. At home she had Anita, but they seemed to have grown apart somehow since going in their separate directions to study. She had hardly seen her best friend at all over the four weeks of the Christmas holiday – although she suspected Joe might have something to do with that.

She and Anita had exchanged the odd letter this term – apparently Anita now had a Goth boyfriend who came from Leeds. Megan wondered if the two of them would end up catching the train together over Easter: her to see Jen at her auntie's house and Anita to spend an afternoon listening to The Sisters of Mercy whilst wearing dubious black eyeliner.

For her part, she'd written to tell Anita about the kissing fiasco with Matt, something she still hadn't mentioned to Jen. It seemed incestuous, somehow, to be telling Jen what Matt was like at kissing.

"When we come back after Easter, it'll be properly Spring." Matt volunteered the information, uncharacteristically talkative tonight.

"Some of the daffodils are out already," Sue reminded him.

"But when we come back in April, all the trees will be in blossom," Matt continued, almost as if to himself. "And didn't you say there are ducklings on the lake every year? It might be quite romantic for walks." He smiled shyly at Megan, who, at this moment in time, thought the idea sounded more irritating than anything else.

"There are goslings too," Sue agreed. "And last year a couple of swans came and nested. If you like nature-watching, there's plenty to see." She would have to make the most of it this year: next Spring she would be stuck on a French campus in Rouen, counting down the days until she could see Ged again. It really was tiresome that one had to spend a year abroad if one was doing a Languages degree.

Two hours later, the rehearsal was over. Glad that she wasn't a soloist, Megan fervently hoped that everyone's voice would last out until the end of the performance on Wednesday evening.

Climbing the slight hill back to High and Ridge, she wondered how the others had got on in the bar tonight. There had been a minor sensation in both halls the previous evening when Helen Appleyard, the girl Phil had pointed out to them in the first term, had streaked through the High/Ridge bar clad in only a towel. Several rumours abounded concerning her whereabouts after this, ranging from spending the night in the bath with the Treasurer of High Hall's JCR to seducing one of the post-graduate Floor Tutors, students a few years older than themselves who wangled a free place in Hall by promising to keep an eye on everyone else's antics.

As they arrived at the bar, Sue plonked herself onto Ged's knee and sat there proprietorially. "Give me alcohol!" she declared. "I'm parched!"

Ged looked enquiringly at Matt. "You may need to get these. I've got a lady in my lap."

"Of course." Matt hurried to the bar counter, pulling out several five pound notes.

"Now *that*," whispered Sally to Jen in a very audible aside, "is how to get someone else to pay for the next round of drinks!"

The evening was over. Phil looked at Jen. "Do you want to come back and see my etchings?"

"Mmmm." Jen pretended to consider the invitation. "That depends: would the etchings in question star Arnold Schwarzenegger?"

Matt turned to Megan. "Shall I walk you back to your door?" The eagerness in his tone suggested he was hoping to try kissing her again.

"I don't think so." She made her tone neutral, aware Sally was watching them. "I think between the three of us, Sue, Sally and I should be able to take care of ourselves."

"And don't forget wee Geddy," Sue broke in, squeezing her boyfriend's arm affectionately. "Years of rugby training should mean he can tackle any miscreants to the ground!"

If Ged looked slightly alarmed at this, everyone else was too polite to comment.

She didn't want him then. Matt felt deflated as he walked back to High, alone. He would try again tomorrow, and the next night; but if Megan still didn't show any definite signs of being interested, he would fix his attentions elsewhere the following term.

*

When Megan premiered her purple skirt at breakfast the following morning, Phil choked on his cereal. "You look like the kind of woman my mother told me to stay away from!"

"You're not wearing *that* to campus!" Sally sounded scandalised.

"Why not?" Megan was genuinely puzzled. She was wearing the skirt over thick, black tights to ensure her legs were adequately covered, so she couldn't see what all the fuss was about.

Jen bit her lip. Maybe on anyone else, the skirt wouldn't have looked so bad; but Megan's long, flowing hair, combined with the flimsy material and all those beads, somehow managed to suggest that she was a girl who wanted to misbehave.

"I think maybe it's not really appropriate for lectures," Jen said at last, looking to Sally to back her up.

Sally was looking at Megan with a curious mixture of disgust and envy. She would give anything to be so pretty and ethereal herself. No wonder men were always falling for Megan when she flitted about like Tinkerbell, fluttering her eyelashes and sprinkling them all with 'come hither' looks!

"You really don't have a clue, do you?" she said slowly.

"What?" Megan was still bewildered; Matt's eyes were out on stalks.

It was time she stopped wasting her energy on Matt, Sally told herself as she stumped back to her room, because she knew for a fact that he would never look at her the way he'd been gazing at Megan just now.

*

The School of Music was packed to the seams with the audience for the St John Passion. Ged had found a seat as close as he could to the front. He had a surprise for Sue: Ted nestled inside his jacket, wearing a black bow tie and looking very dapper. Ged was planning to take him out and wave his paw at Sue once she started singing.

As the orchestral intonation began, Megan was aware of a sick, nervous feeling in the pit of her stomach. She looked across at Matt, standing with the other tenors, and he gave her a reassuring smile. While the crescendo of notes merged into the chorus of "Herr, unser Herrscher", Megan lifted her voice and sang with the others, letting the music carry her beyond her disquietude. Somewhere in the second row, a little bear was waving his paw enthusiastically.

*

It was all over. Megan couldn't help a somewhat anti-climactic feeling filling her soul as they left the Music School for the last time that term and walked back to hall with Ged. The oratorio had been so beautiful, so inspiring that everything else now seemed flat by comparison. Perhaps that was why, when Matt turned to her in the Ridge foyer and asked if he could come for a coffee, she said yes.

Sue and Ged disappeared into the room next door together. Megan wanted what they had: that feeling of belonging together, of knowing instinctively how the other one felt. She looked at Matt and sighed. He was *nice*, but he always tried too hard.

"Tea? Coffee?" She wasn't offering him wine this time, even though she had a third of the bottle of Lambrusco left. It was currently hidden in her wardrobe, away from prying eyes.

"Tea, please." Matt seemed extra nervous tonight, beads of perspiration on his brow, a slight tremor in his hands.

For a moment she pitied him. His discomfort was almost engaging – almost, but not quite. She thought again, as she had so many times this term, of Mike and his cool self-assurance, of the way he'd kissed her time and time again without bothering to ask her permission first.

I can't do this! she thought in a panic. *I can't let Matt kiss me when I'm thinking of someone else.*

But, wherever he was, Mike was almost certainly *not* thinking of her. The memory of Rose, touching his face outside the Muirhead Tower, came unbidden into her mind and she hardened her heart. If Mike was getting intimate with someone else, why shouldn't she?

She poured hot water into two mugs, desperate for something to do, then realised she'd forgotten the teabags. Hastily popping them in and hoping Matt hadn't noticed, she tried to make polite conversation.

"It was a good performance, wasn't it? I think that's the best we've sung yet." Grabbing a teaspoon, she stirred each mug feverishly, trying to stretch seconds into minutes. "I'll just go and get my milk from the fridge." She was gabbling again, suddenly as nervous as Matt.

As she moved towards the door, Matt stopped her. "Megan," he began awkwardly, catching hold of her arm.

Instantly she froze, unsure of who should make the next move.

"Can I kiss you?" The words tumbled out in a rush, infused with uncertainty.

She nodded, a deer caught in headlights.

Very gently, Matt took hold of her shoulders, looking into her eyes. "I'm going to kiss you now." He was trying hard not to overwhelm her, needed to give her the chance to say no.

This time, it was a little less terrible than before. Matt still kept his mouth closed, but his movements weren't quite as staccato. Maybe, Megan thought miserably, he would improve with time and practice. Could she endure months of ineffectual kissing in the hopes that one day she would learn to enjoy it?

She noticed his eyes were closed. He was obviously concentrating hard. The idea made her feel terrible.

"Matt?" She pulled away slowly. "I really do need to get that milk." She escaped into the kitchen, yet she still felt totally trapped by Matt's infatuation with her.

The tea had been drunk. Megan and Matt sat in awkward silence, he on her bed, she on a chair. Neither of them knew what to say.

"Thank you." Ever the gentleman, Matt's manners prevailed. "For letting me kiss you again," he added. "It was a special moment."

She had slept all night in Mike's arms. "For what it's worth," he had told her, "that was incredibly special."

She would never be able to have a relationship with Matt until she had let go of Mike completely

*

Matt left a few minutes later. Megan was relieved to see him go: she was going to take Phil's advice and get Mike out of her system for good. First, though, she needed a drink to steady her nerves. She retrieved the Lambrusco from her wardrobe and swigged it from the bottle defiantly.

She also needed to change her clothes. The outfit she'd worn for the performance tonight wasn't the least bit seductive: the girls had all worn long black skirts and white blouses (Megan's smart skirt and her old school blouse – how lucky she'd needed it for her St Trinian's costume!) but that wasn't likely to get Mike's pulse racing.

Rummaging through the clothes in her wardrobe, she found the French maid's costume Jen had given her. She wouldn't wear the cap and apron, of course, but the little black dress would be perfect. Wriggling out of her choir attire, she pulled the dress over her head, finding to her alarm that it clung to every part of her. She needed black tights too, but they were all dirty: she had soiled her last pair when she stepped in a puddle on her way home from the concert tonight.

Okay, she would have bare legs then. She took another swig of wine, aware that she needed to finish the bottle if she were to lose her inhibitions enough for what she had planned.

A quick spray of Anaïs Anaïs, a hurried tour of her mouth with the toothbrush and she was ready. She slipped out of her room furtively, not wanting anyone to see her and talk her out of it.

Luck was on her side. Even so, she decided to go round the outside of the building rather than through the bar, just in case Jen and Sally were still there.

Reaching High's main entrance, she wondered, for a moment, if she was doing the right thing. If she wanted things to work out with Matt, why was she on her way to sleep with someone else?

Jen's voice echoed in her ears: *"You've put sex on a pedestal so it becomes this unattainable thing you long for but can't have."* Unless she slept with Mike, she would always wonder. And if she was always wondering how it would be with Mike, she wouldn't be able to concentrate on being with anyone else.

A few High Hallers who were making their way back from the bar seemed very pleased to see Megan in her skimpy outfit. One of them called out a few suggestions that made her blush: she wasn't quite sure what the words meant, but the intention was clear.

She was just debating the wisdom of stepping into a lift with four inebriated and rather horny strange men when another voice cut through the ribald comments. "If any of you touch her, I'll break your legs!"

Megan spun round to be confronted by Big Ron – happily without an axe. He nodded gravely to her. "I'll keep an eye on you. Don't you worry," his arrival so timely that Megan briefly wondered if he were really there at all. Perhaps she had drunk more than she thought?

"Floor Ten, please," she said breathlessly as they entered the lift. Ron punched the buttons, adding that he was on Floor Five but would see her safely to her boyfriend's room first. This small act of kindness touched her: she could easily have fallen for Ron had he seemed more intelligent.

Mike's room was ten-o-six. Ron waited with her until the door started to open before disappearing back into the lift. "Don't do anything I wouldn't!"

As the door opened fully, Megan realised she had caught Mike by surprise. He was dressed only in boxer shorts, wearing reading glasses and with a book in his hand. Once he saw Megan, he quickly grabbed a tee shirt and pulled it over his head. "These rooms get far too hot at night," he began; then, as his gaze took in what she was wearing, "Holy shit, Megan! Where on earth have you been?"

She'd been drinking again: he could smell it on her breath. She staggered slightly and clung to him for support.

"I was singing in a choir."

"Dressed like that?" Perhaps he should start taking an interest in choral music?

"No, silly." That dress really was alarmingly short, he thought. "I put this on for you. I want you to make love to me."

*

For a moment he thought he'd misheard; then, as her hand started stroking his arm, he realised she was serious. She was also very drunk.

"Megan, Sweetheart, you know I'd love to, but we'd both regret it in the morning."

He would probably kick himself later for turning her down, but she wasn't the kind of girl who went in for casual sex. Besides, he liked her too much to do that to her.

"Don't you find me attractive?" Her lip wobbled and he hoped she wasn't going to cry.

"Incredibly attractive," he said honestly. At the moment, painfully so. "But you'd hate yourself afterwards, Megan. We both would."

By way of response, she ran her finger down his chest, stopping just short of where things would have got interesting. "I need to get you out of my system, Mike." She looked up at him, her eyes slightly glazed by alcohol. "I can't enjoy kissing anyone else," she breathed, "because all I can do is think about kissing *you* – and about what happens after the kissing."

At that moment, there was nothing he wanted to do more than to pick her up, carry her over to the bed and let her try to get him out of her system. But he couldn't. She was too vulnerable; too drunk.

"It's not what you really want." He tried to let her down gently.

Standing on tiptoe, she pulled his face down towards her own and kissed him slowly, passionately.

It really wasn't a good idea, Mike told himself, kissing her back, lost as always in the intensity between them. But, after all, he was only human …

So, in the end, he decided to give her what she wanted.

Chapter Twenty-Six

Just as he was about to pick her up, carry her over to the bed and finally finish this thing between them, she pulled away from him, her face suddenly green.

"I'm going to be sick!"

There was no time to get her to the bathroom or even to the sink in his room; instead he thrust the metal waste bin at her. It wouldn't be the first time it had been used for this purpose.

She vomited, and the sound spattered on the metal. The moment had very definitely passed: desire had vanished.

He waited until she had finished heaving, holding her hair out of the way, then thrust a tissue at her. "Wipe your mouth."

She did as she was told.

Opening the drawer beside his bed, Mike pulled out a toothbrush, still in its plastic wrapper. "Clean your teeth. It'll help to get the taste out of your mouth."

He left her with brush and toothpaste while he went to empty the bin. Pouring the contents down the toilet bowl, he pondered the recent events. Perhaps it was just as well that nothing had happened: his feelings for Megan were confusing enough already without sex complicating the issue. The cleaner kept bleach in the end cubicle. He sloshed a generous measure of it into the bin, swirled it around and then rinsed several times with water. He'd take it back, just in case she needed it again.

When he returned, Megan was still pale but her breath was minty fresh. She looked mortified.

"I am *so* sorry …"

It must be the first time she'd thrown up in front of someone else. He tried to reassure her.

"Last term, I was sick in the washbasin. It clogged the plughole. I had to use the end of a coat hanger to unblock it."

"That's so *gross* ..." But her lip quirked as she said it.

"How are you feeling now?" he asked her next.

She hesitated. She didn't feel quite as fuzzy headed as she had before, but her mind was still slightly blurred.

"I think I need to lie down," she said in a small voice, realising as she did so that the room was swaying. Then, registering her outfit, "Jen's dress! Have I been sick on it?"

There was a small, almost imperceptible stain near the hem. "That should rinse out, no problem," Mike told her. "You should do it straight away, though."

She began to wriggle out of the clingy, black material, then stopped. "Close your eyes."

It was almost ridiculous how coy she was being now, considering she had come here to seduce him; nevertheless, he found it endearing.

Turning away from her, he did as she had asked. A moment later, "You can look now," she said.

Megan had slipped under his duvet, the bedcover protecting her modesty. With any other girl, he would have taken this as an invitation; with her, it was different. He felt strangely paternal towards her.

He took the dress from the end of the bed. "Do you want me to do it for you?"

She nodded. "I just need to close my eyes for a moment," she murmured.

Within seconds, she was fast asleep.

Mike gazed at the tiny figure in his bed. They'd slept in each other's arms before, but that was when Megan was much more adequately clothed. He wondered if he could manage to sleep in his chair.

As he rinsed the offending spot from the hem of Megan's dress, Mike contemplated his next course of action. He was tired of waiting for Amanda to end things: he would tell her it was over when he saw her at Easter, no matter how upset she appeared to be. Once he was a free agent, he would give things a proper go with Megan, see if whatever it was between them was more than just sexual attraction.

He placed the dress over his radiator and turned off the light, trying to make himself comfortable in his easy chair. It wasn't working. He altered his position and tried again, without success.

Eventually he gave up and lay down next to Megan, trying hard not to let his body come into contact with hers. The last thing he wanted was for her to think he'd tried anything on; then again, dressed in boxers and a tee shirt, he was far more decently dressed than she was, he thought, stealing a quick glance at her surprisingly lacy underwear. Desire flickered, but he quickly extinguished it. If there was to be any chance of him and Megan getting together, he had to do things properly now. Turning his back on her, he rolled onto his side and waited for sleep to overwhelm him.

Megan was having one of her recurring dreams about Mike, although this one seemed much tamer than normal. They were both still in their underwear, for one thing. She stretched out her hand and ran it down his chest. What was he doing, wearing a tee shirt in bed? Her hand slid under the material, savouring the lean, muscled hardness.

Mike opened his eyes slowly, aware that his body was tingling all over. Someone was running her hands all over him. For a moment he wondered whether he was awake or dreaming; then as Megan's hands moved lower, he decided he didn't care. Pulling her into him, he crushed her mouth with his own. Passion flamed between them.

This was definitely one of the best dreams Megan had ever had. Every touch was charged with sexual energy; every kiss an explosion of desire. Pretty soon, flesh met flesh, all clothing discarded. Her skin burned wherever Mike touched her.

"Megan! We need to stop." Mike made a half-hearted attempt to halt the inevitable journey, but she ignored him, intent on seeing this dream to its conclusion. She *had* to have him. Seconds later, they were moving as one, her hands gripping him tightly, almost urging him deeper; then she found herself falling into a whirlpool of pleasure, each dizzying sensation stronger than the one before, until he finally collapsed on top of her, his breath coming in short, ragged pants that echoed her own.

The room swam. Exhausted by love, they clung to each other, sleep quickly taking them both. For the next few hours, there was silence.

*

When Megan next awoke, she felt strangely disorientated. Her body ached in places she had been previously unaware of and her naked limbs were tangled with the bedclothes. Not just the bedclothes … She was waking up in Mike's arms, as she had done several times before, but this time it was different. The events of her dream came back to her with horrifying clarity as she realised what had happened: she had seduced Mike after all, waking him from his slumber to have her wicked way with him. She had acted like a cheap whore.

Mortified beyond belief, she slid away from him, carefully climbing over his sleeping form so she wouldn't wake him. She could never see him again, not after this. She would be too embarrassed ever to look him in the eyes again.

Grabbing her discarded underwear from the floor and her dress from the radiator, she hurriedly clothed herself, wondering what time it was. Mike's watch stood on the bedside cabinet, the hands pointing to quarter to six. Silently she stole towards the door, opening it noiselessly and closing it quietly behind her. What had she done? *What had she done?*

By the time she reached Ridge, she felt sick. She couldn't let Jen or anyone else know about this. She was too ashamed. Tapping on the door for Gordon to let her in, she knew that Phil had been right: sleeping with Mike had effectively ruined any chance of her ever wanting to see him again. She tried not to remember the exquisite sensation of feeling him inside her, the overwhelming delight that had rippled through her body as their love had reached its climax.

Love. What had happened between them wasn't love: it was mere physical desire, something that could have happened with anyone, given the right set of chemicals.

So why did the thought of never seeing him again fill her with despair?

*

Mike stirred some time after Megan had left. His first instinct was to reach out for her, to stroke her hair and tell her what last night had meant. She wasn't there. He gazed at the empty bed in confusion: had she ever been there at all?

The faint smell of bleach lingering in his bin told him that his memory was correct: Megan had come to see him last night, come onto him and then puked her guts out. He'd looked after her, put her to bed. And then ... And then she'd woken him up in the night to give him one of the most sexually intense experiences of his life. He grew hard just thinking about it.

It was only seven o'clock. He had plenty of time to think about Megan before he finally got up ...

*

Slipping inside her room as quietly as possible – the last thing she wanted to do was to attract her friends' attention – Megan peeled off her black dress and underwear, knowing she could never wear them again.

She quickly wrapped a towel around herself and headed for one of the shower rooms. Standing under the stream of hot water, she scrubbed her skin furiously, trying to erase her shame.

She couldn't face the others for breakfast. When Sue knocked on her door at eight o'clock, Megan opened it, clad in her nightshirt and clutching a hot water bottle. "You'll have to go without me. I don't feel well this morning."

She wasn't due on campus until ten: time to sneak into breakfast on her own later and eat in solitude, away from concerned yet prying faces. Not that she thought she could keep food down at the moment. She still felt sick to her stomach when she remembered what had happened.

A knock sounded at her door again at eight thirty. Megan ignored it. She couldn't talk to anyone right now.

Moments later, a folded piece of paper slid under her door. Megan waited for another ten minutes before retrieving it – just in case anyone was listening outside.

"*Dear Megan,*" the note read in small, neat handwriting, "*Sue said you are unwell this morning. I hope last night's performance didn't wear you out! Matt xx*"

She smiled grimly when she read it, knowing that she *had* been affected by last night's performance, but not the one Matt meant!

Perhaps a piece of dry toast would settle her stomach. Breakfast would be served until nine.

Dressing hurriedly, without paying attention to what she was putting on, she stole out of her room, hoping she wouldn't bump into anyone she knew.

The dining hall was almost deserted when she arrived. Megan grabbed a piece of wholemeal toast and a cup of tea and headed for the nearest empty table. Although hardly anyone was about, she couldn't help glancing about her nervously, sure that anyone who spotted her would know instinctively what she had been up to the night before.

Feeling slightly fortified, she left the dining hall, returning to her room only to clean her teeth and grab her rucksack. She was aware that she probably looked haggard from lack of sleep, but she didn't care. She had more important things to worry about today than her outward appearance.

Megan walked slowly into campus, her body reminding her with every step what it had done. She felt physically and emotionally bruised.

They were moving as one, her hands gripping him tightly ...

She pushed the memory from her mind, knowing it would return to haunt her over and over again.

Chapter Twenty-Seven

Jen was feeling worried about Megan. She'd missed breakfast, claiming a headache, but had made it into their ten o'clock English lecture. Now she sat there listlessly, not making notes (*most* unlike Megan!), staring into space as if there was something more pressing on her mind.

She would have grabbed her for a coffee and chat straight after the lecture, but Megan had a French Literature tutorial at eleven on Thursdays.

"Meg!" She called out to her friend as the blonde girl tried to vanish into the crowd streaming out of the lecture theatre. "Let's go for lunch at twelve. The Salad Bar."

Had she heard her? She wasn't sure.

Meg had caught Jen's request but knew she couldn't go. Jen was sure to ask probing questions and Megan was afraid she would buckle under pressure. She couldn't tell Jen about last night. She couldn't tell anyone.

She reached the Muirhead Tower and paused. Luckily, neither Mike nor Matt would be in her tutorial, but she couldn't risk bumping into them in the lift. She dived into the Ground Floor toilets. She would hide in a cubicle for a few minutes until she could be sure she was safe.

There was a sticker on the back of the toilet door for Niteline. Megan stared at the telephone number it listed and remembered what Sue had told her at the Freshers' Fayre: *"Student Advice is just advice, but Niteline listens to your problems too."*

Would they listen to her? What would she say? *'I've been lusting after a boy on my French course since December but now we've had sex I feel guilty'*?

Somehow, she didn't think they'd take her seriously.

A toilet door banged and she came to her senses with a start. What was she doing still in here when her tutorial must have begun already? She scrambled out of the cubicle and hurried to the lift.

As the lift approached, Megan began to feel sick again – not just because of last night but because, even after two terms, she still didn't trust the paternosters. She had first encountered these bizarre, continuously moving elevators when she'd come for her interview in December 1984. A student guide had led her to the open shaft and she had seen the lift approaching, expecting it to stop. "You just have to jump in while it's moving," he'd told her. It had been one of the most frightening experiences of her life. (Along with jumping out of the still moving lift when she reached her designated floor.)

As she stepped cautiously into the box for two, she had a sudden flashback to lying in Mike's arms at the end of the Autumn Term. Having exhausted French and German literature, they'd moved onto discussing the French Department and its associated lecturers, and then Mike had extolled the virtues of his two favourite things about the course: the Coffee Lounge and the paternosters.

"The first week we were here, I decided not to get off at the Fourth Floor," he told her, stroking her shoulder while he talked. "I wanted to stay in the lift and see what happened when it reached the top. Someone said it flipped over and I wanted to see if they were right."

She had felt horrified at the prospect. "What happened?" she asked him. "Did you try it."

He grinned. "It's on some sort of pulley system. When it gets to the top, it just shunts to the left and starts going down again. It's no big deal."

A term later, she'd mastered the art of stepping out smartly when she needed to; nevertheless, she couldn't help feeling apprehensive every time she used them.

She exited the lift now, wondering how late she was for her tutorial. Since she never wore a watch, she had no way of knowing what the time was. She pushed her tutor's door open nervously and went in.

As soon as she entered, she felt uneasy. The tutorials this term were built around modern French novels and this week's topic was André Gide's *'L'Immoraliste'*, a novel full of repressed sexuality. Megan found the conversation excruciatingly pertinent as the rest of her tutorial group talked of how Michel, the central figure in the book, had cheated on his wife, Marceline, to indulge his sexual appetites with others. Michel was French for 'Michael', and Marceline wasn't a million miles away from 'Amanda'. Megan felt as though it were her own sordid affair with Mike that was under scrutiny: further proof, if she needed it, that she could never tell anyone else what had happened.

(She was also slightly embarrassed to realise that she had completely missed the subtext of the novel, not having registered that Michel was a latent homosexual. One of her friends in the Sixth Form had been gay, but he had never felt the need to talk about it: everyone accepted that this was who he was.)

Leaving her tutorial at twelve, she bumped into Heather outside the lifts. When Heather asked her if she wanted to go for lunch, Megan hesitated: she liked Heather, but it was a reasonably superficial friendship. Still, there would be fewer awkward questions from her than there would from Jen.

"Okay," she told her, knowing that she needed to eat, "but let's go somewhere different: I don't feel like the Guild today."

She was anticipating a five minutes' walk into Selly Oak to grab a sandwich from one of the shops there, but Heather led her past the Guild to the Chaplaincy.

"What are we doing here?" Megan was mystified.

"They have a Hunger Lunch here every Thursday," Heather explained. "My room mate's in Ang Soc – the Anglican Society – and she brought me here a few weeks ago. You get soup, bread, cheese and pay whatever you want. All the money goes to charity."

It seemed like a worthwhile cause, but Megan still felt uncomfortable entering the building. Would they serve her if they knew she was a scarlet woman?

Heather led the way into a large dining area where several smiling Christians stood behind a long counter. Their wholesome faces and conservative clothing made Megan feel even worse. She queued silently behind Heather, hoping that there would be no enforced conversation: she wouldn't put it past any of this lot to try to win souls whilst they had a captive audience.

Seconds later, she became aware of a rather attractive young man standing nearby. She idly wondered what he was doing there. His dreadlocked hair and tie-dyed trousers made him look as if he belonged in some hippie music festival, not a Church hall; yet when he started speaking to her, Megan was surprised to discover he belonged to the CU. Maybe Christians weren't all as boring as she'd thought, then; nevertheless, she was sure this Jonathan would judge her if he knew her secret.

Heather seemed quite taken with Jonathan - who joined them at their table while they ate - confessing privately to Megan that although he wasn't strictly her type, she could fall quite easily for someone so easygoing and charismatic. Jonathan, it appeared, had quite a few stories to tell. He was a Second Year Geography student but had taken a year out before University to join a team of teenage evangelists on a floating hospital, which he described as a 'Mercy Ship'. They had sailed around Africa, going from village to village with medical supplies and even providing surgery in some cases, all free of charge – although Jonathan was quick to point out that the unqualified volunteers such as himself hadn't been allowed to take on any medical responsibilities.

It was all so fascinating that Megan almost forgot her inner turmoil.

"What did you think of Jonathan?" Heather asked eagerly as they walked back to the Muirhead Tower.

Megan considered the question carefully before answering.

"He seems genuine," she said at last.

Heather was bursting to tell her something. "He asked me out!" she exclaimed, eyes shining. "Well, it's not exactly a date: he's giving a talk to the CU at one of their Friday evening meetings in May and he asked me if I was interested in going along to hear him."

Privately, Megan thought Heather was reading too much into this; but it seemed churlish to say so.

They were about five minutes early for their two o'clock lecture on the French novel, the companion to her tutorial this morning. It seemed silly to have the tutorial first and not the lecture: Megan always found she understood the text much better once it had been explained to her by an expert. Perhaps they did it this way to stop students plagiarising what the lecturers said?

Her mind still occupied by Heather's potentially unsuitable attachment to Jonathan, she totally forgot that Matt would be looking for her. She only remembered, too late, as he slid in beside her, mentally kicking herself for leaving a vacant seat for him.

"Are you better now?" Matt's concern was touching, if a little misplaced. How could she explain that guilt and not nausea had kept her from joining her friends at the breakfast table that morning?

"I'm better than I was," she said guardedly, "but I don't think I'll be up to socialising tonight."

Matt's face fell. "But it's our last night!" he protested. "We go home tomorrow."

Megan felt mean when he said it, but she was still too vulnerable to spend an evening in the bar with her friends, aware that if she spotted Mike, her face might give her away and then there would be awkward questions.

"You must come," Matt repeated. "We won't see each other again after tomorrow until the middle of April."

Did 'we' mean the whole gang or just herself and Matt? she wondered.

She was still looking at him, trying to formulate a reply, when she felt a strange sensation in the pit of her stomach. Without turning round, she knew that Mike had entered the lecture theatre. She suddenly felt sick again.

Every instinct told her to get up and leave. Sitting here, knowing he was somewhere behind her, was causing an extremely unpleasant physical reaction: her stomach churned, then tied itself in knots.

She half rose to leave, but caution held her back: what if he followed her? She wasn't sure which of the two men she dreaded talking to more.

Somehow, she managed to get through the hour long lecture, although she wasn't convinced that her notes made any sense. As everyone began to move, she turned quickly, trying to locate Mike before he spotted her. She was disconcerted to find him looking straight at her, a peculiar expression on his face.

Mike, meanwhile, was feeling racked with uncertainty. He'd actually made it to the breakfast hall for the first time that term, wanting to catch Megan before she left for campus. He knew she usually ate early – unlike him, she attended all her classes – but although he sat there nursing a cup of coffee from eight until eight thirty, she didn't surface. In the end he had to hurry off to campus without seeing her, although he desperately needed to talk to her.

Now, walking into his two o'clock lecture, he had been hit by the sight of her sitting with Matt, the guy who followed her around, looking longingly at her. Mike shouldn't have felt jealous, but he did. Although he knew he was better looking than the other man, he worried that Matt was more Megan's type: he was so ridiculously clean cut, for goodness' sake! His only consolation was that Megan had told him Matt was a terrible kisser.

She was gone before he had the chance to catch hold of her and ask her to go for a coffee. Not that he could be sure she would have agreed: she always avoided him on campus, as if whatever it was that simmered between them existed only in his room. Was he her guilty secret?

Matt was still prattling away, oblivious to Megan's discomfort. She let his nervous chatter wash over her whilst she debated what to do next. She had agreed to come to the Guild Coffee Shop with Matt, not because she wanted a drink but to get away from Mike. Did Matt think this constituted a date? she wondered. She didn't think now that he could ever be her boyfriend – and if he knew about her and Mike, he wouldn't want to be; but she needed someone 'safe' she could spend time with: anyone to distract her from running back to Mike's room, to his arms.

She realised Matt had been asking her something. Too embarrassed to admit she hadn't been listening, she smiled and nodded.

"Great! I'll book the tickets then!"

What had she just agreed to? Her panic rose.

This time, she gave him her full attention and found that he had planned another theatre trip, to see *'The Scarlet Pimpernel'* in April. It would be good to go out again as a group, she decided, thinking that, by then, she might have forgiven herself enough to be able to enjoy her friends' company.

*

As Megan boarded the train at New Street the following day, she tried not to dwell on recent events. She had managed to avoid the last get together in the bar, pleading her headache, swearing it was turning into a migraine. (She'd also told Jen that was why she hadn't seen her for lunch.) Sally had looked vaguely suspicious, but they had allowed her to spend the night in her room alone.

At some point in the evening, a note had been slipped under her door. Mike had simply written, *"Megan, we need to talk. I'll be in my room all night. Mike."*

Megan knew what 'We need to talk' meant: it was code for 'It's over.' *Could* something be over if it hadn't really existed in the first place? It didn't matter because she didn't respond.

*

And now she was sitting on a train again, her suitcase packed with enough clothes for five weeks at home. She'd left some of her more interesting outfits locked in her wardrobe in Hall, knowing instinctively that her mother wouldn't approve of the purple skirt. This time, she hadn't shared a taxi to the station with her friends: Sue was being picked up by her parents, and Jen would be leaving the following morning: apparently she and Phil had plans for this evening. That only left Sally, never Megan's biggest fan. She *could* have asked the other girl if she wanted to split the cost of a cab, but that would have meant having to endure each other's company, so in the end she'd enlisted Matt's help to lug her case to Fiveways station. She could manage easily at the other end.

No she couldn't! She'd forgotten that she had to travel between stations once she arrived in Manchester. Bother!

With perfect timing, just as she was bemoaning her lack of foresight, an almost familiar face appeared in front of her. "We'll have to stop meeting like this!" a voice exclaimed.

It was the boy from her English course, the nice one who had been so helpful at the end of the Autumn Term and whom she'd ignored completely ever since. What was his name? Something that began with H ... Or was it J?

"Not wearing your mini skirt today?" he continued cheerfully.

Megan blushed. "I think my parents prefer me in jeans," she muttered.

"That's a pity ..." The young man, whatever his name was, looked mildly regretful. "I especially liked the purple one you wore to lectures the other day."

Had he really taken an interest in what she was wearing?

He grinned at her. "It was noticed," he said gravely.

Megan wasn't sure whether to feel pleased or flustered. In the end, she settled for a combination of both.

"You've forgotten my name, haven't you?" he said suddenly, making her feel guilty.

"No," she lied. "It's Harry ... I mean, Henry ... Jason ..."

"Justin," he corrected her.

"And you live in Bolton!" she cried triumphantly. "See! I *do* remember you!"

"And I seem to remember telling you I'd ask you out for a drink some time – only it never happened." He gazed at her with mock sorrow. "You broke my heart, Megan. I'll never trust another woman again!"

"That's hardly my fault if you didn't ask me!" she replied with spirit, relishing the easy banter between them. It felt good to carry on a mildly flirtatious conversation with someone who didn't worship her, the way Matt did - or do peculiar things to her hormones, like Mike.

"It's time we put that right then." His voice immediately sounded more serious. "There's a buffet car further down. I can get you a cup of tea if you like."

She hesitated, unsure whether she would be betraying Mike or Matt if she accepted. But it was only a cup of tea, not a marriage proposal!

"Thanks," she said, smiling up at him. "I'd like that, Justin. Milk and no sugar."

It was amazing how quickly two hours passed when there was someone to talk to. Megan felt surprisingly relaxed with Justin, despite his obvious interest in her. As the train reached Piccadilly and began to slow down, Justin scribbled something on a scrap of paper and handed it to her.

"That's my phone number." He was suddenly shy. "If you want a proper drink some time, let me know. Littleborough's only thirty or forty minutes' drive from Bolton and I can borrow my dad's car."

"Thanks." She was flummoxed by his offer. After all, they had only just met each other – you couldn't count the Cheese and Wine at Freshers or the hasty walk to Victoria last December. But she took it anyway. Perhaps she *would* give him a call. It would give her something to do while her parents canoodled.

Unwillingly, she forced herself to remember that this time she would have both parents under the same roof. She still wasn't sure how she felt about it, wondered if her mother was rushing things along too fast. Her dad was still a relative stranger to her: how would it feel to have him sharing the bathroom, the television, her mother?

"Penny for your thoughts."

She came to with a start, realising she was ignoring Justin. "Sorry," she apologised. "I've got a lot on my mind."

"Perhaps we should have that drink now, then, before we go our separate ways?"

"Steady on!" she joked. "You've bought me a cup of tea already!"

Turning up smelling of alcohol would *not* impress her mother.

"Some other time, then. But at least let me help you with your case."

He heaved it out of the overhead luggage rack as easily as if it had been filled with air.

"Come on. Let's get you to Victoria."

Chapter Twenty-Eight

Megan lay on her bed, staring moodily at the ceiling. She had now been home for a grand total of – she made a rapid calculation – two weeks and three days and she was bored.

She had another 5,000 words essay to write over Easter. The title was to "Write a pro-feminist essay on any text that takes your fancy", which left the essay wide open to any and every possible interpretation. She would have loved to have written her essay on *'Tess of the d'Urbervilles'*, one of her all-time favourite novels; but she was afraid that to do so might ruin the book for her forever.

Jen claimed she was writing about *'Five on a Treasure Island'*, the first Famous Five book. "George is obviously a repressed transvestite," she'd argued when Megan called her out on this. "Look at how she always dresses as a boy and refuses to answer to the name Georgina. And Anne and Aunt Fanny are just typical representations of downtrodden women in a patriarchal society: they're always cooking or sewing."

Megan was slightly alarmed by this explanation, having accepted the tale at face value as an old-fashioned adventure story when she'd read it at the age of six. And then she'd caught Jen's eye and realised that all her friend's comments were tongue-in-cheek.

They'd been given a reading list of suitable feminist critics whose opinions they might want to include in their essay. None of them were in the local library in Littleborough, although there were a couple of volumes by female scholars she'd never heard of before. She'd spent the greater part of the last fortnight sitting in the library's reading room, scribbling down notes for her essay. She could have taken the books home, but the reading room was more conducive to writing than her cramped bedroom was.

Justin's phone number lay on top of her chest of drawers. She hadn't rung him – yet. She wasn't sure if she would.

She'd seen Anita, briefly, towards the beginning of the first week. Her friend was obviously channelling her new boyfriend's Goth vibe because Anita had dyed her hair black and matched her clothing to her hair. She looked striking and a little scary. Megan wondered what Joe thought about it all.

A letter had arrived from Matt the day after she came home. It was more of a card, really: an excruciatingly whimsical offering depicting two teddy bears cuddling on the front. It was the sort of card you sent to someone when you were both revoltingly in love, she thought: when you called each other names like 'Pumpkin' and 'Snuggle Bunny' and spent hours on the phone saying, "No, *you* hang up." It was not, she thought, appropriate coming from someone who had kissed you twice – and both times very badly. Of course, she felt guilty straightaway for thinking this, but it couldn't alter the fact that Matt was far keener on her than she was on him.

Her parents weren't helping either. Still at the stage of wanting to impress her formerly-estranged husband, Mrs Jackson was over-compensating for all the times she'd left Megan to her own devices, trying to be Cool Mum and pretend an interest in her daughter's love life. She had fooled no one. Worse still, Megan had to invent imaginary male friends so she could give her mother a sanitised version of her life in Hall. Getting drunk and throwing herself at first Matt and then Mike was not a story she wanted to share with anyone, least of all her mother.

She had tried to confess all to Anita, though – from force of habit rather than anything else. She got as far as telling her that she'd dressed up in a tiny black dress and gone to Mike's room to persuade him to sleep with her, but when she mentioned passing out after throwing up, Anita had seemed relieved.

"Thank goodness for that!" she'd exclaimed. "It would have been a total disaster if you'd actually slept with him!"

Once she'd said that. Megan had been too embarrassed to tell her what had happened only hours later.

Letters and cards continued to arrive from Matt: one every two to three days. She was beginning to feel smothered by his intensity. After the third card, she wrote back: nothing heavy, just a brief note thanking him for writing and saying that she was very busy with an essay right now. The next day he sent her a picture of his cat in his garden – at least, she assumed it was *his* cat and *his* garden. On the back of the photo he had written 'March 1986' and drawn the outline of a heart. She found his devotion wearisome.

She tried to think of Mike as little as possible. Sometimes she would go several days without remembering the night they'd spent together; at other times she would lie in bed at night, replaying the video in her memory, then feeling ashamed all over again.

Perhaps her father was more perceptive than her mother, despite not really knowing her, because he started asking her about the cards and letters she was receiving, wanting to know if there was anyone she felt serious about. "I know you don't tell your mum everything," he said, "and I'm not expecting you to tell me either; but if you do need to talk at any time, you know I'll always listen." She confessed that Matt was rather keen on her but that she was still making up her mind. "Someone else in the picture as well, eh?" he commented astutely. "Just make sure *you're* happy, Megan. That's what counts."

He was surprised when she hugged him fiercely after that.

Jen called her a few days later to say she would be arriving at her aunt's for the Easter weekend and staying until the third of April.

"They've got a massive house so we always end up going there for Easter," she explained. "It was okay when we were younger: Auntie Sandra always did an Easter egg hunt in the garden and all of us kids used to sleep in the attic and tell ghost stories in our sleeping bags; but now we've grown up, it's not as much fun." She paused. "I don't think they want me borrowing the car either. I know we said you could come over to Leeds but I might be better coming to see you instead. How far are you from your local train station?"

It was decided that Jen would take the train to Littleborough on the Tuesday – at least it'll get me away from my cousins' awful April Fool's Day tricks," Jen said practically – and that Megan would meet her at the station.

"If it's nice weather, we could walk up Blackstone Edge," Megan said hopefully. "There's an old Roman Road. It's part of the Pennine Way."

"I'm not promising anything." Jen's voice crackled over the phone. "But I'll wear my trainers, just in case," she added.

The first was a gloriously sunny day, most unseasonal for a British April. Jen would be arriving at eleven. Megan made sandwiches and found some fruit. She had tried baking scones the night before, but they hadn't risen. She had felt quite insulted when her father asked innocently if they were biscuits.

Jen arrived promptly, looking full of the joys of Spring. Phil had been to stay with her in Devon, she explained, as they began walking up the hill. He had got on well with her family and they had been to the seaside and the local donkey sanctuary. Megan tried not to feel jealous of her friend's good fortune, but she couldn't help wishing that she, too, had a boyfriend who seemed so perfect.

That reminded her: she hadn't told Jen about meeting Justin on the train, or his offer to take her out some time. When she recounted the tale, Jen shrieked at her. "You idiot! Why haven't you called him?"

"I didn't want to hurt Matt's feelings," Megan confessed.

"And how's he going to know?" Jen shot her a withering look. "Honestly, Megan, you're so pathetic sometimes."

She explained about Matt and his barrage of cards and letters (which now totalled nine, including an Easter card). She had written back to him once.

"It *does* seem a bit excessive," Jen said doubtfully; then, "Are you sure you haven't encouraged him?" she asked suspiciously.

Megan hung her head in shame. "I let him kiss me after a Choir Rehearsal, and it was awful. He just sort of *pecked* at me."

Jen broke into hysterical laughter. "Sorry, Meg, but that's hilarious! Every time I see him now, I'm going to think of Woody Woodpecker!" Wiping her eyes, she became more serious. "Hang on! Was that the night we caught you in your room with Mike, just before you passed out?"

Megan's silence spoke volumes.

"So," Jen said slowly, "you kissed Matt for the first time, and then you had a massive snog-fest in your room with Mike. If it was anyone else but you, I'd be calling you a slapper!"

Megan said nothing. She thought her behaviour probably warranted the epithet.

"I let him kiss me again after the concert," she said in a small voice.

"And?"

Megan chose her words carefully. "It was a bit better than before," she said eventually, "but compared to Mike ..."

"Mike doesn't love you," Jen said gently. "I know the two of you have this physical attraction thing going on, but you can't build a relationship on that. Matt's absolutely devoted to you, Meg. So what if he's not the world's greatest kisser? He's faithful and he's loyal and he'd do anything for you. And it's not as if the two of you don't get on …"

Jen was right, of course. Megan thought for one last time of how it felt when Mike kissed her: how he made her bones turn to water when he touched her; how her heart lurched whenever she saw him. And then she thought of faithful, dependable Matt, trotting after her like a little dog, always eager to please. Mike belonged to someone else: always had done; Matt was hers and hers alone. He loved her so much: surely he deserved a proper chance?

"Matt's the one then," she said softly, not realising she had spoken aloud until Jen gave her a hug and told her she was very happy for her.

They didn't talk much after that, needing their energy for the climb, which was steeper than Megan remembered. Jen admired the view at first, but as they left the main road and began winding their way over the moors, following the Roman Road, she looked less enthusiastic.

"It's a bit bleak, isn't it!" she commented, staring at the barren landscape.

Megan was surprised at Jen's response. Growing up in Littleborough, she had always been surrounded by these hills and found their presence comforting, if a little rugged.

"Can't we head back down the hill a bit," Jen suggested after a while. "We passed a pub with picnic tables outside. We could sit and eat our sandwiches there – and maybe get a drink while we're at it."

Megan acquiesced immediately. After all, Jen *was* her guest. She felt vaguely disappointed that Jen didn't appreciate the hills as much as she herself did, though.

Walking back later on, after enjoying white wine for Jen and a cup of tea for Megan at the pub, Jen broached the subject of Matt again.

"Why not take it slowly this next term?" she suggested.

Megan thought that if she and Matt took it any slower, they would be asleep. Still, she listened to what her friend had to say.

"Matt's never had a girlfriend before," Jen began, "and he doesn't really know much about kissing, from what you've said – so why rush the physical side of it? Why don't you start going out properly and let things develop at their own pace in terms of the hand holding and kissing – and whatever else you feel happy getting up to?"

It seemed like a sensible plan. And perhaps if she and Matt watched a few romantic films together, he would get an idea of what kissing was supposed to be like. She would have to ask Phil if they could borrow High Hall's video recorder.

She supposed this meant she wouldn't be ringing Justin after all. If she had decided to make Matt her boyfriend, she couldn't very well go for a drink with another man – or could she?

"I don't see why not," was Jen's response. "You won't be seeing Matt until we go back in ten days' time, and what he doesn't know won't hurt him." Noticing Megan's expression, she added, "It's just a drink, Meg. And you're not even going out with Matt at the moment."

She was right again. Megan found herself looking forward to ringing Justin and arranging an evening out. Perhaps Anita and Joe would go too and then it would seem less like a date and more like a night out with friends.

It was a pity Jen couldn't stay longer. Megan would have liked to introduce her to Anita, or even take her along as moral support when she saw Justin. But Jen had a train to catch, back to Leeds and the bosom of her family.

"It's only another ten days until we're back in Birmingham," she said as she hugged Megan goodbye. Then, lowering her voice, she added, "Keep me posted on what happens with Justin!"

Megan walked home in a glow of contentment, feeling much more positive about her life now she had talked to Jen. *Except you didn't tell her about your night of passion with Mike,* a small voice whispered in her head. She ignored it. Mike was history; Matt was her future. If he only he wasn't quite so irritatingly keen ...

*

She rang Justin the following day and tentatively arranged for him to come over that Friday evening. She would see if Anita was free too. Another card had arrived from Matt, but she tried not to think about him while she was talking to Justin.

Anita was unexpectedly available and so was Joe. Megan wondered if Anita had told him about the Goth boyfriend in Leeds.

They arranged to meet up at The Fisherman's Inn: it was practically next to Hollingworth Lake, which should make it easy for Justin to find. "At least the lake's on the map," Anita argued when Megan speculated whether or not this was the best venue.

When Friday evening came, Megan dressed with care, wearing her double shirt combo with black leggings and her Victorian boots. She added her trilby for the finishing touch. Anita was impressed with the hat *and* the boots. "You're turning into quite the little bohemian, aren't you?" she commented when Megan entered the pub.

Megan was relieved to see that her friend had toned down the Goth image for tonight: her hair was still black rather than dark brown, her natural colour; but Anita was wearing red lipstick instead of a more funereal shade, and her ankle length tie-dyed dress was predominantly purple, patterned in black. As ever, she looked striking. Joe appeared to be struggling to tear his gaze away from her.

"How are things going with Luke?" Megan asked as they waited for Justin to arrive.

Anita shrugged. "Okay. I went over to Leeds last week and we went to a gig: a band called 'Fields of the Nephilim'. They're a sort of Goth-rock mixture."

It all sounded very different to the St John Passion. Not for the first time, Megan was conscious that she and Anita were growing apart.

And now here was Justin, walking shyly through the door, peering round, looking for her. Megan swiftly made the introductions, presenting both Anita and Joe as friends from the sixth form. Hands were shaken and a round of drinks was bought, Megan sticking to orange juice. She'd had enough trouble letting her mum agree she could meet the others in a pub without exacerbating the situation by returning home smelling of alcohol.

Justin quirked an eyebrow at her when he realised she wasn't drinking. "My dad's an alcoholic," Megan explained. "He hasn't had a drink for years, but my mum's still massively anti-alcohol, so it's easier if I stick to soft drinks when I'm back home."

"And if I asked you out again, when we're back in Birmingham, would you go for a proper drink then?"

His question surprised her: she hadn't been anticipating it.

"I don't know," she said, momentarily flustered. "I'm sort of seeing someone at University."

"That's a pity," Justin's eyes met her own, "because I was hoping that tonight might be the start of something for you and me." He gave a short, self-deprecating laugh. "Stupid of me, isn't it? I haven't seen you all term, apart from across a crowded lecture hall, but just because you take me up on the offer of a drink, I think there might be something in it. Anyway," he downed the rest of his drink in one, "I'm getting another. Anyone else fancy one while I'm up?"

Once Justin had vanished in the direction of the bar, Megan turned her attention to Anita.

"Not bad," Anita jerked her head in Justin's direction. "That's not the one you were telling me about, is it? The one you nearly slept with?"

"No!" Megan tried to hide her consternation, aware that her cheeks were flaming at Anita's casual remark. "Justin's on my English course," she explained. "I met him properly for the first time at the station in Manchester last December. He helped me find my way to Victoria. We sat together on the train coming home this time."

"Funny that you haven't mentioned him before …" Anita paused deliberately.

"There's nothing to tell," Megan protested. "After I bumped into him at the station in December, I didn't see him again until we were both on the train back to Manchester a few weeks ago."

"Well, one of you's a fast mover then!" Anita commented. "It's not like you to go for a drink with someone you've only chatted to once or twice! It's the equivalent of anyone else getting off with someone they've just met in a nightclub!"

Did Anita *really* think her so prim and proper? She had no chance to find out because Justin returned with the drinks and the conversation moved on.

The evening was drawing to a close. Megan was feeling slightly sick after an overabundance of orange juice. At least it was healthy.

As the four of them made their way outside, Justin turned to her. "Do you want a lift home?"

"Haven't you been drinking?" she asked him, puzzled.

He gave her a sheepish look. "Only alcohol-free lager. I wouldn't have driven here otherwise."

"Can you take Anita and Joe too?" she asked next. However, Anita and Joe had plans of their own, already disappearing down the road, hand in hand. Megan bit her lip. She hoped Anita wouldn't do anything silly.

"I live about a mile away," she told him, climbing into a car which was so much smarter than the one Joe's brother had driven. "Turn right out of the car park and keep going straight on. When we get to the railway bridge, I'll tell you where to go next."

For a few minutes they drove in silence, Justin concentrating on the road, Megan mentally weighing him up against Matt.

"Follow the road round to the left here," she broke in as he reached the end of the road, "and keep going, and left again under the bridge, then right at the traffic lights. My house is half a mile up that road there."

It seemed no time at all before Justin was pulling up next to her mother's driveway. "Door to door service," he said with a flourish.

Megan looked at him.

"Thanks for the night out," she said hesitantly. "It's been nice getting to know you."

He grinned. "Same here. Maybe one of these days we'll get further than a chat and a drink."

She fumbled momentarily with her seatbelt. When she looked up, his face was moving towards hers. "Good night, Megan."

The kiss he gave her was slow and surprisingly gentle. There were no earthquakes like there were with Mike; but it was definitely a vast improvement on Matt's clumsy attempts.

Catching his eye, she smiled. "That was nice too. Good night, Justin."

She couldn't be sure, but she thought she saw him punch the air before driving away.

*

Not having arrived home until almost eleven the previous evening, Megan decided to sleep in on Saturday morning, deliberately not setting her alarm. By the time she surfaced, it was almost ten o'clock.

She mooched around idly for some twenty minutes or so, enjoying the freedom of an empty house. Both parents were out grocery shopping together. She wondered if her father had realised he was signing up for all of this.

Thinking back over the four weeks she'd been at home, it seemed her mother had domesticated her father pretty quickly, indoctrinating him into her rules for washing up – "dirty things on the left; clean things on the right. Let them drain: tea towels are covered in germs" - and teaching him how to hoover properly. She would probably be getting him to take an inventory next of all the soap and toothpaste that were stockpiled inside the large cupboard on the landing. Would her father see this as domestic bliss or conjugal hell?

Another card lay on the doormat. Without looking at the envelope, Megan knew who it would be from. She sighed. Although she appreciated the effort Matt was making on her behalf, he did seem to be overdoing it.

She decided to make the most of her parents' absence by enjoying a long and decadent soak in the bath. As she began to turn on the taps, she was hit by the recollection of the last time she had enjoyed a lengthy wallow, when she'd taken her Short Loan book into the bath with her after spending the night lying in Mike's arms.

She breathed in sharply. Oh, to turn the clock back to the time when it was all so relatively innocent between Mike and her! But time marched forwards, never backwards: it couldn't be reset or rewritten. She had played with fire and been burned; and now she could never see Mike again.

She was stuck with Matt, then: sweet, dependable Matt with his awkward mannerisms and clichéd cards: Matt who worshipped her as a medieval knight adored his lady: Matt who would never hurt her, never cheat on her. If Mike had prompted a sea of raging hormones within her, Matt was the gentle breeze after the storm, a safe haven where she could heal. He had won her by default of not being Mike, but she would make it work – *had* to.

For one brief second, she wondered if Mike ever thought about her at all.

*

Her parents returned home while she was still in the bath, re-reading *'Tess of the d'Urbervilles'*. She heaved herself out of the lukewarm bubbles with ill-grace in response to her mother's insistent tapping on the door. "Megan! What are you doing in there? It's nearly twelve o'clock!"

Flouncing into her room clad only in a towel, she remained in this state of undress, intent on finishing the next part of the story. Tess was currently being wooed by Alec d'Urberville, all wicked grins and twirling moustaches, after being abandoned by her husband, Angel. Megan had never liked this part of the story: she thought Angel had treated Tess far too harshly after discovering that she had been seduced against her will years before he had married her. She also thought him a total hypocrite for not forgiving Tess even though he had confessed to "eight and forty hours of dissipation with a stranger" himself. It was one rule for men and another for women, she thought crossly. Perhaps she should write her essay on *'Tess'* after all?

She was so engrossed in her reading that she didn't hear the doorbell and was totally surprised by her father putting his head around her door to tell her that she had "a visitor". "I'd get dressed first though, Love," he added, "unless you want to give the poor lad a heart attack!"

Megan stopped dead in her tracks. She had assumed her visitor was Anita. Had Justin driven back to see her again now that he knew where she lived?

Quickly pulling on her jeans and a clean tee shirt, she raced downstairs. Sitting at the kitchen table, drinking a cup of tea, was Matt.

Chapter Twenty-Nine

Megan stared at Matt in disbelief. What was he doing here in her house? Her brain struggled to register the reality of the situation.

"Matt," she said at last.

"Hello, Megan," he said quietly.

Her mother looked at her expectantly.

"Mum, this is Matt." She hesitated. "A ... *friend* from University. Matt, this is my mum."

"You might have told me you were expecting him." Mrs Jackson's voice was tight.

Matt looked embarrassed. "Megan didn't know," he said quickly. "I wanted to surprise her."

Yesterday evening, it had seemed like the perfect way to win Megan's heart. What could be more extravagant, more romantic than turning up on her doorstep, clutching a bunch of flowers? He'd checked the train times carefully and left the house at eight this morning to catch a train to Waterloo and then brave the underground to Euston. At least it wasn't a week day: he had an idea the London part of his journey would have taken much longer in the rush hour. At Euston, he'd managed to buy some flowers – which he'd then inadvertently left on the train to Glasgow in his haste to scramble off at Manchester. Then had come the nightmare of realising that the train to Littleborough (final destination: Blackburn) left from a totally different railway station, so he'd had to take a taxi to Victoria. It had been one of the most stressful days of his life.

It would have felt worth it, had Megan appeared pleased to see him. Instead, she was doing that thing that women did when they weren't happy with you: it was the sort of face his mother made at his father when he forgot to put the bins out.

"You should have warned me," she said at last. "What if I'd been out?" What if Justin had been there?

Matt looked crestfallen. In his imagination, his escapade had taken on epic proportions, something akin to Romeo sneaking into the Capulets' orchard by night for a glimpse of Juliet or Orpheus travelling to the underworld to regain his lost love, Euridyce. Now he saw his dramatic gesture through Megan's eyes, as something embarrassing and somewhat inconvenient.

"I'm sorry," he said at last, finishing his tea and rising to his feet. "Perhaps I should leave."

"Don't be daft!" Megan's voice was surprisingly warm. Despite her shock at seeing Matt in her kitchen, she was actually quite touched. He'd come all the way from Wimbledon, for Heaven's sake! He must like her if he was prepared to do that.

She turned to her mother impulsively. "Can Matt stay for lunch?"

"Well, he won't be able to get home in time for it," her mother said drily. "Just before you came down, he was telling me he comes from London."

Dragging Matt away from her mother's disapproval, Megan took him out into the garden, glad that the weather was behaving. There wasn't really much to see, but she thought he would appreciate a respite from the awkwardness in the kitchen.

"I'm afraid I've upset your mother," Matt said uncomfortably.

Megan shook her head. "She's like that with everyone."
Silence.
Matt tried again. "I bought you some flowers …"
"That's really sweet of you."
"… Only I left them on the train."

"Oh, Matt!" She hugged him suddenly, taking him by surprise. "I'm really pleased to see you," she said, realising that she meant it.

Matt began to relax. Perhaps this wasn't such a disaster after all.

From the kitchen window, Mrs Jackson watched her daughter with the young man who'd turned up so unexpectedly. "Do you think he's her boyfriend?" she asked her husband.

John shook his head. "Not yet," he said cryptically.

Julia was intrigued. "What makes you say that?"

"Body language," John explained. "He's unsure of her, keeps looking at her for approval."

"What about that hug?"

"She's fond of him," John said thoughtfully, "but she hasn't decided yet."

He wouldn't tell her he'd had this conversation with Megan over a week ago. If his wife wanted to think he was an expert in psychology, he was quite happy to further the illusion.

Lunch was a somewhat stilted affair. Mrs Jackson produced her standard 'visitor food': cooked meats, shop bought quiche, green salad, crusty bread. It was just as well she'd been shopping that morning, she thought, worrying as usual about whether her hostess skills would come up to scratch. Entertaining didn't come easily to her: she found it very trying.

Luckily, Mr Jackson was keen to play the devoted father, although Megan wished he wasn't quite so enthusiastic about eliciting information from Matt. His constant questions must be making the poor boy feel as if he were at a job interview.

"What are your plans for this afternoon?" Julia asked, once the meal was done.

Megan considered the possible options. It would be nice to show Matt something of her home village, she thought; then again, there was the walk up Blackstone Edge – he might not complain as much as Jen had done; or the canal.

"How long are you here for?" she asked, thinking that would give her an idea of how much to try to pack into an afternoon.

Matt looked slightly embarrassed. "I hadn't actually thought that far ahead," he confessed, avoiding her mother's steely gaze. "I just grabbed a return ticket and hopped on a train." An unspoken question lingered in his eyes.

"Mum," Megan began carefully, "can Matt stay here tonight? It took him four hours or more to get here today. It's not fair to make him do two trips in one day."

"Nobody *made* him come here," Mrs Jackson began, but her husband silenced her with a look.

"I think we can manage that," he said evenly. "We do have a spare room, Matt – unless you'd rather share with Megan?"

His daughter coloured at the suggestion. Surely her dad didn't think she and Matt were …

Meanwhile, confusion filled Matt's face. He *thought* Megan's dad had just offered to put them in the same bedroom. Surely not? But he couldn't get the image out of his mind.

"We're not … *involved* like that," Megan said quickly.

Her mother breathed a sigh of relief.

*

In the end, Megan decided to take Matt on a tour of the village, starting with the primary school near the park and the library, then moving on to her old secondary school and walking across the playing fields and onto the old carriage drive that had been in use in a bygone age before cars and buses and main roads.

"This is where we used to do cross country." She led him up a heavily wooded slope, weaving in and out of trees until the ground levelled out by a public footpath. Sunlight filtered through the trees, casting shadows at their feet. Here and there daffodils peeped out; it was still too early for bluebells.

Megan wondered if she should tell him that this was where she and Dave had come in the summer for 'alone time'. She decided not to: after all, she wouldn't like it if Matt started showing her the places where he'd kissed other girls.

She faltered suddenly, remembering the last time Matt had tried to kiss her. What if he never improved? How long would she have to go out with him before deciding whether or not it was going to work out?

"Are you okay?" Matt's voice was full of concern.

"I'm fine," she lied. "I just tripped."

His hand stole into hers, wrapping his fingers tightly about her own. Emboldened by the fact that she had let him do this, Matt said casually, "We can stop for a rest if you like." What he actually meant was, We can stop and have a kiss.

"No, let's press on." Megan didn't mind Matt holding her hand, but that was as far as she was going to let it go for the present. She remembered Jen's counsel to take things slowly and resolved that she would let events evolve naturally this time.

They walked on in silence.

After a while, Matt spoke. "Are we officially going out now?"

"I suppose we are." He had written her countless cards, travelled over two hundred miles to see her. Surely that merited boyfriend status?

He paused walking for a moment and turned to face her. Instantly she panicked. As his mouth came towards her, she tilted her head so that his kiss landed on her cheek. "Was that a butterfly?" she asked desperately, pretending she'd been distracted by nature. Without waiting for a reply, she hurried on.

If Matt was slightly disappointed not to be able to practise his kissing technique, he kept quiet about it. As the footpath merged into a field, he let go of her hand. It all seemed too public here for romance.

The two of them wandered past numerous sheep, none of which registered their presence. Matt was relieved: he felt nervous around wild animals. "They roam all over the place," Megan told him. "Sometimes I'd find one in the garden when I came home from school."

It was all very different to Matt's home in Wimbledon. He hadn't realised before that Megan lived so much in the country.

When they finally returned home an hour later, Mrs Jackson was wondering what to make for tea. The problem was solved when her husband suggested that they all went out for dinner. "You liked the *Bella Vista*, didn't you?" he asked, referring to the meal they'd been for in December, in honour of Megan's birthday.

"Perhaps Matthew doesn't like Italian food." Her mother could always provide a cloud for every silver lining.

Matt assured them that he liked both pizza and pasta.

*

As they sat in the restaurant that evening, sipping mineral water and eating garlic bread and olives, Megan contemplated how much her life had changed in a few short months. Who would have thought last September, when she started at University, that in six months' time she would be sitting down to a meal with both her parents *and* her boyfriend?

Matt was her boyfriend. She tried the phrase in her mind: it still seemed unreal somehow.

Meanwhile, Mrs Jackson was warming to her daughter's new friend. Matthew had lovely manners and was so charming. His parents were obviously well to do, too, if they lived in Wimbledon. Yes, all in all he was a much better choice than that dreadful Dave person.

Matt was feeling slightly overwhelmed. Coming to see Megan on the spur of the moment had seemed like a delightful adventure at eight o'clock this morning. He had now been here for – he checked his watch – a little over six and a half hours – and in that time he had met Megan's parents, been for a romantic walk with her, holding hands, and was now sharing dinner with her too. He would have assumed the day couldn't be any more perfect were it not for the fact that he was actually spending the night in her house. It felt wonderful to have her parents' seal of approval (and how fortunate that he'd had the foresight to travel with a change of clothing and a toothbrush, just in case).

When they returned home after stuffing themselves with far too much pizza and pasta, Julia made Megan help her prepare the guest room for Matt. Since this involved moving most of the junk from the spare room into Megan's own room for the night, Megan was not particularly happy.

"I'm sure Matt wouldn't mind sharing his room with the Christmas tree and decorations," she grumbled, wondering whether there would be anywhere for her to sleep with all these extra boxes.

"It's only one night, Megan," her mother said patiently.

"So why not let Matt put up with it for one night instead of me?" Megan wanted to know.

"Because he's a guest," came the reply. "Now, help me with this duvet cover."

While Megan and her mother sorted out the bedding, Mr Jackson decided to have a 'man-to-man' talk with Matt.

"Megan's very innocent," he remarked, looking at Matt out of the corner of his eye.

So am I! Matt wanted to reply; instead he told her father that he would look after her.

"Make sure you do. And be careful," Mr Jackson said meaningfully.

Matt tried to work out whether this was a talk about safe sex.

"I respect your daughter," he said at last.

"You'd better," came the response, "because I'll be coming to Birmingham looking for you if you don't!"

Luckily, Julia interrupted them both by asking if they'd like hot chocolate before bed. Seizing his opportunity, Matt fled for the sanctuary of the spare room where he spent the next hour lying in bed and thinking about Megan before he finally fell asleep.

*

The next day dawned bright and sunny. Megan decided to take Matt for a walk by the canal. It wasn't too far from the railway station, so they could kill two birds with one stone.

"How did you sleep?" she asked politely as they breakfasted on tea and toast.

"Fine, thanks." Matt didn't mention the disturbing dream he'd had about Megan coming into his room, taking all her clothes off and climbing into bed with him. He felt hot and bothered whenever he thought of it.

"Can you manage another walk before you go back? The train station's near the canal. I thought we could go and look at the ducks."

Matt was keen on the idea – as long as the ducks didn't come too close.

He took her hand again as they walked down the main road, away from her mother's, heading in the direction of the station. As they neared the village centre, Matt spotted a small off-licence.

"Should I buy your parents a bottle of wine, to say thank you for having me?"

"They don't drink," Megan said shortly. She didn't feel ready to tell Matt the ins-and-outs of her family situation just yet.

They crossed the road by the antiquarian bookshop and passed the municipal flower beds. Walking past the station, they crossed another road, finding themselves next to the canal.

"There's a way onto the towpath over here," Megan called, letting go of his hand and forging ahead.

For a while they walked in silence, soaking in the atmosphere. Ducks dabbled on the surface of the water; red billed moorhens swam busily. To their left, a long row of terraced houses backed onto the path. They must have been weavers' cottages at one time, Megan thought.

An abundance of flowers grew around their feet: yellow celandine and coltsfoot stood out against the white of cow parsley and wild garlic. Megan remembered a school project from years ago when one of her primary school teachers had brought them out here on a nature walk. She had drawn each flower carefully in a small blue notebook and labelled them in her best handwriting.

"How far does this go on for?" Matt asked some time later.

She gave him an amused look. "If we could keep walking, we'd come to Hebden Bridge and then Mytholmroyd – the village where Ted Hughes was born. That's probably ten miles away or more – and we run out of towpath long before that."

"Oh." Matt felt confused. Why were they walking along here then?

"I just wanted you to see it." She felt suddenly shy. "I know you like the lake on The Vale. I thought you'd enjoy the canal too." She checked her watch. "We should probably head back now, though. You've got a long journey ahead of you."

It was on the tip of his tongue to tell her he could stay longer, but he decided not to. This was Sunday, after all, and in a week's time they would both be back in Hall together. He wondered if she would let him stay over in Ridge sometimes, like Ged did with Sue.

Megan was starting to get cold feet – metaphorically speaking. Matt's coming here to see her had been a wonderfully romantic gesture, but she could see herself becoming easily annoyed with him when the reality of student life resumed.

"What are you going to do in the last week of the holidays?" she asked him.

Matt was thoughtful. "I'll probably visit my grandmother at some point. She'll be so pleased when I tell her that things are working out for the two of us now."

Matt's grandmother knew about them? Megan's feeling of claustrophobia grew.

"I told her about you after the first term," Matt continued, completely unaware of Megan's sense of panic, "and then at the start of the holidays I told her we were getting closer and I'd kissed you."

His grandmother had always told him her own stories of the hearts she'd broken at the balls she'd attended just after the First World War. Born in the 1890s, she was a true Victorian at heart. She had startled Matt's younger sister when she was thirteen by asking her if she'd "started wearing corsets yet?" and often reminded him that he should act like a gentleman at all times. Apart from insisting on clean fingernails, her only other ambition now that she was in her nineties was to see both her grandchildren settled down happily before she died.

He realised Megan was speaking to him. "Sorry," he apologised. "I was miles away."

"I said, What else have you told her?" Megan's voice sounded strained.

"Only that I'm in love with you and have been since the first time I saw you." Matt stopped walking. "I fell in love with you at Freshers. That's six months ago and the feeling hasn't gone away."

She couldn't reciprocate. She liked him, thought it was worth seeing whether they worked as a couple, but she wasn't in love with him. Not yet; maybe not ever.

He noticed her hesitation. "I'm not asking you to fall in love with me right away," he said awkwardly, "but you need to know how I feel."

She had known for months: seen it in his puppy-dog eyes; heard it in his courtesies and compliments. He needed no love poems to declare his interest in her: it was written all over his face.

"Don't rush me," she said softly. "I do like you, Matt, but all this is a bit too intense. Let's just carry on as we are and see how it develops."

It wasn't the answer he wanted, but it would have to do.

*

After she had seen Matt off at the station, Megan took herself back to the canal and wandered up and down the towpath on her own, ruminating. She had a boyfriend: surely that would stop her from running back to Mike again in the future? She had felt bad enough cheating on the unknown Amanda, but she couldn't be unfaithful to Matt: it would break his heart.

Perhaps her best friend would know what to do? Anita and her family usually enjoyed lazy Sundays, lying in bed until noon and then slumping in front of the TV or reading the papers and colour supplements, so she was likely to be in if Megan called round. She would have to pop home first, though: she and Matt had spent almost two hours walking and talking and Mrs Jackson would be expecting Megan home for lunch. She could do that now and ring Anita at the same time, just in case she was busy doing something with Joe.

Anita was not only in but was most disgruntled to be woken by Megan before midday. She was instantly alert, though, once Megan explained in a lowered voice that she needed boyfriend advice. "Give me half an hour to get showered and dressed and then come over," she instructed. "We can walk to The Triangle and chat there."

Megan had already had enough fresh air to last her the rest of the week, but she complied with her friend's wishes, turning up on Anita's doorstep about forty minutes later. Anita's estate had been built on the land owned by a farm and some of the fields still remained. No doubt they too would be built on at some point in the future, but for the time being they provided a useful place to walk and think. The Triangle comprised a small three-sided area with a bench, beyond the back of the estate and towards the remaining fields. It had been a favourite spot for both girls for years: most of their teenage problems had been discussed there.

Anita had brought apples and Jaffa cakes. They sat and munched the food while they talked.

"Hang on!" Anita's cheeks were flushed by the April wind, her black hair tied back in a ponytail. "It's not Justin you're on about then?"

Megan told her of Matt's unexpected visit.

"Get you!" Anita sounded impressed. "You go out with Justin on Friday and Matt comes to see you on Saturday. You're juggling two men at the same time!"

"It's not like that!" Megan protested. "Justin's a friend – I'm not going out with him; and Matt ..." She paused. "Matt's been chasing me for ages," she said at last. "I suppose I thought he deserved a chance."

"That makes you sound like a charity!" Anita observed, crunching her apple core noisily. "You should be going out with him because you like him, not because it's a reward for persistence!"

"I *do* like him!" Megan insisted.

"Have you kissed him yet?"

Megan was silent.

"No!" Anita sounded scandalised as she suddenly put two and two together. "He's not the one you wrote and told me about, is he? The one who was the lousy kisser?" She looked at her friend incredulously. "You *can't* go out with him, Meg – not if he doesn't turn you on."

But she had made that mistake already with Mike, falling for him just because of a strong sexual magnetism between them. And physical attraction didn't mean anything if it was *all* there was.

"Matt loves me," she said heavily. "I know he won't cheat on me, like Dave did, and he won't try to push me into sex before I'm ready for it either." She took a Jaffa cake and bit into it at a leisurely pace before continuing. "He's not the greatest kisser at the moment, but that can all change, can't it? I mean, if we practise enough, he's bound to get better."

"Rather you than me," Anita said slowly. "Just as long as you're careful." Catching her friend's eye, she elaborated, "Be careful with your heart, Meg. These things have a way of going wrong."

Part Three: Summer Term

*"Th'expense of spirit in a waste of shame
Is lust in action ..."*
Shakespeare, Sonnet CXXIX

Chapter Thirty

It was good to be back at University after so many weeks at home. Megan had been dreading telling Sally that she was going out with Matt, but the other girl seemed to accept the news with a philosophical attitude. "It was always bound to happen," she commented when Megan apologetically told her of Matt's journey up north. "Just make sure you look after him. I wouldn't want to see him get hurt."

Once Matt had returned to Wimbledon, Megan had worked hard on her essay, completing it by the Wednesday lunchtime. She hadn't written about *'Tess'* after all: one of the library books she'd found had made some interesting comments on *'The Waste Land'*, T S Eliot's long and baffling poem. She'd studied it for A level so felt she knew it well enough to write about it in depth.

It was just as well she had finished her essay when she did because Matt had started posting her a card every day. Between reading these and making sure all her French notes were up to date, there had been time for little else in the last week in Littleborough.

Justin had rung her on the final Friday (they'd swapped numbers the week before), asking if she wanted to go out again and trying to ascertain which train she would be taking back to Birmingham. She made a feeble excuse to get out of going to the pub with him a second time – not because she hadn't enjoyed herself before but because she knew Matt wouldn't like it now they were 'officially' an item; but she told herself that travelling back to Birmingham with Justin wouldn't be a crime: if anyone saw them together, she could claim she had bumped into him by chance, like she had on the journey there.

As she unpacked her books and other items from the trunk she'd left behind over Easter, her fingers closed around the tape Matt had made for her the previous term. She still hadn't listened to it, she thought guiltily, remembering how she'd intended to take it home with her and play it on her Walkman. (She'd left her radio-cassette player in Hall, locked in her wardrobe.)

She would put it on now, she decided. That way, if Matt asked her about it, at least she could say truthfully that she'd heard it. And it would be company while she unpacked.

As she had expected, Phil Collins and Alison Moyet featured heavily. The tape began with *'Against All Odds'*, which seemed an appropriate title given that she and Matt were now going out. This was followed by *'You Can't Hurry Love'* – she would quote that back at him the next time he seemed to be trying to move things too fast! – and then *'Easy Lover'* (or *'Hopeless Kisser'* as she rechristened it in her head, feeling mean instantly when she did so). After this Phil trio, the playlist moved onto Alison Moyet's *'For You Only'* and *'Where Hides Sleep?'* She knew what he was trying to say with the first of these, but the hidden meaning (if there was one) of the second eluded her.

It was as the next song started, Phil Collins singing *'One More Night'*, that she found Mike's copy of *'The End of the Affair'*. For a moment she simply stood and gazed at the book as the juxtaposition of both titles hit her with a double blow of irony. Her affair with Mike was well and truly ended: there would never be "just one more night". Regret overwhelmed her, the soulful words of the lyrics piercing her heart: "I know there'll never be a time you'll ever feel the same."

She didn't hear any of the songs that followed: she was too busy grieving over what might have been.

*

Phil and Matt were both excited about the first disco of term. They'd initially been planning to make it a toga party until Sally had pointed out, practically, that it was the start of term and they wouldn't have any spare bedsheets.

"Why not make it the second week?" she suggested. "The cleaner leaves clean sheets on a Friday. If we only put one used bedsheet out instead of two, we can hang onto the other one for a toga."

"It's all right for you girls having two sheets each," Phil grumbled. "*We* only get one."

"Yes, but *you* have duvets. *We* have to make our beds properly," was Sally's reply.

It was decided that there should be enough sheets to provide togas for those who wanted them.

"After all," Phil said with a sigh, "we know only a few people will bother dressing up anyway."

Matt had spent most of the previous week working on his playlist. Having learned from the last term's discos, he had included plenty of tunes that were good to dance to. He rarely saw Megan on the dancefloor, though. He picked up one of the recent singles - Samantha Fox singing, "Touch me (I want your body)" - then thought better of it and put it down again, not wanting Megan to get the wrong idea. He'd seen her only briefly since arriving back at Hall today: they'd both been busy unpacking and then he'd had to start getting the music ready for the disco. He'd been so busy he hadn't even had time to eat, although apparently the girls had shared takeaway pizza a little earlier.

He checked his watch. Seven thirty and time for the first record. He knew that most people wouldn't be turning up until nine, but he didn't care. He took his position seriously and made sure he always started on time – even if the hall was empty. Within seconds, *'The Power of Love'* was blasting round the room. Matt sang along to Huey Lewis and the News, truly believing every word.

It was just after nine by the time the girls and Ged found their way over to the disco area. A few brave people were dancing to Sinitta's *'So Macho'* but the rest of the room was deserted. Megan felt sorry for Matt and Phil – and the rest of the Events committee.

Matt looked relieved to see Megan at last. He had been waiting for ages to play *'Love Comes Quickly'* by The Pet Shop Boys for her. He particularly liked the words "... when you least expect it/Waiting round the corner for you": it summed up how he felt about finally being Megan's boyfriend.

"Is everything he plays from now on going to be as soppy as this?" Jen murmured in Megan's ear.

But Megan had been transfixed by the line "Taste forbidden pleasures". Was *every* song she heard tonight going to remind her of Mike?

Another excruciating hour and it was all over. Megan thought sadly of the books in her room and of how she could have spent the last hour reading. Still, Matt looked happy, despite the lack of people on the dance floor.

"Well done!" she said politely.

Matt beamed. "Did you like the song I played you?"

"Which one in particular?" There had been so many that Matt seemed to have invested with special significance. He had gazed meaningfully at her every time the word 'love' was mentioned.

Before he could answer, a raucous cry went up from the bar area overhead. Megan swivelled her gaze to see what was going on. A pretty girl was draping herself over first one man then another.

"Who's that?" Sally asked disapprovingly.

Phil chuckled. "That's Troy. He's on my floor. Every so often, he likes to dress up as his alter-ego, Helena."

"That's not really a woman?" Jen's voice dripped disbelief. Troy was certainly very convincing.

Megan watched, fascinated. With his androgynous looks and killer cheekbones, the young man certainly had a face to launch a thousand ships. His lithe body looked good in that skin-tight dress too.

"Troy's girlfriend hates it when he dresses up," Phil told them, "but that's because he's much prettier than she is!"

Mike would look good in drag too. The thought popped into Megan's head before she could stop it. He had the bone structure for it, like Troy.

Beside her, Matt slipped his hand into hers. "Time for a quick one?" He looked at her hopefully.

"Pardon?"

His face reddened. "Sorry, I meant, Time for a quick coffee before bed?" Then, as he realised the possible implications of the last two words, he flushed again. "I mean, before you go to sleep in your bed and I go back to High to go to sleep in mine."

Mike had only needed to look at her, or to utter the words "My room" and she had been putty in his hands. Now, with Matt burbling inanely, she found herself completely devoid of any desire for her boyfriend.

"Maybe another time," she said firmly, removing her hand from his and pushing her hair away from her face. "I'll see you at breakfast," she added swiftly, noting his crestfallen look.

He leaned in to kiss her and, as before, she turned her face so the kiss fell on her cheek.

"Good night, Matt."

"Good night, Megan."

As she walked away, he wondered what he'd done wrong.

*

He was at her door before eight the next morning, waiting to take her to breakfast. Megan felt peeved, liking her usual routine of wandering down to the dining hall with Sue, Jen and Sally. One couldn't indulge in a good girly gossip with Matt present.

At breakfast, Matt was annoyingly attentive. "I can butter my own toast, thanks!" Megan snapped at him at one point. She was beginning to regret upgrading him to boyfriend status.

When Megan stomped off to get more tea, Jen had a quiet word in Matt's ear. "Don't try so hard. You're getting on her nerves."

Matt looked startled. "I'm only trying to show her how I feel," he protested in an injured tone.

"Well, you're overdoing it. Give her some space."

Jen had noticed Megan's body language both last night and this morning. If she wasn't mistaken, her friend was feeling suffocated already.

*

Although she didn't have anything scheduled before her two o'clock French Literature lecture, Megan decided to hit campus at ten anyway. She would hand in her English essay and then check her pigeon holes in both the Arts Faculty and the Muirhead Tower before deciding what to do next.

Matt knew she was 'free' until the afternoon, but he wasn't. He would have asked her if she wanted to meet up for lunch at one but thought of Jen's warning and decided not to. Maybe she would be more pleased to see him in their afternoon lecture together if she'd had the opportunity to miss him earlier. "Absence makes the heart grow fonder," he muttered to himself.

Megan took a leisurely stroll down to the university long after everyone else had left. She was enjoying her alone time: it was a welcome respite to the relative noise and bustle of Hall. After completing her admin tasks, she mooched around the Dillons bookshop on campus, checking the availability of any texts she hadn't yet bought, indulging herself by browsing the classics.

In the Graham Greene section, she found a brand new copy of *'The End of the Affair'*. Should she buy it? It would enable her to return the one Mike had lent her all those months ago. She put it back hurriedly, not wanting to give herself an excuse to visit his room again.

"I've heard that one's quite good." A voice in her ear made her jump. Spinning round, she came face to face with Mike, just as dangerous and as forbidden as ever.

An instant chemical reaction fizzed in her bloodstream; her heartbeat quickened; her throat became dry.

"How was your break?" he asked her.

"Fine. Yours?"

"Not bad. Do you want to go for a coffee?"

She should have told him that she was now going out with Matt, but all the pent-up longing of the past five and a half weeks suddenly overwhelmed her. Matt wouldn't like it, but Matt didn't need to know. This was just coffee, for goodness' sake! She wasn't going to kiss Mike or do anything else that was stupid.

He didn't take her to the Coffee Bar in the Muirhead Tower: instead they found a café in Selly Oak, away from prying eyes, and ordered something hot and caffeinated which resembled neither tea nor coffee when it came.

Megan gazed about her, at the dingy formica-topped tables and the worn vinyl chairs, and felt ashamed. Why were they skulking in a place like this, amidst the smell of hot grease and bacon fat? It all seemed rather sordid somehow, as if they were having an affair.

"I've missed you."

Last term his words would have made her heart sing; now they pulled her chains of guilt tighter.

"I've got a boyfriend now," she burst out, needing to see his reaction.

For a moment, Mike didn't respond; then, ripping open a sachet of sugar and pouring its contents into the dark, bitter liquid in front of him, he regarded her coolly. "I'm very happy for you," he said neutrally.

Inside, he cursed the timing. He had brought Megan here to tell her that he and Amanda were through. He wasn't expecting her to fall into his arms straight away, but he had wanted her to know that he was now a free agent, so that if they got together again she wouldn't be running away from him as soon as guilt got the better of her.

He took a sip from the steaming mug in front of him. "So, who is he? Someone back home?"

She didn't meet his gaze.

After a moment, she mumbled something indistinct.

"Pardon?"

"I said, I'm going out with Matt." Her attitude was a strange mixture of defiance and embarrassment.

Matt. That was the guy who hung about with her in lectures. The one she'd been looking for when he'd found her in the High foyer, drunk, and taken her back to her room.

"He came to stay with me over the Easter holidays." Her eyes met his now, challenging.

Mike showed no reaction. "That must have been nice for you both," he said, non-committally.

Had Matt held her all night like he had? Had he seen Megan's eyes grow dark with desire, heard her moan in the throes of ecstasy? An overwhelming jealousy took hold of him. He had finished with Amanda, *for her*, and now she was with another man. He gulped down the rest of his coffee. It was too painful to sit here with Megan, knowing he couldn't have her.

"I've got a twelve o'clock," he said shortly, getting up. It was a lie, but Megan wasn't to know that.

She stayed sitting where she was, nursing her drink as if reluctant to let go of it. "You go ahead then. I'm finishing this."

Did she mean the coffee, or this thing between them? He turned and left the café.

Once he had gone, Megan let the tears fall. He had never loved her, had shown no emotion at all when she told him she was with Matt.

Did you expect him to challenge Matt to a duel over you? she asked herself mockingly. He'd claimed to be "very happy" for her: that was code for 'I'm relieved you've stopped chasing me.'

Still, at least it was now definitely over. She wouldn't be going round to his room anymore now she had a boyfriend. You could say, really, that she'd just used him as a boyfriend substitute before and she didn't need one of those now she had the real thing.

Was Matt the real thing? It was still too early to tell; but at least when she kissed him now, she wouldn't be thinking of Mike.

Scrubbing her eyes with a tissue, she resolved not to think about him again, then blew her nose and headed back to campus.

*

She deliberately tried to blot Mike out of her memory for the rest of the day. She and Jen had agreed to meet up for lunch at twelve thirty, to avoid the one o'clock rush. As they queued for salad – again – in the Cellar Bar, Jen asked casually how things were with Matt.

"I haven't seen him since breakfast," Megan confessed. "We've got French at two, though."

"You don't look as happy as you should at the idea of seeing your boyfriend," Jen commented drily.

Megan hesitated. "I'm wondering if I've rushed into this," she said slowly.

"Are you nuts?" Jen couldn't believe what she was hearing. "You've known he's liked you for months and months; you get on well together; he travelled two hundred miles to see you over Easter – and you think you're rushing things?"

"Well, maybe I'm going out with him for the wrong reasons, then." Megan felt weary of the conversation already. "I *do* like him. I just think maybe it's a mistake to try to force yourself to love someone, just because he's in love with you."

"Give it time," Jen urged. "Have you got anything else after this lecture at two?"

Megan shook her head.

"Then go somewhere, just the two of you, and spend time getting to know each other properly," was Jen's suggestion. "Even if you just end up going for a coffee" – Megan thought, fleetingly, of Mike – "or having a walk in The Vale, you need to find out what he's really like as a boyfriend. You've only known him as a friend before – the boundaries have changed."

"I'm still worried about how things have changed," Megan confessed. "Now we're going out, Matt keeps wanting to kiss me all the time."

"What's so wrong with that?" Jen was puzzled. "It's what boyfriends and girlfriends do."

Megan looked at the table.

"What if it never gets better?" she asked in a small voice. "What if I never feel the spark with him that I felt with Mike?"

He made her bones turn to water when he touched her …

"And what if you end up feeling something much stronger for Matt?" Jen said practically. "What if you actually stop thinking about Mike and comparing everything with anyone else to a handful of times when you had a drunken snog – and concentrate on learning how to be with Matt?" She paused meaningfully. "Sometimes you have to work at the physical side of things. But the more you practise, the better you get."

Megan left the Cellar Bar feeling her resolve strengthened by Jen's pep-talk. She *would* make this work with Matt – had to if she wanted to stop thinking about Mike.

Arriving five minutes early for their lecture, she saw he was already there. He gave her a grateful smile when she sat down beside him. "This morning, I thought you were cross with me about something."

"I was just tired." The white lie made his face glow with relief. It was so easy to make him happy, she realised: a kind word here, a smile there. Again she was reminded of a puppy.

"Are you busy after this?" she asked softly, trying to make her voice a seductive whisper. "Because I thought we might take a walk on The Vale together …"

His large spaniel eyes looked at her trustingly, the way any dog's would if his mistress said 'Walk'. And now she couldn't get the image out of her mind. Perhaps she should buy him a collar?

She was so busy mentally throwing him a stick, watching him chase a ball, that she didn't even notice when Mike entered the room.

*

Matt stretched out happily on one of the benches by the lake. Afternoon sunlight caught the water, ripples of gold spilling in concentric circles. Several families of ducklings were swimming past, tiny balls of fluff bobbing busily.

"We should feed them," he said suddenly. He sat up and looked at Megan. "If we saved some of our toast from breakfast – or just took the bread – we could bring it out and feed the ducks together."

His parents had taken him and his sister to the park to do just that when they were younger. The memory covered his mind like a warm security blanket, a relic of a happy childhood. "Didn't you do that when you were little?" he asked.

Megan grinned. "I'm still little. Feeding the ducks sounds like fun, though."

She leaned into him, making an effort. His arm stole around her, hugging her against his chest. The combination of the weather, the lake and Megan made it an almost perfect moment.

Would he ruin the atmosphere if he tried to kiss her? He glanced at her tentatively. "Megan?"

This time, he took hold of her face, keeping her still so she couldn't turn away. He let his kiss linger on her lips instead of letting nervousness dictate his speed. Quality, not quantity, he told himself.

Although Megan had stiffened instinctively when Matt first touched her, she soon began to relax. It wasn't unpleasant. Perhaps her body was learning to adapt to him after all?

Matt's eyes were closed, his senses tingling. Kissing Megan was one of the most wonderful things he'd ever done. Her lips were so soft. He released her face and let his hands drift down to her shoulders, stroking her hair, letting the liquid sunshine spill through his fingers.

Cautiously opening one eye, he realised that she was staring at him. He thought that he had never seen anything so beautiful in his life.

"Have you seen the goslings?" she asked, her words breaking the spell.

He followed her gaze to the fluffy, grey chicks, following their parents to the water's edge. Maybe one day he and Megan would look like that, he thought dreamily, his mind already projecting a future where they were surrounded by their own brood of children.

"I didn't realise I'd have all this on my doorstep when I came here." She was still talking. "I didn't see The Vale until I arrived at the start of Freshers."

Matt let her words wash over him, drinking in Megan's face, her hair, the warmth of her body against his. After a while she fell silent. They sat there for some fifteen minutes more, watching, enjoying nature.

Eventually, Megan stirred. "I suppose we'd better get back to Hall. I don't know about you, but I've got reading to do."

She rose slowly from the bench, feeling pleasantly rested – not just physically, but emotionally too. *This* was what she needed: this calm companionship; not the agitation of hormones whirling round her body, of desire holding common sense hostage.

When he rose too and took her hand, she let him hold it all the way back to Hall.

Chapter Thirty-One

They spent a lot of time on the Vale over the next few weeks. Now it was the Summer Term, the evening menu in Hall started offering a salad option every day and there were bread rolls too. Matt and Megan took rolls every night to save for the ducks.

"It doesn't matter if they go stale overnight in our rooms," she told him, "because I think I've read something somewhere that said hard bread is better for them."

"Actually, birdseed, peas and sweetcorn are a lot better than bread," Sally interjected, gatecrashing the conversation. "And you can't give them mouldy bread: it can kill them."

Matt frowned. This was all much more complicated than he'd thought. Would he be able to fill his pockets with peas and sweetcorn? he wondered. It would be much messier than just carrying bread out of the dining hall. Maybe he should invest in a few tins of corn? It would be worth it if it helped him spend quality time with Megan.

He gave up totally on the bread after a disturbing incident on their fourth day of feeding the ducks. Momentarily sidetracked by how pretty Megan looked in her purple skirt, he forgot what he was doing and threw a whole bread roll in the direction of the water. To his horror, it actually hit a duckling on the side of its head. The tiny creature sank instantly. Had he killed it? Luckily it resurfaced a minute later, coughing and spluttering, but it was enough to deter him from throwing bread again from now on.

Megan was doing her best to let Matt distract her from thinking about Mike. Every day they walked in The Vale then sat on a bench by the lake and practised kissing. Matt was definitely improving, she thought: as he gained confidence, he was learning where to put his hands, how to open his mouth. She would only kiss him outside, though, mindful of how easily she had been carried away by passion in Mike's room, on his bed. Although she couldn't really see any of that happening with Matt, surely it was better to be safe than sorry?

From time to time, she glimpsed Mike in the dining hall or in the Muirhead Tower. Since she was always with Matt on these occasions, she felt safe: having a boyfriend sent a clear message that she wasn't interested. Mike would be unlikely to talk to her ever again now he knew that she wouldn't be visiting his room. If she sometimes felt a pang of regret or a faint memory of desire, she squashed it instantly. She was Matt's girl now.

*

"We should all do something tomorrow night." Sally, buttering toast at the breakfast table, looked at the others. "What about a film?"

"Ooh!" Jen looked animated. "I really want to see 'A Room With A View' and it's just come out."

Everyone else looked blank, even Megan.

"We can't do this Saturday," Matt cut in, before Jen could elaborate. He nudged his girlfriend. "Megan and I are going to the theatre."

Megan looked startled. She remembered Matt talking about theatre tickets some time last term, but she'd thought he meant the whole group of them. Still, it might be fun to have a proper date night. So far, she and Matt had done little else but walk around The Vale or kiss on a bench.

"What are you seeing?" Sally again.

Matt looked as if he would burst with excitement. "It's *'The Scarlet Pimpernel'* – with Donald Sinden!"

The name sounded familiar and then Megan remembered: she had seen him in two sitcoms, playing an English butler to some American woman back in the 1970s (she must have been only nine or ten at the time) and, more recently, as a snooty antiques dealer in a show called *'Never The Twain'*. From what she could recall, he had a very theatrical voice.

The conversation moved on as Sue haughtily asked why they couldn't still go to the cinema even without Matt and Megan, and Sally wanted to know if there were any other films worth watching.

"I think *'Jagged Edge'* is still on," Jen said thoughtfully. "I saw it over the Easter holidays, but I don't mind seeing it again."

Upon learning the film was a courtroom thriller that involved the trial of a possible rapist and murderer, Megan felt relieved to be going to the theatre instead. She had a nervous disposition at the best of times.

"We'll definitely see *'A Room With A View'* next Saturday," Jen promised.

The next day, Megan indulged in a fairly lazy morning, having little to do except for her laundry. After two terms, she knew how to use her time wisely: the washing machines were located in High Hall's basement area, but there were several benches where she could sit down and read while she waited for the cycle to finish. Armed with fifty pences and a copy of Muriel Spark's *'The Comforters'*, she set off, half-dragging, half-carrying the ridiculously large bag of dirty clothes that she had managed to accumulate in just one week.

The laundry room was deserted when she entered, although the noise of several machines told her that others had already been in and started their washload. There were still a couple of empty machines. She chose the nearest one and began stuffing in coloured tights, underwear and leggings. Putting her money in the slot, she started the forty minutes synthetics cycle. Minutes later, she was lost in her book.

Perhaps fifteen minutes later she heard the sound of someone else entering. Without looking up, she was suddenly aware of Mike's presence. Peering round the edge of her book, she saw that she was correct: he was crouching by one of the machines, pulling his damp clothes out of it.

After days of telling herself that she was over him, she was annoyed to find that she still retained some sixth sense that alerted her to his appearance. Had she subconsciously recognised his aftershave? she wondered.

As if feeling her gaze, he turned round. "Looks like you dropped something." His voice was flat.

She followed the direction of his eyes and saw what he had just spotted. Awkwardness enflamed her cheeks. Why couldn't she have dropped something sexy? she asked herself petulantly. Instead, her Minnie Mouse knickers lay on the ground, in full view of not just Mike but any other boy who happened to wander in. It was all highly embarrassing.

She reached for them at the same time he did. Their fingers touched inadvertently, a familiar flicker of electricity passing between them. At that moment, she knew that nothing had changed; she still wanted him, despite Matt, despite Amanda. She wanted him; and the knowledge made her ashamed of herself.

For a moment, he held her gaze, the longing in his eyes reflected in her own. If he had kissed her now, she would have kissed him back. Instead, he turned his back on her once more, pulling the rest of his clothes out of the washing machine and stuffing the still slightly wet garments into a carrier bag.

Without saying anything more, he left.

*

Back in his room, Mike cursed his timing. He'd returned to the laundry room with the express purpose of drying his clothes, but he hadn't been able to spend another minute in there with Megan. If anything, she looked even more delectable now she was definitely off-limits.

It wasn't just the way she looked though: there was something deeper than that pulling him towards her. He had thought it was mutual but obviously he had been mistaken. She'd traded him in effortlessly for a guy who was so clean cut he made Cliff Richard look edgy.

He had to forget about her. Rose had made it quite clear that she wouldn't say no to second helpings, but he wasn't after anything casual. Nor was he ready to rush into anything too intense after the way he'd been burned by Amanda. He'd been the one to finish it in the end and she'd seemed relieved; but he was wary now of getting close to anyone else. At one time, he'd thought Megan was someone he could open up to. How wrong he'd been! She didn't really care about him: wouldn't have got involved with someone else otherwise.

Megan waited for her washing to finish, trembling a little. Seeing Mike had unsettled her. What was the point of her spending the best part of a week kissing Matt to get Mike out of her mind if he was going to turn up unexpectedly like that and throw her hormones into confusion again? She felt even guiltier when Matt arrived ten minutes before the end of the spin cycle, having been alerted to her whereabouts by Sally and Jen.

Matt was unusually talkative as he helped Megan unload her washing and place it in one of the driers – although that could have been because he was trying to hide his confusion at the sight of her underwear. Handing her an exciting pair of navy lace knickers, he wondered whether she would wear anything like that tonight – not that he would know if she did: they were still only at the kissing stage.

How long did the kissing stage last? Perhaps Ged or Phil could give him some advice. He still felt hot and bothered when he thought about doing things to Megan, but he didn't know whether his fantasies were disgusting or normal, due to his lack of experience. He could do with a friendly chat with someone who knew how it all worked.

As his fingers came into contact with a silky bra – it was the first time he'd seen or touched one of those! – he found himself picturing Megan wearing her underwear and nothing else. He imagined cupping her breasts with his hands and squeezing her soft flesh, then stopped himself, horrified at his perversity. Megan was so sweet, so innocent he doubted whether he would ever get to touch her.

Megan, meanwhile, was trying to pretend that Matt didn't have his hands on her underwear. It was kind of him to want to help, but she would have preferred to do it on her own.

"It's nice doing this together, isn't it?" Matt's voice intruded on her thoughts. He paused. "The sort of thing we'd be doing if we were living together – or married."

A slight sensation of panic began to creep through Megan's mind. They had only been going out for a fortnight, so why was Matt talking about a future together? She liked him, but it was a huge step from dating to marriage. The idea scared her.

Unaware of her consternation, Matt blundered on. "We could share a house together in our Final Year, couldn't we? None of the others will be around except Sally – she'll have a year abroad like us. That would be nice, wouldn't it: you, me and Sally in a student house somewhere?"

Megan knew, instinctively, that the last thing Sally would want would be to share a house with a man she liked but couldn't have and his girlfriend. And even if, in two and a half years, Sally had moved on and was no longer in love with Matt, who was to say that their relationship would still be intact that far into the future anyway?

"All that's a long way off," she said diplomatically. "Neither of us knows how we'll feel next month, let alone in a few years' time. What if you meet someone else on your year abroad? What if I do?"

The wounded gaze Matt turned on her radiated hurt. "I'd *never* go off with someone else. Anyway," his face suddenly brightened, "what's to stop us choosing the same place in France? Wouldn't that be wonderful, spending a year in Paris together, or in Nîmes, or Montpellier?"

"Don't do this, Matt!" Megan's tone was sharper than she'd intended. "I can't think about something so far into the future. I have enough problems trying to plan my outfits for the week or get all my essays done on time without you putting pressure on me about things that are years away."

Checking that everything she had placed in the drier was safe and that she wasn't going to be inadvertently shrinking any of her clothes, she pushed her coins in the slot and picked up her book.

"If you don't mind, I've got reading to do. I'll see you later."

She knew he would be upset, but she suddenly found it difficult to care.

*

She was still fuming thirty minutes later, when her laundry was dry, but it was herself and not Matt she felt angry with. If it had been Mike who was talking about the future, she knew her heart would have been racing – although she suspected that, for him, the future wouldn't reach further than inviting her out for a drink in a few days' time. She should feel flattered that Matt thought so much of her that he was desperate to plan their next five or ten years together; instead, she found it claustrophobic and rather annoying. There was nothing like someone being really keen on you to make you feel the opposite way about them.

And now she would have to spend a whole evening with him too, she thought grimly as she carried her clean clothes back to Ridge. She would have to be firm with him, make sure he understood that any 'soppy talk' was off the table for tonight.

She deliberately confined her conversation to the girls when lunchtime came and they hit the dining hall as a group for the legendary 'rat burger', a King Rib that was actually quite tasty. At least Matt had the sense to leave her alone, talking instead with Phil about their plans for the toga party disco the following evening.

"What's up with you and Matt?" Jen mouthed at her as they stood up to take their dirty plates away.

Megan pulled a face. "He's getting far too clingy. This morning he was talking about us living together in our Final Year!"

"That does seem a bit extreme," Jen agreed. Looking at Megan's worried face, she added, "He'll probably calm down a bit once he gets used to the idea of going out with you. Don't forget, he spent six months pining over you before anything happened – he's bound to be over-excited to begin with."

As she placed her used crockery and cutlery on the trolley provided and turned to leave, Megan spotted Matt hovering awkwardly near the door to Ridge. She sighed. "What do you want?"

"I … erm … I was just checking that we're still going out tonight …" Matt was terrified that his romantic evening would be ruined.

"I suppose so," Megan said ungraciously.

Matt breathed an audible sigh of relief. "If we leave at half four, we'll have time to go for food first. The play starts at seven thirty."

"Okay. I'll be ready on time. I'll meet you in the foyer."

Matt watched her leave, frowning to himself. She seemed tense, but he couldn't think why.

Behind him, Phil gave a sardonic laugh. "Bloody PMT! At least it's only a few days every month."

Matt nodded, although he didn't have a clue what Phil was talking about.

*

He had planned to take Megan somewhere special for dinner, but they ended up at Pizza Hut because it was convenient for the theatre and reasonably cheap. Megan seemed to relax as she attacked garlic bread and an olive and anchovy pizza. He remembered now that her parents had taken them both out for Italian food too: it must be her favourite.

There were plenty of other options that would have ranked higher for Megan than pizza, but she didn't care. She had a sudden craving tonight for olives and anchovies, not caring when Matt pulled a face at the mention of both of them.

They finished their food in plenty of time to find the theatre and their seats. Matt had managed to procure an excellent view of the stage and Megan enjoyed the first half of the play immensely, relishing Donald Sinden's over the top performance.

After the interval, as the curtain began to rise for the second act, Matt felt sufficiently emboldened to put his arm around Megan. She shrugged it off irritably, wanting to concentrate on the drama unfolding before her. He tried again a moment later, with the same result. Phil had obviously been right with his comment: Ged had helpfully explained about women's hormones when Matt asked him what the letters stood for.

Walking back from Fiveways Station at the end of the evening, Matt felt deliriously happy, despite Megan's moodiness. He had spent a whole week being her boyfriend at University, spending time with her, now taking her out. He envisaged the wonderful months ahead and smiled to himself.

They reached Ridge and Megan paused in the foyer. "I had a really nice time," she said simply. "I'm sorry I've been a bit grumpy: I think I'm just tired."

He was expecting her to invite him in for coffee, so he could finish the evening by kissing her to his heart's content, but instead she gave him a quick, awkward hug and turned towards the Ground Floor corridor.

"I'm really sleepy," she said with a yawn. "I'll see you in the morning."

He watched her leave, feeling curiously cheated.

Chapter Thirty-Two

Megan tried hard in the following week not to find Matt so annoying. She knew his heart was in the right place, but it was wearying being worshipped so much.

Saturday evening saw the whole gang taking a trip to the cinema to see 'A Room With A View', to keep Jen happy. It was a sumptuous production and very funny, with Maggie Smith and Judi Dench on fine form as elderly English spinsters. Megan could tell that Matt was enjoying the romantic scenes more than the other boys were and wondered if he were making mental notes on kissing techniques.

It was only much later on in the film – about two thirds of the way through – that Megan realised why Jen had been so keen to see it. The young male characters had met up near a river and suddenly decided to go skinny dipping. Megan peeped between her fingers at the sight of three attractive naked men frolicking in the water and then chasing each other through the bushes. Could this film *really* be a PG certificate with so many male dangly bits on display?

Matt had entered his customary hot and bothered phase: not because he was embarrassed to see so many unclothed men on the screen (he had, after all, been to a boys' boarding school) but because he had a very disturbing mental image of what it would be like if he too were naked and chasing Megan through the bushes.

Since they had caught an early showing, the seven of them headed for The American Food Factory once the film was over. It was the first time they had been there as a complete group since their initial outing over Freshers. While Megan busied herself with deep fried potato skins and chicken fajitas, the rest of the group discussed the previous Sunday's toga party disco. Megan had made a half-hearted attempt to support Matt, turning up in a bedsheet that covered far more of her than most of the outfits she wore on a daily basis, but the event as a whole had been woefully underattended. It seemed that Phil was now trying to persuade Matt to let him be in charge of the music the following evening.

"It's not that we don't appreciate all your hard work," he was saying, "but I think you need to be a bit more adventurous with some of your song choices. There are a lot of Rock Soc people in Hall who never leave the bar on a Sunday evening because you don't play any of their stuff at the disco."

"Hang on!" Sally interjected in alarm. "We don't want the whole evening to be non-stop Iron Maiden and Black Sabbath!"

Megan listened with only half an ear, too busy thinking about the impending dessert menu to feign any interest in something she knew nothing about. Then, as she caught her name, she sat up and concentrated.

"So, let's do a swap," Matt continued. "I'll help with all the setting up for the disco, but you can deejay for me – and in return you let me use your room for a romantic evening with Megan. Jen says you taped a film over Easter that Megan wants to watch."

And what if Megan didn't want a romantic evening in with a video? she wanted to retort, irked that Matt should be making plans without consulting her first. But he and Phil were already shaking hands to symbolise a done deal. It looked like there was no escape.

Jen was grinning at Megan, obviously expecting her to be pleased. "It's *'The French Lieutenant's Woman'*! You'll love it."

She *had* wanted to see the film, now Jen mentioned it. She'd been devastated to learn it had been on TV over the Easter holidays and she'd missed it.

Smiling up at Matt, she thanked him for his consideration, adding, "But don't start it too late: I like to be in bed by ten thirty."

*

By the time Matt had worked out which buttons to press to switch on Phil's colour TV and the High Hall video recorder, and then found the tape with the film on and managed to eject the one already in the machine, it was past eight o'clock.

"I'm sorry," Matt muttered contritely. "I'm not very good with gadgets."

Phil's single room was as narrow as all the others Megan had been in. (She tried not to think of what had happened the last time she had been in a room in High Hall.) He had organised it so the desk sat under the window, across the width of the room, and the bed was at a right angle to it. This meant that Matt and Megan were forced to sit side by side in a space that was only three feet wide in order to see the television screen. It was going to become very uncomfortable very quickly.

"Why don't we move back a bit?" Matt shuffled backwards until he was leaning against the headboard. "This feels much comfier." Since Megan looked uncertain, he added, "I'm not trying to seduce you!"

Of course he wasn't. Matt was a gentleman. Megan joined him at his end of the bed and lay back against the pillows.

"How come Phil has so many pillows?" she asked suspiciously, a moment later.

Matt blushed. "I brought the two from my room," he confessed. "I just wanted to make sure you'd be comfortable."

He still wasn't sure what he'd been hoping to get out of this evening, apart from being alone with Megan in a place where it was possible to stretch out for a proper cuddle. The bench by the lake was too hard and too public, and she never invited him back to her room for coffee these days.

The moment the film started, Megan was captivated. She had never read the novel upon which the film was based, so the entire story was unknown to her. As she avidly followed the tale of the Victorian biologist, Charles Smithson, and his fateful obsession with Sarah Woodruff, the enigmatic 'French Lieutenant's Woman' of the title, Matt struggled to keep up with the plot. He had read too little Victorian literature to recognise the conventions portrayed in the film; and he found the metafictional aspect – the story cutting to the affair between two actors playing the lead roles in a film being made of the novel – impossible to grasp.

"I suppose they're the grandchildren," he said at one point to Megan as the two actors, Mike and Anna, lay in bed indulging in a post-coital discussion of a particular scene they were about to film.

Megan was enjoying the film too much to let Matt's chattering put her off, although she *was* beginning to wonder why everything she read or watched seemed to involve at least one love triangle. Charles had begun the film by proposing to Ernestina yet rapidly developed a tragic fascination for Sarah, regarded as a fallen woman by all and sundry. After a dramatic disappearance by Sarah, Charles finally tracked her to a hotel in Devon, where he let his passion for her get the better of him.

Matt, who had been dozing off, was suddenly wide awake at this point, mentally studying Charles' masterful handling of Sarah as he kissed her passionately, swept her up in his arms, carried her over to the bed and had his way with her.

"He's a bit desperate, isn't he?" he commented as Charles collapsed after only a moment of intense thrusting.

Megan said nothing, transported back to that fateful night when she, too, had become a fallen woman. On screen Charles was apologising for his behaviour, having realised that Sarah was not the loose-moralled woman everyone thought her to be and that he had just rendered her unmarriageable by making love to her. Her reply was simply, "I wished it so," uncomfortably reminding Megan yet again of her own encounter with Mike.

She saw further parallels as Sarah disappeared once more after her evening with Charles, just as she, Megan, had disappeared from Mike's life (no more trips to *his* room!). But here any similarity ended, for Charles, after breaking off his engagement, then spent years trying to find Sarah again, exemplified by the large and bushy beard he grew over the time he searched fruitlessly.

Megan watched events unfold, a growing sadness in her heart as she reminded herself that Mike would never pursue her like that. When Matt's arm found his way around her shoulders and hugged her into him, she let it happen, her sorrow as much for herself as the unhappy couple on the screen.

As the final credits rolled, she knew she should be making a move; but a combination of tiredness and emotion overwhelmed her into sleep.

*

Matt was the first to wake the next morning. For a moment, he was puzzled: this wasn't his room. Then he became aware of the warm shape lying next to him and realised he had spent the night with Megan lying in his arms. Well, perhaps 'lying in his arms' was an exaggeration: he had spent the whole night with her lying on top of the arm he had draped round her, crushing it to the point where he could now no longer feel it at all.

He carefully moved his other arm to glance at his wristwatch. The hands stood at six fifteen: time to be up and moving. He idly wondered where Phil had spent the night with his own bed occupied.

Megan was still fast asleep. He nudged her gently. "Megan." No answer. He tried again. "Megan, you need to wake up."

This time she stirred, rolling off his arm, then sitting up slowly. "What time is it?" She sounded sleepy.

"Quarter past six. You need to get back to Ridge."

Her eyes widened in horror. "Why did you let me fall asleep?" What would Jen say, or Sally, if they knew she'd been in High all night? She could tell them that nothing happened, but would they believe it?

"I couldn't help it. I fell asleep myself." Matt sounded defensive. "Nothing happened," he muttered.

"That's not the point." Megan knew she sounded petty, but she felt angry that she'd put herself in a compromising position.

A cloud of resentment enveloped her as she grabbed her room key and opened the door. Matt watched her leave, his heart flooding with disappointment over the now ruined romantic evening. Would he *ever* get it right?

He was still lying on the bed, brooding, when Phil entered the room at seven.

"Good night?" His apparently casual question was loaded with meaning.

"Megan's just left." Matt let Phil draw his own conclusions.

Phil's eyebrows shot up. "She spent the night, then?"

Matt nodded, aware of what Phil was thinking, determined not to contradict him with the truth. He was tired of being seen as a 'nice' boy: why not let the others think he had made a conquest?

"Where did you go last night?" Matt was curious to know why Phil hadn't returned to his room.

Phil shrugged. "A load of us went back to your place for a bit of a Rock Soc party after the disco. Not Jen – she and the others said they'd had enough of the heavy metal in the disco." He looked proud. "I still can't believe I got away with playing as much as I did last night. You should have seen it, mate: loads of headbanging on the dance floor, and that was just the girls in Ridge!"

"It's not really my kind of music," Matt said hastily.

"No, you like your Phil Collins, don't you? Mind you, the new Genesis album'll be out in a couple of months and that sounds like Phil's solo stuff. We'll have to get the first single for the disco: I think the release date for that's some time in May." He looked at Matt. "I'm not being rude, but I need to take a shower. I'll see you later."

As he left, closing the door behind him, Matt wondered if he would be able to borrow Phil's room again.

*

Jen couldn't believe what Phil had just told her. "No!"

"It's true," Phil insisted. "They did it last night. Matt told me."

Jen hesitated. Matt wouldn't lie about something like that, but Megan hadn't said anything to her and surely she would ... And then she thought of how secretive Megan had been when she was seeing Mike. Perhaps she was the sort of girl who didn't confide in anyone?

There was Megan now, arriving at the breakfast table, looking tired.

"You look knackered this morning!" Jen said cheerfully. "Didn't you get enough sleep last night?"

Megan blushed, instantly confirming Jen's suspicions. "Not really," was all she would say by way of explanation. Then, as Matt approached their table, she stood up. "I'm not really hungry at the moment." Without any further conversation, she was gone.

Matt put his tray down, looking puzzled. "Was that Megan? Why was she leaving?"

Jen and Phil looked at each other.

"Did you sleep together last night?" Jen asked bluntly.

Matt knew what she meant; but, technically, they *had* slept together, side by side, so why shouldn't he answer in the affirmative?

"Yes, we did." He tried hard to sound casual. "Do you think she feels embarrassed about it?" he asked next.

Jen paused. She knew that, for Megan, sex was a big deal. She had romanticised it to the extent that anything less than perfection would crush her completely. If she were unable to face Matt now, it must mean that whatever happened hadn't been very good.

"I don't know," she said slowly. "I'll see if I can talk to her later."

Megan hadn't been lying when she said she wasn't hungry. She must be suffering the after effects of not enough sleep because she felt nauseous whenever she thought of food. She would go in to campus early, she decided, and work in one of the stacks in the library, away from prying eyes. She still felt irrationally angry with Matt: he had spoiled the film for her by allowing her to fall asleep in Phil's room. Moodily she pushed books into her rucksack and set off on her way.

*

She worked solidly until eleven, then felt sufficiently hungry to want something to eat. The Mason Lounge tea lady didn't open on Mondays, so her custard creams weren't an option. Perhaps she could grab a coffee and something light in the Guild?

First, though, she would check her pigeon hole. Making her way up the stairs in the Arts Faculty, she bumped into Jen coming down.

"Megan!" Jen sounded pleased to see her friend. "Come for a coffee with me. I've just had an hour of Bibliography and I need caffeine!"

Jen waited while Megan scanned the 'J' pigeon hole, wondering exactly how to broach the subject of Matt. In the end, she decided a direct approach was what was needed.

"So," she began as they sat down in the Guild café with cups of coffee and slices of cake, "how are things with you and Matt?"

Megan looked at her coffee cup.

"You spent the night with him, didn't you?" Jen persisted.

Megan nodded miserably, unaware that they were at cross purposes. "I feel terrible about it now," she said in a low voice.

"What makes it all so bad?" Jen was sympathetic.

Megan took a mouthful of cake and chewed carefully while she considered.

"It all happened too fast," she said eventually. "I didn't mean for it to happen: it just did."

Maybe, in an ideal world, she and Matt would have spent months getting to know each other, letting the physical side of things develop slowly, before spending an innocent night together, lying in each other's arms, talking, kissing, like the way she'd done several times with Mike before things went too far. Maybe. Any chance of that was now ruined: she'd slept next to Matt, and now he might think that this was the next stage of their relationship and that she would curl up with him every weekend. Even that was too much of a commitment for her at this stage.

She looked at Jen, her eyes dull. "It was a mistake; but what if he expects it to happen all the time now?"

"Matt loves you," Jen said gently. "I'm sure he won't put pressure on you to do it again."

"I was trying so hard," Megan said bleakly. "I was making sure that we only kissed out of doors, so there was less chance of getting carried away, and I wasn't letting him come back to my room. I only went to Phil's room with him because I really wanted to watch that film. It's my fault: I led him on."

"You didn't do anything wrong," Jen insisted. "You like him, don't you?"

Megan nodded. "But I'm not in love with him," she added.

"Falling in love takes time," Jen told her. "I know you feel bad right now, because you think it happened too quickly, but in a few months you might feel differently about him." She paused. "Waking up with someone you know you're in love with is one of the best feelings in the world."

Megan couldn't help a warm glow from stealing over her as she relived Mike's kisses; nor could she blot out the memory of waking up in his arms.

She knew than that things would never work out with Matt, lovely though he was. No matter how hard she tried to forget Mike, she was imprinted with the memory of him. No matter how shallow and meaningless it had been to him, for her it had been real. Mike had stolen a piece of her heart and no one else was capable of retrieving it.

She looked steadily at Jen. "I think I need to let Matt know it's not working out."

Chapter Thirty-Three

Jen was, understandably, upset over Megan's decision. She still thought her friend needed to give Matt a chance to prove himself. He was exactly the sort of person Megan needed, she thought desperately, knowing that if she were single again, Megan would probably end up running back to Mike.

In the end she managed to talk Megan into waiting a week or two. "You've hardly been together five minutes," she argued. "At least spend a bit more time together before you rush into anything." Not wanting her to make a snap decision based on one night of inadequate sex, she added, "You can hold back on the physical side if you don't feel comfortable with any of that. I'm sure Matt loves you enough to wait."

She would have words with him herself, she thought grimly as Megan headed back to the library. While she didn't doubt that Matt was head-over-heels in love with his girlfriend, she could easily understand that he might have rushed her the previous evening. Men were often like that: they thought sex proved you loved them.

She knew Matt had a two o'clock lecture with Megan. It was only just gone twelve now, and there were no English classes today. She would go over to the Muirhead Tower and see if she could find him.

Just as she was about to exit the Guild, she caught sight of a familiar figure in the shop. Matt was standing by a rack of greetings cards, obviously looking for something.

Jen tapped him on the shoulder. "Buying Megan a card?"

Matt started guiltily, almost dropping the card he'd been holding.

"Let's have a look." Jen scrutinised it carefully. On the front was a teddy bear holding a bunch of flowers, accompanied by the words, 'I'm Sorry.'

"What are you apologising for?" she asked, as casually as she could.

"I ...erm ..." Matt's eyes were downcast. Embarrassment emanated from him. "She's not happy with me," he said at last.

"I know," Jen said shortly. "We've just been having a chat and she told me all about last night. What were you thinking?"

Matt looked at her helplessly. "I just wanted to hold her."

Why were men so useless? Jen wondered to herself. How long would it be before they realised that you could hold someone and feel close to them without having to take your clothes off to do it? It was on the tip of her tongue to say this to Matt, but she bit the words back.

"You just need to go slowly with Megan," she said carefully. "What you did last night was something very intimate ..." She tried again. "I mean, I know lots of girls don't care how many people they sleep with, but Megan's not like that. For her, it's something special. It means everything."

Matt was feeling confused. Was Jen talking about lying down on the same bed with someone, or having sex? As far as he knew, he and Megan definitely hadn't done the latter. Unless ... His mind whirled. Could he have done it in his sleep without realising? The thought was too horrible to entertain.

"I don't want to make love to Megan unless it's what she wants too," he said at last. He also wanted to make sure they were both conscious. He still felt traumatised by the idea that sex had possibly happened last night and he had slept through it.

"Just take it slowly," Jen repeated. "And don't tell her we've had this conversation!"

*

"Megan …" Matt began slowly. Their French lecture was over and she was packing away her things.

"Yes," she said, without looking up.

"I think we need to talk. About last night."

Heather, sitting on the other side of Megan, pricked up her ears. This sounded juicy. She knew the two of them were now going out, but Megan had always seemed physically distant towards Matt. She certainly didn't act like a woman who was having her needs fulfilled.

"Not here," Megan said quickly. "Let's walk back to The Vale and sit by the lake."

She might as well take Matt to a place where he felt happy.

Heather could tell when she wasn't wanted. Matt and Megan had been content to let her tag along as they trudged along the path back to the Halls of Residence, but once they reached The Vale she knew she was surplus to requirements.

"I'll leave you two lovebirds alone, then," she said as she left them by the lake and took herself off to Wyddrington.

Matt found a suitable bench and gestured to Megan. "Shall we sit there?"

She seated herself, leaving a noticeable gap between them. "What do you want to say?"

Despite the warmth of the sun, he could detect a chilliness in her manner towards him. "Megan, I'm sorry," he began in a rush, then stopped, feeling confused.

"What are you apologising for?" She sounded weary.

"I … erm … I know you aren't very happy with me at the moment." He was trying to catch her eye, but she was avoiding his gaze, staring out over the lake at something indiscernible in the distance.

He tried again. "I talked to Jen earlier. About you and me."

Megan suddenly gave him her full attention. "What did you say?"

The words came out slowly. "She said you were upset about what happened last night." He hesitated. "It's all a bit of a blur, really. I remember falling asleep with you cuddled up to me and then waking up hours later. I didn't do anything else, did I? Anything I've forgotten?"

"Like what?" Megan was genuinely puzzled.

Matt breathed a sigh of relief. Evidently he wasn't a somnambulant rapist after all.

"Why are you cross with me?" he asked next.

Megan sighed. "It's not you: it's me." Looking at his questioning face, she elaborated, "I was angry with myself for falling asleep instead of going back to Ridge. If anyone had seen me leaving Phil's room at that time in the morning, they would have assumed we'd been at it all night. I don't want to get a reputation for being that sort of girl."

Matt was astounded. Was *that* what all the fuss was about?

"No one would ever think anything like that about you," he said earnestly, quite forgetting how he'd misled Phil into thinking exactly that when he'd spoken to him earlier.

Megan gave him a wobbly smile. "I'm sorry I've been so uptight recently," she said in a small voice.

Without warning, Matt closed the gap between them and enfolded her in a hug. She relaxed into it, too tired to fight him now. Anyway, she reasoned, he deserved a bit of a cuddle after she'd been so mean to him all day. He was trying so hard to make her happy: the least she could do was to make a bit of effort herself.

*

For the next few weeks, Megan tried hard to wind down the relationship a little at a time. She liked Matt and didn't want to hurt him, so she tried to remove the romantic side of things gradually whilst still retaining the friendship. Surely, she reasoned, it was possible to get to the stage where they were 'just friends' again without anyone being hurt.

Exams were looming. It was now the fifth week of the Summer Term and Exam Week took place in the sixth. Jen popped round to Megan's room before dinner and confessed that she was finding it all very stressful.

"Sally doesn't get phased by exams so she doesn't understand why I do," she told her, "but I can tell I'm worried because I'm two days late," she confided, adding, "My periods are always like clockwork, apart from around exam time."

"I'm late too," Megan said without thinking. She had a ridiculously erratic cycle and could easily wait six or seven weeks instead of the usual four. She wasn't actually worried: by now she was used to her body's idiosyncrasies. Besides, she must be about to come on soon because she had all the usual pre-menstrual symptoms: tender breasts, heightened emotions, feeling nauseous when she woke up.

Jen shot her a concerned look. By her calculations, it was just over a fortnight since Megan and Matt had slept together. She hadn't asked Megan whether they'd taken any precautions, but remembering her words – "It all happened too fast" and "It was a mistake" – she thought they probably hadn't.

"I'm going to do a pregnancy test," she said slowly. "Not because I think I am – I know I'm not - but because if I see a negative result, it will be one less thing to worry about." She looked carefully at Megan. "I think you should do one too."

Megan opened her mouth, ready to protest that she didn't need to, that six or seven weeks was nothing, then closed it again, remembering that not only had she not had a period this term, she hadn't had one over the Easter holidays either. A sudden panic gripped her: ten weeks was much more serious than six or seven. No, it was longer than ten weeks: her last one had been several weeks before the end of term. She counted rapidly. Could it really be three months or more?

Jen was busy making plans. "We can go to the Health Centre on campus. I'll pop in after lectures tomorrow and make the appointments." She chose her words carefully. "Even if we both think it will be negative, it's better to make sure."

After her friend had gone, Megan sat on her bed for quite a while, trying to work out what to do. There was still a chance that she wasn't pregnant, but she knew it was far more likely that her night with Mike had reaped unexpected consequences.

Pregnant. The word seemed like a death sentence. What would her parents say? And her friends? There was no point asking herself what Mike's reaction would be: she knew that already. He would probably shrug and tell her that it wasn't his problem, that it had been an isolated incident that was "pretty special at the time".

And then her heart stood still as she realised she would have to tell Matt that she was pregnant with another man's baby.

Jen told her the following day that they both had an appointment with the nurse on Wednesday. "We have to take a sample." She pulled a face. "They gave me these little bottles. You're supposed to do it as soon as you wake up."

Megan looked at the tiny receptacle and wondered how any woman could aim at something so small. It was all right for men, she thought crossly: they were built totally differently and could just point and shoot.

Her fears were confirmed the following morning. She was sure more of it had ended up on her hands than in the bottle. Still, at least she had the required amount.
She scrubbed her hands furiously under the tap, wishing she could wash her unwanted pregnancy away too.

She would be lecture-free after her twelve o'clock tutorial and so would Jen. Their appointments were at one fifteen and one twenty-five. Sitting in the waiting room together, they tried to talk of unimportant things. Jen didn't tell Megan that her period had started that morning. She didn't want her friend to know she was the only one who needed a test.
Megan's name was called first. Jen gave her an encouraging smile. "You'll be fine. Do you want me to come in with you?"
Megan shook her head.

The nurse's room was white and sterile. A few alarming posters issued dire warnings about sexually transmitted diseases and a box of tissues and some rather nasty looking metal instruments stood on the desk. Megan swallowed hard as she sat down.
The nurse consulted her notes. "Megan Jackson. You're here for a pregnancy test – is that right?"
Megan nodded.
"Have you brought a sample?"

Without speaking, Megan handed it over. She knew already what the result would be, yet even so, a tiny part of her hoped that it was all some ghastly mistake and that the nurse's verdict would be "Negative."

She watched in silence as the nurse thrust a cardboard stick into the bottle. "It usually takes a couple of minutes," the woman said cheerily. Megan wondered how many girls like her sat here each day, waiting to find out if their whole future had changed.

She watched the clock on the wall, the seconds dragging by as if reluctant to elapse. After what seemed an interminable age, the nurse turned back to the sample.

"You're very definitely pregnant." Her tone was neutral.

Megan stared at her in disbelief, her one shred of hope now completely eviscerated.

"You're going to have to make some decisions, Megan." The nurse's voice was now surprisingly gentle. "Most girls choose a termination and we can arrange that for you, if it's what you want. That can happen any time before you reach twenty-eight weeks, but the longer you leave it, the more complicated it will be."

Still unable to take any of this in, Megan said nothing.

The nurse scribbled on the pad in front of her. "If you decide you're going through with it, you'll need to start taking folic acid. You'll also need to see a doctor, so you can have a proper check-up." She paused. "I'm not trying to influence you one way or the other. What you do next is up to you."

As Megan stumbled back into the waiting room, her ashen face told Jen all she needed to know.

"Let's go back to Hall now," she said, getting up. "I think you and I need a talk."

Chapter Thirty-Four

Jen could tell Megan was in a state of shock. She sat her down on her bed and made her a cup of tea, but Megan stared past her, her eyes blank and unseeing.

"It was positive, wasn't it?" No point in pretending otherwise.

"I can't have a baby." Megan's voice sounded hollow.

"Then don't," Jen said practically. "It's not as if you don't have a choice."

Mike's mother had tried to get rid of him by sitting in a hot bath and drinking gin.

"I can't get rid of it." She looked at Jen miserably.

"Why not? It's just a foetus, just cells."

Megan shook her head. "There's a baby," she said in a tight voice, "growing inside me. A little person. Have you any idea how scary that is?"

"You're in shock," Jen said automatically. She gestured at Megan's mug. "Drink your tea. It might help."

But drinking tea wouldn't stop her being pregnant. Jen didn't understand what she was going through.

"It's not fair!" she said, thinking aloud.

"What isn't fair?" Jen was trying to be supportive.

"It only happened once." Megan looked at her wildly. "How can I be pregnant after just one time?"

Jen wisely said nothing.

"People will think I'm a slut," Megan went on urgently. "They'll think I got pregnant because I was sleeping around." Her gaze was suddenly fierce. "You can't tell anyone."

"If you're serious about not getting rid of it, I won't have to," Jen said practically. "You getting bigger is going to give the game away for a start." She put an arm around her friend. "You're not thinking about this properly, Meg. If you had the baby, what would you do? You couldn't stay in Hall and just keep it in your room with you. And how would you go to lectures with a screaming baby?"

Megan hadn't thought about any of this. Her primary concern at the moment was what she would tell Matt.

And then the thought stuck her: if she *didn't* have this baby, then she wouldn't have to tell him about it. Nor would she have to say anything to her parents, or to anyone else.

But she couldn't abort Mike's baby, even if she didn't really want it. A perverse part of her whispered, *If you can't have Mike, at least you can have a part of him.*

No, that was crazy. Jen was right: she couldn't have a baby; but she couldn't get rid of it either. There must be another way ...

"What if I fell down the stairs?" she asked, her mind desperately trying to think of a workable solution.

Jen looked at her as if she were mad.

"If I fell down the stairs and had a miscarriage," she was gabbling now, "then it wouldn't really be my fault, would it? Not like having an abortion."

"I think you need to have a rest," Jen said evenly. "You're not thinking straight at the moment." She hugged her awkwardly. "I've got some work to do for Bibliography. I'll see you later."

She opened the door, and all of Megan's hope left with her.

*

She wasn't sure how long she slept, aware only that she'd been asleep when a frantic knocking sounded on her door. Matt stood there, wild-eyed. She caught his breath and realised he'd been drinking.

"You're pregnant." He said it flatly, as if the words were too terrible to invest with meaning.

Megan dragged him inside hurriedly. This was no doorway conversation.

He turned and faced her, hurt and anger fighting for dominance. "You're pregnant." He enunciated the words again. Confusion streamed from him: he was a little boy trying to make sense of something he didn't understand.

"How did you know?" There was no point denying it.

"Jen told me. She seemed to think it was my baby and that I should be responsible and help you to make the right decision." He grabbed hold of her suddenly, seizing her shoulders and shaking her. "You're my girlfriend but it's not my baby. How many men are you sleeping with?"

She had never thought she could be frightened of Matt. Now, as he stood there, gripping her so hard it hurt, she was suddenly afraid.

"Matt," she tried to keep her voice steady, "you're hurting me. Let go. Please."

He pushed her away as if she were contaminated. "How many?" he repeated.

"Only one." Her voice was a whisper. "It only happened once."

"Who was it? Dan? Mike? That guy with the guitar?"

He sank to the bed, his hands covering his face in despair. "You're my girlfriend. Why are you sleeping with someone else?" At this moment, he sounded utterly broken.

Despite the pain in her shoulders, despite the fear she'd just experienced, she had to look after him. "Matt?" She put an arm around him tentatively, but he shrugged it away.

"I haven't been cheating on you." She took a deep breath. "I made a mistake, but that was last term, before you and I got together. I haven't seen him since, not in that way."

A cup of coffee in a seedy café; a brief moment of looking at each other in the laundry room; and, even now, her heart still beat faster whenever she thought of him.

"It was Mike, wasn't it?" Matt said the words slowly, as if reality were only just dawning for him. Perhaps it was.

She nodded. There was nothing else to say.

"Where? When?" His voice was fierce.

"Does it matter?" He was only torturing himself.

"Yes, it does." He regarded her coolly. "I'm your boyfriend and I have a right to know exactly when you were screwing someone behind my back."

"It wasn't behind your back." She tried to keep her voice calm. "I started seeing Mike a long time ago, back in December. We saw each other two or three times and we kissed, nothing more."

"Then why are you pregnant?"

"I saw him again in the Spring Term," Megan continued, a sick feeling rising in her throat. "It wasn't a relationship – he's got a girlfriend at home – but from time to time, we just got together."

"Slag!" The word burst from Matt in an explosion of hatred.

"It wasn't like that." Tears filled her eyes as she tried to explain. "When I went to see him, it wasn't for sex. We used to talk about things …"

"What things?" Matt sounded jealous.

She shook her head. "Books. Our families. He's had a tough time recently."

"So you slept with him to cheer him up?" Matt had every right to sound bitter.

"No." This was the hard bit. "I'd started thinking about *you* and whether we should try going out. I didn't want to be going out with you but be thinking about Mike, so …" How on earth could she explain what she'd done? "So I got drunk and went over to his room and asked him to make love to me," she finished in a rush.

Matt had never felt more devastated. Megan – his sweet, innocent Megan – was no better than a whore.

"When was this?" he said at last. It was an effort to get the words out.

Her reply was a faint whisper. "The night we performed the St John Passion."

The room spun momentarily. That was the night Matt had kissed her for the second time. He had sat in her room and drunk tea and kissed her; and then she had run to Mike and opened her legs for him like a common prostitute.

He didn't register what he was doing until his fist had hit her.

For a moment, Megan saw stars. Matt's blow had caught her on the side of her jaw. She felt it tenderly: there would be a bruise later.

Matt was staring at her in horror. "Megan! I'm sorry! I didn't mean …"

She pulled him towards her, tears rolling down her cheeks, cradling his head, trying to hold him through the pain. "It's all right," she heard herself say, over and over again. "It's all right."

Matt nestled into her and cried like a baby.

She released him some time later. His sobbing had subsided; her jaw ached.

"You know you have to get rid of it." Matt's voice, flat and hard.

She said nothing.

"You have to," he insisted, his tone harsh. "Mike won't want to play happy families with you, and I'm not bringing up someone else's bastard."

What had she done to him? She recoiled in horror. This was Matt – sweet, gentle Matt – and she didn't recognise him at all.

"I can't have an abortion." The words wrenched from her, as painful as removing a tooth.

"You have to," he repeated. "You're *my* girlfriend. You can't have someone else's baby."

Tears in her eyes, she looked at the face of a man she no longer knew. "I can't kill another human being."

"You have to," he said for a third time, "because if you don't, you'll be killing *me*." Silence while they both looked at each other. Then, "I'll throw myself under a bus," Matt said desperately.

It was the drink talking, she told herself. Matt wouldn't really do anything stupid, would he? And then she thought of his fist hitting her face and realised that he was totally unpredictable. And it was all her fault.

He was still there, half an hour later, lying in her bed in a semi-drunken stupor, when a faint tapping on her door signalled someone else's presence. Megan answered it quickly. Jen stood there, her face full of concern.

"How are you feeling?" Her eyes fell on Matt, prone, unconscious. "I take it he's not happy?"

"Why did you tell him?" Megan couldn't keep the sense of betrayal out of her voice.

"I had to tell him, Meg. It's his responsibility too." Jen looked at her friend's tear-stained face. "You shouldn't have to go through this on your own."

Now was the time to tell Jen about Mike, but she couldn't. Matt's last words to her, before he collapsed into oblivion, had been to make her swear not to tell anyone that it wasn't his baby. "I don't want people looking at me, laughing," he'd slurred, taking another swig from the bottle in his backpack. "Get rid of it and no one will know it ever existed. But if you're really going to be stupid enough to keep it, you've got to let people think it's mine."

This was what she had driven him to, she thought woodenly, looking from Jen to Matt. She'd used him to try and get over Mike, not thinking about Matt's own feelings, wanting only to fill her time with someone who could help her forget. It had been a mistake ever to try to be more than friends – and both she and Matt were paying the price for that now.

"He's not handling it well," she told Jen now, her eyes filling with tears.

"What did you expect?" Jen didn't mean to sound uncaring, but she couldn't help the frustration that escaped with her words.

"I really do have to get rid of it, don't I?" Megan said miserably. "It's destroying Matt just thinking about it."

As Jen put her arms around her, Megan let her tears fall once more.

*

She wandered through the next day in a daze. She still couldn't believe that she had been so stupid – or that Jen, by being helpful, had made the situation even worse.

She couldn't face breakfast. Now she knew she was pregnant, her early morning nausea made sense. It also gave her the excuse to hide in her room instead of going to the dining hall with the others. She knew Matt would be there and things were too tense, too fragile between them. He'd apologised again for losing his temper and hitting her when he'd finally come to, but she was aware that things would never be the same again between them. She had hurt him too much for him to forgive what she'd done.

Before leaving for campus, she examined her face in the mirror. There was a bruise on her face but it was almost unnoticeable unless you knew where to look. If anyone asked, she would say she had walked into an open door.

She slipped out of Hall without waiting for anyone else, unable to face either girly chatter or Matt's stony silence. He was still putting pressure on her to abort her child. She knew it was the only practical solution; even so, she flinched from the idea.

Somehow she got through her ten o'clock French Lit tutorial, although she couldn't remember anything anyone had said. Exams started on Monday and this was her last day of classes this week. She had to focus, but she couldn't.

Eleven o'clock and English. Jen slipped into a seat beside her in the lecture theatre. "The others missed you at breakfast. I said you had a headache."

Megan *did* have a headache, brought on by all the stress of her current situation. "How was Matt?" she asked in a small voice.

"Hungover." Jen gave a terse reply. "He must've really knocked it back last night. I've never seen him like that before."

Inside Megan's stomach, guilt grew: a heavy stone, weighing her down. "I've really messed up, haven't I?" she said bleakly.

"No," Jen was honest, "you've just been unlucky. It could have happened to anyone."

Anyone twisted enough to sleep with another girl's boyfriend after leading on someone else who liked her, Megan thought bitterly. She deserved everything she got. Perhaps God was punishing her?

For the next fifty minutes, she tried to concentrate, writing things down whether or not she understood them. The lecture would be done by twelve and then she would have two hours to wait until French Lit and Matt – *if* he wanted to sit with her after the way she'd treated him.

As David Lodge made his closing comments, Jen turned to her. "His books are so funny – how come his lectures are so dry?"

Megan made no reply, her mind already preoccupied with thoughts of doctors and hospitals. She wondered if an abortion hurt.

And then, unbidden, an image of herself holding a newborn baby popped into her mind. She *couldn't* get rid of it – but it was the only way.

Two o'clock. Jen had taken her for an early lunch after their lecture together, making sure that she ate and drank something. Sitting in the Cellar Bar – where else? – Megan had felt terribly alone despite the hustle and bustle all around her. Everyone else was carrying on with life as normal, whereas her life had stopped the moment the nurse told her she was pregnant. She couldn't do this. It was too much for her to handle.

She felt the same way now, sitting in the lecture theatre. Heather sat beside her, filling her ears with unimportant drivel. There was a tiny person growing inside her, for goodness' sake! She didn't need to know about shenanigans in Hall or what someone else had seen on the way to campus.

"So you'll come with me then?" Megan tuned back in, aware that Heather had just asked her something.

"Sorry," she confessed. "I was miles away."

"The CU tomorrow. Jonathan's doing his talk. He told us about it at the Hunger Lunch, remember?"

Megan cast her mind back to the last Thursday of the Spring Term. She couldn't forget that lunchtime, coming hard on the heels of her fatal indiscretion. She had been racked with guilt then; but that was nothing compared to the way she felt now.

"I can't go," she said bluntly. Sitting amongst a group of shiny, happy Christians whilst she knew herself to be a degenerate sinner, was more than she could bear.

"*Please.*" Heather looked at her imploringly. "I can't go on my own: I'll feel out of place."

And she, Megan, felt out of place everywhere right now. She sighed. She might as well suffer in the chaplaincy as in the Hall Bar. At least she wasn't likely to bump into anyone she knew.

"Okay," she said unwillingly. "But you owe me one."

Chapter Thirty-Five

Megan barely touched her food at dinner that night, pushing it around her plate as if she had other things on her mind. Jen watched her and sighed inwardly. She knew things were still strained between Matt and Megan: the latter had reported that Matt had blanked her totally in their lecture that afternoon, sitting with a couple of girls who also did French and Drama. Megan knew who they were because Matt had pointed them out to her before, in another lifetime when he was still speaking to her.

Phil and Ged had joined them at their usual table, but Matt was conspicuously absent. Jen spoke privately to Phil. "Do you know where he is?"

Phil shook his head. "I knocked on his door, but he didn't answer."

He was probably drinking himself silly again, Jen thought in a flush of anger. She was very disappointed with Matt's behaviour. *He* wasn't the one who was pregnant, for Heaven's sake!

"Has something happened between those two?" Phil asked curiously. "I thought they were all loved up after the other Sunday."

"It's complicated." Jen would say no more and Phil didn't press her. He didn't mind Jen sharing her own touchy-feely stuff with him, but he didn't want to hear about anyone else's.

Megan spent the rest of the evening in her room, trying to read. She'd left Heather after the French lecture and gone to the library, thinking they must have at least one book on pregnancy and birth. The volume she found had been written in 1970 and seemed rather dated, but it did tell her how to work out her possible due date and it also had a helpful section on what size the foetus was throughout every week of the pregnancy.

Megan grabbed a pen and began to jot down dates. She didn't have a clue when her last period had started, but she did know when the child had been conceived: in the early hours of Thursday the sixth of March. Conception was supposed to take place two weeks into one's cycle. She counted backwards. One week before was February 27th; two weeks before was February 20th. That meant her child would be born towards the end of November, which put her at just under three months pregnant. According to the book, the baby was now three to four inches long, weighing in at about an ounce. There was also a much smaller risk of miscarriage now she had got to this stage.

She placed her hands on her still flat belly and tried to imagine the tiny heart beating inside her. "It's not that I don't want you," she told the unknown inhabitant of her womb. "It's just that I can't see any way of keeping you."

Again, a sudden mental image of herself cradling a baby. This was *her* child, a part of her. How could she possibly destroy it?

A knocking on her door. Matt, as drunk as before. She let him in, wondering how fragile his state of mind would be tonight.

"Don't leave me, Megan." He had already reached the weepy stage. "Whatever happens, don't leave me."

He had noticed the pregnancy book. His mood changed suddenly, Mr Hyde appearing in full force.

"You're keeping it. aren't you?"

He had grabbed hold of her again, the sour stench of his alcohol-soaked breath assaulting her nostrils.

"I don't know."

She managed to wriggle free of him, but he lunged at her again. "You want that baby more than me."

"That's not true." But inside she thought it might be.

He pushed his face close to hers, his eyes full of hatred. "You. Are. Not. Having. Mike's. Baby." Every word was a knife in her heart.

Slowly, very slowly his hand reached out. She flinched, half expecting another blow. Instead, he stroked her face, his fingers tracing the bruise he'd given her. Instinctively she stiffened.

"Megan." His voice now full of anguish. "Please get rid of it. Can't you see what it's doing to me? To us?"

What 'us'? she thought wildly. She and Matt weren't a couple anymore. How could they be after what she'd done?

Turning her face back towards his, he kissed her very deliberately on the lips, as if trying to stake his claim on her. "I still want you," he said simply.

By the time Matt left, Megan's emotions were in even more turmoil that they had been before. Matt and alcohol did not mix well; however, she was equally aware that he would not be drinking to excess were it not for her. She felt trapped by his obsessive need for her.

She slept badly again, her mind too full of recent events. When morning came, bringing with it the now familiar nausea, she didn't even bother getting up. Friday was lecture free. She would rest while she had the chance.

Jen tapped on her door later, asking how she was. "The others are starting to ask questions," she told her. "I've said you're under the weather, but you can't make that excuse indefinitely."

She dozed fitfully until noon, emotionally drained by the past few days. She still didn't know what to do. Common sense told her that keeping the child was impossible, but in her mind's eye she still saw herself rocking it to sleep in her arms.

It was with a heavy heart that she walked to the University Health Centre that afternoon to make an appointment to see the doctor on Monday. She would talk to him about a termination: it was the only viable option.
She cried all the way back to Hall.

*

Entering her room to be alone with her tears, Megan spotted a note on the floor. Someone had taken down a phone message for her: "Heather says it's a seven o'clock start. She'll be waiting outside Wyd at six thirty."
The last thing she wanted in her present state of mind was to go out anywhere, but if she stayed in her room, Matt would appear again. She couldn't not let him in: it was her fault that he was so unbalanced at the moment. If she went for her evening meal at five thirty, as soon as they started serving, she could meet Heather as requested and escape for a few hours.
She didn't let herself think about what would happen when she arrived back in Hall at the end of the evening.

Heather was waiting for her with a face full of expectancy. "Thanks for coming."

She spent the entire walk to the Chaplaincy chattering about Jonathan and how much she liked him. Megan thought this was a little extreme: after all, Heather had only met him once, at the Hunger Lunch in March. When she mentioned this, the other girl coloured.

"Actually, I bumped into him in the Guild last week and we went for a coffee," she confessed. "That's why I remembered about tonight: he asked me if I was still going along to listen to him."

"You didn't tell me you'd seen him." Was everyone as secretive as she herself was?

"I was going to." Heather sounded defensive. "But when we met him the first time and I tried telling you how much I liked him, you said I was reading too much into it and that he'd only talked to us because he was trying to convert us!" She paused. "You weren't very supportive."

Megan thought guiltily of the number of secrets she'd kept from Heather, knowing that she couldn't claim to hold the moral high ground.

"I'm sorry," she said quietly. "I had a lot on my mind that day."

They had reached the Chaplaincy. Megan wondered if any of the Christians would have a sixth sense that alerted them to fallen women. She felt as conspicuous as if a large sign had been hung around her neck, bearing the word "Whore".

Loads of students have sex, her mind argued. *Look at all the free condoms we had at Freshers!*

But those students had the sense not to get pregnant; and the common decency not to traumatise their boyfriends by telling them they were having another man's baby. She wasn't just immoral: she was a terrible person.

Heather looked as nervous as Megan felt, hovering at the back of the large room which had been filled with chairs. Noticing music stands and a drum kit near the front, Megan felt alarmed. Was this a talk or a concert? Was Jonathan going to *sing* his life story to them?

As the room gradually filled up, Heather grabbed two chairs at the back for herself and Megan. "If it's really dire, we can just slip out," she muttered. Megan was relieved to know that Heather was as apprehensive as she was.

The music started. Megan counted two guitarists and two singers. The drummer was Jonathan.

"Did you know he could play?" she whispered to Heather.

The other girl shook her head. "He kept quiet about that one."

As the band launched into their first song, something about majesty and sacrifice, with a chorus about worshipping God, Megan decided that this was definitely one of the most bizarre moments of her life so far. The music was catchy, though, and the words were projected onto the back wall to encourage everyone to sing along. She was half-tempted to join in herself.

Another song, and then a girl with glasses and a terribly Christian outfit stepped forward. "Let's pray."

Megan was expecting the room to fall silent for a few moments, but instead various people began to speak out loud, addressing their prayers to a God who seemed like a best friend. The speakers ranged from chatty to passionate; it was like nothing else Megan had ever experienced before.

And now Jonathan was striding forward, taking the microphone and addressing the crowd. "I'm here tonight to talk to you about God's love," he began, "but before I do that, I want to give you a few facts." He paused for effect, his dreadlocked countenance offset by his commanding presence. Everyone wanted to hear what he had to say.

Six million," he enunciated slowly. "That's the number of Jews killed by Hitler in the holocaust. It's the number of babies killed since the 1967 Abortion Act."

The words twisted like a knife in Megan's gut. *Six million babies.* She couldn't add to that number. She just couldn't.

She had no idea what else Jonathan said that evening, sitting there with tears streaming down her face as she thought of the little life inside her and how she had to protect it at any cost.

Some time later, she was aware of the music starting up again and Heather nudging her gently. "He was amazing, wasn't he?"

Just one song this time and people began to file out, heading in the direction of the room where they'd had the Hunger Lunch. Several students were presiding over the serving hatch, offering tea, coffee or squash. Megan found herself being carried along by the crowd, unable to find a safe place to hide.

"Come on!" Heather tugged at her again. "There's Jonathan. Let's go and say Hi."

"I'll catch up with you in a minute," Megan told her. "I'm just going to the loo."

Spotting the signs for the toilets, she fled for sanctuary, too fragile to make small talk. Once she had reached the safety of a cubicle, she pushed the bolt across and cried as if her heart would break.

Megan had never thought much about God before, beyond a vague awareness that she believed in a generic Higher Power that rewarded you for being good and punished you for getting it wrong. A prayer of some sort spilled from her now: a gut-wrenching, soul-shattering prayer. "Please, God," she begged the unknown deity, "please keep my baby safe. Tell it how much I love it, how much I want it." Her tears fell afresh as she whispered the words. "Please let it know that even though it wasn't planned, it's still loved. And please give me the strength to go through with this, even if it means doing it all on my own."

There was no blinding flash of light to tell her God had heard; no earthquake; no plague of locusts. But inside, she felt an overwhelming sense of hope. She was going to have this baby, no matter how hard it was.

She quickly added a PS: "And please help Matt to cope with all of this. Help him to understand why I can't kill my baby."

Wiping her eyes on a piece of toilet paper, she left the cubicle and went to find Heather.

Chapter Thirty-Six

Matt gazed at Megan in disbelief. "You're *what*?"

"I'm not getting rid of it," she repeated. "There's a little life growing inside me. I can't kill it."

"Mike won't want to know." He sounded desperate.

"This isn't about Mike. It's about me."

He turned away from her in disgust. "And I'm supposed to watch you getting fatter and fatter, knowing his baby's inside you, knowing how it got there?"

"I'm sorry I've hurt you," she began, but he turned on her fiercely.

"You haven't hurt me: you've ripped out my heart, stamped on it and now you're trying to force it down my throat! I *loved* you; but you've ruined it. You've ruined everything."

He was as drunk as he had been the previous evening, and the one before that. She wondered if he would ever be sober again.

"What about adoption?" His words startled her.

"What?"

"What about adoption?" he repeated. "I let you have the baby, but you give it up for adoption."

She couldn't give her child away, not when it had spent months growing inside her, but maybe Matt would change his mind once it was born? Surely, she told herself desperately, when he saw a vulnerable, helpless little baby he would want her to keep it?

"You can't tell anyone it's not mine," he said slowly. "Jen already thinks it's my baby, so we let her go on thinking that. And I start staying over, so we look like a proper couple."

He was taking charge, steamrollering her into being part of the story he longed for. She wanted to say no, to protest that she would do this on her own, without a pretend boyfriend, a pretend father; but guilt stopped her mouth. She had hurt him so much already: what harm could it do if she indulged his fantasy until he was strong enough to face the truth himself?

She looked at her alarm clock: it was past eleven. She had left a note on her door for Matt when she went out with Heather, telling him she would be out until late (she'd returned at quarter past ten) and that he should look for her tomorrow. Instead he'd staked out her doorway, sitting on the floor in the corridor, waiting. She suspected he'd thought she was with Mike, so she'd hastened to reassure him, telling him about Heather and the CU but not her cry for help in the toilets.

"I really need to get some sleep," she said apologetically.

Matt didn't move. "Then I'll stay with you." He looked at her drunkenly. "If you don't let me stay, I'll go back to Hall and tell Mike you're pregnant. And I'll tell him you've slept with so many men, you don't know whose it is."

Her heart stopped. How could Matt say those things? How could he hate her so much?

Grabbing her nightshirt, she fled the room. Would he have gone by the time she returned from the toilet? She stayed there much longer than she needed to – she could always blame an unsettled stomach – but he was still there, stretched out on her bed, fast asleep.

In the end, she took the easy chair, removing the throw from the top of her trunk and wrapping it around herself for warmth. Despite her uncomfortable posture, exhaustion soon overcame her and she slept.

*

She was stiff when she awoke the following morning. Sunlight streamed in through the curtains, a golden shaft in her eyes suggesting that dawn had arrived some hours ago. For a moment she wondered why she wasn't in her bed, then the sound of gentle snoring alerted her to Matt's presence. He was still supine on her bed. He hadn't moved at all in the past – *how many* hours?

The clock on her bedside cabinet said five to nine. That couldn't be right! But it was. She had slept for almost ten hours and, for once, felt refreshed. Maybe she could manage some breakfast this morning?

No, the sick feeling at the back of her throat told her breakfast wasn't an option. How long had the book said this stage lasted?

A light tapping at her door. Jen stood there with an enquiring look. "Can you face food this morning?"

"Not today." Megan tried to obfuscate Jen's view of the room, standing in front of her to block her field of vision. She should have remembered the other girl topped her by five or six inches.

"Is that Matt?" Jen's tone sounded peculiar.

Megan stepped outside the room, holding the door to so she wouldn't lock herself out.

"He popped round," she said defensively.

"Last night or this morning?" Jen was relentless.

"Does it matter?"

Jen decided to be blunt. "If he's pressuring you into anything you don't want to do, then yes. I know things are … more complicated now, but that doesn't mean you can't say no."

"He's not making me do anything," Megan said quickly. She knew Matt was under a lot of pressure. He wouldn't use emotional blackmail under normal circumstances: his threats last night had just been words.

But now Matt was stirring. She could hear the creak of bedsprings as he moved and sat up. He appeared unexpectedly in the doorway behind her, placing a hand on her shoulder proprietorially, telling the whole world he was her boyfriend.

"Morning, Jen. Did Megan tell you we're having a baby?"

*

Once Matt had decided to go public, it was amazing how fast the news travelled in their little circle. Jen broke the news to Sally herself before breakfast – she thought it would be better coming from her.

"I see." Sally's mouth looked tight. Jen knew this must be difficult for her.

They walked to the dining hall together in a group, Megan as well. Her stomach was churning but Matt told her she needed to make an appearance. He had planned an official announcement and he wanted her to be part of it.

"Didn't you wear that shirt yesterday?" Sue asked suddenly as they sat down. Matt was always so meticulous about his clothes.

"I spent the night with Megan." Matt looked at the others, daring anyone to comment. "Actually, we've got some news for you." He paused for effect. "Megan's pregnant."

Phil looked totally stunned; Ged upset. Sally said nothing.

"And you're keeping it?" Sue sounded scandalised. "What about your degree?"

"We haven't fine-tuned any of that yet." Matt was still answering for both of them. "We just thought you should know as soon as possible. Megan's suffering from morning-sickness. That's why she hasn't been to breakfast recently."

Megan wished the whole world would open up and swallow her. It was one thing to decide to go through with the pregnancy; another to have Matt highjack it and start acting as if he were in charge.

"Please don't tell anyone else yet," she begged hurriedly. "I've only just found out and I'm still getting used to the idea. I just thought all of you should know what was going on."

Later, Phil took Matt aside for a man-to-man talk. "It must be tough, mate," he said quietly. "God knows how I'd react if Jen was pregnant! Are you sure you can handle this?"

Matt's eyes were bleak. "I've loved her since the moment I saw her," he said heavily. "I can't let something like this take her away from me."

Jen had been right, then, Phil thought: Megan was the one who wanted this baby, not Matt. Still, at least he wasn't running away from his mistake, like so many others their age would have done. Phil suddenly found he had a lot of respect for Matt.

He had less respect for him when he caught sight of him again in the afternoon. Matt hadn't joined the others for King Rib and Megan had said she didn't know where he was. She looked as if she'd been crying. Phil finally tracked him down in his room, where he was lying on the bed, swigging from a bottle of red wine. He'd obviously indulged in a liquid lunch on his own.

"What are you playing at?" Phil liked to come straight to the point. "Megan's been worried about you."

Matt's ensuing comment regarding Megan was extremely uncomplimentary.

Phil removed the bottle from Matt's hand and gave him a hard look. "You need to make your mind up: either you're in love with her or you're not; but drinking on your own doesn't help. You're scared – I get that - but you can't spend the next nine months hiding in a bottle."

"I don't want her to leave me." Matt's voice was muffled by alcohol.

"Then don't give her a reason to do it," Phil said practically.

Sally tapped on Megan's door. "Can I come in?"

Megan opened the door warily. Sally was the one she knew least out of all the group and she always felt that the other girl was judging her.

To her surprise, Sally gave her a hug. "I feel it's my fault."

Megan stared at her in surprise. What was Sally on about?

"I shouldn't have given you such a hard time over Mike." Sally looked shame-faced. "Jen told me that one of the reasons you started going out with Matt was to get Mike out of your system. Matt's always found you irresistible: I used to watch him looking at you in the bar, in our first term."

Megan tried to decipher this muddled stream of consciousness. "You didn't push me into going out with Matt," she said slowly. "He wore me down, turning up at my parents' house in the holidays, sending me cards and letters all the time. It got to the point where I thought he deserved a chance." She faced Sally steadily. "I know you like him, and I felt bad when we started going out because I didn't want you to be upset."

"He'll never look at me the way he looks at you," Sally said stoically. She sighed. "I'd give anything for a man to love me like Matt loves you."

She couldn't know the irony of her words.

Matt tried really hard to take Phil's words to heart. Deep down, he was terrified that Megan would leave him. He couldn't bear to lose her now, even with someone else's baby inside her.

Thinking about the baby made him itch for another drink. She was compliant now, but that was because he was letting her go through with the pregnancy. It might even run in his favour, because the bigger she got, the more she would need him to look after her. If she found herself relying on him, she was less likely to tell him to leave.

No, the next six or seven months wouldn't be a problem, but what came after that could be tricky. Would she still stay with him once she'd given the baby up for adoption? She wouldn't need him anymore. Should he make her keep the baby, then, to prolong her reliance on him?

For a moment he indulged in a wild daydream: him and Megan living together with her baby, both carrying on the deception that the child was his. He couldn't do it. Every time he looked at her, saw the child suckling on her breast, he would be forced to remember that it wasn't *his* child. It would look at him with Mike's face, taunting him ...

Sweating slightly, he grabbed another bottle from the stash beneath his bed and let the friendly liquid carry him into oblivion.

Jen was worried about Megan. She was sure that there was something her friend wasn't telling her, but she couldn't force Megan to talk about it if she didn't want to.

She took her aside after lunch. "Is Matt treating you properly?"

"What do you mean?" Megan stalled for time.

Jen tried to word it delicately. "Is he ... making demands on you?"

Megan's silence confirmed her suspicions.

"You don't have to let him, you know. Tell him that 'no' means no. If he forces himself on you, that's rape."

"He's not doing anything like that!" Megan looked alarmed. "He's just ... He keeps turning up at my room when he's drunk and then he tries to talk me into doing what he wants. He's not letting me have any time on my own."

"I think you both need a night off from each other." Jen was thoughtful. "Why don't we do a girls-only night? You and Sue can come to our room and we'll order pizza. If Matt turns up at your room, you won't be in."

She would also ask Phil to keep an eye on him, she thought, and either take him out for the night or keep him safe in High.

Phil wasn't particularly keen on the idea of an evening with Matt, but he agreed with Jen that Megan needed a break. He and Ged took Matt on The Harborne Run: by the second pub, Matt was too inebriated to continue, so they stayed in The Green Man for the rest of the evening, sipping pints whilst Matt cried into his wineglass, and took a taxi home at the end of the evening. Between them, they managed to carry Matt to his room and left him there to sleep it off.

Meanwhile, Megan and the other girls relaxed with pizza and ice-cream, swapping sixth form stories and shrieking with laughter. It really was most enjoyable.

"That must be one of your pregnancy cravings," Sally said at one point, gesturing towards Megan's olive and anchovy topping. "I bet you wouldn't have eaten that a few months ago!"

"What other cravings have you had?" Jen asked curiously.

Megan considered the question. "Easter eggs," she said at last. It was true: ever since coming back to Hall after the Easter holidays, she had found herself craving the thin, substandard chocolate. If she'd realised this was going to happen, she would have stockpiled them over Easter, when they were actually available in the shops! she thought crossly.

Sue sniffed sceptically. "I thought pregnant women were supposed to want to eat coal! Or spread pickle on a cream cake, or anything else equally disgusting."

"My mum had a craving for salad when she was pregnant with me," Jen said instantly.

"That's probably why you always want to eat in the Salad Bar," Megan grinned.

"Have you thought of any names yet?" Sally butted in eagerly.

Anxiety clutched Megan's heart. Matt was still talking about adoption, but she knew she couldn't give her baby away. He couldn't make her do that, could he?

"I don't know whether it's a boy or a girl," she said at last.

"You could still make a list," Sue protested. She paused. "You know we're all expecting to be godparents, I hope?"

Since Megan was still coming to terms with the idea of the pregnancy itself, a christening was the last thing on her mind. For the meantime, she just smiled at Sue and murmured something non-committal. There would be time to think about the social implications later on.

When she awoke the next morning, it was with a sense of contentment. It was amazing how well one slept after a pleasant evening with no visits from an unreasonable boyfriend.

Maybe she was being too hard on Matt, she thought as she cleaned her teeth. After all, it was perfectly reasonable to him feel upset over what she'd done. She was sure that most girls' boyfriends would have ended the relationship, not agreed to stay with the mother of someone else's child.

But did she *want* Matt to stay with her? she asked herself now. He had been getting on her nerves before she knew she was pregnant, and she knew that she would never feel the same urgent attraction for him that she felt for Mike. Was she strong enough to go through this pregnancy on her own?

And then she thought of Matt's wild eyes and his panic at the idea of losing her, and she knew that she couldn't end things yet – not while he was still in shock. She would have to take things slowly until she was sure he could survive without her. Maybe, she thought, allowing herself a spark of hope, he would go off her as she grew bigger? Surely he wouldn't still be attracted to her once she was the size of a house?

After breakfast, Sally tapped on Megan's door. "I know you can't face food first thing in the morning at the moment, but I thought you might be hungry later." She handed her some fruit, some toast and a couple of boiled eggs. "They're hard boiled, so they should be safe. I'm popping to Tesco later, so I'll see if I can get you some chocolate. I can't promise Easter eggs, though!"

Megan found herself welling up at the other girl's kindness.

"And if you've got any laundry that needs doing," Sally continued, "Jen and I are taking ours in about ten minutes and we don't mind putting yours on as well."

She had seriously misjudged Sally, Megan thought as she finally closed the door behind her. She had been so busy deciding that Sally didn't like her that she had completely overlooked the other girl's positive qualities. Maybe with friends like her and Jen – and Sue – she wouldn't need Matt's help after all.

She spent the rest of the morning trying to prepare for her French Lit exam the next day. It was a good job she'd been so obsessive about attending lectures and taking notes: at least she had plenty to revise from now.

A part of her wondered whether all this preparation was unnecessary. If her baby was due in November, then she couldn't see herself coming back for the Second Year of her course – she was pretty sure the seats in the lecture theatre weren't designed to accommodate an eight months' bump.

Once exam week was over, she would go and talk to her various tutors and apprise them of the situation. Surely she couldn't be the first student to become pregnant partway through a degree course?

When Matt woke up around midday, he tried to remember what he'd done the night before. Had he seen Megan? He didn't think so. Did he want to see her now? Again, he wasn't sure. He knew he loved her, but the way she'd treated him was tearing him apart. She'd slept with another man, for goodness' sake! He couldn't get the thought of the two of them out of his mind: of Mike throwing Megan roughly on the bed and tearing into her the way that Victorian chap had done in the film. Why hadn't she let *him* do that to her?

Thinking about it all made him reach automatically for the bottle under his bed. It wasn't there. Had Doug stolen it? Or Phil? He knew Phil had been here yesterday, but his memory was clouded. It was all Megan's fault, he thought desperately. He'd never been a big drinker before, but she had hurt him so much that he just needed something to make the pain go away.

He decided to walk to the nearest corner shop for more supplies.

Sally had forgotten that Tesco would be closed on a Sunday. Trying one of the few shops that *was* open – a little local newsagent's-cum-off-licence – she was unsurprisingly unable to find any Easter eggs. She grabbed a couple of Wispas instead. Maybe these would do?

Standing in the queue for the counter, she spotted a familiar face in the drinks section. The shop wasn't busy, so Sally left her place in the queue and went to talk to Matt. "Fancy meeting you here!" she said, not bothering to think of an original conversation starter.

Registering the embarrassment on his face, she peered into his basket and realised why. "Having a party?" she asked drily.

Matt blushed. "I've … um … been under a bit of strain recently," was all he would say.

Sally gazed at the face she used to dream about, marvelling how quickly you could fall out of love with someone. She still thought Matt was good-looking, but he'd gone down in her estimation ever since she'd learned Megan was pregnant. She'd always thought Matt a gentleman, but he was obviously just like the rest of them: someone who would jump on you first and ask if it was okay afterwards. She still felt uneasy whenever she thought of Rudi, her German boyfriend who'd seemed delightful until he'd revealed his baser instincts. It was just as well he'd returned home to Düsseldorf when he did, before Sally took up kick-boxing.

However, she smiled at Matt, giving him her usual friendly grin and asking how everything was going.

"It's not great with Megan," Matt told her, thinking it was a relief to be honest. He gestured at the bottles in his basket. "I've found that having a drink or two helps to take the edge off it."

"Sometimes talking helps too," Sally told him. She paused. "You know where I am any time you need someone to listen."

Matt felt confused. Sally was his friend, and he loved Megan, so why was he suddenly picturing himself kissing her and not his girlfriend? Was he simply trying to get his own back; or was there some sort of connection with Sally?

He had a lot to think about as they walked back to Hall.

Megan had just stretched out on her bed for a nap when Sally tapped on her door. "I've brought you some chocolate."

"Thanks," Megan started to say; then her eye caught sight of Matt, skulking behind Sally. "What's *he* doing here?"

Sally tried to be diplomatic. "We bumped into each other at Tesco. Why don't we all have a cup of tea and a chat?" She had a feeling that a third party would be useful if these two were going to have another intense conversation.

For the first five or ten minutes, the atmosphere was strained. Megan was attempting to make polite conversation; Matt was monosyllabic. Sally felt like knocking their heads together.

"Why don't you say what's really on your mind, Matt," she said at last. Sally believed strongly in talking things through. She had joined Niteline three months ago, although Jen was the only person who knew this. Sally had been forced to tell her why she wouldn't be sleeping in their room every so often.

Immediately, Megan felt herself grow tense.

Matt stared at his tea.

"How do you feel about recent events," Sally persisted.

Matt looked up. "Angry," he said at last. "Angry. Confused. Betrayed. Hurt."

"Why do you feel angry?"

"Because this baby's ruining everything," Matt said in a small voice. "We were getting on really well and now it's all gone wrong."

"How do *you* feel, Megan?"

Tears stood in Megan's eyes. She blinked furiously, desperate to hold them at bay. She knew Sally was trying to help, but she couldn't do this in front of her.

"I feel like it's all gone wrong too," she whispered eventually. "I'm too young to be pregnant. The timing's rubbish!" She looked at Sally in despair. "But I can't kill my baby."

Sally was momentarily at a loss. The Niteline training had included a talk on abortion and how to support someone who had made that decision; but no one had mentioned what to say to a woman who went through with her pregnancy. It had been assumed that no one would want to do that.

"I think you both need to support each other," she said at last. "Matt, you said you feel betrayed, but Megan didn't get pregnant on purpose and she didn't do it to hurt you. Both of you are still in shock about what's happened: you don't feel ready for it; but at least you've got months and months before the baby arrives." She took a breath. "You need to make the most of what you have now, before there's another little person demanding all of Megan's time and energy."

Matt was about to say that Megan wasn't keeping the baby but thought better of it and said nothing. He had a feeling he would have to talk Megan into adoption.

"Megan," Sally continued, "you need to share this properly with Matt. Let him feel involved. Matt, be honest with Megan if you think she's shutting you out; but tell her nicely. Her hormones are going to be whizzing around all over the place so don't take it personally if she shouts at you or bursts into tears. Just give her a hug and let her know how much you love her."

Matt looked at Megan. "I'm sorry I've let my feelings get the better of me." He was hoping that this would convince Sally that everything was okay. If she thought that, perhaps she would go and then he could have time alone with Megan.

Megan watched Matt mistrustfully. The words sounded convincing, but did he mean it? He'd demonstrated such extreme behaviour recently that she was afraid to believe him.

Sally felt delighted that she'd effected a reconciliation. She'd known all along that Matt and Megan just needed to talk things through. Maybe she should think about a career in relationship counselling?

"I'll leave the two of you alone then," she said, getting up and going to the door. Stepping out into the corridor, she felt a warm glow at knowing she'd brought the two of them closer together.

Matt looked at Megan as the door closed. "I still haven't forgiven you for cheating on me," he said abruptly. "You've put me through hell these past few days."

Megan said nothing. She had no defence. Matt carried on.

"I want it to be like it was with Mike. No more turning away when I try to kiss you; no more sending me back to High at the end of the evening. You're my girlfriend, so start acting like it."

Megan felt dead inside. How could she kiss someone who was issuing demands like this? But she had cheated on him, destroyed his self-worth. She owed it to him to show him she was sorry. Besides, her mind argued, at least Matt was loyal. How many other men would have agreed to stay with her after what she'd done?

She made no protest as he came towards her, pushing her back on the bed. She let him kiss her, feeling nothing, going through the motions to keep him happy.

Caught up in his desire for her, Matt was oblivious to Megan's own lack of passion. Emboldened by the fact that he was finally lying down with her, he pushed further, allowing his hands to wander. She sat up abruptly. "Not there. I'm too tender."

It wasn't a lie: her breasts permanently felt as if they were on fire. However, she was relieved to have a valid excuse to halt Matt's advances.

She faced him now, her heart beating fast. "I can't … you know what." She faltered. "It might harm the baby," she said delicately.

Since Matt had already been replaying the scene from the film in his mind's eye, this was not welcome news. As soon as he'd started kissing Megan, he had been overwhelmed by the urge to plough into her. The idea of holding her down and taking her roughly excited him.

"I bet you never said no to Mike," he muttered sulkily.

"It only happened once," Megan said wearily. "Most of the time we just talked." That wasn't strictly true, but she didn't want to annoy Matt further.

"I'm coming back here tonight." It was a statement, not a question. Deep down, Matt was sure that if he was persistent, Megan would gradually give in. After all, he hadn't given up on her before, when she had kept him on a string for months and months before finally agreeing to be his girlfriend. Surely kissing her like that would break down her defences? He couldn't believe that he was the only one who felt turned on by it.

"I'll see you at the disco then." She looked tired. "I really need to rest now, Matt. I feel worn out." She ushered him out of the door seconds later.

Walking back to High and discovering Doug was absent, Matt lay down on his bed and thought about Megan. In his fantasies she never said no.

*

Before the disco, Phil had another quiet word with Matt. "You've got to ease back on the drinking. I know you've been knocked for six by this pregnancy but being permanently drunk isn't doing anyone any favours." He paused. "You've got exams tomorrow, haven't you?"

Matt hadn't thought about French or Drama since hearing Megan's news on the Wednesday evening.

"I'm assuming you have to pass these to be allowed to stay on for your Second Year?"

When Matt didn't say anything, Phil began to feel frustrated. "I'm doing the disco tonight. You're too much of a loose cannon at the moment."

"I'm not drunk," Matt said defensively. "I bought another couple of bottles earlier on today, but I haven't touched them yet."

It was true. A combination of kissing Megan properly and having a very satisfactory daydream about her had made him feel much more positive. Still, if Phil was offering to do the disco, Matt could spend the evening slow dancing with Megan. They would look just like all the other couples out there. And then he would take her back to her room and ...

He came to, realising that Phil was still talking.

"... but you can still help to tidy up at the end."

"Sure." Matt nodded, not having a clue what he'd just agreed to. He was finding it hard to focus when his mind was so full of Megan.

Phil sighed and started to sort out the playlist.

*

By the time the disco ended, Megan was dead on her feet. She hadn't felt like socialising, still emotionally drained from spending time with Matt, but Jen and Sally had whisked her down to the hall 'to cheer her up'. She'd been somewhat disconcerted to discover Matt waiting for her, an orange juice in his hand, and even more alarmed to understand that he wanted to dance with her. She'd made the effort, though, swaying with him to some of the slower numbers and sitting out the headbanging ones entirely. Matt *seemed* fairly stable at the moment, but she was aware he could flip suddenly. At least he was sober tonight.

"It's my birthday next Sunday," Sally remarked as the evening wound down.

Sue looked indignant. "Why didn't you tell us sooner?" She would have planned a party had she known.

"I was thinking," Sally continued casually, "about going out somewhere – for a proper dance, I mean. The Hall discos are still rubbish – no offence to Matt and Phil – but isn't there a nightclub at Fiveways?"

Everyone looked at Sue. "Well, as you know, I'm not really one for clubbing," she began self-consciously, "but I think you'll need to go into Birmingham for anywhere decent. There's a new place called The Dome that opened last year, and another one called The Hummingbird, and there's Bobby Brown's on Gas Street, but I'd go for Edwards Number 8 – it's a lot cosier."

"I'm not booking it for a private party!" Sally said in alarm. "I just thought we could all go along together. I'll invite other people from my course too, and we can ask people on the corridor."

And so it was settled. They would go *en masse* to the nightclub on the following Saturday, Jen having decided it would be tactless if so many of them disappeared on the night of the Hall Disco. "Besides," she argued, "we want Phil and Matt to come too and there's no way they'll be able to get out of doing the disco here."

It would be a fun way to wind down after exams, Sue thought. Besides, she really needed to make the most of her time with her friends: Jen would still be here when she returned from France and Germany for her Final Year, as would Ged and Phil, but the others would be doing their own Year Abroad.

A sudden thought struck her. "How are you going to do your Year Abroad with a baby?" she demanded.

Megan looked startled. "I hadn't really thought about that. I need to see my tutors and work out what happens with the rest of my course."

"Rather you than me," Sue said feelingly.

Jen shot her an exasperated look. "Let's all get through Exam Week first, shall we?" she said.

Chapter Thirty-Seven

Luckily French Lit was an afternoon exam so Megan had plenty of time to recover from morning sickness before walking to campus with Matt.

He had stayed over the night before, insisting on sharing the narrow bed with her. Clad in a pair of pale blue cotton pyjamas, he had been decently dressed and she had retained her underwear beneath her modest nightshirt; even so, he had been worryingly tactile, trying to kiss her long after she wanted to go to sleep and sulking when she refused to let him fondle her.

"It's not that I don't want to," she'd told him – actually, that was exactly what it was: she couldn't bear the thought of him touching her – "I just feel too tender everywhere. I expect it's a hormonal thing," she added recklessly, gambling on the fact that Matt knew less than she did about pregnancy symptoms.

Matt was sufficiently suspicious to grab the pregnancy book to check. Unfortunately, he opened it at the photo of a baby's head crowning and that disturbing impression put him off the idea of sex for the rest of the night.

Now, as they walked hand in hand along the path to campus, he tried a more subtle approach. "I could give you a massage tonight, if you like."

Megan stopped in her tracks. "Pardon?"

"I could give you a massage," Matt repeated. "To help you relax," he added. In his mind's eye he was picturing a naked Megan stretched out on the bed while he slowly rubbed oil into her soft, white flesh. It was such a distracting image that he almost walked into a lamp post.

"Maybe a neck rub." Megan thought she knew what he was thinking. "I'll probably feel stiff after sitting writing for two and a half hours."

If she was honest, the thought of Matt touching her anywhere, even just holding her hand, made her skin crawl. The subconscious memory of him hitting her made her flinch from his touch. Lying next to him all night had been extremely unpleasant: she couldn't help comparing it to the easy way she and Mike had slotted into each other's arms and so often fallen asleep without realising.

She couldn't afford to torture herself with recollections of Mike. He was history now. He was also sitting just in front of her in the Great Hall when she arrived for the exam. She gazed at her allocated seat number in despair. Mike wasn't directly next to her: his seat was in the vertical row adjacent to hers but two horizontal rows ahead. That meant she could see him, but he wouldn't be aware of her unless he turned round. Which he did.

For a moment, they stared at each other. *What would you say,* Megan thought, *if you knew about your baby?* and *What would Amanda say?*

The thought was still bouncing around inside her head when he dropped his gaze and turned away.

Mike had actually revised for this exam. He had enjoyed studying The Modern French Novel – in particular Marguerite Duras's *'Moderato Cantabile'*: he liked the novella's ambiguity and its austere style – but after seeing Megan, he found it difficult to concentrate on anything else. She was still breathtakingly beautiful, but it was more than that: there was some sort of connection between them, some sixth sense that had alerted him to her presence when she entered. That was why he'd turned round. He couldn't be sure, but he thought he'd detected a longing in her eyes that mirrored his own.

Megan tried hard not to think about Mike for the next two and a half hours as she wrote about feminine angst and violent imagery in *'Moderato Cantabile'* and repressed sexuality in *'L'Immoraliste'*. She couldn't help drawing a parallel between her clandestine coffee with Mike at the start of term and Anne Desbaresdes' furtive café-meetings with Chauvin. Literature, it seemed, whether it was French or English, was nothing but secrecy and love triangles.

At the back of the room, Matt scribbled furiously, desperately trying to recall what little he could of the texts he'd studied this term. He was aware that he'd spent too much time in lectures thinking about Megan and not enough making notes. If he failed this exam, he thought angrily, it would be her fault: first she'd distracted him; then she'd traumatised him. He was beginning to wish he'd had a drink before coming here.

*

Walking back to The Vale, her hand clasped in Matt's vice-like grip, Megan began to feel stifled. She could understand that Matt felt nervous about letting her out of his sight – she couldn't run off to Mike if he kept tabs on her, he'd said – but his insecurity was beginning to feel like a cage. She wouldn't put it past him to find a pair of handcuffs somewhere.

For once, though, he left her at the door to Ridge. "I'm coming back. I just need to go over to High first, to get supplies." She quirked an eyebrow enquiringly. "Socks. Pants. A clean shirt for tomorrow."

He was moving in to her room, she thought dully, and the more he managed to assimilate himself into her life, the harder he would be to evict. She had to end it now – or at least, next week, once the exams were over.

Matt, meanwhile, was thinking about the couple of bottles under his bed. He'd promised Megan he wouldn't drink, but she wouldn't know if he kept it in High. He wasn't going to get drunk anyway: he just needed something to take the edge off how he felt right now.

"I'll see you later." She turned her face dutifully for his kiss.

Walking to her room, Megan stopped in the corridor. Someone was playing something rather catchy and it was coming from Jen and Sally's room. Tapping on the door, she walked in. Phil was stretched out on Jen's bed, his head in her lap. They looked very cosy.

"Sorry. I'm interrupting." Megan started to walk out but Jen called her back.

"Don't be silly! Come and listen to this."

'This' turned out to be the new Genesis single. "It came out today," Phil explained. "It's called *'Invisible Touch'* – the same name as the next album and the concert tour. I had a morning exam, so I popped into town afterwards and picked it up. What do you think?"

Megan listened, trying to make out the lyrics. Why did everything have to remind her of Mike these days? she asked herself bitterly as she heard the words *"reaches in, grabs right hold of your heart"* and *"It takes control and slowly tears you apart."* The next words, though, could have applied to both Mike and his baby: *"Though she'll mess up your life, you'll want her just the same."*

Instinctively, she put her hand on her belly, knowing how much she wanted this child, even if it did complicate her life.

"Do you want to hear the 'B' side?" Phil asked Jen. "It's less Phil Collins-y than *'Invisible Touch'*."

Jen nodded; Megan was indifferent. But as the music started, she was gripped by the poignancy of the words:

"In silence and darkness
We held each other near that night
We prayed it would last forever."

Instantly she was transported back to that night in March when she and Mike had finally given in to the longing that had always simmered between them. *They were moving as one, her hands gripping him tightly, almost urging him deeper ...*

With a terrible irony, the lyrics continued: *"Now see what you've gone and done"*, followed a moment later by:

"Do you know what you have done?
Do you know what you've begun?
In silence and darkness
Hold each other near tonight
For will it last forever?"

As she listened to the song, she couldn't prevent the tears from pricking at her eyes.

*

The rest of the week passed in a blur of exams and emotional tension. Matt was very demanding as a bedfellow, hogging the covers, taking up far too much room and snoring. Megan was amazed that anyone could think sleeping together was a romantic thing to do.

He was still pushing for greater intimacy between them, running his hands over her as they lay side by side, kissing her whether she wanted it or not. If she rolled onto her side away from him, he would roll over too and then she would feel something hard poking her uncomfortably in the small of her back. She didn't like to think what that meant.

Somehow, she managed to survive the week. Apart from the Monday, she had two exams every day, all of them literature exams apart from the French Prose and Translation papers. She was relieved that they didn't move onto writing compositions until the second year of the French course.

Friday saw her sitting her last two English papers: Elizabethan and Jacobean Literature in the morning and Modern Fiction (1900 – Present Day) in the afternoon. She had reluctantly agreed to let Matt have lunch with her and Jen (what on earth did he think she could get up to with Jen in tow? she wondered crossly), but instead of meeting them in the Cellar Bar as arranged, he came tearing up to her as they exited the Great Hall.

One look at his ashen face told her there was a problem. "What's wrong?" she asked, with genuine concern.

"I've just had a call from my parents." He was shaking as he stuttered the words. "My grandmother's had a fall. They think it's serious."

"Can we do anything?" Jen asked practically.

He shook his head. "I'm taking a train to London now. I need to get there as soon as possible, just in case …"

He bit his lip. Despite the state of their strained relationship, Megan reached for him, holding him close. She knew how much Matt loved his gran. He must in bits over all of this.

"Do you want me to come with you?" she asked gently. "I've got an exam this afternoon, but I could take a train after that."

Again Matt shook his head. "I appreciate you asking," he said in a tight voice, "but it's a family thing. You don't know her." He knew he would probably cry when he saw her and he didn't want Megan to see his vulnerability.

She hugged him again. "Do you know when you'll be back?"

"I've got a Drama exam on Monday." He released himself from her embrace. "I'll probably come back on Sunday evening, but I might go back again after the exam if she's still in hospital.

Now Jen stepped forward to give him a hug. "Take care," she said simply. "We'll be thinking of you."

He walked away from them both without looking back.

*

Although she was sorry for Matt, Megan couldn't help feeling relieved that she would have the luxury of a couple of nights to herself. What bliss it would be to stretch out in bed without another person there, or to drift off to sleep without fighting off roving hands.

It did rather put a dampener on her plan to tell Matt it was over though. How could you reject someone when their grandma was dying? She'd never met the woman but she found herself fervently hoping that she would get better.

Saturday dawned, golden and stress-free. Megan stretched lazily and contemplated her day. Breakfast first. She really fancied eggs and bacon and ... She paused suddenly, aware that she was actually hungry. Was her morning sickness finally over? There was only one way to find out!

Grabbing her towel, she quickly showered and dressed and then knocked on Jen and Sally's door. Jen opened it, clad in her dressing gown and looking at Megan blearily. *No one had the right to be so bright eyed and bushy tailed first thing in the morning - especially not someone pregnant!*

"I was just seeing if you fancied breakfast." Megan came bounding into the room then stopped as she caught sight of Phil, bare chested beneath Jen's sheets and blankets. "Oh! I'm sorry ..."

She was backing out in embarrassment, but Jen caught her arm. "Don't be silly. Phil stayed over last night."

So where had Sally slept? Megan wondered, realising that she hadn't seen Jen's room mate since the previous morning. When she'd asked where Sally was at tea, Jen had made some vague comment about her being 'busy all evening'. Had she acquired a boyfriend, then: one she found so irresistible that she had spent the whole night with him?

Phil was sitting up now. "Pass me my tee-shirt. And my boxers." Jen did as she was asked. Phil pulled the tee-shirt over his head and wriggled into his shorts under the cover of the bedclothes. "I'm going back to High for a shower." He kissed the top of Jen's head before pulling on his jeans. "See you at breakfast."

"I'm so sorry I disturbed your morning cuddle," Megan began hesitantly, but Jen brushed her off.

"We'd been awake for a while. Don't worry about it." No point in embarrassing the poor girl further by telling her what she'd interrupted. On reflection, perhaps it was just as well Megan had arrived when she did, because otherwise she and Phil might not have got out of bed at all.

Megan enjoyed an indolent, Matt-free day. She could get used to this, she thought later on as she sat by the lake with a book. Idly she pictured herself in a year's time, sitting here with a pram. Her baby would be about six months by then. What would it be like?

Whenever she tried to picture the child, she always saw herself talking to a little girl. She would have blonde hair like her own, but the brown eyes would be Mike's. "Stay safe in there, little one," she murmured. "Mummy's looking forward to meeting you."

As she whispered the words, she was hit with an unbearable sadness. Her baby would grow up without a father, just like she had. Should she tell Mike after all? Surely he deserved to know he'd fathered a child.

Maybe later, once Matt had been tidied away. She still felt guilty when she thought about ending things, but she knew she couldn't let them carry on. He might think he was in love with her, but the way he felt was too possessive, controlling. She would wait until his grandmother was safely out of danger and then tell him the truth. At least he'd have the summer to get over it.

Walking back to Ridge, fluffy white clouds in a brilliant blue sky overhead, trees covered in pink and white blossom, Megan felt almost happy. Nature always lifted her spirits: the sun warmed her heart as well as her skin.

She had completely forgotten about Sally's party so it came as a shock when Sue knocked on her door thirty minutes later to ask if she was ready yet. Megan stared at her aghast. She didn't like nightclubs and had naïvely assumed she wouldn't be expected to go, given her 'interesting condition'.
"You can't not go," Sue argued. "It's Sally's birthday!"
And now here was Sally herself, joining the conversation, reiterating that Megan *had* to go and that everyone would be mortally offended if she didn't. "But mostly me because it's *my* party," she added.
Eventually Megan was persuaded. She would wear her sunshine yellow shirt with white leggings, she decided, thinking that she needed to make the most of her tight-fitting clothes whilst she was still able to wear them. Pretty soon she would be the size of a house, reduced to wearing maternity tents and waddling around like a duck with haemorrhoids.
Jen whistled when she saw her. "No one would think you were pregnant!"

The nightclub was noisy and smoky. Realising she had a tailor-made excuse not to dance – what if she slipped or was knocked over – Megan persuaded her friends to go and enjoy themselves on the dance floor whilst she sat near the bar, minding their jackets. After a while she felt thirsty, so she decided to get an orange juice. The jackets would be okay for a few minutes if she left them.

A voice in her ear made her jump as she stood waiting to be served. Without turning round, she felt the familiar prickle that told her Mike was nearby. "I've missed you," he said.

Chapter Thirty-Eight

The room seemed to spin with her as she turned round. Mike was as heart-stoppingly attractive as ever, but it was too late now.

His eyes were drinking her in, lingering on her hair, her face, her eyes. "You look good," he told her, his gaze now resting on her outfit, "but then you always did wear nice clothes."

She was too riveted by the sight of his long legs encased in what looked like spray-on denim to register the banality of his comment. Inwardly Mike cursed himself. Megan looked wonderful, sexy, amazing – and he'd said she had 'nice clothes'. What was wrong with him? He tried again.

"I'm not with Amanda anymore. I finished things over Easter."

Was he mistaken, or did she catch her breath?

"I'm not telling you this so you'll dump your boyfriend and go out with me instead," he said hurriedly; although, if that *did* happen ... "I just wanted you to know."

Megan felt like bursting into tears. Why couldn't Mike have told her this before? Before she tried so hard to make a go of things with Matt. Before she let people think it was Matt's baby. Before Matt's grandmother threw a spanner in the works by ending up in hospital.

She rapidly put the brakes on her train of thought, made it come screeching to a halt. It was her own fault and no one else's that she was in this mess. Even so, her heart lurched just looking at him.

It was as she stood there, consumed with longing just to be held by him again, that the idea hit her. Matt was in Wimbledon, far, far away. What he didn't know wouldn't hurt him. What was to stop her going back with Mike tonight, lying in his arms, telling him about their baby? If he rejected her afterwards, at least she'd be no worse off – and she'd have a clear conscience. But if, by some miracle, Mike wanted to be involved in his child's life, then perhaps he would be willing to be involved with her as well. Hadn't her parents ended up together again, even after so many years?

He was still speaking. "I haven't slept with anyone else this term. I can't stop thinking about you and what happened …"

"I think about it too," she said softly.

He made her bones turn to water when he touched her …

"So," he was moving dangerously closer, "what do we do?"

One endless moment when the world stood still, when she actually thought that he was going to kiss her. She would have melted into his arms instantly: she knew that beyond the shadow of a doubt. She would have kissed him there and then, not caring who saw, who told Matt. Except, she didn't get the chance.

"Megan! There you are!" With unbelievably inappropriate timing, Jen was at her side. "I'm just getting drinks. Help me carry them."

She whisked Megan away from danger, thanking her lucky stars that she had spotted the two of them in time.

Megan opened her mouth to protest, but Jen silenced her with a look. "I hope you remember," she hissed, as soon as they were out of Mike's earshot, "that you are pregnant with Matt's baby. No matter how you feel about him at the moment, you *cannot* go off with another man. It would kill the poor guy!"

"I wasn't going off with him," Megan protested but the excuse sounded hollow in her own ears.

"Maybe not," Jen sounded more gentle now, "but you were looking at him as if you wanted to. Why are you so hung up on him, Meg? Watching the two of you just now was like winding the clock back to last term. You just can't say no to him, can you? When you look at him, you're all lit up inside." She thought it tactful not to comment that she had never seen Megan look at Matt like that.

"Is it that obvious?" Would Matt have noticed, had he been there?

Jen studied her carefully. "To me it is, yes, but that's because I know what it's like to want someone that badly. Her voice was suddenly sympathetic. "It's not just a physical thing, is it? You're in love with him."

Fate was cruel, Megan thought sadly as she sat slowly sipping an orange juice – she didn't want to be kept awake tonight by pregnancy heartburn, thank you very much – and listening to her friends' conversation with half an ear. Mike no longer had a girlfriend. He and Megan could have been seeing each other all term. Instead she was stuck with Matt, sweet, gentle Matt who had turned out to have a darker side after all.

She was suddenly tired of thinking about Matt. She would tell him it was all over as soon as he got back from London, even if his granny was still unwell. She couldn't put her life on hold just to make him happy. He had been good to her – well, mostly – but that didn't mean she owed him anything. Matt was a big boy now: he would have to learn how to cope with disappointments in life.

She scanned the room rapidly, trying to see where Mike had gone. Beside her, Sally twitched irritably. "If you're looking for Mike, he's probably outside getting off with someone else."

But he had told her he kept thinking about her. Suddenly she was unsure. Could she trust Mike? Had he told her the truth, or was he still with Amanda after all?

Reading the uncertainty in her eyes, Sally decided to be brutal. "If you go off with Mike this evening," she told her, "none of us will speak to you ever again." Before Megan could respond, she added, "You're our friend, but so's Matt. We can't let you do that to him."

"I won't speak to Mike again tonight." The words dragged from her unwillingly.

"Good girl!" Sally said approvingly.

Megan was suddenly struck by a possible loophole. What if she went round to High just after midnight? Technically, that wouldn't count as 'tonight', would it?

Beside her, Jen spoke softly in her ear. "I know it's hard for you, but you have to think of what you'd be throwing away with Matt. And even if it turns out that Mike wants you, do you really think he'd be happy helping you bring up someone else's baby?"

"Maybe I need to talk to him about it." Megan looked hopeful.

Jen sighed. "Maybe you need to talk to Matt first. I'm sure he'd be horrified if he thought you were unhappy."

Now Megan felt more confused than ever. Which man was Jen telling her to be with?

It was almost midnight by the time the crowd of people from The Vale began to wend their way home. Megan found herself chatting to people she hadn't talked to in months: Meryam, the Turkish girl on her course, who didn't know Sally but had just happened to be having a night out; Deena and Chandra, two girls from their end of the corridor - they didn't know them very well, but they seemed a fun-loving pair. There were also various people from Sally's German course who lived in Wyddrington and Mason.

Who had Mike come with? Megan wondered. He hadn't given any explanation as to why he was there that evening, and she knew for a fact that Sally wouldn't have invited him. Her heartbeat accelerated at the thought of popping round to see him once they reached Ridge.

The train from New Street to Fiveways was packed with weary partygoers, some of them definitely the worse for alcohol. Megan wondered briefly if Matt was okay. She had been worrying about his drinking for the past week and a half.

That wasn't a reason to stay with him though. She knew now, after seeing Mike, that she couldn't fool herself any longer. Even if Mike didn't want her, she couldn't settle for someone she felt no attraction for, no matter how sweet he was.

Matt *was* sweet, she mused. There was something endearing about his hopelessness; but it had been a mistake to substitute fondness for love. She hoped there was a girl somewhere who would appreciate him for what he was, someone who would love him back with the same intensity he felt for her.

She was so busy thinking about her tangled love life that she failed to register where they were until they had sped past Fiveways. "Shouldn't we have got off at the last station?" she asked in alarm.

Jen patted her reassuringly. "The University's the next stop. We'll get off there. Some of Sally's friends are in UH – University House. It's a bit far for them to walk from Fiveways. It's closer for us too."

Of course. Megan vaguely remembered making the same choice when Dave had come to see her and been so awkward about the walk back to Hall. That was seven months ago already. How things had changed since he'd come to visit her!

Reaching the University a moment later, they tumbled off in a horde and began making their way back to Halls. It was a clear, starlit night, the gibbous moon a silvery shape in the sky. Megan soaked in the camaraderie, knowing that she wouldn't have been enjoying herself half as much had Matt been present.

They were finally at The Vale. Goodbyes were said first to the Masonites, then to the inhabitants of Lake and Wyddrington. Now only the Ridgeites and High Hallers remained. Megan noticed that Sue and Ged were holding hands as they trudged up the slope. She thought they looked genuinely happy together. Phil walked with his arm around Jen: since he was only a few inches taller than her, this was an arrangement that worked well. Megan was struck by how relaxed both couples seemed with each other: it was a million miles away from how she felt when Matt held her hand.

As they reached the Ground Floor corridor of Ridge, Sue turned to Ged. "You're staying, aren't you?"

It must be wonderful, Megan thought wistfully, to be going out with someone you genuinely wanted to spend the night with. And then she remembered Mike and felt hopeful once more.

She placed her key in her lock, ready to unlock her door. To her surprise, Jen opened it for her, marching in and grabbing Megan's nightshirt and toothbrush.

"What are you doing?" She felt too stunned to speak.

Jen pulled the door shut behind her and pocketed the key. "It's for your own good," she said, looking at Sally. "We've decided to keep an eye on you tonight to make sure you don't do anything silly like running off to Mike."

Megan started guiltily.

"Or, rather, Sally will be keeping an eye on you. I'm going over to Phil's, so you can have my bed," Jen continued. "The sheet's clean: I changed it this morning."

Megan wasn't sure whether to feel angry or touched. On the one hand, she felt annoyed that her friends were taking control of her life; on the other, she felt strangely moved that they would go to such lengths to protect her.

"You can't stop me going round another night," she said at last.

"Maybe not," Jen agreed, "but at least Matt will be back by then. He deserves you to be up front with him, Meg. Just imagine how bad you'd feel if he came back from London to tell you his grandmother had died and then found out that you'd cheated on him as well."

"I can't believe you're still lusting after Mike," Sally muttered sourly. "Matt deserves a lot better than that."

Jen shot her a quick look.

There was a frosty atmosphere as the two girls changed for bed. Megan thought sadly of how nice Sally had been to her the previous Sunday, when she'd brought her a picnic breakfast and gone to Tesco to find her some chocolate. All that kindness was now forgotten: Sally said nothing, but she seethed with unspoken resentment towards Megan. All in all, it was most unpleasant.

As Megan lay in the unfamiliar bed in an equally unfamiliar room, she pondered her next move with Matt. Was there a specific amount of time one should wait before ending a relationship if the other person was in mourning? And if Matt's granny wasn't dead but seriously ill, was she supposed to wait until she'd "shuffled off this mortal coil"- as Hamlet had put it – before telling Matt that their relationship was equally dead?

Sally's voice suddenly sounded in the darkness. "I think you're being incredibly selfish."

Megan waited for her to elaborate.

"You more or less told me a week ago that you're not really interested in Matt," Sally continued. "You were just using him as a Mike substitute. Well, did it ever occur to you that someone else might genuinely want him? Except, now you've done the deed and ended up pregnant, you're stuck with him, aren't you? If you'd left him alone in the first place, none of this would have happened."

There was really no answer to that. Megan was tempted to reply that she would still be pregnant, Matt or no Matt, but she had promised him she wouldn't tell the truth – not yet, anyway. She desperately wanted to know how Mike would react to her news, but, in all fairness, she should let Matt know what she intended to do before she did it. He wouldn't be happy, but that couldn't be helped.

Anyway, she thought, suddenly fizzing with righteous indignation, Matt was the one who'd decided to lie, not her. It was ridiculous, really, when you came to think of it: pretending the baby was his just to save face. She was sure their friends would have had more respect for him if they knew he was standing by her when the baby wasn't even his; instead, everyone regarded him as a fool, an idiot who hadn't had the sense to take proper precautions.

Still musing on what to do next, she eventually fell asleep.

*

Sally was still in a bad mood the following morning. It was only as Megan rushed back to her room to find her towel and go for a shower that she remembered today was Sally's actual birthday. Instantly she felt contrite. Poor Sally, being forced to share a room with the girl who had stolen the love of her life!

Sue met her in the corridor as she emerged from the shower. "There you are! Come and sign Sally's card!"

There were flowers too: a large bunch of pink and red carnations, white and yellow chrysanthemums and a rather orange-y gerbera, with a handful of ferns thrown in for good measure. "We bought them yesterday," Sue explained. "Ged had the bright idea of how to keep them fresh."

She pointed to her metal waste bin which, filled with water, made an excellent makeshift vase.

"All mine were too small for such a huge bouquet," she added.

Megan hoped the flowers would improve Sally's mood.

Sally declared herself touched by both the card (which the rest of her friends had signed) and flowers. By the time Jen and Phil arrived to escort everyone to breakfast, she was almost smiling.

"Why isn't Matt's name on the card?" Megan whispered to Sue while Sally was queuing for boiled eggs.

"I didn't buy it until yesterday," Sue hissed in return. "Can't Matt sign it when he comes back?"

"Got anything special planned for today?" Ged asked as Sally sat down with her heavily laden tray.

Sally hesitated. "Why don't we all go out for a late lunch?" she said at last. "I know Phil will be too busy setting up the disco to go out this evening, but there's a pub on the Bristol Road that does Sunday lunch for £3.99 each. I'm not promising it'll be any good, though."

Megan mentally checked her bank balance, calculating that she could afford a cheapish lunch - especially since she was now saving money by drinking soft drinks in the bar. It seemed pregnancy had its advantages.

"Does anyone know what time Matt's getting back?" Sally tried next.

"Probably not until this evening," Phil commented. "He asked me to start the disco off if he was late, but he probably won't be in the mood to do it if he's spent all weekend in a hospital. I was pretty much planning on doing the whole thing."

"It's a shame you're not Music Rep instead of Matt," Sue commented drily, "since you seem to be doing his job for him every Sunday at the moment."

Privately, Megan thought that Phil probably did a better job than Matt, despite the odd forays into heavy metal, because he knew more about music. The last time Matt had deejayed he has still been choosing songs based on their meaningful titles rather than choosing tunes that people wanted to dance to.

Since all her exams were now over, Megan spent most of the morning on various necessary tasks: doing laundry, writing to Anita, making a list of things she needed to say to a) Mike and b) Matt. She was able to combine all of these by taking her writing pad to the laundry room.

How convenient it would have been, she thought wistfully, if Mike had also decided to do his laundry now. They could have indulged in meaningful conversation whilst their clothes whirled and danced in the machines.

Instead, she penned Anita a quick note, not mentioning the pregnancy in case anything got back to her parents before Megan had the chance to break the news herself, asking how things were with Joe and telling her that she didn't think things with Matt were going to work after all.

Once this missive was completed, she set about the earnest task of composing what she would say to Mike and Matt. At the top of the 'Mike' list, she wrote: 'Baby' followed by 'reaction?' Underneath that, she scribbled, 'If pleased, suggest we go on date to talk things over properly; if horrified, explain you don't need any help and can do it on own.'

Matt next. She headed his piece of paper with the words 'How to end it tactfully' and then sat chewing her pen for several minutes while she cogitated what to do. In the end, she wrote, 'It's not you: it's me', then immediately crossed it out since it was far too clichéd. This was followed by 'I really like you as a friend' – rejected for a similar reason – and 'I love you but I'm not in love with you' – equally unsatisfactory. There really was no way to do this without hurting his feelings, she thought in despair.

She was still trying to think of a sympathetic way to say goodbye when the spin cycle ended some twenty minutes later.

Sally's birthday lunch was not a roaring success. They had to wait ages for a table and by the time the waitress finally arrived to take their order, the only meat left was chicken. Megan, who had experienced a sudden craving for roast beef – the baby must be wanting iron, she decided – felt distinctly put out.

Jen, aware of the simmering hostility between her two friends, was trying her best to pour oil on troubled waters. "It was a good turn out last night," she began valiantly. Loads of people turned up."

"Including some people who weren't invited," Sally said pointedly.

Megan began fiddling nervously with her hair.

The food, when it appeared, was rather lacklustre. Megan poked at a sorry looking roast potato and contemplated the week ahead. She needed to see her tutors as soon as possible to ascertain whether it were possible to put her Second Year on hold. Once she knew where she was academically, she would have to tell her parents that they could expect a grandchild in six months' time. She had a suspicion her mother would not be impressed. (Her father was still too much of an unknown quantity.) She would have to live at home for the next year and the prospect filled her with dismay.

After such an unappetising meal, no one could summon up any interest in pudding, not even Sue. The six of them paid their bill and left the pub, all of them somewhat deflated. Megan found herself feeling sorry for Sally who must surely be disappointed with the day so far.

Matt arrived back in Hall just before six, looking much more positive than he had on the Friday. He hadn't had a drink all weekend and his grandmother had a broken hip but was on the mend. She had seemed quite cheerful with her hospital room permanently full of visitors.

She hadn't asked about Megan and Matt had been relieved. He was still determined to make this thing work, but he found it stressful to think about her at the moment. Once his Drama exam was out of the way on the Monday morning, he would concentrate on his girlfriend. He was sure he could talk her round to accepting his plans for the future.

Since he had a lot of preparation to do for the next day, he was quite glad of the reprieve from running the disco. He'd realised after the first few weeks that he was out of his depth, but he'd ploughed on, desperate to impress Megan. All that had changed since discovering she was pregnant: he was the one in control now: she had to convince him that she was worth staying with.

He idly debated whether to go to her room tonight. The exam was important, but it was days since he'd held her. Perhaps she would be more responsive after not seeing him for a few days? He knew she wanted sex – why else would she have slept with Mike? – but she was still playing games with him, pretending to be coy, not letting him touch her where he wanted to. Were all women like this? He would have to check with Phil and Ged.

Matt managed to keep off the wine for the best part of the evening. Doug was out – probably head banging away at the disco – so he had peace and quiet to read through his notes for the exam. He was relieved that he'd already completed the performance module at the end of last term, aware that he'd not really been at his best these past few weeks.

At ten o'clock, he put down his pen and thought about Megan. He needed to hold her, to fall asleep in her bed with her. There were other things he wanted to do as well, but she was proving remarkably resistant. Maybe he should be more forceful, not take no for an answer? He'd overheard guys he didn't know in the bar, claiming that 'No' often meant 'Yes': girls just liked to pretend they weren't interested, to make it more exciting.

Opening one of the bottles of wine he'd bought on his way back to Hall, he took a deep swig and instantly felt reassured.

Megan had gone along to the disco with the others, mainly to support Phil but partly because she didn't want to be in her room if Matt called round. Now, as he made an appearance just as the evening was ending, she felt a sense of panic building inside her. She wanted her life back, and that included being able to shut her door on the outside world and go to sleep on her own.

Matt's eyes were unnaturally bright; his breath smelled of toothpaste. Had he been drinking again? she wondered.

"Megan!" He crossed the room and came towards them. "I've missed you so much!" he said, wrapping his arms around her and turning her face towards him for a kiss.

She couldn't struggle in front of the others, so she endured his display of ownership while it lasted. "I'm coming back to your place tonight," he continued, in front of all their friends. "I need some TLC after the weekend I've had."

Inside, Megan fumed. If she turned him away now, she would look like the bad guy. Her reputation with Sue and Sally was already at an all-time low thanks to her being seen talking to Mike on Saturday. If she said no to Matt, they were bound to think she was sneaking off to the tenth floor of High again.

"You can come for a chat," she said ungraciously, "but I'll have to chuck you out afterwards. I need my sleep."

Walking back to Ridge *en masse* – sans Phil, who was staying in High – Megan became aware that Matt was playing to his audience. "It was a really stressful weekend," he was saying as they neared the Ground Floor corridor. "I'm going to need plenty of hugs just to calm me down."

Except, these days with Matt a hug was never enough, Megan thought sourly. If she put her arms around him, he usually took that as a cue that she wanted something more. She was fighting him off more often than she'd had to fend off Dave.

As they reached the end of the corridor, Megan turned to Jen. "Would you mind knocking on my door in about half an hour? I know what Matt's like once he gets talking – we'll both lose track of time if we're not careful."

She hoped Jen would understand her coded message: wasn't she the one who'd told Megan she didn't have to let Matt pressure her into doing anything she didn't want to?

As they entered her room, Matt switched into clingy boyfriend mode. Seating himself on her bed, he patted the covers. "Come and sit with me. I need to tell you how much I've missed you."

Instead, Megan hovered suspiciously by the easy chair. "How's your grandma now? Did you say she was on the mend?"

"She is, but it was extremely worrying." He looked at her beseechingly. "Why won't you sit next to me? I need a hug."

Megan felt torn. She knew Matt was being manipulative, but at the same time she was genuinely sorry he was having such a tough time.

"One hug then," she said with resignation, sitting next to him as he'd asked.

As she turned towards him, Matt grabbed her, pulling her so close that she almost fought for breath. "Don't leave me, Megan," he murmured into her hair. "Don't leave me."

"Matt, you're hurting me."

He was kissing her now, desperately, trying to cover her entire face with his lips. Women *liked* being kissed. If he carried on for long enough, would he ignite the passion that had been absent from their relationship so far?

"Matt!" With an effort, she heaved herself away from him. "You've got to stop this," she told him. "You can't just kiss me into submission like someone in a film."

"Why are you so cold?" He sounded hurt. Angry.

"It's the end of the night and I'm tired. I need you to go so I can get some sleep. You know the baby's making me feel tired at the moment."

That was evidently the wrong thing to say. At the mention of the baby, he flashed her a look of total contempt. "It's ruining everything between us."

No, she wanted to tell him, it's not the baby: it's you. She couldn't say the words. He was too volatile to be faced with an unpleasant truth.

"Please go," she repeated.

As if on cue, a tapping sounded on the door and Jen's voice called out, "Don't forget the time, Lovebirds!"

"I think that's your exit." She wouldn't look at him.

When he didn't move, she made her way to the door and opened it. Jen stood there, a strange expression on her face.

"You heard what she said, Matt." Megan tried to jolly him along. "Pumpkin time for you!"

As Matt stalked out of the room, Jen thought she had never seen anyone look so venomous.

Chapter Thirty-Nine

Jen was still worried about Megan as they walked to breakfast the next morning. "I gather Matt didn't want to leave last night," she said bluntly.

Megan flushed. "I wasn't being mean. I just needed a decent night's sleep."

"No one's judging you," Jen said gently. "And even though Matt's going through a tough time, it doesn't give him the right to force you into anything. You're allowed to tell him you don't want him to stay over."

Megan was silent. She was aware that her guilt had probably allowed Matt to get away with far too much, but she hated the idea of him drinking to excess because of what she'd done. Deep down, he was still a sweet and gentle young man – just a boy, really – who felt betrayed and rejected. Could she blame him for being so clingy, for needing to feel loved?

Matt wasn't at breakfast. Jen wondered if he'd been drinking again. Phil had already voiced his concern that Matt was using alcohol as a crutch. For someone who was usually a light drinker, this was unsettling, to say the least. He should be looking after Megan, she thought angrily, not adding to her stress.

In his room, Matt was nursing a hangover. He hadn't intended to drink heavily the night before an exam, but by the time he arrived at his room after being forced to leave Ridge, he had worked himself up into such a state of indignation- and resentment-fuelled anger that he had to have a drink to calm down. That had been followed by another, then another, until he realised he'd emptied both bottles. It was all Megan's fault! He'd only ever been a social drinker before: he would take a glass of wine or two, three at the most, throughout the course of an evening in the bar and he definitely wouldn't drink on his own; but she had driven him to this with her adulterous ways! Was it adultery if you weren't married? He wasn't sure. He closed his eyes again, attempting to sleep off his headache.

*

Despite having no lectures until her two o'clock French Lit, Megan went into campus early, needing to see her tutors and break the news of her impending motherhood. At the start of the year she had been assigned a personal tutor: he was supposed to be her first port of call for any pastoral matters. She decided to go and talk to him first.

Doctor Timothy Holroyd was a pleasant man in his mid to late thirties. He had an engaging smile and a somewhat dishevelled appearance. She remembered him lecturing on symbolism in Victorian literature: his enthusiasm for the topic had appealed to her. When she tapped on his door to see if he were free, he ushered her in and sat her down in a comfortable armchair. "What can I do for you, young lady?"

Some women would have bristled at the appellation; not so Megan. She found Dr Holroyd's old-fashioned term of address charming – or perhaps it was the way his warm brown eyes seemed to crinkle kindly at her? Whatever it was, she began to relax, sensing that she could trust him.

"I wanted to ask about the possibility of deferring my Second Year," she began carefully.

Dr Holroyd's nod invited her to say more.

"I'm having a baby in November." The words came out in a rush. "So, you see , I can't really carry on with the course – not to begin with anyway."

Instead of replying immediately, her tutor flicked the switch on the electric kettle that stood on his desk. "I think this is going to take a while," he remarked pleasantly. "Tea or coffee? And I think I've got some biscuits somewhere."

Megan left Tim's room half an hour later feeling far more positive. She had also developed a slight crush on the man, due to his endearing personality.

"My wife and I married at the end of our Final Year," he told her. "We were both carrying on with our studies – her MA involved the portrayal of women in Chaucer – and we were as poor as church mice, but it didn't matter." He sighed heavily. "It was wonderful to be so young and so much in love. She had to abandon it of course when she found she was pregnant. That was fourteen years ago and she still talks of going back and completing her thesis, but we have three children now – thirteen, eight and five – and she finds them a full time job."

Did that mean she, too, would have to give up her academic aspirations? Megan wondered.

Tim gave her an encouraging smile. "It might be easier for you. The University has its own nursery – for staff and students. If you're thinking of taking a year out, you could book a place for October '87. It's not free, but the fees are cheaper for students. One of my Third Year tutees is a mature student with three year old twins and she put them both in there at the age of six months, when she started her course."

Wrapped in a warm glow of optimism, she hurried to the Muirhead Tower to look for Professor Burns. He seemed as dithery as ever as she sat in a chair opposite his desk and told him that she would have to take a year out.

"So, you plan to start your Second Year in 1987 and then do your Year Abroad in 1988," he murmured, scribbling on a piece of paper.

Megan looked at him incredulously. "I can't do the Year Abroad with a baby!"

Professor Burns appeared to be genuinely surprised. "Can't you take it with you to lectures?" he enquired. "I'm told they sleep a lot when they're small," he added helpfully. Noting Megan's raised eyebrows, he tried again. "The students who do two languages sometimes spend a year in one country and then do a four weeks' intensive French course at the University of Montpellier. That might be an option, if you're really sure you don't want to take your baby to France for a year – although I would have thought it an excellent opportunity for the child to be bi-lingual."

He really didn't have a clue, Megan thought as she began to leave his office. Thank goodness for tutors like Tim Holroyd who were in touch with reality!

*

She hadn't checked her French pigeon hole in ages. She might as well have a look now since she had to pass it anyway to get to the lifts, although she hardly ever had any correspondence here: anything to do with Combined Honours always found its way to her English pigeon hole instead.

She reached the small foyer and stopped suddenly. Pinned to the wooden structure was a note with her name on, and the handwriting was unmistakably Mike's.

With trembling fingers, Megan detached the note and unfolded it. *"I can't stop thinking about you,"* it said. *"I'm free tomorrow at 11. I'll be waiting in the First Floor Coffee Bar."*

She had a lecture at ten on a Tuesday, but then she, too, would be free after that. She would be free to tell Mike about his baby; free to see if he was still interested in her once he knew.

Then she thought of Matt and her heart sank. She *wouldn't* be free – not until she'd told him it was definitely over. If she was going to speak to him, she had to do it today. Even if Mike didn't want her, she knew she couldn't carry on being Matt's girlfriend. His constant demands were destroying her.

The time was now ten to eleven. Jen had gone to a ten o'clock Bibliography lecture and would be finishing soon. If Megan went back to the Arts Faculty, she could grab her friend for a coffee and ask her advice about how to handle Matt. After this morning's conversation, she felt sure Jen would be supportive.

"Let's try the Guild Coffee Shop," Jen suggested as they began descending the first floor staircase.

Megan was so busy thinking about what cake she would order that she mistimed her step, slipped and plummeted down the rest of the flight, landing heavily on her back. Pain surged through her body, an agonising fire across her lower abdomen. Something damp was seeping through her leggings: had she wet herself in shock?

"Don't move!" Jen sounded frightened. She turned to a nearby student. "Run and ask the office to call an ambulance."

As the pool of blood around Megan slowly increased, she found herself drifting into unconsciousness.

Chapter Forty

When Megan woke up, some time later, in the hospital bed, she knew at once what had happened.

"I've lost it, haven't I?" she said in a tiny voice.

From the chair beside her bed, Jen nodded.

Megan wept then. She wept for the child that would never be, that had slipped away before she had a chance to hold it, to love it. She wept for Mike and the thought of how she had lost both him and his baby. She wept for Matt and the pain she had put him through over the past few weeks; and, finally, she wept for herself.

Throughout all this, Jen held her hand tightly, tears streaming down her own face. "I'm so sorry, Meg," she whispered. "I am so, so sorry."

Megan's grief was beyond words: it felt as if she were made of tears, as if her very skeleton consisted of pain. She let it consume her, feeling a visceral need to cry out her agony in heart-wrenching sobs.

"Meg ..." Jen sounded worried.

A nurse appeared then, administering a sedative, and Megan slept. Sleep brought no comfort, however: she dreamed of holding a blood-stained baby that looked at her with Matt's eyes, full of hatred. When she awoke again, she was shaking with fear.

Jen had gone. Megan rang the bell for the nurse and asked where her friend was. It was only when she explained that Jen had gone back to Hall for her evening meal that Megan realised it was evening. Had she really been in here for six or seven hours?

She wanted to talk to someone about her baby, but she was still too raw. The hurt was locked inside her somewhere, in a place she couldn't reach at the moment. She knew that was the only way she could get through the next few hours and days – if she pushed reality away and didn't let herself think about it.

Jen came back later on, bringing flowers and chocolate. Megan ignored both of them. Gifts wouldn't bring her baby back.

"I asked Matt to come with me," Jen began hesitantly, "but he said he couldn't." She paused. "I know he's probably in shock. He must be grieving too."

"It wasn't his baby," Megan said abruptly. What need of secrecy now? Tears welled in her eyes once more. "It wasn't his baby. He'll be ecstatic now I'm not pregnant anymore."

Jen was perturbed. Megan was obviously delusional. She knew things had been strained between the two of them, but at least Matt had stood by Megan, despite the baby being unplanned.

"I'm sure he's as upset as you are," she began carefully, but Megan cut her short.

"It wasn't his!" she repeated.

All of a sudden, things began to make sense. Jen now knew what her friend had been doing at Sally's party. "Does Mike know he's the father?" she asked quietly, followed by, "And does Matt know he's not?"

"I never slept with Matt." The confessions came tumbling out, one by one. It was such a relief to finally tell the truth. "He knew it wasn't his because we never had sex."

"But you spent the night together," Jen began in surprise, "and then the next morning he told Phil he'd made love to you. And when I asked you about it, you said you had."

"I fell asleep next to him when we were watching 'The French Lieutenant's Woman'," Megan admitted, "and I felt guilty because I didn't want to lead him on."

"How would falling asleep with him lead him on?" Jen was puzzled.

Megan lowered her eyes. "I was already having second thoughts. The last thing I wanted was for him to start thinking we could share a bed on a regular basis, even if it *was* relatively innocent."

"You must have slept with Mike before that, then." Jen knew her friend well enough to understand how her mind worked. Megan wouldn't have cheated on Matt.

"The end of the Spring Term." The words came out slowly.

"Before or after we caught you and Mike in a drunken clinch?"

"I decided to take your advice," Megan said in a small voice. "Remember? Both you and Phil said I should sleep with him to get him out of my system."

"Go on." Jen's voice was steady.

"So, after the concert, I went round to see him." She looked ashamed. "I dressed up in your maid's outfit –"

"You did what?" Jen sounded scandalised.

"Only the dress," Megan hastened to reassure her. "I wanted to look seductive. I went to his room and I asked him to make love to me – I was a bit drunk at the time – well, a lot drunk."

"He shouldn't have taken advantage of you," Jen said sternly, thinking Sally's initial observation had been right and that Mike was a sex-crazed, sexist pig.

"He didn't." Megan looked embarrassed. "He told me he wouldn't, so then I kissed him and I think *maybe* he might have done something about it, but I threw up and I think that put him off." She looked at her friend steadily. "Mike looked after me and put me to bed. He acted like a perfect gentleman."

"So, when did you …" Jen paused delicately.

"I woke up in the night." This bit was so hard to explain. "I used to dream a lot about Mike, about *doing things* with him." She coloured, thinking this was far too much information. "Anyway, I'd been quite drunk when I went to bed, so maybe I was still a bit fuzzy – I don't know – and when I found him in bed next to me, I just started doing what came naturally. And then he woke up and it just went on from there."

There was a dreamy expression in her eyes. Jen knew, without being told, that it had all been very satisfactory.

"So why on earth did you start going out with Matt?" she asked at last.

The answer was heartbreaking: "Because I couldn't have Mike and I couldn't bear to keep on thinking about him."

"I wish you'd told me about Mike when it happened," Jen said a while later. "I wouldn't have kept pushing you into going out with Matt if I'd known."

"I thought I couldn't have him." Megan looked suddenly bitter. "He had a girlfriend and I didn't think he'd ever leave her, so I sort of settled for Matt. Only, he broke up with his girlfriend in the Easter holidays. We could have been together all term if he'd told me."

"Did he know you were pregnant?"

Megan shook her head. "Matt wouldn't let me tell him. He said Mike wouldn't want it anyway; and then …" Her voice wobbled. "And then he threatened to tell Mike I was pregnant but that I'd slept with so many men I didn't know whose it was."

She started crying again. Jen was shocked. How could Matt say something so vindictive? It wasn't like him at all. Perhaps you could blame some of it on the alcohol; but even so …

"I think Matt might need help," she said slowly. "From what you've said – and from what I've seen – he's developed an obsession with having you as his girlfriend – or with keeping you as his girlfriend. No one should treat you like that, Meg. You're worth more than that."

Megan began wiping tears from her eyes. "I've felt so guilty about what I did to him," she confessed. "I knew he was in love with me and I really tried to be in love back, but I couldn't: the spark just wasn't there. I was trying to break up with him before I knew I was pregnant."

"You didn't do anything wrong," Jen said automatically. "Sleeping with someone else before you were going out with him isn't cheating. And you're not Matt's property either. No one has a right to try to control someone else."

She put her arms around her friend and held her tight. "I'm so sorry you've had to go through this on your own," she murmured.

Later still, Jen broached the subject of the baby. "How are you feeling physically?"

"Drained," Megan told her. "And sore." She swallowed. "I've got to have a scrape tomorrow, so they can check there aren't any bits of baby left inside me." She looked as if she might cry again. "Do you think God's punishing me?" she asked next.

"Why would He do that?" Jen's voice was gentle.

"I talked about falling downstairs, remember? I said I couldn't have an abortion but what if I fell downstairs and had a miscarriage." Her eyes were wild and staring. "I didn't do it on purpose. I just slipped."

Jen was at a loss to know what to say. Would grief counselling help? she wondered. Perhaps she could ask the nurse on her way out.

Thinking of the nurse reminded her of something else. "What about your parents?" she asked. "Do you want me to give them a ring?"

Megan shook her head. "They didn't know I was pregnant. They wouldn't know how to handle it if you told them I'd had a miscarriage."

Jen looked at her friend's tear-stained, defiant face. "You don't have to go through this on your own, you know."

"I'm not," Megan said simply. "I've got you."

Jen choked back the tears forming in her own eyes.

*

For the next few days, Megan slept: a deep, sedative induced sleep that allowed her body to start healing from its ordeal. There was nothing to help with her inner pain, though. Every time she thought of her lost baby, her heart broke a little bit more.

Sue and Ged visited; Sally too. Matt was conspicuous by his absence. At Megan's request, Jen hadn't told the others the truth: they assumed Matt was too upset to visit at the same time as them, imagining him to be suffering, like Megan, from grief. "Although he's probably relieved too," said Sally, voicing what they were all thinking.

On Thursday afternoon, Megan was discharged. Jen walked up to the maternity hospital, just off campus, to meet her. They would take a taxi back to Hall. As they left, Jen noticed Megan staring at the heavily pregnant women who were coming in for ante-natal checks and thought of the ache she must feel inside.

"Let's get you back to Ridge," she said softly.

*

Back in her room, Megan paced nervously. No one else had known she was pregnant, apart from her immediate group of friends. That meant there would be no awkward questions, no unwelcome sympathy.

Tomorrow she had no lectures, but she would have to go through the heartache of seeing her tutors and explaining that she would be back in September after all. The pregnancy book had said miscarriages were less likely after three months, so what had she done wrong? She couldn't forgive herself for tripping on the stair. If she'd been more careful, her baby would still be alive.

She didn't feel like anything to eat but she made herself go for tea with the others, forcing herself to eat food she couldn't taste. She caught sight of Matt in the distance, uncharacteristically sitting with a crowd of High Hallers. She wasn't sure if he'd seen her.

Then, later, a quiet tapping on her door. Matt: contrite, sympathetic, apparently sober. She let him in. She was going to have to tell him he was history.

He pre-empted her, sitting down on her bed, pulling her towards him by the hand. "I forgive you," he announced uncertainly.

Megan's mind whirled. He forgave her? For what?

He was carrying on nervously, almost as if it were a pre-prepared speech he had learned for a play. "I forgive you for your unreasonable behaviour and I think, given recent circumstances, that we can get back to normal; but it will take time for me to trust you again after what you did."

She stared at him in disbelief. There had been no word of apology, no 'I'm sorry for your loss.' He was magnanimously declaring her to be forgiven as if he were the wronged party!

Jen's words echoed in her brain: *"You didn't do anything wrong"* and *"No one has a right to try to control someone else."*

"Could you please leave?" She kept her voice steady. "I'm really tired, Matt. We'll talk another time."

She didn't let her tears fall until he was gone.

Chapter Forty-One

Back in his room, Matt seethed with frustration. Megan should have been welcoming him with open arms, not fobbing him off with some excuse about being tired. Didn't she realise how lucky she was that he'd stuck around? It was more than most men would have done, given the circumstances. Tomorrow he would be more forceful. It was time she understood that their relationship had changed.

Megan lay awake for a long time that night. She felt empty: acutely aware that something was missing. Despite the knowledge that a baby would have irrevocably complicated her life, she still mourned over what might have been.

*

The following morning, Megan didn't want to get up. The idea of going for breakfast with friends who knew of her loss was too much for her to bear. She didn't want to talk about what had happened; nor did she want to see people deliberately avoiding the subject. After a while, she blutacked a note to her door. It said simply, "Not going to breakfast today."

After this, she dozed again, trying to compensate for the sleep she'd lost. Early morning sounds pervaded her consciousness: doors banging, the quiet hum of corridor conversations, water running for baths and showers. Underlying all of this, the persistent ticking of her alarm clock relentlessly measured the time, second following second with a grim inevitability, a reminder that life would continue to drag on.

When she finally surfaced, everything was quieter. Ten o'clock: she had managed to sleep after all. Jen had pushed a note under her door. *"Had to go in for Anglo-Saxon. Do you want to meet for coffee at 11?"*

Knowing that she had to face campus sooner or later, Megan forced herself to shower and dress. May sunshine warmed the air; nevertheless, she clothed herself in her baggy black jumper and jeans, the sombre colours reflecting her mood.

Jen hadn't suggested a meeting place, so Megan headed for the Arts Faculty. She would wait for her friend to come out of her lecture. As she approached the building, she looked up. Mike was coming out of the library and he was heading in her direction.

*

For a moment time stilled. She stood, rooted to the spot, watching his approach, unable to move or think or feel. As he reached her, he nodded uncertainly. He was as apprehensive as she was.

"You haven't been in lectures this week." His eyes searched her own, seeking answers.

"I was in hospital. I had an accident." She couldn't tell him the rest: if she did, she would cry.

His face registered concern. "Are you okay now?"

No, she wanted to tell him. *No, I'm not okay. I have a huge hole inside me where something's been ripped away.* To her horror, she felt her eyes well with tears.

He hesitated. "Coffee?"

She nodded. "Not here, though. Somewhere private."

*

Together they walked through campus, down into Selly Oak, to the little café where he had taken her at the start of term. Mike ordered coffees and carried them to their table. In the almost empty room, a fly crawled over the formica counter top, following a trail of previously spilled sugar.

"So," Mike was looking at her intently, "tell me about this accident."

"It was Monday." Megan made her voice sound detached, but the narration tugged at her heart, the sharp pain of pulling a plaster off a wound. "It was Monday and I was walking down the stairs in the Arts Fac. I slipped and fell." She paused. "Before I fell, I was pregnant. Now I'm not."

A stunned silence. Megan wished she knew what was going on in Mike's mind. Was he judging her?

"I'm sorry," he said quietly. "That must have been hard for you."

She nodded wordlessly. He allowed silence to envelop them both.

After a few moments, she spoke again. "I'd only just found out. I took the test a couple of weeks ago." Truth spilled from her lips, tinged with the rawness of it all. "It wasn't planned, but I still wanted it." A tear rolled down her cheek.

Instinctively, Mike reached across the table and held her hand. He wanted to comfort her, hold her close, but he was also jealous: Megan had walked away from him after one night but taken the time to make a baby with someone else.

"How's your boyfriend taken all this?" he asked eventually.

She looked at the table. "It wasn't his." The words came out as a whisper. "I've only slept with one person."

One endless moment as comprehension dawned. "It was *my* baby?"

Again, she nodded. "I wanted to tell you, but I was afraid."

"My baby," he repeated, reaching out his other hand, gripping hers. She was amazed to see pain in his eyes. "I would have stood by you," he said bleakly.

She shook her head. "No, you wouldn't. You're the French Department's resident sex-god: a baby would have ruined your image."

"Maybe I'm not a sex-god anymore," Mike insisted. "Maybe I was never one in the first place."

Megan snorted. "Do you know how many girls fantasise about you?"

"But none of that matters," he told her softly, "unless I can have you."

And in that moment, something passed between them, and for the first time she read his heart.

Minutes ticked by and still they sat there, holding hands, the untouched coffee growing cold in its cups.

"You feel it too, don't you?" He already knew the answer. "This *connection*, whatever it is we've got. It's not just physical ..."

And yet the magnetism between them was, at this moment, so strong that the air almost crackled with it.

"My baby," he repeated again later.

"*Our* baby," she corrected him.

His hands were still closed over hers, the sexual charge between them only building in intensity, both of them completely unaware of anything but each other.

"I wish I could take you back to my room right now," he murmured. Qualifying it, he added, "Not for sex. I just want to lie and hold you. I think we both need that."

She couldn't blot out the memory of waking up in his arms ...

*

"Why do we keep fighting this?" he asked after a while.

"Timing?" she suggested. "You had Amanda; I had Matt."

She still had Matt, she realised. He'd been unreceptive the previous evening, but he would have to listen to her today. She would have to be a big girl and learn to ignore his emotional blackmail.

"Amanda's history."

He was waiting for her to say the same about Matt. She had to be honest.

"I've been trying to finish things with Matt for weeks. I knew I'd made a mistake as soon as we started going out."

"This is the one who's a terrible kisser, right?" He was enjoying teasing her.

"I've been trying to tell him it's over. He just doesn't want to hear."

Mike took a deep breath. "Seriously, Sweetheart, you have to try. I wasted a whole term letting things drag on with Amanda because I felt guilty about hurting her."

And now she noticed something she hadn't registered before. "You've stopped smoking!" she said in surprise.

He gave her a lopsided grin. "It was a woman who got me to start smoking and a woman who got me to stop." He hadn't touched a cigarette all term. If Megan wanted clean cut, he would show her he could do that. "Not that I haven't wanted to," he added honestly. "I was supposed to be giving up in January, but I felt so stressed about my parents that it didn't last long."

"How are things now?" She remembered clearly every word he'd said in that deserted basement room. "How was the Easter holiday for you and your dad?"

"He's not moved anyone else in," Mike said shortly, wishing he'd not given up after all. He always felt stressed when he thought about the divorce. "His girlfriend stayed over a few times, but I don't think she liked me being around. She kept asking if I was going to stay with my mum for a few days."

"Did you?"

A negative headshake. "She doesn't want me around either. She's too busy 'discovering herself' and 'getting her life back'." He sighed. "I can't blame either of them. I'm not a kid anymore: I can take care of myself. They must have hated staying together just because of me."

"Do you think we would have ended up like that?" The question came from nowhere. "If things had been different … with the baby."

"I don't know," he said honestly. "I'd like to think that we would have made a go of it – lived together next year, worked something out for the year after that."

Briefly he imagined himself curled up with Megan, a baby sleeping peacefully in a cot beside the bed. It was easy to romanticise it; he knew the reality would have been far more challenging.

"All I know," he said slowly, "is that we need to get to know each other properly – no more of this sneaking around. I think we've got something: we're great in bed together, but we can talk too. You're the only girl I know who's read *'Slaughterhouse 5'* and *'The End of the Affair'*. You *get* books. You understand me."

He would never forget Amanda. She had changed him as a person, been his first love; but he couldn't talk to her the way he could talk to Megan.

Could he and Megan make a go of things? There was only one way to find out.

*

They walked back to campus slowly, hand in hand. He let go at the foot of the steps to the Muirhead Tower. "I've got a German seminar. I'll see you this evening."

She nodded, unused to the idea that she warranted a pre-planned assignation. He *wanted* to see her.

"I'll be in my room," she said softly. "Come and find me."

He kissed her briefly on the mouth, the gesture a promise for later. She watched as his long legs carried him into the building, no longer unsure of his feelings for her.

She should have gone to see Professor Burns, to let him know that she no longer needed a year's maternity leave. She couldn't do it: the pain of admitting her baby wasn't there anymore was something too tender to poke at now. She would wait until Monday instead.

Jen's voice, calling to her from the patch of grass in front of the library. "Where have you been? It's almost twelve!"

Hurrying towards her friend, Megan decided to tell Jen the truth. Jen wouldn't try to talk her out of seeing Mike: not now; not when she knew Megan's heart had never felt complete with Matt.

As they walked to the Guild Coffee Shop, Jen listened quietly as Megan told her about the unexpected meeting, noticing the hope in her eyes, hearing the longing in her voice. "I think we should have let you follow your heart when you fell for him months ago," she said slowly. "I thought we were doing the right thing: Sally said Mike was bad news, so we were just trying to protect you."

Megan wondered whether she should mention Mike's comment about Sally disliking him because he'd ranked her bottom of his bonk-list but decided not to. She didn't want to remind Jen of anything that could be construed as 'bad boy' behaviour.

"I might need your help convincing Matt it's over, though," she said now. A thought struck her. "Is Sally still keen on him?"

"You are *not* palming him off on Sally!" Jen tried to sound stern, but Megan thought she detected a slight smile. "I'm not convinced she'll want him anymore," she said thoughtfully, "if she finds out how he's used emotional blackmail to get you to stay with him."

Remorse overwhelmed Megan, and not for the first time. *She* had done this to him. Matt had been so sweet, so lovely – before she ripped his heart out and shredded it with her betrayal. He had worshipped her and she had turned out to be a false idol. No wonder he was so angry.

"Do you think he'll ever get over this?" she asked sombrely.

"I think you need to think about yourself," Jen told her. "You've only made yourself miserable by trying so hard not to hurt Matt." She looked at her watch. "I've got Popmobility with Sue at one, but I'm free after that so, if you like, we can put our heads together and think about the best way to tell Matt it's over."

"Thanks." Megan felt reassured. "I'm going back to Hall now, so come and find me when you're ready."

They hugged briefly. Life was beginning to take an upward turn.

*

It was amazing how hope altered your outlook on the world. The sun's rays seemed warmer, the sky brighter, the trees greener – and all because she knew Mike had feelings for her. A bud of optimism had sprouted in her heart, a seedling that could grow and flourish. Megan may have walked back to Hall but she skipped inside.

Her heart still sang as she reached her room, switched on the kettle, made a cup of tea. Her grief for the baby was still there but muted somehow: she was aware of it, but it was now a dull ache, no longer an agonising, gaping wound. Mike would enable her to heal: she wouldn't have to hide her true feelings the way she had with Matt. It was the first day of a more positive future.

*

When the knock sounded on her door a little later, she assumed it was Jen. Opening the door, full of gratitude to her friend for coming round so quickly, she found herself staring instead at Matt. His face was sheer fury. He was also very drunk.

Instinctively, she tried to close the door, but he was too strong for her, barging his way in, flipping the catch to lock them both inside.

"Why have you been lying to me?"

The accusation wrenched from him, as if the words were too painful to utter.

"I don't know what you mean." Megan tried not to let him know she was afraid.

"How long have you been seeing him behind my back?"

She started guiltily, realising he must have seen her with Mike earlier.

"I bumped into him by chance," she said at last. "We just went for a coffee. That's all."

"Liar!" Matt was glaring at her now, his gaze full of hatred. "You're still sleeping with him. I saw him kiss you." Questions burst from him like machine gun fire. "How long has it been going on? How could you do this to me? Have you been laughing at me behind my back?"

"It was just coffee," she repeated, but his alcohol-fuelled anger deafened him to her protests.

"All this time," he grabbed hold of her drunkenly, "all this time you kept telling me you couldn't do it because it would hurt the baby. Well, the baby's gone, so what's your excuse now?"

"Matt," she tried to fend him off, but he was having none of it, "you're hurting me."

He paused momentarily, staring at her as if unable to comprehend what she had just said, and then he was forcing her back onto the bed, pushing her down, anger lending him the strength to pinion her to the mattress so that she couldn't escape. One hand was tearing at her clothes; the other resisting all her struggles to move, to cry out. And then his knee prising her legs apart, keeping her prisoner whilst he fumbled with his own jeans, his boxer shorts, saying nothing, letting his actions shout his hatred.

Tears rolling down her cheeks before, during, after …

Oblivious to her silent sobbing, or maybe spurred on by it, he thrust into her, taking her savagely, tearing at her in his haste to punish her for the perceived infidelity. It was every nightmare she had ever had, rolled into one and intensified.

A combination of fear and pain made her retreat into herself, almost as if she were a detached observer, as if she were watching this happen to someone else. Snippets of *'The Waste Land'* echoed through her mind: *"Philomel …So rudely forced … Well now that's done: and I'm glad it's over."* This wasn't Matt: it was someone else. It was happening to someone else: not her.

A sudden jerk, followed by shuddering as he emptied himself inside her, his face a twisted gargoyle of hatred and release. And then he was hurriedly redressing, still saying nothing, contempt still burning in his eyes. Without looking back at her, he strode over to the door, unlocked it and was gone.

*

Megan lay there for some time. She was in a state of shock: her body bruised; her heart torn.

"So rudely forced."

Outside, the sun was still shining, the birds still singing, whilst in here this dreadful thing had happened.

"So rudely forced."

It had happened to someone else: not her. *It had happened to someone else: not her.*

Somehow, she managed to crawl off the bed, to reach the door and lock it. She knew then that she would never open it again.

Chapter Forty-Two

Megan lay on her bed in a scrunched-up ball, hugging her knees to her chest in a protective foetal position. She was aware that her heart was thudding far faster than it should have been doing, that her body was trembling, that she was unable to comprehend what had happened.

Footsteps along the corridor. Knocking. Jen's voice: "Megan? Are you there?"

She hugged herself tighter; the door remained locked. It was safer that way.

Gradually, the room darkened as dusk set in. Still she did not move. Her breathing was coming in quick, short gasps; her pulse raced.

Matt's face, the hatred in his eyes, was burned into her brain. He had pinned her down. He had violated her. She wanted to be sick.

Jen's voice echoed in her mind: *"Matt's absolutely devoted to you, Meg. So what if he's not the world's greatest kisser? He's faithful and he's loyal and he'd do anything for you."* But that wasn't the person who'd come to her room earlier. The hands that had forced her had belonged to someone cold and brutal. He had ploughed into her, taking what he wanted, acting as if she were merely a thing to be used.

More footsteps. More knocking. The sound of voices outside her door. Jen, full of concern: "I don't know where she is. I haven't seen her since lunch time."

A quiet hum of conversation. Mike's voice now, his anxiety replicating Jen's. "When I saw her earlier, she said she was coming back here. Hasn't anyone seen her?"

Megan lay very still, hardly daring to breathe. She was aware of the ticking of the clock, of the lingering, sour smell of wine, of the stickiness slowly seeping from her body into a damp patch beneath her. Matt had invaded her world, robbing it of safety, of sanctuary. Nothing existed anymore except her fear. She huddled into it, reliving the nightmare.

After a while, the voices moved away. Later still there was more knocking. Still she lay immobile, unable to move or speak or think or cry. She was dead inside. There was nothing left.

Eventually she slept, exhaustion taking its toll. In her dreams he was there again, *pushing her down ... tearing at her clothes ... his knee prising her legs apart ... his actions shouting his hatred*. She struggled but he was too strong for her. *Tears rolling down her cheeks before, during, after ...* She jerked awake, rushed to the basin and was violently sick.

The hands on her clock pointed to eleven and three. Silently she slipped out of her room, opening the door quietly so that no one would be alerted to her presence. She hadn't used the bathroom in over twelve hours. Now she sat there, shaking, feeling tender, bruised, alone. Her tears fell noiselessly. She didn't flush: she couldn't risk anyone hearing her.

Back in her room, the door locked once more. Even so, she knew she wasn't safe: she would never be safe again. Burying her head in the pillow, she cried into it, letting it muffle her sobs. The pain was overwhelming. She wanted to die.

Sleep overtook her again. At one point she cried out, reliving the nightmare, unable to escape. When she finally opened her eyes once more, light was streaming through her window, cold and harsh, no longer full of life and promise.

*

More tapping on her door. As before, she ignored it, willing the voices to go away. And then, a key turning in her lock. She froze in terror. What was Matt doing now?

Jen stood there with the Floor Tutor, anxiety emanating from her. "Where have you been? I've been looking for you since half two yesterday." Then, as Megan did not reply, Jen's tone became frightened. "Meg! What's wrong?"

Paralysed with fear, Megan said nothing, hiding her dirty secret, her dirty self. Her eyes were wild, her face haunted. Jen had never seen her look so terrible, not even when she was in hospital just after losing the baby.

Instinctively, she moved towards her, reaching to give her a hug, but Megan flinched away, unable to trust anyone's touch.

"Meg, you need to talk to us." Jen's voice was gentle, beseeching. "We can't help you if you don't tell us what's wrong."

The Floor Tutor murmured something Megan couldn't catch. Jen's eyes widened in horror.

"Has someone hurt you?" she demanded. "Who was it? Was it Matt?"

At the mention of his name, Megan heaved.

"Megan." Jen was speaking slowly and deliberately. "If Matt forced you into anything, we need to know. He needs to be reported."

No. She couldn't report him because then she would have to admit what happened. Saying the words would make it real: she wasn't prepared to do that.

More low, urgent whispering between Jen and the Floor Tutor. Megan thought she caught the phrase "can't *make* her report him." She shuddered. What she wanted was for all of this to go away, for it never to have happened in the first place.

The Floor Tutor left, leaving Jen alone with Megan. Megan didn't look at her friend. She was too raw for questions, for explanations, for sympathy.

Respecting her silence, Jen made her a cup of tea. "Drink this. You mustn't get dehydrated." She picked up Megan's room key and placed it in her own pocket. "I know you don't want to see anyone right now, but I need to get in and check on you. I can't drag the Floor Tutor out every time."

Megan tentatively stretched out a hand towards the mug. Slowly picking it up, she was aware of the weight of it in her hand, of how easy it would be to dash it to the floor and break it into a hundred tiny pieces just as Matt had shattered her. Things that were broken were swept up, discarded. That was all she was fit for now, to be thrown away like anything else that was finished, worthless.

She put the mug down again without taking a sip. Her hand trembled and some of the liquid spilled onto her bedside drawers. She stared at it aghast then burst into tears.

It was a relief to cry openly. At some point, she was aware of Jen's arms around her, of gentleness, care, concern. She wept as if her heart would break, trying to evict the guilt, the shame, wanting it to leak out through her tears.

Jen was at a loss to know what to do. Obviously something terrible had happened. The way Megan was crying now could only mean one thing; even so, she struggled to believe it.

"Do you want me to find Mike?" she asked at last, but Megan shook her head violently.

"Not Mike." She couldn't see him ever again, not after what had happened with Matt. She was dirty, disgusting. How could anyone want her after that?

Jen tried again. "Do you want me to bring you some food? I can get you something from the dining hall – or I can go out and buy you something."

She couldn't eat. She still felt sick to her stomach, liable to vomit again at any given moment.

Eventually Jen left and Megan slept again. It seemed as if this was all she would do for the rest of her life: sleep, dream, wake, cry, repeat. She curled herself into a ball once more and shut the world out forever.

*

Some time later, the sound of her key turning in the lock woke her. Jen must be back. She sat up groggily, wondering what her friend wanted this time, but the figure striding through the door was very definitely male.

Megan gazed at Mike in shock. What was he doing here, in her room? Without thinking, she shrank away from him, from the hands that could potentially hold her down, the strength that could take what it wanted.

"Megan, Sweetheart." Mike's voice was gentle. He was approaching her as one might a frightened animal, edging forward slowly, cautiously; keeping his distance so he didn't scare her. "I'm not going to hurt you," he continued, gesturing behind him. "I've left the door open, so you know there's a way out; and Jen's just outside. She won't let anything happen."

As he neared the bed, the scene of her violation, she started to panic. "Stop," she croaked, her throat dry with anxiety.

He did as she requested.

"I'm going to sit on your chair," he told her, noting the fear in her eyes and avoiding the bed. At this slightly safer distance, he began to talk to her again, his voice calm, hypnotic. "What happened? What did he do to you?"

The words were a stone inside her, too heavy to be lifted out. She turned her dead face towards him, gazing blankly with eyes that saw only pain and betrayal. How long before Mike attacked her too?

And then Jen was entering, sitting beside her on the bed, placing an uncertain hand on her shoulder. "You need to talk, Meg. You're safe now. No one's going to hurt you."

But she would never be safe. Not while Matt was walking around, barging into her room, pinning her down. Panic took hold of her again, crushing her windpipe, rendering her unable to speak.

Jen looked at Mike in despair. His face hardened. "I could go and look for him. Make him tell us what he did." He wasn't violent by nature, but at this precise moment, he wanted to break Matt's legs.

Megan leaned forward, drawing up her knees, wrapping herself into a tight, safe ball. "He thought I was cheating on him," she said dully, her voice unnaturally high. "He was angry I wouldn't give him what he wanted – so he took it."

Well now that's done: and I'm glad it's over.

There was a sharp intake of breath from Jen. Mike swore softly, under his breath. "I'll kill him," he said.

And then Megan began to cry again, each tear a reminder of what had happened, each sob a desperate plea for help. She cried until she couldn't cry anymore, Jen's arms around her, holding, comforting. At some point, Mike must have moved from the chair because she sensed another pair of arms gently wrapping around her so that she was cocooned between the two of them, feeling the hurt and the grief ebb away, if only temporarily. She let herself be held; she let the pain leak out.

*

It was hours before she felt ready to talk again. Her brief confession was all she could safely handle for the time being. It was enough they knew Matt had hurt her; any further information was irrelevant at this stage.

Mike and Jen stayed with her all morning – or was it all afternoon? Time had lost meaning for her. They were there, and that was enough.

They made her cups of tea and forced her to drink them. At one point, Jen sent Mike for food. Megan knew this had been done on purpose, so that she wouldn't alone in her room with a man. She could tolerate Mike's presence while Jen was there, but she didn't think she would ever want to spend time with him on her own again.

"You still need to decide what you want to do," Jen told her as they waited for Mike to return. When Megan looked at her blankly, Jen elaborated: "Are you going to report Matt?"

"I don't want to talk about it." Megan retreated back inside herself.

"You're going to have to," Jen said gently, "because if you don't, he might do it again – whether it's you or whether it's someone else."

Hot tears spilled from Megan's eyes. She couldn't let anyone else go through this. She couldn't go through it again herself.

"He's not normally like that," she heard herself whisper. Sweet, gentle Matt who loved her so much that he had forced her down, torn her clothes, prised her legs apart. Matt who had placed her on a pedestal, worshipped her and then violated her.

"He's not been himself for a while," Jen argued. "Look how possessive he's been; how controlling. He's obsessed with keeping you as his girlfriend." She paused. "You have to report him," she said bluntly. "He needs psychiatric help."

But it was her fault, not his, Megan thought wildly. She had tipped him over the edge with her pregnancy. He wouldn't have started drinking if it weren't for her. Like Frankenstein, she had created a monster and was appalled by its appearance.

Eventually, though, she gave in and let Jen take control. As she automatically went through the events of the previous afternoon, from Matt's arrival to his departure, she felt hollow inside. *It had happened to someone else: not her.*

Jen wrote everything down. "You'll probably have to say this all over again to the police," she said apologetically.

Megan's heart squeezed. When Jen had talked about reporting Matt, she had imagined her friend meant reporting him to the Floor Tutor or to the SCR. This was much more serious.

"Do we have to tell the police?" she asked in a small voice.

Matt wasn't a bad person, just a very confused one. She still thought of him as a puppy, but a puppy who didn't know his own strength, who didn't realise that his game was too rough.

Jen put an arm around her. "I know this is hard for you, but we need to keep you safe."

"He didn't mean to hurt me."

"Maybe not," Jen agreed, thinking that Megan was a classic case of someone being in denial, "but he did. He can't make a habit of that, Meg. That's why it has to stop now." She looked Megan in the eye. "I'm going to make a phone call. I'll look out for Mike in the foyer. Don't open your door if anyone knocks."

Once she had gone, Megan felt totally alone. She sat and waited, knowing that Jen was doing the right thing.

*

Matt was nursing a hangover, but it didn't stop him thinking about Megan. He was still trying to piece together the events of the previous day, when he'd drunk far too much before going to see her. Even now he was slightly hazy about it all. He'd been angry – he remembered that much – angry because he'd seen her kissing Mike on campus, flaunting her infidelity. She'd given in to him in the end though. He'd finally made love to her, although he thought he remembered being rough with her. That was okay: girls liked it rough sometimes. They liked their boyfriends to be manly, to show them who was in charge.

Thinking about her now, about making love to her again, made him realise he had to stop drinking. He'd only drunk the day before because he'd seen her with Mike. She'd broken his heart but then he'd shown her he was still in charge. But there were too many gaps in his memory after the second bottle of wine and he wanted to remember it all, to savour the recollection of how she'd felt as he moved inside her.

She wasn't answering her door even though he knocked for ages. He wondered where she was. He called out, in case she was sleeping, but there was no reply.

Stumbling back through the Ridge foyer, he spotted Jen and Mike, deep in conversation. Megan wasn't the only one Mike was after then. Perhaps he should tell Phil to keep an eye on his girlfriend.

*

In her room, Megan sat and shivered. Hearing Matt's voice outside her door had brought it all flooding back to her. Did he really think she would let him in after what had happened the day before?

She felt suddenly angry. *He* had done this to her: he had violated her, and now she was a prisoner in her own room, afraid to go out, afraid to do anything – because of him. She tried to harness her anger, to hold it in check until she could leap on its back and ride it to retribution. How could she have thought it was her fault? *He* was to blame: not her.

The sound of her key in the lock. Jen and Mike entering, faces serious. She would have to make a statement to the police, they said, expecting her to crumble, to dissolve into tears as she had earlier on. Now, however, Megan stuck out her chin defiantly. Shock had given way to anger; anger was ready to act.

"We'll go with you," Jen declared, liking this braver version of Megan.

The other girl hesitated. "I'd like *you* to come …"

"What about me?" Mike asked, trying not to feel hurt she didn't want him.

Megan sighed. "I don't want you to hear what he did to me," she said simply.

"I don't think we're allowed to be in the room with you when you make your statement," Jen told her. She caught Mike's eye. "Mike knows that what happened wasn't your fault."

Megan's face registered signs of an inner conflict. She had waited for Mike for so long, but would he still want her when he knew the full extent of what Matt had done to her? Would he blame her for not struggling harder, for not managing to fight him off?

Mike reached for her but she shied away, unable to trust any man right now.

"This is what I'm on about, Megan." Mike's voice was full of frustration. "How can I ever have a proper relationship with you if you're afraid to let me touch you? You have to admit what he did to you: it's the only way you'll stop being afraid."

The three of them took a taxi to the nearest police station. Jen and Mike waited whilst Megan went into an interview room and told her story. She could remain detached, impersonal because she didn't know any of these people she was talking to. It all seemed slightly surreal.
What would happen to Matt? she wanted to know.
There were no actual witnesses to the event, but Jen had reported the condition Megan had been in the following day. (Was that really today?) If she wanted to press criminal charges, a forensic medical examination would determine whether there were traces of Matt's semen on her clothes or her skin. She was also advised to let the medical officer check her over for any traces of STIs – and then there was the possibility of pregnancy.
It was this last piece of information that floored her. Not a baby. She couldn't have Matt's baby. That would be too cruel after losing Mike's. She stared at the medical officer in disbelief.
"We can give you the Morning After Pill as a precautionary measure," the older woman suggested.
Megan shook her head. She'd read somewhere that the pill caused a spontaneous abortion and said so now.
The doctor sighed. "An ECP is *not* an abortion pill: depending on the type you're given, it merely prevents ovulation or fertilisation."
In other words, a baby would be prevented from starting in the first place. Surely that was okay, under circumstances such as these?

As if in a dream, she watched the doctor hand her the small white pill and swallowed it down with the glass of water provided.

"It's around 75% effective," the doctor sounded factual, clinical, "so I'd watch out for possible signs of pregnancy in a week or two: nausea, tender breasts, delayed or absent menstruation."

So why was she taking this thing in the first place, Megan thought wildly upon hearing this, if she might still be pregnant after all?

Chapter Forty-Three

Megan didn't want to think about Matt and what he'd done once she was back in Hall. Jen reported that he had been asked to give a statement to the police and that he had been officially banned from entering not only Ridge but all the other Halls of Residence. The gossip grapevine was producing fresh rumours every day, but Megan wasn't interested in any of it. She wanted to forget, to put the past behind her, to prove to herself that Matt hadn't won.

"He's gone home a few weeks early," Phil informed them at breakfast a day or two later. "I don't know whether he'll be coming back in October."

He'd seen Matt just before he left. For once, he was sober: the shock of being interviewed by the police and being charged with sexual assault had convinced him that his drink problem was more serious than he thought.

"I didn't want to hurt her," he told Phil. "I just needed to know she loved me."

"You shot yourself in the foot with that one then," Phil said with his characteristic bluntness. "Girls don't like being attacked in their bedrooms and forced into sex. If you'd asked me or Ged, we would have told you that," he added, not without a touch of irony.

"Will you give her this?" Matt handed Phil a letter. "It's not sealed, so if you or Jen want to look at it, you can. I just need her to know I'm sorry."

Phil took the envelope awkwardly. He had no words for an occasion such as this.

Matt walked away without saying goodbye.

Jen waited a few days before giving Megan the letter Phil had passed on to her. It was a brief missive, more of a note really. It said simply, *"I'm sorry I hurt you. I hope you can forgive me at some time in the future. Matt."*

Megan read the note and then screwed it into a ball. "I don't want to think about him anymore," she said.

It was true, she didn't want to think about Matt; but at the back of her mind lurked the possibility that he had left something of himself behind, inside her. She watched the calendar anxiously, desperate for the crippling pain in her lower back that would tell her it would all be all right.

Mike had somehow slotted into the space left by Matt in the friendship group. He and Jen had developed a healthy respect for each other after supporting Megan through the longest day of her life. The rest of them didn't know it had been his baby: Jen thought it better if Sally wasn't disillusioned about Matt, and Mike didn't know the rest of them well enough to let them feel sorry for him. He was still grieving for a child he'd lost before he'd known of its existence.

He and Megan sat with the others in the Hall bar every evening. It had become a public courtship but that was because he knew she was still uneasy about being alone in her room with him or any other male. Occasionally they joined in with their friends' conversation; the rest of the time, they talked to each other about books, their parents, sixth form life, their respective family homes. She was aware that she should invite him to visit her over the summer, but the idea of him being in her parents' house, where anything could happen, currently overwhelmed her. The bar was safe: they were in full view of everyone else.

Gradually, he had begun inching closer to her as they sat beside each other, allowing a light touch on the arm, a meeting of fingers. She didn't back away from him as she had before, the last time he'd been in her room. After a few days, he asked if he could walk her back to her room. He kissed her chastely on the cheek as they reached her doorway. A couple of days later, he held her hand as he walked her back. This time, when he moved towards her, she turned her face and let him kiss her briefly on the lips. Small victories, but each one told her that she was beginning to heal. And when she realised, thankfully, that she wasn't pregnant, she knew she could finally begin to forget Matt.

After a week, Megan invited Mike and the others back to her room for coffee. When the others tactfully declined, Jen whispered to her that it was time to see if she could handle this. "You can keep your door open if it makes you feel safer," she advised. "And Sal and I know he's in your room, so we can come and check on you every ten or fifteen minutes."

It was a huge step to take, but she was determined not to let Matt ruin this for her. After twenty minutes and two cautious heads checking she was okay, she felt able to close the door with Mike inside the room. He sprawled on her bed, obviously wanting her to lie down next to him, or at least sit, but she opted to stay in the easy chair while they talked. She wasn't ready to revisit the scene of Matt's crime, the bed where he'd forced her. Sleeping in it was one thing; lying down next to Mike was another matter entirely.

"I know you're being very patient with me," she said abruptly, even though he hadn't complained, "but just having you in here with me is enough for the time being."

Mike crossed the room to where she sat, perching on the edge of her chair, gently stroking her hair away from her face. "How's that?"

His touch was as light as thistledown, his fingers tracing the contours of her face as if she were a precious piece of porcelain.

"Don't put me on a pedestal," she said suddenly, not wanting either of them to make the same mistake as Matt. When you had wanted someone for what seemed like forever, it was all too easy to idolise them, to think they were perfect, and then to crumble when you found they weren't.

"So," Mike pulled her to her feet and tentatively wrapped his arms around her, ready to let go if she appeared distressed, "why don't you tell me what your flaws are, then?"

His arms were so gentle, so secure, that Megan knew she was safe. "I have a tendency to fall for bad boys," she told him, looking him flirtatiously in the eye.

He bent his head and kissed her properly. "That's unfortunate since I'm a reformed character now. But if you want me to start smoking again …"

"Don't you dare!" she said with feeling, kissing him back and realising that sitting on the bed together might be more practical after all.

Taking his hand, she led him to the most comfortable place in the room. The best way to erase Matt was to make sure she associated this bed with someone else.

As he kissed her again, her skin tingled at his touch, the rightness of him obliterating any fears she might have had. She wouldn't let him stay tonight, but maybe next week …

And she knew then that, no matter how long it took, she and Mike would be okay.

Printed in Poland
by Amazon Fulfillment
Poland Sp. z o.o., Wrocław